little black dress
· IT'S A GIRL THING ·

Dear Little Black Dress Reader,

Thanks for picking up this Little Black Dress book, one of the great new titles from our series of fun, page-turning romance novels. Lucky you — you're about to have a fantastic romantic read that we know you won't be able to put down!

Why don't you make your Little Black Dress experience even better by logging on to

www.littleblackdressbooks.com

where you can:

- ♥ Enter our **monthly competitions** to win **gorgeous** prizes
- ♥ Get **hot-off-the-press** news about our latest titles
- ♥ Read **exclusive** preview chapters both from your **favourite** authors and from brilliant new writing talent
- ♥ Buy **up-and-coming** books online
- ♥ Sign up for an essential slice of romance via our **fortnightly email** newsletter

We love nothing more than to curl up and indulge in an addictive romance, and so we're delighted to welcome you into the Little Black Dress club!

With love from,

The *little black dress* team

T0349140

Five interesting things about Samantha Scott-Jeffries:

1. Samantha has a Master's degree in Investigative Journalism, but it didn't take long for her to realise that she was better suited to writing about 'gorgeous, lovely things' than reporting from the front line.

2. She can only drink two glasses of wine without falling over, but will eat most men under the table and still have room for dessert. She loves to cook and bake but doesn't understand the meaning of the word 'share' when it comes to cake or sushi. Only the word 'seconds' registers with her in that context.

3. Samantha doesn't get sport, but loves watching *World's Strongest Man* on TV. She's not sure why.

4. She once ghost-wrote a book about pig farming for a TV personality and couldn't bring herself to reveal that she is, in fact, a vegetarian.

5. Samantha is small in stature but has a big laugh. Her husband labelled it 'architectural' as soon as they met, convinced that it had the ability to move buildings.

I Do, I Do, I Do

Samantha Scott-Jeffries

little black dress

First published in 2009 by
LITTLE BLACK DRESS
An imprint of HEADLINE PUBLISHING GROUP

A LITTLE BLACK DRESS paperback

2

Cataloguing in Publication Data is available from the British Library

ISBN 978 0 7553 5282 1

Typeset in Transit511BT by Avon DataSet Ltd,
Bidford-on-Avon, Warwickshire

Printed and bound in Great Britain by
Clays Ltd, St Ives plc

Headline's policy is to use papers that are natural, renewable and
recyclable products and made from wood grown in sustainable forests.
The logging and manufacturing processes are expected to conform to the
environmental regulations of the country of origin.

HEADLINE PUBLISHING GROUP
An Hachette UK Company
338 Euston Road
London NW1 3BH

www.littleblackdressbooks.com
www.headline.co.uk
www.hachette.co.uk

For Grant, who's shared my real-life adventures and has always believed in my fictional ones.

Acknowledgements

With enormous thanks to Robert Caskie for his unwavering belief and support, to Grant for his endless encouragement and keen eye over my first drafts, and to Alice and Penny Scott, my first readers. A huge thank-you also to Claire Baldwin and the Little Black Dress team. You all made this book possible.

On Fire

'**Y**ou've almost reached Ray ... if you're hot, leave a message ...'

It had been one hell of a week and all I wanted to do was call the best gay friend a straight girl could have, but all I could reach was his voicemail. Ray had been on a shoot all day, which was really bloody inconsiderate of him – office life was just plain dull when he wasn't around. An Asian babe with a slick London style and a reputation as the best young director in the company, Ray had a tongue which was always as sharp as his haircut. Today I'd missed his witty emails between attending to the whims of my deluded boss Maddy Davenport-Parker, the formidable head of Independent TV production company On Fire. I'd also missed the 'ciggy' breaks we usually took together, huddled outside the impressive building we worked in, gossiping. Despite the fact that I didn't even smoke, fag breaks were the very best way to find out what was really going on and I never missed one. This week, everyone in the five-hundred 'strong and growing' company was officially depressed. There'd been a big contract with the BBC we'd been closing and lost, a final edit with the commissioning editor of our supposed next big hit series which now had to be completely re-cut, and a hardline talk on the company cutbacks being made. The total sum of this had put Maddy in the foulest of moods. And it was only Thursday.

Out in the real world, beyond the big glass doors etched with flames, a tube strike loomed due to a 'security threat', it hadn't stopped raining since Saturday, and my so-called boyfriend hadn't returned my calls all week. To top it all off, I'd just run to the deli at the end of the road for a salad and it had cost me £14.75 and given me a blister from my new heels. How I hated to love Notting Hill.

'Ray, it's Izz, call me when you've wrapped,' I tried to chirp, phone squished under my chin, salad in one hand, brolly in the other, pushing the staff-kitchen door open clumsily with my foot.

The kitchen was deserted. The faint smell of microwaved soup and post-lunch scrapings were a familiar greeting. I dodged the overspilling bin stuffed full of empty food cartons and the well-thumbed pile of magazines and papers as I shook off my soggy trench. I unwrapped the white cardboard carton and dipped a plastic fork into a no-fun pile of organic alfalfa sprouts. To liven things up I flicked through the *Daily Mirror* in a pretence of brainstorming new TV ideas for a meeting later that afternoon. Really, I thought, this was not so different to any other week and I wasn't sure if that was a good or bad realisation.

'Isabelle . . . get me Conrad's office, Channel Four, on line one.' It was Maddy, standing behind me, interrupting my search for the latest Posh and Becks story. In true D-P style, she'd left her desk and walked down three flights of stairs to find me in the kitchen on another grab-what-you-can lunch break, just to ask me to dial a number. Before I could turn round, she'd started to sashay back to her office, eating the banana I'd just bought for dessert and clutching the only decent glossy that had been in the pile. That was Maddy. I'd been her PA for three years. I was used to her and didn't flinch. I was used to going to board meetings, hearing about cuts in budgets, before having to convince the accounts department that Maddy's 'Bliss' facials, lunches at Le Caprice and lavish gifts for her daughter were genuine business expenses. I was used to her creative whims – her unpredictable u-turns in edit suites, commissioners' offices and meetings, where a new trend, one-liner in a Sunday supplement or whisper from a rival company fuelled a decision that made everyone gasp at her supposed genius and forgive her snooty behaviour. These ideas were usually self-consciously un-PC, or 'edgy', which really meant that they were ideas for shows designed to humiliate the public they featured. For this reason, I was dreading the three p.m. brainstorm. I peeled myself away from the paper and tottered after Maddy, heels still rubbing, realising that I had just twenty minutes to come up with some killer ideas for the meeting.

'I want a counter-intuitive multi-platform concept,' Maddy announced pretentiously twenty-one minutes later, to blank faces. Every uncomfortable seat around the vast glass boardroom table was filled, the surface littered with skyscraper lattes. 'A big, landmark show.' The faces remained poised for some tangible information. 'Real people don't want to watch derivative programming, car crash versions of ITV shows on Five,' she claimed in her public-school voice, reiterating the mantras of channel executives, before reeling off a list of shows that were just about to be made and sounded exactly like every other show we'd all already seen before. The faces looked baffled. Then, as she paused to open up the debate, eager executives, producers and directors began a frantic pitching session, jostling to talk, to build on each other's ideas, take something in a new direction, impress the boss, their colleagues, and preen their egos. Maddy gazed at her scarlet Smythson notebook, pouting through poker-straight blond hair, and at every suggestion her expression was as bored as a heavily Botoxed face can manage. Five minutes later, she took a call, turning her back on the table, but it didn't stop the flow of eager conversation.

'So, I was thinking . . .' a particularly unlikeable producer started when he had her attention once more, putting one leg on the table, twirling his BlackBerry in his left hand. 'Why don't we conduct a social experiment, take benefits away from single mums who refuse to work . . . see what they do, how they survive!'

'Yuh, sort of *Wife Swap* casting, with *Big Brother* values, but out of the studio . . . err, out of the home,' added another, hedging his bets.

A female director turned to me to whisper, 'Do these guys hate women or just poor people? I can't tell.' I gave her an apologetic, watery smile and let out a giggle.

'Yes, Izzy, what do you think?' someone asked as the rest of the room fell silent. Ooops. The last thing I wanted was to be put on the spot.

'Maybe they could have . . . mentors, famous single mothers, JK Rowling, Kerry Katona – OK, so maybe *not* Kerry Katona, but you know what I mean,' I stammered. It was all I could think of. Maddy caught my embarrassed gaze with her dead-fish stare. It was the first time we'd made eye contact in months.

'So where's the entertainment in the format?' she sneered. 'Three years ago I would have said that a makeover is what they need,' she added, addressing the room. 'So the question is,' she announced grandly to all, 'what's the new makeover?'

Single mums need a makeover to change their lives? What's the new makeover? I mulled. Was she serious? But the majority around the table were locked in concentration, others furiously scribbled notes.

I gazed out of the window, at the grey sky and the street lined with smart stucco-fronted townhouses. There were times in the office when I got caught up in these questions and thought them desperately important, then times when over a cocktail and 'you won't believe the day I've had' exchanges that I'd realise how ridiculous it all was. To think I'd studied documentary and film-making at Uni and had ended up taking the minutes in meetings where Maddy and her entourage thought how best to tread over the public to create their next big hit and climb their way to the top of entertainment ratings. As I doodled, I reminded myself that Maddy's world was centred completely round a small slice of the elite London media. She claimed to know what 'real people' wanted in these meetings but at other times referred to them as 'civilians'. The simple fact was that Maddy was famous for launching a bitchy 'cheffing' duo five years ago and a TV format that ran for three years, where each episode reduced the homeowners to tears. She was still living off the kudos. Nothing On Fire had produced since had been anything like that hit and word was that she was at the end of her career. Maybe it was the pressure that had created the monster? Or was it years in the industry that had killed off her last humane brain cells? This, after all, was the woman who had to be stopped by the company lawyers from making three hour-long 'revisit' specials, out of the two divorces and one mental breakdown that had emerged once the cameras had finished filming series twelve of her biggest hit.

My mobile buzzed on the glass table and I glanced at the display panel. Recognising an excuse to leave the room on the pretence of an urgent call for the boss, I made a swift exit. Perfect.

'Izz, what the hell's up, honey? You've jammed my mobile with twenty missed calls. What if someone hot really does want to leave a message?!' It was Ray. I shuffled through to the corridor as quietly as possible, the pristine white walls and battered stripped wood floors a relief from the colourful atmosphere of the boardroom.

'You can only live in hope! Look, can't talk right now,' I whispered back, checking over my shoulder at the boardroom door. 'I'm brainstorming counter-counter-intuitive ideas!' I drawled in my best Maddy impersonation. 'Anyway, when are you back? Can we meet for last orders at the local? My treat,' I added desperately.

'Will try, my best girlfriend, tube strike permitting, but I thought you were meeting that unreliable idiot you call a boyfriend tonight. What happened to dinner?'

'Long story, Ray, long story. We had plans, but he's not returned my calls all week, he's driving me crazy . . .'

'Sorry, caller, can't hear you . . . the line's breaking up,' Ray mocked. He'd heard it all a million times before.

'Oh, you know you're the only decent man in my life, Ray. See you at the bar,' I giggled. Clicking my phone shut, I took a deep breath and headed back to the boardroom. Later, I'd have the task of summarising the brainstorm for Maddy and circulating a document, so that the relevant people could work up their ideas into possible TV formats. I had to get back to take notes.

'Isabelle?' It was Maddy. It was five-forty-five and she was back at her desk, summoning me from mine, placed right outside of her door, which she kept slightly ajar.

'As you know, I have a nine-thirty at TV Centre tomorrow. Some of the ideas from today might be useful to drop into conversation. I'd like to take them with me,' she announced whilst writing an email.

'Sure, I'll email them,' I replied, teeth clenched behind a smile, as I realised that my night out had probably just been cancelled. 'Tea?' I added, reluctantly.

'That's all,' she replied, signalling that I was to leave. 'I'll be going to The Electric at six, dinner at eight-thirty, so please tell the Nanny to feed the kids without me.'

I wasted no time. Carefully closing Maddy's door behind me, I sent a text to Ray with one hand on my mobile whilst dialling a car to take Maddy a five-minute walk away with the other. Then I tapped out a quick email to the PA at home before starting on the notes. I was fed up with my evenings being taken up with prepping for Maddy's meetings. I promised Ray I'd be in Zoom by ten and got on with deciphering my scrawl and cutting out the TV talk to get to the nub of the ideas. But it wasn't easy. By eight, the cleaners were hoovering the office, clearing the water glasses from the desks and tiptoeing around me. A runner barged through with kit from a shoot and tapes of rushes to take straight to the edit house. My phone beeped with a text from Ray: Just got 2 bar. Cute guy in corner, if ur late, might hv 2 pull!

Great. Just when I wanted Ray to be sympathetic and there just for ME. I sped things up and continued in bullet points.

It was nine-thirty before I finished and I knew that if

I ran, I could still spend five minutes fixing my face in the ladies and make it to Zoom before ten. I darted into Maddy's office for my tidy-up routine, straightening the magazines on her marble-topped coffee table, changing the water in the huge vase of flowers and checking if I needed to buy fruit on the way in tomorrow. Then I had to tackle the desk. Despite her personal appearance and air of organisation, Maddy was chaotic and messy, in a bohemian, creative way. So it was part of my job to keep her in-tray and out-tray in order, her desk tidy, and to save any Word documents before closing down her computer, keeping a blind eye to the contents, of course. This was a routine I had to perform every night, because Maddy's car always beat my bus to the office in the mornings.

First, I checked that my own email with the brainstorm notes had come through, knowing that Maddy would pick it all up at home. It was then that I noticed there was an email in her drafts folder. Maddy never kept drafts. Interesting. I was now running late, but curiosity got the better of me and I spared a minute to look at who she'd composed her un-sent item to: Ian Leighton, BBC commissioning editor extraordinaire, her nine-thirty. She must have prepped it for the meeting tomorrow and had forgotten to send it, I thought whilst glancing at the clock opposite. Very her. Must be important, I figured. I moved the mouse over the yellow envelope icon and without a second thought, clicked send before I shut down. Done.

I finally made it to Zoom just gone ten and found Ray sitting at the neverending white leather bar. How irritating; despite having come straight from a ten-hour outdoor shoot on the other side of London, he looked immaculate. He was wearing skinny Dior jeans, a trilby hat at a jaunty angle and a battered vintage T-shirt and was perched on an over-designed stool. He had a Mojito waiting for me on one side of him and someone who I guessed was probably the 'cute guy' on the other.

'Izzy, darling, meet ... sorry, what was your name again?'

Ray was the only man I knew who could get away with being so cheeky. Of course he knew the cute guy's name, it was so obvious they'd been chatting and he was playing hard to get. The barfly took umbridge and sloped off to the gents in a strop.

'Prima donna!' Ray laughed, his eyes following his butt as he strutted into the crowds.

I took a slug of the Mojito. 'Thanks for this, just what I needed. So how was the shoot?' I asked, clinking the ice in my glass, changing the subject.

'Oh, you know, same old, same old, directing by the book. I find these half-hour formats so frustrating, no room to put your mark on a film. I reckon it's the last one I'll do of these ...Well, if I can afford not to,' he added with a gloomy realisation, finishing a bottle of Ashai.

The bar was heaving. A group of twenty-something girls in Hoxton-style anti-fashion eyed Ray's good looks greedily. This always happened. And it was usually followed with jibes or 'and what's he doing with *her*' glares. I turned back to him. OK, so I looked a bit rough – I was always on the heavy side, but the blister on my heel wasn't helping my posture, my make-up had mostly rubbed off the face that people told me was pretty, and my mouse-brown hair had turned into a giant frizz ball in the rain, but I was past caring.

'Look, Izz, he's still there, in the corner,' Ray said dreamily, nudging me. 'The cute guy.'

'Oh, I thought the guy at the bar was the cute guy,' I exclaimed, wide-eyed.

'Is he checking me out?'

'Not sure . . .' I said. This was getting boring. 'So how was your day, Izzy? Why twenty missed calls?' I prompted.

'Darling, we're not an old married couple yet, are we? When I can't pull guys like that we'll make a pact to marry each other, like in *Friends*, *then* we'll have those "honey, I'm home" conversations, OK?'

'Yeah, sure, you're so right. But don't go getting a beer gut and a wife beater vest,' I added, ordering another round. What I probably needed was to forget about my bad week, the fact that my so-called boyfriend hadn't called, that I hated my job, and just have some fun.

I ended up back at Ray's. His apartment was one of my favourite places in the world, much to Marc's (Ray's live-in-lover) annoyance. It was a tiny but perfectly formed haven on Portobello Road, each room was bright, white and spotless, with polished concrete floors. The large sash window in the living room over-looked the colourful market stalls and swarms of people below. What made it so Ray was the exquisite sari material draped on battered leather sofas and across beds, the jewelled slippers, statues of the Indian god Ganesh and faded pictures of the Raj. Ray was peeling garlic in the kitchen, whilst ordering me to chop onions, so that he could conjure up a Kashmiri storm. This was always our routine. Curry after the bar with a bottle of wine, whatever the hour. Marc made an appearance at the living-room door in a white towelling robe, raised an eyebrow at me, rubbed his head sleepily, and silently turned to go back to bed. Ray and I filled our empty stomachs with fragrant rice and prawns in a sweetly spiced sauce and my silly diet was a distant memory. With *Funny Face* on the big plasma screen, I dozed off cocooned in one of Ray's patchwork quilts. I awoke the next morning to the sound of Marc moodily collecting last night's dishes from around me.

'That's a job too big for Touche Éclat,' he piped cattily, as I opened my eyes. A great start to the day: a bitch before breakfast and another to greet in the office.

I pulled the covers back over my head and waited for Marc to leave the flat. When he'd gone, I grabbed a quick shower, a small bowl of cornflakes and an oversized cashmere sweater from Ray's wardrobe to belt over my jeans. Ray was already on location, so there was no hope of a leisurely stroll through the market and a quick coffee and croissant in Portobello with him before work. Shame. It felt strange to be in the flat alone, but the thought of running across Notting Hill in last night's clothes without the thrill of a one-night stand as an excuse was a bit sad. Luckily, Ray always insisted I make myself at home (as long as I picked up the dry-cleaning bill for anything I borrowed, of course) but, still, I felt uncomfortable hanging around. So, for the first time ever, I found I was early for work and although the thought of spending an extra hour in the office out of choice made me check my pulse, I still headed off, grabbing a skinny soya cappuccino en route.

A surprising number of people were already at work when I arrived and they all eyed me with suspicion. Nikki the receptionist actually stopped chewing her gum, looked up from a copy of *Heat* magazine, and checked the clock on the wall behind her. She picked up two more calls, 'Hello, On Fire, can you hawld?' she sang, fiddling with her big hoop earrings before asking, 'Izz, is there somefing big happening this morning that

I dunno about?' My reputation obviously preceded me.

The upstairs office was completely silent. I turned on my computer, thinking I might read Popbitch and check out the vintage Biba I was watching on eBay before starting some work, when my thoughts of a leisurely start were interrupted by a loud rummaging noise from Maddy's office. I peered through the gap in the door to see who was in there.

A minuscule female frame was changing out of sweatpants. Her pin-thin legs were spray-tan brown and topped with cellulite. It was only from the hair that I realised that the figure was Maddy. In just a sports bra and pants she actually looked her age. She must have come in straight from her Pilates class, a daily seven-thirty rendezvous with Eric. I scurried back to my desk before she could see me, trying to shake off the image of my semi-naked boss. Just moments later I heard her make a call.

'It was soooo wonderful last night, darling. Divine. I had a fabulous time and I just couldn't wait to tell you,' she purred. Even when she was trying her hardest to be nice, she sounded fake. 'No, of course not. I snuck in and Rupert was fast asleep,' she added, lowering her voice instinctively. I paused, the paper coffee cup at my lips poised as I heard her continue. 'Of course he doesn't . . . you know the sense of being caught just turns me on.'

My skin started to crawl. I couldn't believe my ears. I was overcome with a desperate urge to escape before 'Dirty D-P' spotted me. Careful not to ruffle the papers on my desk as I stood up, I slipped off my shoes and headed for the door. Out in the corridor I ran barefoot to the ladies, shut myself tightly in a cubicle and took it all in. Christ! Maddy was married to Rupert Davenport-Parker, Conservative MP. If she cheated on him and news got out, it would be HUGE. Her cosy Islington home life and his career would be wrecked. I took in some deep breaths. From beneath the cubicle door my eyes followed a pair of heels walk in. Black, patent Prada with heavy wooden stacks. I'd only seen her wear them once before, but I knew they were Maddy's. I waited. I'd been in this situation many times. If I happened to be in the ladies at the same time as Maddy I'd stay perfectly still in a cowardly attempt to avoid making polite conversation with the most awkward and anti-social woman in the building, who also happened to be my boss. The routine was always the same. I'd hear the cubicle door close and the lock turn, and, often, the sound of her taking a call (talk about time is money!). I'd then wait to hear the tap run, the sound of her make-up bag unzip and a lipstick case click open, then the heels would totter off and I was free to follow. But today, the dreaded heels headed straight for my cubicle and Maddy banged frantically on the door. Even though I'd seen the shoes come my way first, I almost jumped out of my skin.

'Isabelle, I know you're in there, I need you NOW.' I flushed the chain, opened up the door and nervously beamed my best 'good morning', all smiles.

'Good morning?!' Maddy shrieked back at me. '*Good* morning?' Her cheeks were mottled crimson, her hair wild, her nostrils flared; really not a good look. Her voice raised an octave and boomed.

'Don't you know what you've done, you idiot?'

Maddy's voice echoed in the confined space. Her expression was bizarre and contorted; she looked as if she might burst out of her Botoxed face.

'Err, not exactly, no. I don't know what you're talking about,' I tried to offer quietly.

'The email, Isabelle. The EMAIL. What were you thinking? Don't you understand how this will ruin me? Or maybe that's what you want. Maybe you've got fed up of your sad little role and want to see the tables turned. DO YOU, ISABELLE, DO YOU?'

She was screaming now, her eyes bulging like a bullfrog's. A single contact lens shot across the room as a result, but she just ignored it, her witchy, skinny finger pointing at me – the accused. I froze.

'DO YOU WANT TO SEE EVERYTHING I HAVE GOT GO DOWN THE PAN? DO YOU, DO YOU, DO YOU, DO YOU, DO YOU, DO YOU?'

This was the last intelligible line of our one-way conversation, because at this point Maddy Davenport-Parker, quite literally, went mad. She turned into a ranting ball of hyperbole, her arms flailing in vague time with her screaming accusations, till, just minutes later, she fell to the cold tiled floor, her legs lifeless and askew, her face wet with tears as she sobbed uncontrollably.

I could imagine all those who were already at their desks listening. My brain whirred. What was I supposed to do? I didn't know whether to pass her a tissue, help her up or run for my life. I was completely and utterly petrified. But before I could think of an answer, Maddy got herself together enough to deliver it for me.

'YOU'RE FIRED!' she shrieked, her voice gritty from her now hoarse throat. 'FIRED, YOU HEAR ME? GET OUT!!!'

I squeezed out of the ladies, stunned. Red-faced, I passed my colleagues for the last time. Most pretended they were working, picking up the phone to dial no one, sending 'Are you hearing what I'm hearing?' emails, or making embarrassed conversations about pending shoots with any person next to them. Others openly stared at me, some shooting me an 'Are you OK?' expression, a few looking smug, as I took a long, slow-motion walk of shame, which seemed to last a lifetime, out of the building.

I didn't go to my desk. I didn't even remember to collect my shoes or my handbag. I just kept on walking, fighting back the tears, head held as high as I could manage, my mind whirring as I walked, through those doors etched with flames for the last time.

Outside I took a big gulp of crisp winter air and walked. Halfway down the Portobello Road, however, I suddenly realised that I had to turn back. I was at risk of contracting some weird medieval foot disease walking without shoes on the grubby streets lined with litter and debris from the market. I didn't have a key to get into my own flat, or my wallet to get a stiff drink. But still, I couldn't face a u-turn. I blagged a pound from my regular flower stall, ran to the nearest phone box, and made a desperate, shaky call to On Fire.

'On Fire, can you hawld?' Nikki the receptionist twanged.

'Nikki, it's Izz, don't put me on—' Great, my money was bound to run out. But she soon came back to me, excitedly.

'Izzy, EVERYONE is talkin', babe.'

'Yes, well, it's one for the pub another time. Look, I need you to get my stuff down to me, the phone box on Portobello—' The pips went. 'Road, near Elgin Crescent,' I squeezed in before the phone line buzzed its dead-line tone. I didn't know whether she'd heard me, or whether she would do anything, but I waited.

Outside the box, I hunched my shoulders and raised my eyebrows in an 'I'm crazy me' expression as the immaculately groomed yummy mummies and trendy media types of Notting Hill peered quizzically at my grubby, bare feet. Finally, after an old lady had literally thrown some coppers at me, a young sweaty On Fire runner arrived, fumbling with my belongings, unable to meet my gaze.

'Great, you're a life-saver, thank you soooo much,' I managed to say, my eyes filling with tears, before he could ask questions. He stood awkward and dumbstruck in his baggy jeans before turning without a word, presumably to run back to the gossiping lair of the office.

Suddenly, I felt very alone. Squeezing my mucky toes and still sore, blistered feet into the heels I was beginning to hate, I literally wobbled. The bustling market had become a blur behind my tear-filled eyes and fuzzy head as I tried to navigate which way was home on shaky legs. I ran the scene with Maddy through my mind as I pushed through the busy market crowds with my head down, oblivious to the calls of the traders.

'This is bad, Izzy, really bad,' I kept telling myself as I carried on walking, the cold winter air stinging my eyes and my now wet cheeks. I pulled up the collar on my jacket and huddled into it for comfort. I didn't know where I was going, what I was going to do, or how long I'd been walking, but several hours later my stomach growled, telling me it must be lunchtime. I headed into the nearest newsagents for an emergency chocolate bar and some tissues. It was then that I saw it. The *Evening Standard* seller's board, the early edition in big, bold, black capitals: MEDIA BOSS THROWS HERSELF INTO FIRE. What on earth? I grabbed a copy and rushed back to my flat to read it. I needed space to clear my head. It must be Maddy, I thought, it must be the affair.

Back home I flopped into a heap on the sofa, leaning back on a pile of cushions to read the front-page article. After everything that had happened, I was quite looking forward to learning the details of Maddy's juicy affair, but I was in for a shock. I scanned the page, racing through the lines at double speed as my stomach turned to water. I felt a trickle of sweat on my brow. My mobile phone buzzed with missed calls and started to ring again. I switched it off.

Renowned television producer Maddy Davenport-Parker took on the BBC this morning, having sent a highly defamatory email to Commissioning Editor Ian Leighton. The contents of the email are said to be highly insulting to both Mr Leighton and the channel. Our source said that the comments may have been fuelled by an earlier viewing at independent television production company On Fire where Leighton demanded a new series to be reworked for transmission at the very last minute. The source also speculated as to whether Managing Director Davenport-Parker intended to send the email, as it appeared to be unfinished, unsigned and containing many litigious statements which we can only describe as outrageous, personal slants in the worst possible taste. We wait to see if Mr Leighton or the BBC will take action. Mrs Davenport-Parker is currently unavailable for comment.

I ran to the toilet feeling nauseous and was instantly sick, swiftly pulling my hair out of the way of the torrent. On wobbly legs I made it to bed, and collapsed into a deep, deep sleep, fully clothed, till the early hours of the next morning, when I awoke with a start, remembering that I'd agreed to meet Remi to go shopping, after an early morning yoga class and brunch. It was just what I needed!

Retail to Betrayal

Selfridges, Oxford Street, London. It was a place where I could be anyone I chose, forget everyone else, and eventually leave wondering what time of day it was. There were days when I'd got lost in its sumptuous lingerie boudoir. Times when I'd gone home empty-handed but happy, having spent an hour inhaling the sweet scent of handmade chocolates in the confectionery department. And there were early evenings when a quick flit around the shoes department left me feeling as though I'd visited a sculpture exhibition, as I lusted after the statuesque shapes. I knew it was hopelessly shallow, but I LOVED the store. My knowledge of its layout was as detailed as a London street map, I could target my prey within seconds of heaving open one of the shop's heavy brass doors, scale the escalators without ruffling the ambling tourists and use my trusty bargain radar to swipe my bounty in record time. I joked that Selfridges was my Mecca, but it was more like my therapy rooms and the treatment was just as expensive as Harley Street. After all, it had been my trusty pick-me-up for years and it had never failed me yet; broken heart, bad date, fight with a friend.

Today, surely, it would be perfect. The thought of an afternoon splurge with my plastic and own personal stylist, Remi, preoccupied my mind all the way through my sun salutations at yoga. But somehow, once I was there, something had faded. It was like rediscovering an old movie that you thought was great five years ago and realising that it didn't live up to the memory you had of it. And I just couldn't figure out why.

I didn't care that Remi, freelance fashion stylist, always had to throw in the odd comment about me needing to be 'TTY' (thinner, taller, younger) to 'do real justice' to particular 'garments and accessories'; she may have been half joking, but she still sounded like some kind of fascist fashionista. Of course, as always, she grabbed the coolest stuff in true competitive shopping style before I even knew it was 'like soooo next season'. No problem there. No, it was something else. I'd been fired before (from the nightclub Remi and I had both worked in at uni; for being caught on the dance floor when I should have been stocking up the bar). I'd been skint before, too. I'd even resigned myself to the fact that I'd not heard from Harrisson (the bad boyfriend material) for over a week. There could be only one explanation, I must be sickening for something.

'Ooooh, the new season's Chloé bag in metallics,' Remi cooed, as she artfully mowed down several shuffling Saturday shoppers to reach the butter-soft totes. 'I called one of these in last season for a shoot. Just di-vine,' she added, in a louder-than-necessary voice, patting a matching purse. And, for the first time ever, she actually made me wince.

I gave myself a shake. If I were filling in one of those questionnaires in *Glamour* magazine about my perfect Saturday, I'd be ticking these boxes:

Early yoga session (remarkably few yummy mummies present equals no gooey baby talk or feelings of inadequacy over shoddy yoga gear) – big tick.

Brunch, followed by a quick mooch back along the Portobello Road with a takeaway soya latte, girly chat and advice on my recent workplace disaster – big tick.

Fashion stylist friend offers ride in sports car and to pay parking, whilst we shop in my favourite W1 department store – big tick.

Possible cocktails to follow to dampen guilt over extravagant purchases and forget about office nightmare? Obligatory box.

So, what was my problem? I wasn't musing on yesterday's events, I was welcoming a distraction. I wasn't worried that there are copies of the Chloé bag all over eBay (Remi says they fund terrorism, which I don't quite understand). I wasn't even concerned that it seemed vaguely ridiculous that Remi was even looking at handbags after her recent purchase of a limited-edition Dior which she jumped the waiting list for, having paid off the most hideous sales assistant this side of Bond Street. I must be ill. In my weakened state, I clutched on to a nearby Miu Miu holdall for support.

'Shall we scoot over to Stella for Adidas, to pick up some yoga togs? Or to the sunglasses section to see the new oversized Tom Fords? I can't decide,' enquired Remi, finally putting the Chloé bag down having tried it on both shoulders, checking her perfect profile in front of a full-length mirror. She shamelessly gave a glaring security guard her finest flirtatious smile. 'Just step AWAY from the bag, Rem ... away from the bag,' I mocked.

'Wait up, Izzy darling, I'm not done!' she laughed.

'Oh, Remi, maybe we can skip this bit and head up to that lovely bar for a drink? You know, we always mix our vodka best with Vuitton,' I added in a desperate attempt to appeal to her love of their Moroccan-style Mojitos and my need to escape the madness of the ground floor.

'What? Are you kidding?! We've only got four hours left of shopping time! I've spied the cruise collections over there, then I want to see if they've got any one-pieces in Swimwear.'

I must have looked alarmed as she continued, 'I know it's only January, but if you don't buy now, all the best pieces will be gone . . . and bikinis, well . . . they're so *done* . . .' Remi sounded like a woman possessed.

'God, Remi, what does it matter . . .' I started then, quickly remembering myself, adding, 'if we're a little late back tonight? Let's grab a drink and then resume mission Missioni swimwear?' I caught myself bargaining with a wide-smiling Remi. I'd need at least a double to muster enough courage to 'get my kit off' in front of Miss Perfect. Remi had inherited her Iranian mother's skin, which was the colour and texture of café latte, and a velvety black bob that always had a GHD. From her British father's side she had a tall, willowy frame, sparkling emerald-green eyes and Kensington credentials.

We made our way through the thickening crowds, and past a horde of women dressed head-to-toe in Burkas.

'I don't get it,' sighed Remi, 'why do they bother spending millions on Chanel when they cover themselves up with those ugly hot things?' Even by Rem's standards, this was in bad taste. Usually I laughed at her black sense of humour, but today I pretended not to hear.

We passed through Menswear like girls in a sweetie store, quickly surveying the male shoppers as we drifted on up the escalator.

'Oooh, cute guy in Diesel!' I said excitedly, for the first time that afternoon. 'Oh, maybe not . . . boyfriend in tow, maybe?' I added, before Remi could share my enthusiasm.

'Yup, and man-boobs to boot. Honey, you're losing your touch,' she mocked, her gaze lingering on the couple.

'Come on, Rem, let's get off here for a drink. I'll settle for tea if you like, then I PROMISE we'll do swimwear . . . purrrrrrlease?' I begged like a kid.

'OK, OK, OK! I suppose it couldn't hurt,' she agreed.

'Great.'

We passed the really expensive labels, which I couldn't even afford to glance at, as I spotted Keira Knightley and tried nonchalantly to not make a fuss whilst wearing my 'I've just spotted a celeb!' expression and nudging Remi excitedly. She was less than impressed by my desperate behaviour.

'Sado,' she whispered.

When we sunk into the soft Moroccan cushions on the bar's benches, Remi kicked off her killer wedges. We ordered green tea, her calorie-conscious choice, and I pondered ordering something sweet. Rem wittered on about fashion and all the stuff she wanted in the store, but I still wasn't in the mood. My mind drifted. I sat wondering if this was all our conversations would ever amount to. Would Rem ever tell me how she felt about anything important, or did she always want to be a 'competitive friend' for whom everything was fabulous in her fabulous life?

'Izz, are you listening?' she said crossly. 'I said the guy at work who keeps checking me out from the other side of the office and sending me saucy emails has been having an e-affair.'

'What?' I asked.

'You know the one, I TOLD you about him. Well, I was giving the new work experience girl some tasks on Thursday and I happened to glance at her screen and, well, whaddya know . . . there was a ton of emails from him in *her* inbox.' Her green eyes were wide as she flicked her immaculate bob.

'Oh, right. Sorry, Rem, but I didn't think you were that into him.'

'Well, of course I'm not,' she replied, defensively, 'but I wanted him to be that into me! I feel two-timed, the bloody net-rat. If it wasn't for Dan, I'd be upset.'

'Sure, Rem, you've got a diamond there. Let's get the bill,' I said, not sure whether or not to pity her latest handsome, lap-dog boyfriend with oodles of cash. Before I'd decided, she'd slapped down a crisp twenty, grabbed me by the arm and dragged me down to Swimwear on the ground floor.

'Izz, you don't seem yourself this afternoon, hun, I think you need a splurge,' said Remi, checking if the pants on a white micro-kini were transparent and almost sounding concerned. 'Why don't you try on something fabulous to cheer yourself up? C'mon, I'm gonna keep an eye on my girl. I think you need some TLC after that hideous incident with your crazy ex-boss.'

'Ah, bless you, Remi. I'm OK, just not quite on form today. Sorry if I'm rubbish company. Tell you what, you check out the new bikinis in Agent Provocateur, and I'll head for something – well, you know, more substantial . . . TTY and all that! And I'll meet you in the changing rooms.'

'OK, doll.' She waved, already halfway towards the peek-a-boo bras.

I headed to the more sensible collections, wondering if I should go up a size due to my lingering Xmas spread, or to try on a twelve, hold in my stomach, and pretend that the dark lighting and slimming mirrors were actually a reality. Good old Remi, I mused, maybe I'd underestimated her. Maybe she understood that I wasn't feeling quite up to scratch and she was just trying to cheer me up in the only way she knew how.

I decided against a Melissa Obadash number with a big gold ring instead of material on one side of the bottoms, and opted for a Heidi Klein with more fabric and a kaftan cover-up and made my way to the luxurious changing rooms. After all, it could be fun to see what kind of mad Fluoro one-piece Remi had squeezed her tiny, buffed body into.

The assistant looked at me as though I was mud and handed me a token. I brushed past her and checked the bottoms of the curtains for Remi's shoes. Remi always tried on swimwear or lingerie with heels and, seeing that she probably never went into the sea, I suspected that she remained in them throughout her holidays. I thought about how much better I'd feel in the bikini if I'd applied several layers of fake tan and hoped that a laugh now with Rem would get me back to my swooning affair with Selfridges.

'Rem? You decent?' I whispered outside the curtains I'd spied her Marni wedges and golden ankles beneath. 'Rem?' I said a little louder. Nothing. 'Reeeee-miiiii,' I sang.

Oh sod it, I thought. After all, we'd seen each other in all states of undress over the years. I pulled the curtain back sharply. Whatever state of nudity Remi was in, it wouldn't bother me.

'Shit, Izz!' she shrieked. Remi was entwined with the guy I'd spotted in Diesel. I could see his cute, tight, white bottom reflected in the mirror and instantly panicked.

'Oh! OK! 'Scuse me!' I stammered, racing to close the velvet curtains with a fumble. I took in a deep breath and suddenly felt very angry. 'So much for man-boobs!' I shouted, and ran to the exit, tears streaming down my face, the bikini and kaftan still in my grasp. I threw them at the burly security guard as I steamed out of the doors. Who needed bloody self-obsessed bitches as friends?

I wandered down Oxford Street, dodging the hordes of shoppers by walking in the gutter, daring the traffic to mess with me. The skies were deepest grey. It was dusk, the shop lights lit up the new season's collections in the windows, but they failed to lure me inside. Eventually I stumbled into Bond Street tube station, stopping at the newsagent's in search of some glossies for the journey, but a *Metro* headline caught my eye: DARLING OF TV'S ON FIRE WAGES PUBLIC WAR WITH BBC. I stopped to read the page six story right there and then:

Maddy Davenport-Parker has issued a statement to the press claiming that she didn't ever intend for the now notorious email damning Commissioning Editor Ian Leighton and the BBC to leave her PC. She blames the incompetence of Personal Assistant Isabelle Mistry for the mistake, whom she is said to have fired in an explosive fashion yesterday. However, in a surprising u-turn, Davenport-Parker said that she had 'good reason' for some of the less personal comments she made about the BBC and its commissioning process . . .

I couldn't read on. I paid for a bottle of water, two packs of gum and dived underground.

I got home and did what any grown-up, responsible woman in angst does. I rang my mother. I reverted to a little girl as I explained the whole story in minute detail (leaving out the scene in Selfridges with Remi, which, frankly, might have shocked my straight-laced, well-to-do fifty-something mum in leafy Surrey).

'Well, dear,' she started, interrupting an hour of my pathetic blubbing, 'it's never good being fired and I don't need to tell you that you should never have sent the email . . .' she mustered, less than sagely. 'But really, I don't know why you're so troubled by the newspapers. The story has only appeared in London. You could work anywhere in the country and, besides, not many people will read these papers anyway, they've got better things to do, I'm sure it will all be forgotten by next week. Why don't you come round to lunch with your father and me tomorrow? You need a proper roast dinner, some home comforts, and things will seem much better.'

Typical. Mother neglected to understand the influence of the London papers, especially within the industry. She'd never imagine that I'd seen that very issue of the *Metro* newspaper pass between several strangers' hands as I gazed into my handbag and pretended not to exist on the tube home that night.

'Mum, you don't get it, this is career suicide. I'm doomed. I'll have to get a job as a cleaner, or flee the country, or something. I'm not sure that even *your* roast potatoes, however good they may be, can salvage this one.' I paused. I could sense her raising her eyebrows. 'Look, thanks, Mum, you know I'd love to come over and see you both tomorrow, but I've got plans,' I lied. 'I'd better go now, love to the old man.'

*

I resigned myself to another evening on the couch. As I opened a bottle of cheap wine, I checked the answerphone and immediately deleted two sickeningly sweet and apologetic messages from Remi and thirteen messages from people wanting to know what had happened with Maddy, as well as an anxious voicemail from Ray. Most of these started, 'Izzy, I've seen the papers . . .' So much for my mum's wise words of wisdom. I erased them one by one, just in case I'd missed a call from Harrisson, but although I waited to hear his voice, the last message on the tape was just another, 'Hi, it's me. Is it true?' greeting. The most depressing thing was that I knew that people had only called to find out the gossip.

I turned on the box and sent a text to Ray to tell him that both his cashmere sweater and I were still alive and I read the small ads in a magazine someone had left on the tube. It was called *The Lady*. The name and typeface seemed so old fashioned that I was expecting a subtitle to read 'for the discerning gentlewoman'. There was no photograph on the front, or any cover lines. It seemed to be straight out of the Fifties and inside the pages were filled with small ads. Most were for holiday rentals – 'Pretty cottage in Tuscany, quiet location, small pool . . . call Dorothy' – and adverts for au pairs and nannies. Further down the page, however, something caught my eye: 'Wedding planner wanted to work with small team, organising the perfect day for couples on the island of Majorca. Please send your formal written application and curriculum vitae to Celia . . .' Great job, I mused, circling the ad with a pen; sunshine, flowers, churches, champagne, food, parties . . . but in Majorca? Wasn't Majorca all package holidays, screaming kids and drunken clubbers? I dragged myself off the couch and Googled the island on my laptop. An hour later, my daydreams of five-star hotels by the sea and palaces for sale in the city of Palma were interrupted by the phone. Harrisson? I hoped.

'Izzy, emergency!' Ray rambled urgently.

'You too? This is one hell of a day,' I answered, as light-heartedly as I could.

'Fashion emergency. I'm going to need the cashmere.'

I let out a sigh of relief. Ray sensed the pause.

'So, are you OK, then?' he asked finally. 'I heard. Well, of course EVERYONE heard.'

'Well, kind of . . . thanks,' I said, trying not to well up again. 'But you're not making me feel better!'

'Look. Urgent situation, house party with Marc, arty types on Old Street, very trendy, very nice, but no central heating, naturally, and I've got nothing to wear,' he continued without pausing for breath. 'Tell me it's clean!' he added urgently.

'Yes, of course it is,' I chuckled. I'd left it to air on a hanger, it was fine.

'No marks, no crumbs, none of that vile perfume you insist on wearing?'

'I swear. I put it on at yours, remember, so no, no perfume, and Ray, *seriously*, I've treated it like my life depended on keeping it pristine', I assured him, lying about the second part.

'That's my girl! Can I pop over?' he asked.

I instantly jumped up to perform a speedy tidying routine. Ray always grumbled at the state of my 'slag pad', as he called it. He was constantly tidying my books into piles as we chatted and wiping surfaces with his finger to test for dust whilst I cooked. He always rinsed a glass before using it, and always complained about my appalling taste in cheap wine.

'I'll be there in five,' added the tidy freak.

The line went dead. I had just enough time to remove a pile of dirty washing from my bedroom floor and wash up the morning's pre-yoga coffee cup in the sink. I'd rely on dim lighting and burning a Diptyque candle for the rest.

'Hi, Ray.' I greeted him at the front door with a kiss on the cheek. 'So glad to see you! You won't believe the day I've had. Got time for a quick glass of wine?' I said excitedly, pleased to see a friendly face and hoping for a chat. Ray followed me into the living room and stayed standing.

'Sorry, Izz, Marc's in the Audi, on yellows outside. I'm really sorry, you know, about today and everything . . . but can we do it another time? You should come along tonight,' he added, eyeing my scruffy 'boyfriend's jeans' look with distaste, 'but I guess it's a bit short notice. I should have thought earlier.'

I felt my face fall. Normally, I would have rushed to put on a chiffon top, heels and some lippy in two minutes flat to join him, but tonight I really didn't feel up to it. He should have known that.

'Not really in the mood, Ray,' I sighed, disappointed, 'but I'll grab the sweater if your chariot awaits.' I put on a brave smile. I rushed to the bedroom and folded up the soft Ballantyne jumper to neatly present to him. When I got back to the living room Ray was reading the ad I'd circled in *The Lady*.

'Izz, I know you need to find a new earner, but this is a bit extreme, isn't it, love?' he mocked. '*Majorca*? Are you *serious*?' he laughed, walking out the door.

Why shouldn't I be?

That night, I thought a lot about the ad. I thought about how good it would feel to start a new life, how good it would be to leave the hideous world of television behind. What would I be missing in England? Mum's roast potatoes, a few favourite haunts, a handful of true friends, but would half of my so-called friends and my bad excuse for a boyfriend even notice I'd gone?

I awoke the next morning with cabin fever and decided that I needed breakfast out. This was partly fuelled by a desire to clear my head and get out of my tiny apartment rather than clean it, and partly due to the fact that my fridge was only able to offer a jar of furry mayonnaise. I wandered along Westbourne Grove to Fresh and Wild, the local organic supermarket, and ordered a large carrot juice – realising I needed some nutrients – and a coffee and croissant, which was what I really wanted. Following my warped dieting ethos, I convinced myself that one went some way to cancelling out the other.

It was early, but the place was packed. Ladies who lunched, it seemed, were also ladies who went out for breakfast. They wore designer jeans, sunglasses the size of saucers, statement jewellery and oversized handbags. There were groups of young trustafarians in their skinny jeans and college-kid styles, looking like deliberately dishevelled and nonchalant rock stars. And there were posh mummies, sickeningly radiant with light tans and peachy cheeks, comparing notes on Polish nannies. They seemed incapable of controlling their screaming, spoilt and well-dressed children with ridiculous names.

I felt pasty, podgy and scruffy amidst the Fresh and Wild crowd and not unlike Luke Skywalker visiting the bar of freaks and aliens in *Star Wars*. I nibbled a corner of the croissant and tried not to stare at 'Pixie', a three year old with her fingers in the sugar-free, wheat-free cakes over at the bakery, whilst her mother made a call on her mobile and thumbed a copy of *Vogue Italia*. I fumbled in my bag for something to distract me. I'd brought *The Lady* with me and read through the ad again. I found a half-chewed Bic at the bottom of my bag and started to write out a draft letter on a recycled napkin. After all, I figured, I had nothing to lose. To answer Ray's question, maybe I *was* serious.

Tiffany Blue

I wasn't very good at being a lady of leisure. I didn't feel that I could while away the hours at Tate Modern, contact almost forgotten friends on Facebook or go for long walks in Holland Park. When I contemplated a shopping trip, I imagined 'signing on' in this season's Prada, which just didn't seem right. And when I thought about visiting the cinema for a matinée I just felt like a single, lonely failure. I'd scoured the net for jobs in the media, bought every industry paper and tried to ignore the escalating coverage about On Fire and the BBC. The story had even made the local TV news. I might have been exaggerating my own importance, but I felt like a national embarrassment and so I stayed cooped up in my flat, keeping a very low profile.

On the morning of the fourth day after my sacking, as I devoured mouthfuls of toast and groaned at having just picked up a council tax demand in the post, I found a letter hiding amidst the remaining junk mail. The envelope was a beautiful Tiffany-blue, my name and address penned in an elegant hand, the black ink sweeping and looping, softly curling the tips of the letters gracefully. A letter! How retro! I thought, ruining the elegant envelope with a smudge of marmalade as I rushed to open it. Inside, the thick parchment paper was monogrammed at the top and the same elegant handwriting continued below:

Dear Isabelle,
It was with great interest that I received your application to work as a wedding planner as part of my small team on the island of Majorca . . .

I was surprised at such a speedy response from overseas and expected the next sentences to contain a standard 'we'll keep your details on file' phrase as a result.

After reviewing your covering letter and curriculum vitae, which were most persuasive, I have decided that although you've no direct experience in this field, you could be just the girl for us.

I felt my face beam with a wide smile. How very posh!

As it is a little difficult to conduct an effective interview by telephone, I would very much like to invite you to join us for a trial period beginning the 29th January.

I re-read the last line again. The twenty-ninth of January was just ten days away! Either the woman was testing my commitment or she was desperate for help.

The letter continued, quite bizarrely, to offer accommodation at the place of work during a six-month trial and a meagre salary in euros. But the money paled into significance when I thought about the opportunity to do something new, something in the sun, something that would actually make people happy. It was a crazy idea; accepting a job in a country I'd never visited, for a woman I'd never met, for less money than I'd ever earned. But that was part of the appeal. Acting on impulse and the promise of new experiences was just what I needed. A taste of the unknown, a taste of somewhere different, and now I had an opportunity. There was just one thing niggling in my mind, holding me back. Harrisson. He might be bad boyfriend material, but he had been *my* bad boyfriend material for two years and I had always hoped that he would come good. It was now, or never.

I had left several desperate, pathetic voicemail messages for Harrisson, pleading with him to return my calls urgently. Suddenly, now, he called. He was overseas, shooting a fashion story in icy Sweden. I imagined him surrounded by beautiful Bond blondes. He sounded both busy and cross that I'd interrupted him, which didn't help my vision.

'Izz? Harrisson. Look, babe, I'm in the middle of a shoot and we're starting to lose light. What is it that can't wait?' The babe was obviously thrown in to hide how angry he was that I'd disturbed him. I was holding up the final set-ups and it was costing everyone time and money.

'When are you back in London? I really need to talk to you,' I started, welling up.

'Can't this wait till tonight? I'll be done in three hours,' he offered. 'Look, I'll call you before we hit the bar,' he tried to bargain. But this time, I didn't want to come second to the models, second to work, last on his list.

'Not really. I'm fed up of all of this messing around. All this "Mr I'm Not Bothered", "Mr Art Director". I just need to know where I stand, and I need to know right now, Harrisson.' I surprised myself at how I sounded (fuming and vaguely ridiculous).

'OK, OK,' he mumbled in hushed tones. I could hear him walking, his boots gently creaking through the snow, obviously trying to find some privacy, embarrassed that someone might overhear. 'We're cool, you and me, you *know* that,' he said softly, melting something inside of me.

'Cool isn't enough any more,' I heard myself saying, despite how I felt. 'You didn't tell me you were in Stockholm this week. You said we'd do stuff. I've needed you this week, Harrisson, stuff has been happening, it's been bad. And because you didn't tell me you were away, I've ended up calling you a million times to make plans and now you think that I'm turning into some clingy, desperate bunny boiler. If you don't want to know, then please just—'

'Baby,' he interrupted, pleading in the honey-toned voice I'd heard a million times before. In truth, it was starting to sound fake. 'You know how much you mean to me. I don't know where I'm going to be most of the time, let alone diarise it with you.'

'Diarise? Christ, Harrisson. I don't want a relationship where we *diarise*. I just want a proper *relationship*.' I was starting to sound demented.

'I just thought we were having fun, Izzy. I thought we both knew where we were . . .' He started. These were the very words I had been dreading. 'And I thought we both had realised that we were in love and none of that stuff mattered,' he added softly.

I was stunned. I didn't know whether to be happy or to cry. I had to think. Before I could tell him why I'd called, I hung up. I didn't think to sign off, it was like a knee-jerk reaction, like ducking to save being hit. Without thinking I jammed down the receiver.

Now what? None of those lousy magazine articles, my dubious collection of self-help books or string of disastrous relationships had prepared me for this. I sat dumbstruck, contemplating my fate. If I went away, I might miss out on the love of my life and possibly a relationship in which a man, my man, would finally commit. But if I stayed, then things might just continue the way they always had been with Harrisson and that had never been quite enough for me.

From the moment we'd met, Harrisson had been cool and aloof. Fresh out of uni, I'd come to London and taken the first job that came my way to pay the rent on my grotty flat share – waitressing at The Love Café. I had always thought it was a ridiculous name, not least when the boss insisted we answer the phone with a 'Hello, you're in love' and sign the bill 'With love' for every customer. There were heart-shaped cut-outs to use for sprinkling a perfect chocolate-shaped heart on the top of the cappuccinos. Pastries and hand-made chocolates fashioned in the same heart shape, edible flowers to top healthy salads and cookie cutters to make toast into ... yes, you guessed it ... golden buttered hearts. Whilst the healthy, light food helped tone down my waistline for my new London life, I soon grew tired of living in a perpetually enforced Valentine's Day. Then, somewhat ironically, a cute guy came in. Guys never came in. With a bossy girlfriend dragging him through the doors for hot chocolate at the end of a wintry shopping trip, he made eyes at me whilst she checked out her purchases from local vintage stores. I mistook it for boredom. Then, halfway through her towering glass topped with mini marshmallows, she called me over.

'Do you allow photography here?' she asked, pouting, without meeting my eye.

'I'd need to ask the owner,' I'd answered, noticing that the heart-shaped fried eggs and ham were ready to deliver to table four.

'Can you? Great. I'm a food photographer. Shoot for all the Sundays. I'm thinking this will make a great story. I'm *sure* your boss will be delighted.'

I put the woman in touch with the owner and before I knew it, he had not only agreed to photography in the café the next day, but also had said yes to a healthy, happy waitress appearing in the pictures, enjoying The Love Café's food. As all of the other waitresses were far further on their way to achieving tiny London waistlines, 'healthy' was me and 'happy' was the promise of a token fee. Keen to keep my job, I reluctantly turned up for the shoot and to my surprise the cute guy was art directing.

He was a lot more fun than the photographer and bored at waiting for the kitchen to prepare endless heart-shaped food to shoot. Eventually we got chatting. His name was Harrisson and he was way too good-looking, I figured, to be interested in me. Between receiving calls on his mobile and tweaking the odd set-up for his photographer girlfriend, he started to tell me more about his job. Then, when I told him about my degree, he told me that he had a friend at a TV production company, On Fire, who had mentioned that one of the top people there was looking for a PA. I scribbled down the details on my waitressing pad, grimaced a forced smile for the 'happy waitress' shots and called the TV company straight afterwards. After a terrifying interview, I landed the job. But what surprised me more, was that when he heard, Harrisson called me at the café and said he'd buy me a drink to celebrate.

Although he'd seemed distant and preoccupied on our date, he asked me for another, checking his Filofax to arrange it. When I spotted the receipt in the fold of the book that read 'With love, Izzy' amongst a bundle of photographer's cards I agreed, thinking that he must be a romantic.

Yet, even now, I felt that we were still stuck at that same dating stage. I'd wanted more, but he'd kept things cool. I'd never seen another romantic gesture, but despite the on-off course the relationship had taken, where I often felt second to his work and better propositions, I'd fallen for him. Having waited so long for the moment where he told me he had fallen for me too, I wasn't sure if I truly believed it was happening, or if the words were enough any more.

As I finally cleared away my breakfast things and made yet another cup of tea, my head searched for the 'get out of jail free' card; the course of action I could take that would leave all of my options open. Finally, it came to me. The six-month trial. Of course. I wouldn't be saying goodbye to Harrisson, I'd be flitting off like he always did, to another job in a different country. And I could always return. Maybe, I pondered, this was what he needed; to know what it felt like. And, maybe, then he'd come running. But it was here that I stopped myself. I only entertained that scenario for a second. Truth was, I was tired of waiting for Harrisson to come running or, in fact, for any guy. I decided that now I was going to change my life, for me. And if I couldn't be happy with a man, I resolved, in a moment of clarity, I was going to help make other women happy with theirs.

This new way of thinking felt good. It felt positive and different. I went with the moment and wrote back to the wedding planner, accepting her kind offer. I then started to think about how I'd tell my mother that her only daughter was about to emigrate to sunny Majorca. Whilst I figured out what I'd also say to Ray, to Remi and how I'd handle Harrisson, I threw myself into packing. I had to keep up the momentum so that I wouldn't bottle it. I had to focus on the things I needed to sort out, like terminating the rental on my flat, paying up my bills and, of course, finding shoes perfect for Spanish cobbled streets which still oozed glamour.

I eyed up the big lump of dark brown wood in the corner of the bedroom and decided that I could take it on – the wardrobe. I opened the doors and checked out the enormity of the task. Blimey, worse than I'd thought. I had to make a forceful start. I attacked piles and piles of clothes at speed, rediscovering old favourites I thought I'd lost for ever, hugging them like old friends and finding expensive impulse buys that had never been worn, which made my cheeks prickle with guilt. I had to admit there was some vintage that looked as if it had finally had its day, jeans that had never been a flattering cut, and a couple of scary sale shockers that seemed to never fit into any season, amongst the things I most treasured.

Determined to fight the urge to try to squeeze everything I had ever owned into one suitcase by the end of the week, I tried to be strong about slinging the Seventies Ozzie Clarke dress that had never looked good on me, the Chanel handbag that was too worn with wear to keep and the foxy McQueen dress that I'd kept for years but would never, ever fit into again. I tried to divide everything into piles. The best I could do was to have piles for definitely keep, might keep, like but shouldn't keep, should keep but don't really wear, should keep but way too sensible to be fun. It was about as organised as I could be whilst my mind formatted my mental 'to do' list.

It took half a tub of Ben and Jerry's best creamy ice cream to get through the emotional exercise. It was all going so well till I came across them – Harrisson's crisp white shirts. He'd left them there in case an emergency meeting or dinner invite popped up, but really they stayed because he knew I loved wrapping myself in them, my security blankets, to lounge around in. I ran my fingers down the thick white cotton; the shirts were cool to touch, slightly rumpled and smelt of freshly washed laundry. Delicious. I felt a lump in my throat the size of a toffee apple, but I was determined not to stop what I'd started. I grabbed the shirts from their hangers and relegated them quickly to the dump pile and tried to forget that I'd stumbled across them.

Then, it was out with the digital camera before a change of heart on the definitely ditch piles. My aim was to eBay more than half of the total mass, which I could monitor on my laptop from Majorca, and then send on to the lucky new owners. The rest was destined for the Clothing Exchange and the remainder for Oxfam. By the end of the process I had consumed my body weight in 'Cherry Garcia' to ease the pain of losing gorgeous, lovely, coveted things that were just way too fashion, or, dare I admit it, impractical, for a Latino lifestyle.

If I was Remi, I thought inadequately, still surrounded by a ridiculous amount of heavy winter wear, I would now be left with the perfect 'capsule' wardrobe and feel cleansed by the whole process. But I wasn't. I was miserable. And, I admitted to myself, without the armour of my wardrobe, my job, the security of my flat and my man, I was nervous.

It was a feeling that I couldn't shake for the next ten days. I tried to throw myself into all of the necessary preparations, but I knew that they were partly serving as a distraction, to stop me thinking about Harrisson and what could have been. If I tackled cancelling the council tax, then I didn't have to think about how much I already missed him. If I busied myself clearing out my kitchen cupboards and putting the flat up for rent, then I couldn't indulge myself with thoughts of all the good times we'd had. I stayed cooped up whilst the grey skies faded to white and became heavy with snow and, for the first time ever, I became organised.

I defrosted the ice monster that lurked at the top of my fridge, I cleaned the sticky residue off the shelf in the pan cupboard, I wrote letters to the gas board. I finally admitted to myself, as I sipped tea and watched the lacy flakes fall and turn to slush, that if I wandered around Notting Hill or the West End, visiting all of my favourite places for one final time, all I'd remember was the great first date I'd had with Harrisson at Tate Modern, the anniversary dinner we'd had at Sketch, the New Year's Eve we'd spent ice skating at Somerset House.

The same went for my friends. I just didn't want to admit that this might be the end of an era, and I couldn't face any of them. How could I call Ray, who obviously thought that Majorca was a terrible idea? I knew that Remi would have the usual London 'but there's no life South of Bond Street!' snobbery about my plans and that all my other friends would just want to talk about my recent experience at On Fire. I wanted to get on with the future, launch myself into new beginnings. It was only when I found a small leather box, days later, at the back of my underwear drawer containing the mother-of-pearl cufflinks I'd bought Harrisson for his last birthday that I decided, without hesitation, that they had to go and so did the past. I felt OK about it. I knew I was ready.

I spent the last evening in my empty apartment. No telly, no sofa, just my iPod and the trashy novel I was taking on the plane. It felt strange, but I had prepared myself for this moment and I was finally excited. I ordered a Japanese takeaway and wiped the dust off the last bottle of dubious white wine left in the flat and searched for a glass, settling for a cheesy Christmas mug that was destined for the bin. As I played with some cold noodles on a chopstick my conscience got the better of me. There was one call I really had to make. I tried Mum. I self-consciously left a message that wouldn't have her dialling the police when she returned from 'stitch and bitch' (due to the revival, she obliviously clicked her happy needles once a week in the town hall with a group of Queenie gay gossips). I tried to sound as laid back as possible with my 'Guess what? I've been offered a job in Spain' opener, leading up to 'I leave tomorrow! Can you believe it's all been so last minute? Call you when I land!' I knew she'd be furious.

I sat hugging the mug, looking out on to the streets below for the last time. The black iron street lamps bathed the grubby pavements in a dirty gold glow and lit up the pastel-painted facades of the Victorian terraces. A little boy in pyjamas played with a bear in one bay window, a family ate dinner beneath another. Out on the street a young couple scurried to the pub, wrapped in scarves, oversized coats and skinny jeans, vapour trails of icy breath and silver cigarette smoke encircling them. I should be calling Harrisson now, I thought, that could be us down there. I could be having a farewell dinner with Ray and Remi. I'd call them, but they'd be out, I told myself. Truth was, I was a coward. It was easier not to make those calls. A goodbye is so final.

Ticket, Money, Passport

The day I was due to fly to Palma, Majorca I awoke
in a groggy panic. My bedroom was so bare it was
unrecognisable, unfamiliar shadows cast themselves on
the walls. It was freezing. The only glow was from my
travel alarm, flashing 05.40 a.m. in the corner, which I
re-read three times in disbelief. I couldn't ever
remember being awake at this hour, not even for Santa.
Any other day I would have groaned, wrapped the duvet
round myself and rolled over to go back to sleep. But the
words 'ticket, money, passport' raced through my head
like a mantra and my stomach grumbled in anticipation.
My head was heavy with sleep but my body was
brimming with nervous energy, urging me to get up. I
drifted through the routine of getting ready and twenty
minutes later, closed the putty-coloured door of my tiny
flat for the last time.

Out on the street, I couldn't bear to look up at the
house that had been home for two years. I focused on
popping the key, still on its silk ribbon, into an envelope
and posting it through the agent's door on the corner of
the street. I then made my final walk through Notting
Hill. I said my silent goodbyes to Paul and Joe,

Ottolenghi and my other favourite stores and cafés, as West London started to wake up. I saw lights flick on in bedrooms, kids in private-school uniforms eating breakfast in immaculate kitchens and a girl stumbling home in last night's flimsy dress. I wrestled with my ridiculously heavy case on wheels and an oversized shopper over my shoulder, wearing all of my warmest clothes in one go, to avoid paying excess baggage. I kidded myself that I looked totally sensible on an icy, January morning. I was the antithesis of those enviable women who turn up at airports looking groomed within an inch of their lives, carrying monogrammed LV luggage, with a handsome husband and three perfect kids in tow. I waded towards the tube station in my bobble hat and sunglasses, my un-made-up eyes stinging beneath them.

Finally, I spotted a friendly face. It was Winston, setting up his flower stall in the usual spot by the steps to the tube, trying not to bother a sleeping tramp in the process.

'Blimey, is me watch wrong, love?'

'Hey, Winston, no . . . I'm off. Going. Away,' I gulped, trying not to be emotional.

'Holiday, eh? Early flight? Lucky you!' he sing-songed. 'I'll have the first daffs in stock by the time you get back.'

I managed a watery, wavering smile and lugged my case down the steps.

I'd never seen the station so quiet. I joined a carriage of Polish builders, peeled off the hat in mild embarrassment and shrugged off Harrisson's heavy winter reefer (which I'd grabbed, despite myself, at the last minute) and headed to Victoria Station to catch the inappropriately named Gatwick Express.

*

Gatwick was already swarming with people; its atmosphere, as always, was disorientating. Under the stark fluorescent lights it could have been day or night, and with a mix of thirty-somethings going skiing and families in shorts heading for winter sun, it could have been any season. My case felt heavy and I searched for coffee, like a pig snuffling for truffles. I needed just a moment to compose myself, a moment to gather my thoughts, a moment to decide if I was going to give in to my urge to call Harrisson. My phone flashed with a constant reminder of his new missed calls. With my emergency soya latte in front of me, I stared at my mobile, contemplating the call. Tentatively, I picked it up and flicked through the phone book on the tiny screen. God, I was a fool. I willed myself to highlight the number. I sipped on the coffee and kidded myself that I was waiting for the check-in to open whilst I plucked up the courage to press the green button. I listened for the dial tone, the phone at my ear. It seemed to ring for ever, but just before I gave up a sleepy voice answered 'Yullo.' Finally. But then something happened which was out of my control: I froze. I just listened. Listened to Harrisson breathing, I listened but couldn't answer. Eventually, he mumbled something inaudible and hung up. I looked up at the departure board, trying to ignore the tears streaming down my cheeks and saw my flight appear on the screen. I blew my nose roughly on a serviette and took this as my cue to move.

I mustered the courage to join a queue that snaked for miles, weaving its way to the easyJet desks. 'Sod it,' I thought, and pulled myself together, finally, making it to the front of the line. The arrow stuck on the floor pointed to a sourpuss.

'Have you read the current baggage restrictions?' she asked, in a bored monotone.

'Hello, yes, I have,' I answered, forcing a smile.

The attendant's eyebrows were painted on in a surprised expression, her was hair scraped back in a harsh Croydon facelift and inch-long false nails painted easyJet orange were encrusted with diamante, I noticed, as she grabbed my passport.

Talking to someone went some way to breaking my mood. It was a welcome distraction. I focused on the task in hand. After a fair bit of persuading and false compliments on the nails, I convinced her that my bulging bag was small enough to actually be hand luggage. I left the desk cramming my lip balm, gloss and hand cream into one of those ridiculously tiny clear plastic bags before she could change her mind.

As I headed for Duty Free, my mind was racing and the next hour was a blur. I bypassed the perfumes whilst worrying that I hadn't had the chance to say any proper goodbyes, blanked the new season's sunglasses whilst wondering if anyone had even noticed that I'd left yet, and missed the beauty offers, convinced that I shouldn't have been so stubborn and should have told Harrison that I was emigrating. I felt so alone. By the end of it, I didn't know if I was tearful because I had missed the chance to buy two Juicy Tube lip glosses for the price of one, or because I was having second thoughts about my hair-brained plan to suddenly move to a country I'd never even visited and start a career as a wedding planner when I was so obviously hopeless at keeping hold of a man myself. I arrived early (yes, early!) at the departure gate and managed to read the front page of *Hello!* magazine at least five times without taking in a single word and convinced myself that it was because there were two kids constantly whizzing by me on 'Heeleys' and three other darlings thumping the chocolate vending machine whilst their mum screeched abuse at them over my shoulder to stop. Best turn to the latest Kate Moss pics on page eleven, I figured.

The moment I was beginning to dread soon came – flight number EZ506 was called, and as we were told to prepare for boarding, I was determined not to let my bottom lip wobble. I let people barge by and resisted using the sharp elbow-nudging technique I usually reserved for bagging the best bargains at a designer sample sale scrum. I let the rush of eager holidaymakers fight it out for the first five rows of seats on the plane and settled for an aisle seat behind the vending machine family, fumbled with my seatbelt and, for a moment, shut my eyes. 'This is it, Izzy,' I told myself.

The time raced by. After a particularly camp display of emergency procedures, I indulged in several tubs of in-flight Pringles and discovered, thankfully, that three G&Ts really go to your head at thirty thousand feet. One hour and fifty minutes passed before I'd even got to the six-page special on Peter Andre and Katie Price, as I voraciously read trash to stop me thinking about everything I had left behind.

The plane swooped smoothly on to the runway and we filed into the terminal (was that a wink from the slick Spaniard at passport control?). I shuffled through the quiet marble terminal that was long enough to sober up any in-flight boozer, peeling off yet more layers and dragging my luggage behind me. I delved inside my oversized bag and searched for the letter that Celia the wedding planner had sent to me so that I had the address to hand.

The taxi journey through the city was my first taste of Palma and I loved it. Through the open window of the immaculate white cab, the air felt warm and the view was far more than I'd hoped for. I stuck my head out like a kid and tried to take it all in. Far from being a tacky tourist resort, Palma looked like a model village of Barcelona. We sped past the old town with its Moorish-inspired architecture, past historic squares, handsome churches and the impressive cathedral set against the backdrop of the harbour filled with gleaming white boats and yachts. There were people jogging, walking dogs, eating a late lunch outside, and not a drunken clubber in sight. We took the road curving out of the city, racing the locals on a dual carriageway lined with trees and heading up, up, up as we climbed into the mountains that looked like a painted backdrop against the deep-blue sky. All the while, the taxi driver rattled on like a machine gun in Spanish as I switched between nods, shrugged shoulders and confused expressions in response.

Finally, we turned off the main road and headed into a small town. The driver circled an old market square and swerved around the street dogs running through narrow side roads lined with townhouses, bashed-up cars and scooters. In just a blink, we'd passed through Andratx. As a sign appeared with the town's name crossed out, we passed a majestic town hall to climb further into the mountains.

Driving on up and passing a bar perched on the edge of a huge drop, we turned left and headed along a windy country lane – the entrance to a different landscape. Here a few larger houses and working farms lay at the foot of the mountains. The staggered terraces were lined with fields of almond trees budding with blossom and orange trees heavy with fruit. There was a little old man bent double, tending his crops in a field while his goats grazed in another, the sound of the bells ringing out from round their necks. Dogs chased the taxi as we whizzed by. The further we travelled up the steep winding track, the fewer houses there seemed to be. This. Was. Remote. Finally, at the top of the lane an impressive wrought-iron gate halted our progress. Beyond, through the bars, I could see a wonderfully tended garden and a large stone house with green wooden shutters at its windows. The taxi spun its wheels on the gravelled drive. The driver suddenly found his English, dumped my cases in the drive, and put out his hand, demanding forty-four euros.

'Yoga breathing,' I thought, to calm my nerves, and, sounding like Darth Vader, I whispered, 'Here goes.'

I struggled up the precarious stone steps that weaved through exotic plants and a mass of yellow flowers shaded by a luscious canopy of bougainvillea. My arms buckling, I dropped the bags at the end of the path and turned round to get my bearings, taking in the view.

The mountains surrounded the house on all sides, and, amidst the pine trees, stone and terracotta farmhouses were scattered on their terraces. From one chimney a chug of smoke arose and I could hear donkeys faintly in the distance. It was beautiful; rustic, imperfect, but beautiful. Suddenly, I felt a long, long, way from Notting Hill.

'Isabelle?'

A strident British voice startled me. It was round, low in pitch, with each syllable accentuated, the tone enquiring but forthright. I jumped and turned almost simultaneously, then felt something at my ankles . . .

'Pepillo! *Ya basta!*'

A small black mutt backed off, responding to a command in Spanish. I could see that it had only one eye.

'Hi . . . Hello . . . Celia?' I puffed, still out of breath

from lugging my precious possessions like a disembodied tortoise. I looked at the lady in front of me and instantly felt like a scruffy schoolgirl.

Celia was immaculate. Her silver hair scraped up into a stylish chignon, a hint of rose blush on her pale cheeks, and the neatest Chanel suit circa 1968 I'd ever seen. As I sized her up, I couldn't help but weigh up how much it could go for on eBay.

She extended a weathered but delicate hand and looked me straight in the eye. Her eyes were enquiring, twinkling and the clearest blue, the youthful glint of which defied the lines on the rest of her handsome face. She gave me a wry smile before shaking my hand in a vice-like grip that caught me off-guard.

'Please, come inside and have some tea,' she said kindly. 'You must be exhausted.'

Celia was welcoming, but matronly. She showed me to my room so that I could freshen up whilst she put the kettle on. It was a simple, small double, with white-washed walls and gleaming floor tiles that smelt of bleach. I dumped my case on the terracotta floor and sat on the bed for a moment to take things in. The mattress was like concrete, and crisp white sheets were turned down over a single blue blanket. I looked around the room. A plain wooden cross hung above the bed. A large chest of drawers and a chair were the only pieces of furniture, a jug filled with wild flowers was the only luxury, but the view was wonderful. A small window with green wooden shutters next to the bed framed a perfect slice of the valley and the mountains. The little dog scratched at my door and I took it as a sign to try to find Celia in the garden.

As I walked through the vast country kitchen, I found Celia laying an ivory lace tablecloth over a mosaic-tiled table, under the shady terrace. Despite the surroundings, the scene was quintessentially English. She added a delicate china teapot covered in faded blue flowers with a matching milk jug, two cups and saucers in cornflower-blue and a lemon-yellow sugar bowl filled with sparkling white cubes of sugar. I offered to help, but she insisted that I sit down.

Celia had more frosty front than the great British coastline as she served high tea. It seemed strange to be eating scones and tiny squares of cucumber sandwiches in another country, but I got the impression that it was a regular occurrence in Celia's Majorcan home. All I wanted was a long, stiff drink and to ask this intriguing woman all about herself and her life, but I remembered my manners and engaged in polite conversation, not that Celia let the chit-chat last for very long.

'Right, well, tomorrow is Monday,' Celia announced seriously as I tried to ask her how she came to be in Majorca, 'and we need to get cracking in the office,' she added, carefully placing her cup of smoky Lapsang Souchong on its floral saucer.

'Yes, of course,' I replied. 'I'm looking forward to it.' Under the table I could feel the small black mutt brushing against my shins, growling at me for the cucumber sandwich I was about to devour.

'Ignore Pepillo. He'll get used to you,' she offered with conviction, reminding me of a more elegant Barbara Woodhouse. She didn't seem concerned that I might not get used to him.

'January, Isabelle, is a very busy time for the company. We're currently inundated with new enquiries from girls who've been proposed to at Christmas and on New Year's Eve. They'll want to be booking a wedding for the coming year, some for the following. Then there are the weddings this spring to organise. And clients to meet who are visiting the island, and who have already booked, wanting to discuss all manner of details for their big day,' Celia continued, pouring herself more tea.

'So, how many in the team?' I interrupted inquisitively.

'Never mind that,' Celia retorted. 'It will just be yourself and me in the office for now. And my suggestion is that you become versed in the general workings of the business this afternoon, how we operate, our services and our fees. Then, starting from tomorrow, *first thing*, you can deal with some of the new enquiries, reiterating what I've told you to our prospective clients. So that you quickly come to understand the finer workings of the business, I have decided to hand over the first wedding of the season to you. Almost every detail has been organised. It will be a good exercise for you to review the requirements of the bride and groom, check what has been done for them and how. On the big day, you will then lead the event with myself and our team will be there to oversee it with you.'

I took in a deep breath in amazement. The first wedding! I knew nothing about weddings! I'd anticipated a gentle afternoon and a 'getting to know you' session with my new boss and landlady, but I shouldn't have. Celia was seriously old school. For the next two hours, I frantically wrote notes whilst Celia delivered a torrent of information from across the table. I was thankful that I'd learned shorthand for my role as a PA. Celia paused only twice to crinkle her forehead and gauge my attention span, giving me just enough time to flex my now tired finger joints. I wondered how she stored such detailed information beneath that perfect chignon.

As the light over the mountains faded to dusk and

the temperature dropped, Celia's dictation came to a natural end. Silently, as I mulled over a few remaining questions, my mind still whirring and on overload, we cleared the table and headed inside.

The house was a large, traditional country *finca*. Inside, the rough jesso walls were stark white, the ceilings beamed and the floors tiled in heavy flagstone. The living room was generous, with a huge fireplace, and was carefully decorated with French antiques and bohemian British touches. There was a collection of Clarice Cliff ceramics, some art work that looked as if it had been there since the Sixties, and some delicate oriental objects, presumably from Celia's travels. There were chic Spanish shawls draped over a sofa and a large vintage mirror, the glass speckled with age. I wanted desperately to snoop at the many solid silver frames containing Celia's photos, hoping to get an insight into who she was, her family and her life, but for now, she was watching me with equal interest and I became conscious of staring.

'Why don't you change for dinner, Isabelle? I've prepared something for us to eat here this evening,' Celia offered, breaking my snoop.

'That's very thoughtful and very kind,' I answered, forcing myself to turn and look at her, rather than at her personal belongings.

'I was rather thinking that eight-thirty would be perfect,' Celia replied. 'The Lechona will be ready by then.'

'That sounds great, thank you, Celia. I really should start unpacking.' I excused myself mumbling the new word – Lechona, Le-cho-na, realising that I had just one evening to get organised before starting work in the morning.

Upstairs, I found my bedroom door already open

and, bizarrely, a low grumbling noise was coming from inside. As I swung the door wide in one motion, not sure what I would find, I caught Pepillo sprawled on my bed, back legs stretched behind him, dementedly shaking his head from side to side as he wrestled with what I presumed was a ball or a toy.

'Pepillo, NO!' I shouted at the dog, cross that he was making a mess of my bed.

As he looked up at me with his one good eye, I noticed that he was actually devouring one of my favourite Marc Jacobs pumps.

'Ahhhhhhhh!' I screamed, not knowing any obscenities in Spanish, whilst chasing him out of the room.

He stopped at the door and as I went to survey the damage, he turned, flashing me a myopic look of pure glee. My bed was covered in a bristle of tiny black hairs and my shoes were wrecked. For now, he'd won.

A formal dinner in the vast white dining room, with antique silver cutlery and Victorian chargers, seemed ridiculous just for two people, but that was the scene that met me as I came downstairs. It wasn't cold, but Celia had lit the fire; the glow reminded me of Christmas at home, and the smell of olive and almond wood burning was like incense. Despite the formality of the room, Celia seemed more relaxed. The suit had been replaced by a pair of cigarette pants and a honey-coloured cashmere sweater, from beneath which a neat white collar peeked out. Her silver hair was pulled into a neat ponytal which swung gently as she proudly brought in what I discovered was the lechona – a whole roasted piglet. Celia served this with potatoes cooked with wedges of onion and rosemary in the oven and *calabacín* (white courgettes). It was a feast. The smell of pork threw Pepillo into a frenzy, but he soon fell asleep on the cold tiled floor by Celia's feet, which now sported supple black ballet pumps, two cream C's for Chanel entwined on the toes.

I was relieved to discover that Celia's mood had softened. She had finally left work behind and seemed more relaxed. She wanted to know all about my life in Notting Hill, telling me that she'd lived in Chelsea in the late Sixties. Despite my questions she didn't reveal much, but it became obvious that she'd been in the midst of swinging London. I guessed that she'd lived quite a life, but it was one that I'd only find out about in time. For now, I was just pleased to see her smiling. Maybe this would be more fun than I'd first thought. We drank a few glasses of hearty country red and Celia became chatty, though never letting down her guard. I finally suspected, as I suppressed a yawn and helped wash the dishes before bed, that she was thankful for some company.

My first few days with Celia passed by in a blur. In an ample office at the top of the house, I embarked on a steep learning curve. During that first week, I felt glued to my desk; a large teak beast with a heavy matching chair and an old-fashioned phone perched on one corner. The walls were covered with bookshelves and filled with lever-arch files, messy piles of bridal magazines, hotel brochures and discarded CD boxes. There was a small cupboard which was home to some candles and vases and a clumpy wooden filing cabinet brimming so full of paperwork that it refused to close. Aside from the computers, the office looked as though it had been this way for years. If it hadn't been for the picture window, through which we could see the tops of trees and the valley below, we could have been anywhere in the world as the hours slipped by. Yet I was thankful that the busy workload didn't allow me any time to dwell on what I'd left behind in London, or on Harrisson.

The office day started at nine prompt, when Celia brought up her first china cup of Lapsang. There was an hour for lunch at two, but no siesta, and we often worked away till the end of the Spanish working day – around eight. By the following Saturday, I was beginning to get cabin fever. I wanted to get out and explore the local town. The only other person I had seen since arriving at the house was Celia's gardener, Pep. The old Majorcan man came to tend to the garden each morning, flashing me a friendly smile beneath his navy corduroy cap, saying *Bon día* and cursing Pepillo as an idle *'perro de casa'*. Yet my thoughts of a day off were on hold. The first wedding that Celia had spoken about at my arrival was, in fact, booked for tomorrow; my first Sunday.

Saturday afternoon's phone calls to brides to be turned into Saturday evening and I was all talked out by the time Celia emerged clutching her early evening sherry.

'Isabelle, what do you say to an early drink in the town tonight?' she enquired formally, already in a well-cut tea dress, cardigan and pearls.

'Perfect!' I replied, as perkily as I could muster. A quiet drink out was just what I needed to calm my nerves before the first wedding of the season.

As I pulled on a fresh pair of jeans and applied a smear of lip-gloss, I imagined how different the scenario this evening would be to a Saturday night out in W11. Celia and I would share a few quiet G&Ts, over which we might nibble some sweet, oily olives. We'd talk about how the fresh, locally grown lemons (which smelt sharply of sherbert when just picked) made all the difference to one of our favourite tipples and how the liberal Spanish measures nearly knocked our socks off. Until I made some friends of my own, I was happy in Celia's company and her kind gesture to show me the local delights of this rustic little place; it was a bit like going out with a distant, enigmatic aunt.

We arrived at the local rickety bar (the only bar) in typical British fashion at about eight-thirty, after a quick supper at home but, of course, the locals hadn't even thought about dining by then, let alone thought about their evening's entertainment. The place was empty. The floor was still awash with disinfectant, the tables were being scrubbed clean, and the owners were just setting up. It wasn't till an hour and a half later that the bar started to fill. By then, Celia and I had lined up around six empty highball glasses on our small wooden table. In my calculations, having wobbled as I stood up to venture to the ladies and tripped over a growling Pepillo on the way back, they were equivalent to double UK measures, and my pocket still rattled with euros!

I sat happily chit-chatting away to Celia, watching the owners and how they operated. The big mama of the *casa* obviously ruled the roost. She was almost as wide as she was tall, her face brown, round and free of make-up. She crashed around, wiping tables, polishing the bar, pouring drinks and serving tapas like a whirlwind in her apron, pop socks and slippers. She greeted regulars like long-lost friends, kissed their children (momentarily paralysing them by cupping their rosy faces in her chubby hands), and nodded knowing glances at immaculate old ladies out with their husbands whilst refilling their glasses from wine bottles at their tables, as their conversation grew thin. Then she'd turn her attention to her staff, clipping her scruffy son round the ear for eyeing the football, which was blaring from the television in the corner, rather than pulling his weight behind the bar, and screeching commands at her meek husband, whom I could see reluctantly frying a tortilla in the kitchen, fag in his mouth, Mahou beer by his side, as the swing doors from the bar flew open as she barged in and out. She was formidable.

By ten-forty-five, the bar was buzzing with chatter and laughter and it was too loud for Celia and me to talk. Little old ladies sat around gossiping with gusto, their short hair set and their clothes tidy. The men, in their caps, neat jackets and sharply pressed trousers, sat mostly silent at their sides, their faces heavily lined from the sun and backs rounded from years of working the land.

'They all look about three hundred years old,' I remarked to Celia, who nodded in agreement but joked that they were probably just in their twenties.

Kids ran riot. Little girls in their prettiest dresses gave their daddies big puppy eyes in the hope of an ice cream from the giant yellow freezer cabinet that hummed like a friendly monster in the corner. A crowd of boys gathered around the TV, drinking Coca Cola from glass bottles with straws and emulating the goals scored in slow motion replay. Workmen in their soiled jeans gathered at the bar, smoking, jibing at 'mama de casa', to her squeals of delight, and praising the tapas that her husband was still rustling up. Then the entertainment started.

The big mama strode over to turn off the TV in dramatic fashion, shooing the boys outside, to carry on their game in the street. At the very back of the bar, through air thick with cigarette smoke, a man and a woman emerged. The duo before us were full-on

Eighties showbiz. She sported a Wonderwoman hairstyle that was stiff with glittery spray, a skimpy white lace bolero over an industrial balconette bra, legs like sausages stuffed into a miniskirt, and stilettoes. He stood proudly in a burgundy velvet suit, ruffled pink shirt over his puffed-out chest, accessorised with a chunky gold necklace and a cigarette, placed at the corner of his ultra-thin lips. It was then, as I squinted through the smoke, wondering if the ban would ever really hit Spain, that I recognised them from the poster pasted up outside. The picture must have been twenty years old and in an attempt to attract some English drinkers to their special night, it had unwittingly read: TONIGHT, COME SEE JUAN PLAY WITH HIS ORGAN.

And play he did. Our inflated Gloria Estefan had a belter of a voice. To a Flamenco backing track, she warbled and wiggled her way through Latino anthems whilst Juan never missed a note on his Casio or let his cigarette slip. The music boomed so loudly from the little bar that it echoed through the mountains and everyone inside got to their feet. The little girls danced in a circle, older couples held one another in tight embraces as they pushed each other formally around the floor, widows danced merrily with their sisters, and the workmen clapped in furious time. Even Celia nodded along to the beat, her eyes laughing as she clocked my surprise. Then, before I knew it, I was up. A man of about sixty, whom I'd seen arrive in a funny 'Ferragut' van, wearing a thirty-year-old suit, was not taking no for an answer, in any language.

I succumbed to the atmosphere and the knowledge that at least he had his own hair, and I tried my best to copy what the other women were doing, with little success and much drunken flair. Despite his years, the old boy was a real mover. He looked dismayed at my lack of rhythm and clumsy footwork, but he was all smiles and encouragement as he twirled me round, stomping his feet, his hands clapping, his head high as he stayed glued to my side. At the end of the song, I slunk back to my stool. And it was as I regained my breath that I realised that Celia had gone.

My eyes searched the room, scanning a whirr of faces through my gin goggles. Hmmm. Strange. Pepillo was still under my chair, sleeping despite the noise, so I looked again. Celia would never be far from her trusty hound, she must be nearby, I watched and waited.

It was time for the entertainment to take a break. Juan the organist, still looking composed, exited to the bar, a towel draped round his shoulders, like a boxer having gone several rounds.

I decided to check the ladies. A group of young girls broke away from a lengthy queue to greet the now heavily perspiring singer as she slipped off her shoes and hobbled to the mirror to powder her brow and puff up her drooping hair. But no Celia. As music started to boom from a battered old beat box in the bar, the girls ran back to the floor screaming. A Tom Jones intro played full volume. I followed the kids and headed for the bar. Oh, well, I thought, maybe I'll check outside and get a final G&T before heading home.

A hundred Spanish voices lisped passionately and clapped in time to the Welshman, as two ladies danced in the middle of their circle. One was a little old señora who can't have been five feet tall and her hair was dyed brilliant red, her face deeply creased with laughter lines and, when she smiled, I could see she bore no teeth. But now she was whirling around, keeping perfect time, enticing the owner's son as a confident girl his own age might, to come and dance with her. The little girls adored her. As I took the first sip of my final G&T, thinking I'd come a long way to hear a Tom Jones tune, I looked up as the other dancing banshee turned. I saw her face for the first time and realised, to my complete shock, that it was Celia.

The Very Best Man

The next morning I awoke with a start. 'Shit! Wedding day!' The realisation struck my sore head like a lightning bolt. My mouth felt furry, my calves throbbed from dancing and the stuffy room was filled with bright, white sunlight and the discordant sounds of the countryside. Great. So much for aiming to start the wedding season feeling fresh and organised. As I strained my eyes to look at the travel clock, I felt my heart race in time with the flashing nanoseconds. Ten-thirty? Surely not! I hit the top of the clock in anger as I realised that yes, that was actually the time and I cursed as the mechanism flicked on to read 10.31. Bugger. I flew out of bed, rubbed my thudding brow and headed for the shower. It was already ten-thirty-two.

With my eyes still half shut and the clock in my hand, I took two steps out of my room and lost my footing over a sleeping Pepillo, stretched luxuriously across the hallway. I skidded on the slippy marble floor in my fluffy bed socks and landed with a crash against the bathroom door opposite, banging my eye on the door handle. 'Fan-fucking-tastic!' I shouted at the dog – who, I swear, looked quite pleased with himself before scuttling off with his skinny tail between his legs on hearing Celia's heels on the marble stairs.

'Everything all right, Isabelle?' I heard Celia enquire as I crawled into the bathroom before she could reach the landing. Ten-thirty-four and counting . . .

I winced in pain but stayed perfectly still behind the door.

'Isabelle? Are you STILL in the shower? We need to leave in forty minutes and I thought we would have a short briefing beforehand . . .'

'Oh right . . . yes, of course . . . everything's fine, just give me ten,' I yelled back, trying to sound cheery and calm, checking my eye in the mirror and realising that, at ten-thirty-five, I didn't have time for a shower at all. Damn it. My left eye was raging. The white was shot through with red veins, the flesh around it was swollen and the lid was puffy. I fumbled in the drawer for some Optrex, yelped on bathing it and did my best cover-up job around the now dark and tender socket with heavy-duty make-up, the kind used in movies to hide scars. In fact, Remi had bought it for me as a birthday present, in case of 'emergency spots'. Only Remi could think this an appropriate gift, but it had finally come into its own – this was definitely an emergency. I was going to my first wedding of the season smelling of last night's smoky bar, with dirty hair, legs in desperate need of a shave, and possibly a black eye to boot. I felt a lump in my throat. I was so desperate to make a good impression on Celia and this was far from an ideal start. I took a deep breath, reached for a handful of Kirby grips, and stuck them in my mouth, twisting my hair and coaxing it into a ponytail.

'Isabelle, have you eaten anything?' Celia asked kindly, still at the door.

I spat out the grips and watched them shoot like missiles into the sink at the thought of food.

'Not yet,' I said in haste, 'I've been looking at my notes, maybe we could chat over coffee?' I shouted, hopefully.

No answer. I heard Celia's heels turn and walk away. Ten-thirty-six. I tried to focus on getting myself together – and fast.

I washed my armpits, applied liberal amounts of Flowerbomb perfume and tried to focus my mind on conjuring up an outfit that would convey 'efficient and understatedly sexy wedding planner' rather than 'hung-over mess with legs like a Yeti'. I tried to steady my hand long enough to apply some lipstick and simultaneously remember if I'd charged my mobile and printed out my wedding schedule and contact sheets. My brain ached. I gave my eye one final check in the mirror. Thankfully the angry red had dissolved to a watery pink.

Back in my room I dropped my towel and fumbled in my wardrobe muttering the words 'efficient and understatedly sexy wedding planner' as I reached for my chiffon Dolce & Gabbana shirt, smart, high-waisted white pants and spike heels. The sea-green shirt was sheer but had ruffles and a large pattern that concealed everything except a silhouette, but not wanting to take any chances I stuck the ruffles in place over my nipples with cosmetic tape (or, as Remi called, it 'tit tape'). I grabbed some oversized sunglasses and a large white leather tote, big enough to fit my lever arch file into and scurried off to the office in search of everything I needed for the big day. I snuck a reluctant peek at the alarm clock: 10.42. Not bad.

'Isabelle, the agenda?' Celia urged as I tottered into the kitchen, my eyes cautiously searching the floor for

Pepillo, and towards the stove, desperately reaching for the coffee pot.

'Yes, of course,' I said sitting down. I checked my colour-coded documents and listed off the times for Celia in my most convincing tone: 'Midday, flowers arrive, I'll shoot down to the church to oversee the displays then cut back to the reception venue to make sure the flowers for the table are in the right place. Twelve-twenty, bride has bouquet; bridesmaids have crowns in place when they finish make-up at twelve-thirty.' I reeled off the details, having run them through my head umpteen times.

By ten-fifty-seven we were ready to go. I greedily guzzled a glass of water on leaving the house, ignored my growling stomach and gave Pepillo a glare. Outside I sighed with relief and drew in my first welcome breaths of fresh air as I tiptoed down the gravel drive to the car. I'd just got away with it. It was merely a bad start. I'm organised. I'm calm and collected. Nothing can possibly go wrong now, I thought to myself.

Celia had insisted on driving to the wedding and the hour-long journey into the mountains in her convertible Mercedes was filled mostly with silence. I knew nothing about cars but this was a beauty; a sleek white model from the Seventies or Eighties, with navy leather seats and a tan steering wheel. And, of course, it was as impeccable as its owner. Celia was sporting a Hermès headscarf and driving gloves. She passed the oversized wheel through her hands without crossing them once, constantly checking her mirror. She looked like a heroine from an old movie, the kind where a film of the scenery rolls past a static car in the studio.

I tried to strike up polite conversation, finally finding an appropriate lull in the map-reading procedures. 'You looked like you were having a good time last night?' I asked knowingly, as the road narrowed and the rugged terrain gave way to spectacular views of the sea, but Celia just gave me a nod. It might have been my imagination but her watery smile and raised eyebrow seemed to say 'You were drunk' and 'Why do you ask?' in just one cool motion. I drank the remainder of the emergency water supply I'd tucked into my tote to quosh my evil hangover, smoothed my hair back into its ponytail, and looked out of the window at the pines sweeping by. I was more nervous today than I could remember having been for a long, long time. It was time to prove to Celia I could really do the job. Time to show I'd done all of the necessary preparation. Time to make sure I didn't screw up someone else's big day.

Finally, we made our way through a tiny rustic village and pulled up to the church. It was a glorious day for a wedding – sunny, blue skies and a gentle breeze for our English rose of a bride, I thought romantically for a second. I fumbled to grab my bag from the back seat and to get going and, turning quickly, I wondered if I'd just heard the sound of a coin dropping on metal. I was determined to stick to the schedule and to stay focused. I ignored the noise. The sun was shining and I felt the breeze play with the ruffles on the front of my shirt as I slammed the passenger seat of the car tightly shut. I glanced round to see that Celia was already halfway up the church steps, meekly kissing the Spanish priest on both cheeks and lowering her eyes. I rushed to follow her.

'Padre,' I started with a wide smile, which waned to dumb confusion as I saw a look of horror on his face. I automatically followed his expression, which hovered at my chest. I looked down. The button from my shirt had popped off – the single faux emerald sparkly button that was holding those few wisps of chiffon in strategic place, had gone. I stood in front of the holy man with my shirt gaping open almost to my navel, revealing two bee-stung nipples, each barely covered by a strip of doubled-over tape. Celia swiftly stepped in front of me as a distraction and I sped through the open church doors and down the aisle to the priest's tiny office to quickly stick myself back into my blouse. Sod it! I had just a few minutes before the florists would arrive, just a few minutes to make sure I didn't look inappropriate in a house of God. I tried not to swear as I ripped the tape from my nipples and rearranged the shirt.

José, the Spanish florist I'd hired, was an artist. He arrived with an entourage of staff in a refrigerated van filled with raffia, ribbon and roses. He built a glorious tower of white roses, Cala lilies and eucalyptus in front of the altar that looked as if it defied gravity. It smelt divine.

'No Ivy,' I said to him as he put the finishing touches to his creation with a smile.

'No Ivy,' he repeated in his sexy accent. Anna, the bride, hated it and we'd heard these words from her a million times. Satisfied, I grabbed the bridal bouquet and headed to the hotel, to the suite where Anna would be in make-up. Meanwhile, the restaurant staff would be setting up the terraces for the canapé reception and the cake was due to arrive. On route, I just had time to glance down at the perfect ball of tightly woven Cala lilies and white roses to think how I'd feel if this was my wedding day, but the moment didn't last long. I soon found myself in a crowded hotel suite full of hysterical women. I calmed a very tearful mother of the bride and forcefully told a princess of a bridesmaid that if only she had decided that she would like her thin hair in ringlets before now, we could have organised it without making the bride late on *HER* special day.

And there she was. The bride. She looked serene, composed and pampered. The make-up artist was working wonders on her eyes, the hairdresser teasing her hair into a loose chignon. Her skin was glowing like a white peach, lit up by the pearls at her ears. Her silk dress was exquisite; not too showy, pure class. I expected nothing less. Anna was an attractive and successful London lawyer. I proudly presented the bouquet to her.

'Hi, Anna, how are you feeling? You look wonderful! And what about these?' I sang, in my best aiming-to-please voice. And just like that, with forty minutes till the bride was due to walk down the aisle, she lost it.

'The Lilies dominate, Izzy, and I was very, very clear that I didn't want the lilies to dominate.' Her cheeks were burning through the delicate pink blush, her made-up eyes bulged grotesquely as she hissed the words and for a moment, I thought she would burst out of her tightly laced corset. 'I HATE them. Where's José?' she demanded, slamming them down on the make-up table, suddenly a bridal prima donna.

'Anna, I completely understand,' I said carefully, 'but there really isn't any time.' I could see that she was welling up, this wasn't what she wanted to hear. 'José has finished the tower and he has left.' The princess bridesmaid stood behind her, almost looking smug.

'Isabelle,' Anna interrupted, 'I didn't think I'd need to explain to you, of all people, that these flowers will be in my wedding photos *for ever*. They will ruin *everything.*'

Through the hotel window I could see Celia wafting

around the dining terrace below, efficiently ticking things off on a list with her Mont Blanc fountain pen, probably checking my every move.

'If I'm late, well that's fine, that's how it has to be. Call him back, Isabelle. Are you even listening to me?' I was, but I knew that another ceremony was booked in straight after Anna's. I couldn't let her know this, however; it made the church sound like a factory and it wasn't her problem.

It was then that Julia, the make-up artist, interjected, passing Anna a tissue. 'Look, I get it, I don't like the lilies either, but José isn't going to have extra flowers to fix this, even if he comes back. Why don't you let me pull out the largest ones whilst Maria finishes your hair? Izzy, run to the garden and pick me some more roses, and don't let the hotel know – or, for God's sake, let Celia see you . . .' I could have kissed her.

With just a few minutes to go, and with the bride poised once more, the bouquet stripped and rebuilt, I raced down to the church ahead of the wedding party. I remembered to call ahead, to make sure with the kitchen that the cake had arrived. It had. Surely things would be plain sailing from now on?

In the cool, calm atmosphere of the pretty village church I greeted the Spanish soprano, pushed the button on the CD of church bells (the real thing ceased to work years ago, not that anyone ever noticed the difference), and waited for the English minister to put on his robes. The wedding guests had gathered outside and I strutted out in search of the ushers, clutching precisely 120 copies of Anna's carefully prepared 'Order of Ceremony' for them to hand out.

It was then that I spotted him. The best man. Definitely the best man. For a moment, my wedding-filled world went a little hazy. He had big puppy-brown eyes, floppy English school boy hair and a sharp suit. He was helping an elderly lady up the steps and laughing at her jokes. His buttonhole gave him away. It was safe to approach him. A buttonhole on a man at a wedding who wasn't the groom or father said, 'I'm here to help.'

'Hi, you must be—'

'Charlie,' he confirmed, with a grin.

'Right. Izz, wedding planner, sorry to be short, but we start in a few minutes, I need the ushers, and immediate family and you for the front row . . .' I did my best to sound organised. 'Efficient and understatedly sexy wedding planner', 'efficient and understatedly sexy wedding planner,' I muttered to myself.

Between Charlie, Celia and me, we managed to get the ushers in place and the guests seated. Celia made her way to the back of the church, I tried my best to move quietly to the front, to signal the soprano to begin singing when the bride arrived. I stood to the left of the pews, near to the mother of the bride, who was still weepy. I had a great view of Charlie. I was still running the details of the canapé reception through my head whilst checking him out whilst, of course, pretending not to be. I felt mildly guilty at ogling another man, remembering Harrisson for just a minute, but I tried to focus on the finer details of the day. The bride was five minutes late. I could see Celia at the back of the church looking down at her watch. I glanced down at my unruly shirt, checking I was decent. Bloody thing. Harrisson had bought it for me a year earlier to go to a dinner party. He was all gentlemanly about buying me something new to wear and I hadn't been sure if it was a kind gesture, if he had wanted me to feel confident in front of his friends, or if it was an exercise which guaranteed I wouldn't turn up in something completely embarrassing or inappropriate. I was never sure, but it made me think of him once more.

Before I could get into self-indulgent thought patterns, the door opened and the bride, with her father, started her slow, dreamy walk down the aisle. She looked beautiful and no one could ever have guessed that just a short while ago she'd thrown a complete hissy fit. The princess bridesmaid shot me a scowl and gave the best man a flirtatious smile. Her bridesmaid's dress had been yanked down a little lower than the other girls' to reveal a heaving cleavage, her make-up was just that little bit overdone, her fake tan just a little too San Tropez. She looked like she was competing with the bride for attention. But so far, she was failing. A few faces searched the balcony for 'the voice'; the soprano had an amazing tone, which resonated through the building. Everyone else looked at the bride in wonder. Well, everyone except her mother.

I leaned over to give her another tissue. 'I know, it's so moving,' I patronised, trying to calm her.

In return she grabbed my arm and whispered in a shrill hiss, 'It's not that, dear, I can't stand that boy she's going to marry,' through tightly gritted teeth. I instinctively slid a little further down the pews.

Even if the battleaxe wasn't moved by the ceremony, I was. I found myself floating into a dream world ... 'Did I, Isabelle, take the best man to be my lawful wedded husband?' I reached for another hanky, this time for me, as the couple exchanged rings.

Outside the church, the artificial bells chimed and the newly weds were showered in confetti and compliments as the photographer shot the happy scene. I snuck a look at Charlie; he seemed to be on his own. I had just moments to strut back up to the hotel, ahead of the guests, but something about him held me there. He looked at me, twice, a double take and gave me a half-smile. I flashed my best look back, melting, and secretly feeling like I'd got one over on the bridesmaid from hell.

When I made it to the ladies room at the hotel I realised what the look Charlie had given me had meant; my tears had washed away my clever make-up and, to my embarrassment, I was looking in the mirror once more at the wedding planner with the black eye.

After I'd reinstated my camouflage, I checked on Miguel, the maître d'. We'd met before the big day, when the bride and groom had come to sample the food and drink and select their menu, to talk with the chef about alternative gluten-free, lactose-intolerant meals for the faddy eaters amongst the guests, and to plan the best way to use the restaurant for the reception. He was a smart, gentle Majorcan man who ran his team of waiters in a sharp operation, catered to his customers' every whim, and was almost as desperate as I was to make sure the wedding ran smoothly.

'Isabelle! OK, the guests, they come now?' he asked hastily in his best, broken English (which was a million times better than my Spanish), as I paced up the steps towards him.

'Yes, they're about to arrive. Is everything ready for the canapé reception?' I asked nervously and out of breath, pausing to look at the stunning views of the mountains and the sea beyond from the terrace.

'Yes, no problem, we serving the cava when they come. Then the tapas, *claro*.' So far, so good, I thought.

'Is everything else OK with the chef and with you for the dinner?' I checked, pointing to the kitchen and then to the dining table, realising I sounded like I thought he was an idiot.

'Yes, this is good. Good with chef, no problemas. Only one thing I ask you, Isabelle . . .'

'Of course,' I prompted, poised.

'We don't understand when we serve this toast.'

'Toast?'

'*Si*, the toast.'

This was beginning to feel like a scene from *Fawlty Towers*.

'You say me, the waiters, they pour cava, then the speeches, then the toast, then a little pause before starter, and so on. Is this toast to be served to guests in small pieces? And you want bread on the table at the same time, no?'

I spent the next five minutes explaining the concept of toasting at the end of a speech and how it differed from our very British breakfast staple. At the same time, I could see the guests wandering into the hotel gardens and could hear Ramon, the Spanish guitarist I'd booked, start his classical repertoire. I spent the next half of the canapé reception worrying about what else might have got lost in translation as I played with placing the name cards on the reception table in correspondence to Anna's table plans. I carefully folded the crisp, white cards and stood them up, checking each name carefully etched in gold calligraphy, carefully straightening each place setting.

'Isabelle.' It was Celia. 'If you've checked that all is well here, I think it would be good for us to have more of a presence at the canapé reception. You might like to see if Anna needs anything in the half-hour before dinner.'

'Great idea, thank you, Celia, I'm learning so much,' I replied, all smiles. I finished the table with a sprinkling of fresh rose petals and tottered off, feeling in control if not still slightly scared by the prospect of approaching my Jekyll and Hyde bride.

On the lower terrace the reception was already in full swing. Under the lunchtime warmth of the sun, quite a few guests who'd used alcohol to quench their thirst instead of water, were wilting; for others, it fuelled lively conversation. Right, I thought, straining my eyes against the sunlight, swerving a letch of an uncle who'd already had too many cava. Where's the woman in the big dress? She should be easy to spot . . .

There was a tap on my shoulder.

'Thought you deserved this,' said a chocolatey voice. I turned round; it was Charlie, the best man, with a glass of cava for me.

I blushed, blaming it on the weather, and he complimented me on a great party. I told him I was looking for the bride and he jokingly asked if she'd given me the black eye earlier. Embarrassed, I told him I'd love to stop to chat, but that I had to find Anna. He pointed me in the right direction.

'. . . and then I almost choked on the ring, which he'd popped into my strawberry sundae! It was supposed to be romantic, but he'd bought such a big rock I ended up in A&E.' Anna was retelling her proposal story as I approached, courted by a doting circle of family and friends. She had picked up the bottom of her dress in one hand and held a champagne flute in the other, at a high, jaunty angle, the 'rock' now sparkling in the sun. The youngest bridesmaid stood by her side, clutching her bouquet, in awe of this giant 'Fairy Queen', a real-life version of the ones in her storybooks.

'Isabelle, I'm so glad you've popped over, everything's wonderful, thank you,' Anna said, businesslike, but looking like she was on another planet.

'My pleasure, Anna. I just wanted to check if you needed anything before we seat everyone for dinner in thirty minutes?' I asked, shielding my eyes from the sun, discreetly reminding her of the schedule. To my relief, she couldn't think of anything more than handing me a room key to put at her place on the table, giving me my cue to scurry back, clutching my now empty glass.

I careered through the crowds, passing the groom and feeling surprisingly squiffy on one drink. I still hadn't eaten a thing and the bubbly had gone to my head. As the crowds parted, I could see Charlie at the end of the patio, by the fountain. He really was cute. I tried to resist the temptation of spying on him, seeing him animated, chatting, laughing, running a hand through his hair as I walked closer. As another guest moved, however, the full scene came into view. Charlie was laughing and joking with the princess bridesmaid. She was giving it full flirt, playing with the silk at her overexposed cleavage, eyes intently on his before throwing her head back as if he'd just told her the funniest thing she'd ever heard.

'Isabelle, have you met Saskia?' Crap, too late to hide, I'd been spotted.

'Saskia works in PR in London . . . organises all kinds of events. I'm sure you'd have a lot in common.' Charlie was being a gent, I assured myself.

'Yah, hi . . . sorry, didn't catch your name, saw you *working* here earlier,' she drawled cattily, in her upper-class, husky voice. 'Great venue. Love this little peasant village, it's just so . . . *real*.'

I winced on the inside, managing a polite smile.

'Charlie and I stayed near here a couple of years ago,

in Deià,' she announced, taking his arm, territorially. 'Yuh, at La Res, but, seriously, now the place has expanded and has been totally overrun by the Brits, it's just not the same . . .'

Charlie shot me an apologetic look. I made some polite excuses and took a deep breath before marching off to check on things on the upper terrace, keen to escape.

The groom was there waiting, scouring the table plan. 'Edward, hi. Having a good time?' I asked. 'Anything you need?'

'Izzy, yes, of course, thanks, great job. Quiet word?' he asked. 'Just wondered if you could help me with something . . . it's a bit delicate,' he said apologetically, his face full of English reserve and concern.

Edward, it transpired, wanted me to make some final changes to the table plan. The feeling between him and Joyce (the hissing mother-in-law) was mutual, it turned out. She'd been causing a bit of a scene during the canapé reception, he explained, and he wanted to move her as far away from himself and Anna as possible. Seeing as this was an informal wedding with no top table for the bridal party, this wasn't a problem. I scanned the table plan, resisted a childish urge to split up Charlie and Saskia, and swapped Joyce's place with an elderly aunt's – a sweet old lady with bad eyesight, she'd never notice and, even if she did, she wouldn't complain. I also promised to keep my eye on Joyce. He had my word.

On time, on cue, with Ramon now poised to play during dinner, we seated the guests. Celia and I politely directed those too tipsy to read the plans illustrated on our large display boards to their seats. I grabbed Joyce before she could ask, or notice, that we'd moved her, doing my best to chaperone her to her new position. 'Really, dear, I don't understand why you haven't given me a sea view,' she slurred, a little drunk, as I tucked her chair beneath her. Celia, I could see, already had the elderly aunt enraptured with her charming manners.

I glanced over at Edward to give him an 'all done' nod. He was leaning over, whispering diplomatically in Anna's ear. She sat quietly, eyes cast down, fingers fiddling with a rose petal, before slamming her napkin down on the table and dramatically making an exit to the ladies. The princess bridesmaid ran after her, with Charlie in tow. Edward had obviously just told Anna why he'd moved her mother. I shot him a sympathetic look. Strange, I knew the play list Ramon was booked to play, but now, as he strummed a Latino version of 'Fifty Ways to Leave Your Lover', Edward raised an eyebrow and Joyce looked content, tapping a heavily jewelled finger in time to the music. I could guess what had happened there: a request from a little old lady, how could he have refused?

With the bride significantly absent from the table, there was a natural pause in the proceedings. I gently told Ramon not to take any more requests and looked to Celia for advice.

'Isabelle, where's Anna, what's going on?'

'I don't think she's reacted well to our strategic swap-around, Celia,' I replied. 'Should I find her, or just tell the waiters to hold the cava and serve water whilst she's away from the table?' I asked, concerned.

'I'll go to the kitchen; you investigate,' Celia directed, instantly turning on her heels.

Inside, I found that the lavish marble washroom was empty.

'Damn it,' I muttered, willing my heels not to start aching as I took the back route, via the hotel gardens, to the bridal suite. Safely out of the guests' sight, I whipped off my sandals, so that I could break into a run. Vibrant lemon and lilac daisies lined the pathway, leading to a lawn shaded by an ancient olive tree beyond. I jogged past the rose bed I'd raided earlier and headed for the heavy wooden door of the suite. Catching my breath, I took a moment before knocking. But the door was already slightly ajar. I peeked inside. My eyes searched for Anna, but I could only make out a maid who was straightening up the bed, plumping the pillows. I glanced to the left of the door, pausing to think where she could be, and it was then that I saw him, as if for the first time: Charlie, the best man. The sun was catching the golden tones in his floppy hair. He'd removed his tie and left his white shirt slightly open at the neck. He looked handsomely dishevelled and he was beaming.

'Charlie, do you know what's happening? Have you seen Anna?' I asked, urgently.

'Saskia's taken her back to the table. It's all fine. You know, just a little family tension,' he said smoothly, still smiling.

I let out a sigh of relief.

'Look, about Saskie, I didn't want you to think . . .' he started.

'Oh, I thought you were an item?' I butted in, excitedly, unable to stop myself.

'No!' he laughed. 'She's not my type. She's a sweet girl, she took me on holiday with her when I broke up with my boyfriend. She's just got, you know, an unfortunate tone sometimes.'

'Oh, boyfriend!' I mused out loud, feeling foolish.

Charlie took my arm and, like the very best gay friends, told me how much he liked my Dolce & Gabbana shirt.

'Well, there's a story there,' I started as we hurried back to the party. 'But first dish the dirt on Joyce?' I pleaded.

This, I realised, before dinner had even started, was going to be a long night.

Heels on Wheels

There's an occupational hazard that comes with being a single girl who organises other people's big days – post-wedding come down. My first morning-after experience wasn't quite what I'd hoped for. I didn't wake up wearing a fairy godmother smile and feeling a sense of contentment knowing that I'd helped make two people very happy and thrown a damn good party for all of their guests. I didn't even feel a sense of relief that nothing had gone seriously wrong and yes, I could do the job. No, that morning I was exhausted, I felt empty and I found myself checking for further symptoms.

As I stretched beneath Celia's regulation scratchy wool blanket and thick cotton sheets, my legs and feet seemed to be telling me that I'd run the equivalent of a marathon in the skyscraper sandals that had seemed like such a good idea to pop on yesterday. My cheeks ached from holding a beauty-contest smile for hours on end and I was dehydrated, having been so busy making sure that everyone else ate and drank that I'd forgotten to do so myself. I tried my best to remember when I'd last felt this burnt out without hitting a bar. But this was more than feeling rough after a night clubbing in Soho, even during one of Ray's supposed fasts, which I always ended up participating in when he cracked his line, 'Izz, if I have to go dry for Ramadan, you have to do it for the "waistline god".' No, I wasn't just tired. This morning there was something else working away in the pit of my stomach, an irrepressible knot that seemed to be telling me 'that will never be you' as an image of last night's happy bride flashed through my heavy head. I didn't want to think about it. I turned over to find a cool patch of pillow and moaned.

Through the slats of the green wooden shutters at my window, the brilliant white sunlight played with dust, turning it to glitter. I lay there for an hour watching the sparkling particles before deciding to throw open the windows. The sun cast a milky haze over the mountains and a bird swooped over the valley to perch amidst a cat's cradle of telephone wires. I could feel sorry for myself today, I mused, watching the bird being joined by another, but for what? I propped myself up on my pillows and listened. Nothing. Just birdsong and the distant bark of a dog. Just as I was drifting back into a delicious half-sleep, the silence was broken by the growing sound of a tiny engine humming like a mosquito as it came towards the house, then past it, straining to climb the country lane. That was it! A scooter! I realised, one eye now open and an image of Audrey Hepburn in *Roman Holiday* replacing the bride I'd never be in my head. That was just what I needed.

I'd already seen the very one; a Vespino, with bright blue paintwork, parked proudly outside the house at the very top of Celia's lane. It had a cardboard sign reading *Se Vende* fastened over its battered faux leather seat with string, but it hadn't occurred to me that I should buy it. A Vespino ('little wasp' in Italian), on account of the sound of its whiny engine with the strength of a budget hairdryer, was the kind of slow-mobile that was far from cool; a mix of bicycle and old-fashioned moped. I had seen ancient Majorcan men riding them, a small cardboard box filled with a few home-grown tomatoes or oranges on the back, chased by the village *Rattero* dogs as they kicked the motor off to save fuel and drift down hill. But I saw the Vespino as a chance to get out and see some of the town, to ride down to the beach, to carry my groceries back from the Wednesday morning market I was so keen to explore. And with a top speed that was slower than a red bus in Central London traffic, I figured that even I couldn't come to much harm riding one. I had no idea how much it would cost to buy, but I figured it couldn't be that much and I could probably haggle if I offered cash there and then. I wasted no time. Daydreams of scooter rides along the coast got me out of bed and after a quick cup of coffee, I found myself taking a long, slow, morning walk to the top of the lane with a bundle of euros folded in the hip pocket of my jeans and a slice of buttery toast in one hand.

The house that I was heading for belonged to a man I'd only heard Celia refer to as 'Mr Hen'. She told me that he had once ran a co-operative with the same name (Hen's) in the local town, a place where people could buy and sell home-grown fruit, vegetables and grains, but the simple building had now been turned into a coach depot and the days of picking up a bag of just-shelled almonds or shiny red pomegranates was a distant memory. Mr Hen, now retired, devoted his time to tending his own produce and still lived in the large whitewashed house with emerald-painted shutters and a handsome sundial that marked the entrance to the *cami*. The small courtyard at the front of the *finca* was shaded by a canopy of vines under which his cats lazed in the dappled sunlight. Some had curled themselves inside flower pots holding cacti, hibiscus and warm earth, others pressed themselves against a sunny stone wall. Aside from the almost silent presence of the cats, there was no one around. The house was perfectly still.

I wandered past the building to the garage in which I'd often seen Mr Hen stooped over an engine. He owned an orange Citroën 2CV, in which a lady, whom I presumed was Mrs Hen, pottered around town, running her errands. This was a car which Mr Hen often worked on, wearing his spotless navy blue overalls. Unlike most of the cars in the town – dented by negotiating narrow streets and impatient Spanish drivers – the Citroën's bodywork was pristine, it's neat French curves topped with glossy paintwork and its split side windows always polished to perfection. Mrs Hen drove it very carefully, her seat pulled up so that her sweet round face was clearly visible over the wheel. She seemed oblivious to the trail of frustrated drivers forced to go slow behind her. I doubted that the car had ever made a journey as far as Palma. Mr Hen also owned a Mini Moke from the 1960s in fire-engine red and a Vespino of his own. Today the garage door was open, the tools were hung on the wall in an orderly fashion, and the floor was completely clear. There was no one to be seen.

'Perdon!' I called hopefully, a little nervous. 'Hola?' I tried again tentatively through the open garage door, noticing the strong smell of oil and cleaning fluid.

From the far corner of the garage I heard a rustling noise and saw a faded old piece of velvet curtain move. The dark shape that emerged revealed itself to be yet another cat. As my eyes came back to the door, a man was stood silently in front of me, looking a little less than happy. I'd never seen Mr Hen up close before. I'd only seen him pass by on his scooter wearing his Bigglesstyle goggles and helmet, or with his head bowed and his back bent as he concentrated on repairing an engine part. But even now those thick black eyebrows wore the same expression of intense deliberation and he continued to stoop.

'*Hola, buenos días, señor Hen,*' I started, wondering how I was going to make him understand my almost non-existent Spanish, then realising I had called him Mr Hen when that probably wasn't his name at all.

'*Buenos. Dígame,*' he replied, seriously.

'*El Vespino, se vende?*' I asked hopefully, feeling quite pleased with myself for almost making a sentence.

He looked a little taken aback and started to chatter in Spanish or Majorcan, I wasn't sure which. Then Mrs Hen appeared in the doorway, pinny on over a neat dress above pop socks and slippers. She was peering at me over the top of her tiny wire-rimmed glasses, an Alice band holding her short neatly cropped hair in place.

'*Buenos días, señora,*' I said. '*Lo siento,*' I added, trying to apologise for the imposition, without knowing how.

Then another figure appeared. A stocky man with a familiar round face topped with a flat corduroy cap. He beamed me a smile. It was Pep, Celia's gardener. I breathed a sigh of relief. He gave me a friendly nod and told the couple who I was, or so I guessed as I watched their eyebrows raise in recognition, with the mention of Celia's name. Then there was an awkward silence as all eyes fell on me, as they waited for me to speak.

Pep spoke just a few words of English, but despite his reserve, I'd got him chatting several times in Celia's garden, where often, after much laughing and miscommunication, we'd made ourselves understood, so I looked to him for some help with my purchase. I tried to make Pep understand that I was interested in buying the Vespino with an array of hand gestures and single Spanish words in no particular order. Pep was so surprised that he asked me in three different ways to make sure that he'd understood. I assumed that he would then relay the information to Mr Hen and I waited for the words '*cuánto cuesta*?' followed by a price but, strangely, the numbers didn't come.

So far, my basic shopping Spanish wasn't standing me in good stead. A fact that was alarming in itself. What followed was a long, baffling, exchange. I stood watching, trying to pull out some familiar words amidst the fast flow of Majorcan, even just the word 'Vespino', but there was no use. Mrs Hen looked on amused, hands in the pockets of her blue pinny, her head nodding gently. After ten minutes of banter, I wondered if the men had got side-tracked and shrugged my shoulders at Pep. I thought he'd understood what I'd wanted to do. Maybe I'd been wrong? Pep took a pause to give me a smile, then mumbled a fast line to Mr Hen in which I caught the word '*probar*', to try, and after the men had debated for a further few minutes, I accepted a test drive.

Mr Hen wheeled out the scooter from the back of the garage, untied the 'For Sale' sign and reached out a fine, leathery hand offering me the keys. He patiently showed me how to start her up and pointed down the street with a flat palm, signalling the roundabout, by drawing a circle with his index finger, muttering the word '*Estellencs*' (Es-te-yens). He was, I supposed, suggesting a route. I agreed graciously, reiterating his directions in broken English. He started to talk on, at speed, pointing to various parts on the Vespino, but I had no idea what he was saying, so I agreed with a '*si*' intermittently, taking it as a sales pitch, and smiled. Still no mention of a price. When he wandered back to the direction of the garage, I took this as my cue to get going. I was just about to say *'adiós'* to Pep, flick up the stand and drive on to the street, when Mr Hen emerged once more, having pulled a black horse-riding helmet from a peg and he handed it to me with urgency. A riding-hat? I couldn't imagine it was legal, but I pulled on the heavy, velvety object and fastened the strap as tightly as I could beneath my chin.

I thanked everyone as I set off, raising one hand to wave, but only for a second, before putting it straight back to straighten up the handlebars, having almost lost control. I'd seen Mr Hen's look of concern but now I needed to pick up speed. The riding hat wobbled around my head, feeling huge as the wind caught its brim, but I didn't care. It was wonderful to be racing down the slope of the little village with the mountains opening out to my left. I flew past the tiny bar on the right where a small table of men gathered for their pre-siesta drink. I swerved away from a dog, stretched out in the middle of the road, basking in the afternoon sun and refusing to move, and headed past the townhouses that lined the tiny village street towards the roundabout. To me, the Vespino felt fast and light and I drifted into a daydream, planning picnics and adventures to the other side of the island.

Beep! Beeeeeeeep! A small Seat hooted its horn furiously and from the rolled-down window of a white car a man shouted dementedly in my direction, in incomprehensible German. I wobbled, veered to the left and checked over my shoulder in a panic. Who on earth was the idiot behind me, obviously driving so badly? It was then that I realised that I was not only at the roundabout, but was also driving round it the wrong way. I got the bike back on track and pulled over. I took a minute to take a deep breath.

'You're an idiot, Izzy,' I cursed, getting off and straightening my hat with one hand, then I got straight back on the bike before I could change my mind, vowing to remember to drive on the 'wrong' side of the road and, just as importantly, to focus. To practise, I took the roundabout twice, so that I could spot the exit the first time around, and negotiate getting off it, the second.

The road took a gradual incline from the roundabout and the Vespino started to pull a little. I heard a car race up close behind me before tightly overtaking, causing me to swerve. I opened up the throttle and yelled an English obscenity in response as it disappeared round a bend. After all, this was a wide road.

Tall pines shaded the tarmac beneath me and smelt gloriously green as I climbed. The rock of the mountain was close on my left, gnarled with weather-worn scars and bearing the trees towering towards the bluest sky. To my right, the pines were thick and lush, giving way to gravelled drives which disappeared down to private houses concealed from view. As I timidly slalomed the bends, the roadside signs for falling rocks made me gulp with fear and soon the corners became tighter and steeper. Wobbling intermittently and unable to see if I'd meet another car, I started to wonder when the road would end and what I'd taken on. The seat of the Vespino was becoming more and more uncomfortable, my legs and arms were growing heavy and tired, but just one bend later, I forgot myself completely and became absorbed in the view. It was breathtaking. Now, higher up the mountain than the pines had allowed me to realise, I could see that the sea spanned the panorama below, the mountains stretching out to it. This was the only piece of Majorca I'd seen so far that seemed totally devoid of human life. There was not a single house, person or vehicle on the entire vista. It appeared to be completely unspoilt, like the Deià coastline must have looked before the hippies and then the tourists discovered it, I thought, negotiating another bend and marvelling at a vast piece of rock that interrupted the view, like a natural sculpture. This drive, I decided, was beautiful and I now could see why Mr Hen had been so keen for me to take it.

The air was soft and fragrant. It cooled slightly as the road led through a viaduct of elegant white stone arches, framing the sea beyond again and again as I started to descend, sweeping down the curves of the bends, the mountains rising handsomely above me, closing in on the sky. A sign announced them proudly as the '*Tramuntana*' and I couldn't resist, despite my aches and tiredness, seeing where the road so carefully carved into it would lead.

Just five minutes later, in the distance, I could see a town. Its stone buildings were tiered and tightly tucked into several deep mountain terraces, looking out to sea. This, I realised as I drove closer, was Estellencs. I came to the top of the town and slowed to drive down the high street.

The town felt like the last small corner of the island that had been kept a secret. Estellencs's traditional stone townhouses and simple cobbled streets looked like they couldn't have changed much in hundreds of years. In the middle of the single road that spanned the length of the town was the plaza. A pretty church with a bell tower lay at its centre, with a wooden bench and a *farmacia*, with its name painted in ceramic tiles, next door. Further down, to my right, I passed two restaurants built on a slope, with tables and chairs perched precariously on an outside patio. A feral cat hid behind the legs of two diners, sitting opposite each other as if on a see-saw, the cat waiting for anything that might fall from their plates.

As I sped by, a waitress hurled a bucket of water in the cat's direction as it snuck out from beneath the diners' feet. Then, just as quickly as I'd come across Estellencs, there was a sign, with its name crossed through in red, indicating that I'd reached its end. I turned the bike around on the uneven road. It was time to search for a drink.

Driving back through the town, I spotted a signpost that read 'cala 1.2km' and I decided, turning into it, that there could be nothing better at this moment in time, than a long, ice-cool beer on the beach. The steep and rugged country track that led down to the sea was narrow (far too tight for two cars to pass each other) and the biggest test of my riding skills so far. Hairpin bends wound past houses and well-tended plots of land amongst the wilder terrain, where the locals had planted their vegetable gardens. As I negotiated each turn carefully I glanced out to the sea ahead and watched the town, now perched up high on the mountain behind me, start to disappear.

I passed a piece of scrubland topped with a *casita* with three goats, which took a pause in their grazing to run alongside the bike from behind their wire fence. Two bends later, the unexpected sound of an indie rock band practising roared out across the valley from another *casita*, and it was the first time I'd seen one of these tiny agricultural buildings used for anything but farming. As I motored around yet another particularly sharp turn I could see a small orchard of orange trees, just by the roadside, and an old man bent over, picking the rotten, fallen fruit from the ground. Just as I was about to pass, he stood up straight, one hand on his back, waving a gnarled walking stick at me. Startled, I lost my balance, veered out of control and, worried about hitting the old boy, and losing the Vespino completely, careered into the soft grass verge. Embarrassed, I got straight up, peeled off the riding hat and went to pick up the bike, shooting the old man a big smile and an apologetic shrug. He spoke to me in lisping Majorcan, offering me a handful of his best, brightest *naranjas*. I awkwardly declined, not knowing how I'd transport them home.

The track to the *cala* was beautiful but it had started to feel like an assault course, a test littered with distractions and I killed the speed of the bike when I started it up once more, giving her just enough power to make it round the last few corners. Just as my head was starting to ache with concentration and the weight of the riding hat, I realised that I had finally come as far as the narrow road would take me. Relieved to finally stop the bike and walk, I pushed the scooter, bumping it down over the last few terraces and steps that led down to the sea. I hoped that the beach would be big, sandy and worth all of the effort.

The *cala* turned out to be a small, deserted fishing port with a pebble beach, but I was far from disappointed. Twelve fishermen's huts with faded, coloured wooden doors hugged the contours of the rockface. On a hard standing a series of boats and canoes were upturned, tightly packed and stored, and beyond them a cobbled slope led down to the sea. It was rugged, but perfect. Romantic visions of smugglers and fishermen pulling their tiny boats into dry land and bringing their catch to the shelters filled my mind as I watched the waves roll in and turn to foam against the golden rocks.

My eyes followed the curve of the cove. Beyond a

natural waterfall, a long concrete terrace shaded by a straw canopy jutted out to sea. It was decked with tables and chairs and decorated with sea-weathered buoys. Marbled and faded by the sea, they hung from the canopy by thick rope. Finally, a bar! I had never travelled so far to get a drink.

Leaving the Vespino on its stand by the entrance, I made my way on shaky, worn-out legs to order what I'd been dreaming of, a glass of ice-cold beer. It arrived complete with a pearly white frothy top and beads of condensation racing down the side. With just one other couple on a neighbouring table, I took prime position at the end of the jetty, placed the riding hat on the table and lifted the glass to take a thirsty gulp. Delicious.

I sat back on the flimsy plastic chair and took it all in. I couldn't remember feeling more content. The sound of the sea and some soft chill-out beats from the bar replaced the consistent buzz of the scooter. The salty air cleared my head. I felt completely relaxed. This, I realised for the first time since arriving in Majorca, was the moment I had been expecting – the moment I felt as though I'd actually escaped. I was finally alone. I was in a beautiful place. My eyes drifted along the handsome mountains, past the rows of bright green pines bristling on the terraces in the now pale sunlight and out to sea. For now, at least, being alone felt all right. Better than all right. It actually felt like what I needed.

It wasn't till the sun started to fade and I felt a nip in the sea air that I reluctantly returned my glass to the bar. I hadn't been savouring the idea of retracing my steps back to Mr Hen on the Vespino, but I took some comfort in knowing that some strange law of nature meant that the way home usually felt like a faster route than any outward journey. The scooter struggled to climb the steep track that led from the *cala* back to the town, and its tyres slipping on the gravel was the only sound for miles. The old man had gone from the orange grove and the band practice had finished. The goats, I presumed, had taken shelter in their *casita*.

It wasn't long before I was buzzing back down the winding mountain road towards Andratx, heading through the pristine white arches of the viaduct. I finally arrived at the roundabout just before dark and took the final stretch of road up through the village to Mr Hen's.

As I pulled up outside his garage Mr Hen appeared from the shadows and greeted me with a *'Buenas tardes'*, his dark brows raised beneath a full head of silver-grey hair. I went to hand back the riding hat and the keys with a *'muchas gracias'* before trying to find my walking legs to carry me the rest of the way home, but Mr Hen protested. He made me understand that it was getting dark now, that I should put the lights on the Vespino and ride it home. I gratefully vowed to return the scooter in the morning.

I was quite relieved to find that there was no sign of Celia when I finally reached the house. I wasn't in the mood for a debrief on yesterday's wedding. Being met at the door by a barking Pepillo, who sniffed at the riding hat and went crazy at the smell of cats which obviously emanated from it, was just about all I could deal with. He jumped up to chase me and claw at my jeans as I lifted the hat out of his reach and carried it up to my room. Inside, I closed the door tightly and listened to the sound of him scratching at the woodwork as I shrugged off my clothes, pulling my tired feet out of my tightly laced Converse pumps.

*

The next morning I awoke to the sound of sawing. It was Pep, working away in the garden. Celia was already in the kitchen. Ahead of her usual schedule she was already coiffed and groomed. It was Celia who finally brought some clarity to the exchange I'd witnessed between Pep and Mr Hen the day before.

'What you have to understand, Isabelle,' she started, stirring the smoky scented leaves in her perfect china teapot, 'is that there's a different psychology behind buying and selling in Majorca.'

'Really?' I answered, standing before her in yesterday's clothes, the riding hat and keys in one hand. 'I only asked Mr Hen if the bike was for sale, and I thought Pep was going to ask him the price.'

'That's exactly my point,' Celia retorted, eyeing my casual look with obvious distaste. 'In Majorca, it's a *seller*'s market. You don't enquire about the price, as you would in England, you make an offer. The seller will already have been weighing you up whilst you do so; he has the advantage. You might *want* to ask him a straightforward question about what you'd like to purchase, but you will never get a straightforward answer.'

'But that's crazy if he wants to sell. What's the point?' I asked in disbelief, wondering how I'd ever buy anything on the island. 'How are you supposed to know what to bid?' I pulled down yesterday's rustic loaf out of the bread bin and poked it, deciding it would be fine if toasted.

'Well, firstly, you won't want to insult him if you're really interested, so you'll need to wear him down into naming a figure. However, if he does, and it seems a perfectly sensible one, you must not accept it,' replied Celia, pulling open a heavy wooden drawer to find a silver teaspoon.

'Why on earth not, if you don't want to insult him?' I was now more confused than ever.

'Because a Majorcan might not trust you if you do!'

I was completely baffled by the local culture, but at least I now understood Pep's convoluted conversation with Mr Hen. I popped the bread into the toaster and waited.

'If you want my advice on the whole affair, my dear, you must take the motorcycle back and act as if you don't want to buy it. Only then, Isabelle, might he come round to the idea of you buying it. If you look like you really want it, he might well question why he's selling it at all,' Celia added with a laugh.

I had a lot to learn about Majorca. It was far more than just a pretty landscape.

I'd been staring at it for weeks now and hadn't dared to turn it on: my English mobile phone. I'd kept it hidden in the top drawer of my desk and I swore that I could almost feel it glowing, its small green light flashing as if it had its own heartbeat. I wasn't sure if I'd needed to leave it off so that I could give myself a chance to adjust to my new life without any distractions, or if I was just too scared to see who had tried to call. Or, more to the point, if Harrisson hadn't. So far, I'd been good. I'd made one call, the call of duty. I'd rung my mother once, to tell her I'd arrived safely and how wonderful everything was, mostly to deter her from sending an embarrassing SOS food parcel full of WI jam and Tetley Tea. Apart from that I'd remained a coward. I'd effectively run away from home without telling anyone else. Now, I knew it was time to find some courage to check my voicemail. I plugged the phone in to charge and tentatively turned it on.

'You have twelve missed calls and seven messages,' said the awkward, robotic female voice.

'To listen to your messages, press one,' she continued. I hesitated. Did I really want to know? Wouldn't it be best to stay disappeared? Could anything be so urgent? Would I call Harrisson back even if he had left me a message?

Whilst I contemplated, I pressed one. And as soon as I'd done so, I regretted it. The first four messages were from Ray.

'Izzy. Me. Office life today is dullsville. Just calling to tell you you're not missing a thing. On Fire has become an ironic title for a very un-happening enterprise. Call me, I need to bitch.'

'Izz. A drinkette? Tonight? I need to get you out of that house and back into the social media mecca of "the Hill". Besides, cute new guy from accounts is going to be at our usual and my Gaydar tells me he's definitely on the scene.'

'Izzy, it's your dearest. Where are you? Have you gone to detox in some fabulous spa? Sooo jealous. Call me when you've emerged a butterfly from your cocoon.'

'OK, it's me again. You don't call, you don't write. Some lesser men would be offended. I'm coming over. I don't even care about the state of your "slag pit". I just need to make sure that you haven't been murdered in cold blood and your body consumed by flesh-eating maggots. You're never this quiet.'

Now I felt really guilty. For Ray, this was the voice of concern. The next message was from a dental nurse, reminding me of my six monthly check up . . . then several messages without any voicemails, just silence. Just as I was wondering why people did that, it finally came, the voice I'd been dreading.

'Izzy . . . Harrisson. I know you were angry when we

last spoke. And I guess you're still mad at me. What do you say I make it up to you – dinner at Sketch, next Friday?' His voice was sexy and familiar and I felt my eyes sting with tears. Why was I doing this to myself? I placed the phone back in the drawer with a shaky hand. I didn't want to hear any more. As I looked for a tissue, my hand lingered on the handle of the drawer and I found myself opening it up again. 'What the hell?' I mumbled to myself. 'Too late now.' And taking out the phone I pressed one, once more.

'Hi. Look, this is embarrassing.' It was Harrisson again, several days later. 'I can't believe you haven't got the courtesy to tell me this is over for you.' He sounded angry, male pride, I guessed. 'I thought you could have been more, well, grown-up about it, Izz.' Ouch! 'Look, it's fine. Just tell me when I can come and get my stuff and we can both move on. This doesn't need to be so awkward, OK? So call me.'

In my own wimpy way I was pleased. He'd declared it over and so now it was. I hadn't had to take the call. I didn't have to call him back. It had all been done for me. I'd even eBayed his stuff; the cufflinks were with magnus1986 in Sweden. It was all perfectly tidy. It was cowardly, I knew it, but with Harrisson, I needed this to be easy.

Excusing myself from the office for an hour or so that afternoon, I ventured out on my blue Vespino, which already felt like a trusty old friend. I rode down to the town, where shopkeepers were reopening their doors after the siesta. A group of kids just out from school played in the large town square on their bikes, their mamas gossiping whilst they watched them. I parked up and went in search of the cheesiest postcards I could find to send to Ray. He'd said that Majorca was all just

cheap package deals and who was I to convince him
otherwise? Clutching a small paper bag containing
'Magalluf By Night' I pulled up a flimsy plastic chair to
a table, ordered a coffee and thought about what to
write. I didn't know where to start.

Darling Ray,

Having narrowly escaped being consumed by
flesh-eating maggots (spawned by the world of
television, rather than the dead-body-munching
kind), I've fled to Majorca (spa was too spenny).
I'm here working as a wedding planner. Please
stop laughing!!!

I miss you. Promise to get in touch when I
emerge as that butterfly.

Izzy xx

Sitting in the square, I felt it was strange to be writing
to Ray in Notting Hill. It felt like a million miles away
and not just geographically. If I was still sitting at my
desk at On Fire, I'd be juggling Maddy's diary, feeling
stressed and wondering how I'd lose three dress sizes in
three days, ready for my next date with H. Being here,
I realised, I'd stopped worrying about having the latest
iTunes downloads on my iPod, seeing what was new on
YouTube, buying the trouser shape of the season, being
seen at the right parties. None of that seemed to matter
as much as it once had and nor did the people I
associated with it all. I didn't care that Remi hadn't tried
to get in touch. I was far from surprised. It would take
another six months or some Popbitch column about
Maddy D-P for her to even think about where I might

be, and that went for all of the other so-called friends I had tried to keep up with in West London. All those people I'd said 'hi' to in smoky bars over a warm Mojito, but never had a proper conversation with. The good-looking girls a 'friend of a friend' always invited to the right parties, who seemed only to chat when they couldn't get the attention of the guy they really wanted to be flirting with. I guessed I'd put Ray under that same category until now; someone to have fun with, when it suited him, but at least he'd missed me and, I guessed, like everyone, I needed someone to.

The Gooochi!

'Hi, yes, I would like to get married ... Yes, in Majorca. No, I don't know the legalities.'

It was my third new enquiry of the morning and with so much to prepare for Francesca's wedding in just two days' time, I really wasn't in the mood to put on the manner I reserved for trying to secure new business. The caller was Maia, from Norway. She'd holidayed on the island and her boyfriend, a marine biologist who wanted to get married by the sea, had family in England. I chewed on a pencil and intermittently took notes with the phone clamped between my shoulder and ear. I winced as I saw three new emails hit my inbox from Francesca as Maia spoke about a particular stretch of beach she hoped to hold a ceremony on.

'I will send you some information, no problem,' I chirped on autopilot, trying to get rid of her and get back to my planning. I glanced up at Celia. 'Yes, yes, I'll put it all in an email.'

Celia had her back to me. She was teetering on the tiptoes of her caramel-coloured kitten heels, pulling an old file from a high mahogany shelf and with it a thick layer of dust on to her ivory silk pussy-bow blouse. 'Drats,' she cursed.

Celia placed the file on top of her desk. When she turned around to answer me, I could see that she wasn't about to launch into the usual steely advice she reserved for one of her matronly briefings. To my surprise, she was clearly upset.

'Is there anything . . . ?'

'No!' interrupted Celia sternly, before I could finish my sentence, opening the file.

'It's simply this wretched dust,' she announced abruptly, turning to leave the room.

I didn't follow her; Celia wasn't the kind of woman you pandered to. Flustered, I picked up her phone the moment it rang, got rid of the call, and then went straight back to look at the folder she'd been so desperate to grab.

I'd assumed it was a file filled with wedding paperwork, containing a price or a contact she needed to root out, but no. This was more of a scrapbook. An album put together by hand, with a William Morris patterned cover, laminated and bound with string. Inside, on the faded coloured paper there were theatre tickets, postcards, photos of picnics, cards from family birthdays, handwritten notes, sweet wrappers and pressed flowers, all glued in. But there was one particular image that caught my eye; Celia with a very handsome older man, his arm around the shoulders of a young boy. They appeared to be at a very English country fair; there was a steam engine in the distance and a series of old fashion stalls leading out of the shot. The boy was holding up a prized, shiny conker in one hand and a string bag filled with marbles in the other, the combination of which was making him smile. I didn't linger on the book. I paced quickly back to my desk and resumed answering Francesca's email. I just made it in time.

'I'm sorry, Isabelle,' I heard Celia utter in a delicate tone from the doorway. 'I didn't mean to snap.'

It was the first time I'd seen Celia look apologetic and, more to my surprise, vulnerable. She appeared, to my now trained eye, slightly dishevelled. Although her clothes and hair were as perfect as usual, her lips were dry and free of lipstick. There was a watery look to her eyes and a smudge of mascara just below one brow, but, more than that, her posture had changed, her shoulders had dropped, her head was bowed, her guard was down. Celia looked tiny in the doorframe. And, for the first time, I realised that she was an older and more fragile woman than I'd supposed. Yet one with an abundance of stiff-upper-lip sensibility and British reserve, which I felt duty-bound to play along with.

'Oh, don't you worry about that,' I said, trying not to stare over the top of my computer. 'I was just looking at Francesca's schedule for Saturday and thinking that checking through the finer details might be best done with a cuppa. Can I tempt you?'

Celia managed a 'Yes . . . that would be lovely.'

I tried my best to make my way down to the kitchen quietly. I was sure I'd spotted a special packet of English chocolate Digestives hidden in Celia's cupboard. This was a chocolate biscuit moment if ever there was one. Outside, Pep was pottering around in the garden, pruning an oleander bush and chatting away to Pepillo, presuming that no one could see or hear.

As the kettle finally boiled I found the biscuits, buried deep in a heavy brown ceramic jar with a cork top. Predictably, I bumped my head on the roof of the cupboard in a rush to turn off the heat. I rubbed it momentarily before performing Celia's mid-morning tea ritual: two spoonfuls of Earl Grey leaves, one of Mil Flores in the pot; the milk (just a splash) in the lemon floral jug; sugar (with a silver spoon) in the sugar bowl. Not forgetting the tea strainer, 'naturally', I muttered to myself, mimicking the lady of the house.

Back upstairs I carefully negotiated the furniture in the office, balancing the best china on Celia's wooden tray.

'I'll be Mother,' I said nervously, slipping into a saying I'd once used with my grandmother. Along with the tea, it was a comfort blanket of a phrase, designed to reassure, and I immediately regretted sounding so patronising, but Celia seemed to ignore it as she tapped away at an email.

I poured and set a full cup of tea on a saucer at the end of Celia's desk, along with a porcelain plate piled high with chocolatey biscuits. Celia stayed silent and I took this as my cue to do the same. I printed out some notes for Saturday and sent two faxes. Fighting with the doddery machine, from the corner of my eye, I caught Celia nibbling at one of the biscuits, carefully patting the corner of her mouth with a serviette.

'Ready, Isabelle?' she eventually enquired, matter-of-factly, breaking the awkward silence. 'For the wedding this weekend?'

'Yes, Celia, I actually think I am,' I replied with wavering confidence, avoiding the pressing subject of Celia's upset. 'Of course, I couldn't have done it without you, I mean,' I said, finally filing the fax receipts in the rickety drawers that still wouldn't close. 'You really have shown me the ropes and you really have held my hand every step of the way. To think, I have only been here just a few weeks and—'

I stopped in my tracks. Celia was crying. A single tear rolled down one cheek. As she noticed me looking, she gently wiped it away with a silk handkerchief she seemed to conjure from nowhere.

'Oh, silly old me,' she croaked, giving me a weak half-smile. As I caught her eye, she shifted her gaze down to the floor.

'Come on, Celia,' I offered, sitting back down, 'what is it? And I'm not falling for any more dust stories.'

'It, my dear, I suppose, is Patrick,' she answered slowly, still unable to look at me. 'My Patrick. My wonderful Patrick . . .' She paused to take a deep breath, as if to prepare for what she wanted to bring herself to say. 'He died today, this day, in 1982. He was so young . . . it was so unexpected . . .' she paused again, 'that I can't quite believe it, even now. All these years later.'

I really didn't know what to say. I sat awkwardly, playing with the handle of the china teacup in front of me.

'Was it the wedding, that made you realise the date?' I asked, wanting to learn more and wanting Celia to feel as though she could open up.

'Oh no, there's always the date,' replied Celia, looking at me now. 'I prepare myself for that every year. I start to think about not thinking about it a whole month beforehand. No, Tomas decided to get in touch. Today of all days. I guess it's spooked me.'

I must have looked confused.

'Tomas, our son.'

My mind flashed back to the photograph.

'So is it a good or bad thing that he made contact?' I asked carefully, reaching for a biscuit.

'That, my dear, is what I'm not sure about.' And with that, Celia returned to her emails, pausing only to give me a glance to let me know, firmly, that this was the end of the subject.

*

Later that day, Celia uncharacteristically took a break.
From the office window, I could see her in the garden.
She'd changed her heels for Hunter Wellingtons and
thown a sugar-pink cardigan over her blouse. A
patterned headscarf held her perfect chignon in place as
she bent to prune the rose bush she always so carefully
tended. Celia's whole garden was beautiful, but this
seemed to be her prize plant, the one thing in the
garden that Pep wasn't allowed to touch. With her shiny
stainless-steel shears she clipped at it with swift, certain
movements.

The noise of the ringing office phone made me jump
with a start, bringing my mind back to the office. I
answered it clumsily with a cursory 'Hello'.

'Oh, I'm sorry, I must have the wrong number,' said
a man with a public-school air. 'I was looking for Celia
Timms.'

I hesitated. I didn't want to disturb Celia, so
absorbed in her pruning and obviously wanting some
time alone. I fumbled, 'No. I mean, yes, this is the
right number for Celia, she just isn't available right
now.'

'Oh . . . and you are?' asked the voice, quite rudely.

'I'm sorry, I'm Isabelle, I work with Celia in the
business.'

'The business?'

'Yes, the business. May I ask who's calling and the
nature of your call, so that I can help?' I replied
defensively. Francesca was still in need of my attention
and I didn't have time for some stuck-up, nosey guy
asking me a lot of questions.

'Right, sorry, yes, you must think me quite rude. It's
just that I haven't spoken to Celia for a while,' the voice
answered, apologetically.

'As I said, Celia is not in the office at the moment. May I ask her to return your call?'

'You can, of course. Tell her Tomas rang, please,' he said softly, his voice becoming warmer now.

'Thomas?' I repeated, wondering if the voice belonged to Celia's son.

'Yes, without an H, as they spell it in Majorca.' He said Majorca with a 'y' in the middle and rolling the 'r'. The voice, I decided, was quite sexy.

'Do you have a pencil?' he asked, breaking the silence.

'Oh yes, sorry, fire away,' I piped, my mind whirring.

Tomas reeled off his number quickly, then paused. 'Look,' he started gently, 'I know you're just being professional, but I really am very keen to know how Celia is.' He paused again. 'She's my mother.'

'Sure. Celia's fine, just fine,' I replied, unconvincingly.

'Right. Yes, right. OK, well, if you can tell her I called, that would be wonderful. Thank you . . .' Another pause.

'Isabelle,' I reminded him. 'Izzy.'

And then it happened. As it sometimes does. My mouth ran away with me. 'Tomas?' I asked, stopping him from hanging up. 'Look, I might be speaking out of turn here, but Celia does seem upset today. She is . . . well, you know . . . what with the anniversary of—'

'Dad's death,' Tomas stepped in to add, frankly.

'Yes . . . Sorry, I shouldn't have said anything,' I started, regretting my outburst and checking at the window that Celia was still in view. She wasn't. My eyes searched the garden for her.

'Izzy?' Tomas asked again. 'Do you know if Celia is going to be around for the next week or so? I don't want to push you or pry, but it's important, I'm wondering if maybe I should just come and pay her a visit.' His voice was still soft and I started to wonder how the boy in the picture had grown up.

'I really don't think it's for me to . . .' I paused. There was still no sign of Celia. I was standing up now, watching the door.

'I know, Izzy, and I do appreciate that,' Tomas interjected smoothly, 'but just tell me if she'll be there. You needn't mention anything to her.'

I hesitated. 'It's really not for me to comment. I just work for Celia. I'm sorry, I knew I shouldn't have started this,' I said honestly. I could hear her kitten heels tip-tapping their way along the tiled corridor. Now I had to get rid of him.

'OK, OK, she's always here,' I heard myself saying, flapping, as I placed down the receiver and went about trying to look as though I'd been busy for hours. I didn't look up as Celia slipped behind her desk. She started to chatter in Spanish to a catering company on the phone. She was almost fluent, but her upper-crust English accent always gave her away as an *extranjero* or 'outsider'. I took a deep breath and answered email from Francesca.

Firstly, I had to advise her that if she really wanted to extend her canapé reception to two hours, she should lay on more canapés for her guests. I sent another to change the room bookings at the five-star hotel she was staying at, cancelling one single room and finding that I had to find another hotel for further late additions added to her guest list. Then it would be back to the reception venue to change the numbers for dinner before I laid on more transport. Francesca was already emailing me back as I made a start on changing things, and she was apologising for the slide in numbers. I tried not to laugh out loud as I read her first message, in her typically broken English.

'Isabella,' the email started – she always called me Isabella but, in her flamboyant Italian accent, it sounded too pretty to correct – 'more canapés, you worry me. Why do we need umbrellas? You think we are going to have rain?'

'Oh the joys of organising a wedding in Majorca, for an Italian bride with German and Spanish contractors,' I groaned out loud in desperation. Celia shot me a frown and raised her hand to hush me as she strained to hear the person on the other end of her line. This wasn't the first time that our plans had got lost in translation. I was sure it would all seem comical in time but, right now, it felt as though I'd never nail down the final details for Francesca's wedding.

That evening I stayed in the office until late, watching the sun fade over the valley through the window and making sure that I had the last details perfectly organised for the looming wedding day. I was worried about making such last-minute changes. I called the people I'd emailed, to double check they had the current information. I called everyone else involved in the big production, to make sure they had the date, time and their particular role just right. I spoke to Francesca one last time to check her final numbers.

'Sì, Isabella. Giorgio, he's broken off with his girlfriend this year, so he was the single room, but now he's not coming to the wedding,' she fired off quickly as I crossed his name off the list. 'Paolo, now he is coming with Emilia, she's the vegetarian, but she eats the fish. OK?'

'OK,' I replied.

'Fransisco and Marta,' she continued, 'they are also new, to add. And they are staying in the other hotel you tell me.'

'Yes, I'm sorry about that, Francesca, but the hotel is

now fully booked, but the other is also very nice and just a five-minute walk away. I just need a credit card number to secure the room. Anything else you need?'

'Yes, Isabella, I need one extra bed in room three for the guys.'

'OK, but this is still thirty-three guests, so no extra people? How many people in the room? Three?' This was still complicated.

'Three, the same guys as before. No extra persons.'

'But you don't want one of them to have the single room you cancelled?'

'Ah, yes, Isabella, that's good. Just one extra bed, then.'

'It is actually a twin room already, OK?'

'*Si*, Isabella, *si*, this is better, I understand. Just two persons in that room, it is better.'

We ran through it all again one last time. The last thing I wanted was one of Francesca's or Roberto's friends to be without a room or without dinner.

When I'd first met Francesca, she'd made it clear that she wanted a relaxed and informal wedding for her family and close friends. She was laid back, sweet and friendly. But she was also very busy and once she was back in Italy, it had become increasingly difficult to communicate with her, not only because we sometimes misunderstood each other's English, but also because she always left things to the final hour before taking a decision and then changed her mind. What's more, Francesca not only wanted her wedding to feel fresh and contemporary, she also wanted it to be perfect. She was marrying Roberto, a successful interior designer, and the couple had little restraint on their budget and tons of style. They also had very set ideas and exacting standards. It was always going to be a challenge to ensure that each detail met their expectations and would yet seem so effortlessly executed on the day. Not least for someone with my limited experience.

First, there was the food, seven specially selected courses, adapted slightly for an Italian palette. 'Isabella,' she'd write, trying to decide on a dish, 'with this, if it is too much sauce or oil, because it is Spain, then I don't want it. I want to choose another. Let me know about the sauce, please.' I'd then have to work out how to ask a Michelin star chef how much sauce there would be on his sea bass without causing offence or inviting the answer 'As much as is correct.' Francesca's wedding cake was planned to follow: a chic tower of individual New York cheesecakes, the tiers and stand on which they were placed made completely out of milky white chocolate by a very patient cake maker.

Then there was the decoration. Everything, and I mean EVERYTHING, had to be cream. Not just cream in general, but a very specific buttery shade. I was so nervous about getting the wrong colour – a little too milky or a touch too lemon – that I had swatches made, which I carried around in my handbag. I whipped them out in fabric stores as I scoured piles of linen, in the candlemaker's as I chose the exact hue, shape and size for the church and the dinner tables, and, in the stationer's, when the card for printing menus, name cards, seating plans, order of service booklets, had to be just so. Before too long, I had 'Francesca cream' down pat, and I ceased needing to check the now greying and well-thumbed swatches. And it was just as well. When I received a call from the florist, the very best in Palma, telling me that Francesca's flowers had arrived, I raced down to the city to find to my dismay that they were just a tone too white. They just had to be reordered. The flowers were to be hung from the ceiling above the altar in vast hanging glass bowls, for which we had to seek special permission from the Spanish priest, find the strongest stepladders in the city, and a florist's assistant with a head for heights.

Francesca's preparations continued endlessly. She changed the seven courses seven times, asked the priest to wear robes, then a suit, then a robe again, substituted vegetarians for fish-eating vegetarians, and one continuous long table for five round tables of five and one top table of eight, topped with sugar almonds and disposable cameras – all cream, of course. Each night I dreamed that too much sauce was served on the food, the menu orders were wrong, or that the German wedding, scheduled just a few hours before Francesca's in the same church, overran, leaving no time to switch their yellow and red floral displays for Francesca's cream. I was therefore relieved when the wedding day had almost arrived; finally, I could just get on with it and stop worrying. Well, almost. As I prepared dinner for Celia and myself the night before the big day, I received a text from a very panicky Francesca:

Isabella, we have a delay with the connecting flight. Please, you contact the hotel. I am trying for another connection from Madrid to Majorca tomorrow morning. Francesca.

I couldn't believe it. Francesca had insisted on spending the week before the wedding with her family in Italy. Her guests had arrived in Majorca and checked into the hotel, as had the groom, but she, just hours before her wedding, had not. I took the onions off the heat, wiped my hands on my jeans, and called her.

'Francesca. It's Isabelle. Is everything OK?'

'Isabella, I sorry!' she started. 'I cannot believe, the

flight is now leaving Madrid at eight a.m. tomorrow morning.'

'You poor darling. We must find you a hotel room near to the airport,' I said, trying to calm her.

'But the hotel in Palma?' she asked.

'Don't worry, leave it to me. Most importantly, where is the dress? Do you have your luggage with you?'

'Yes, I have it. Hand luggage.' She paused. 'I am so worried that I'm never going to go to Majorca,' Francesca started, sounding teary.

'Look, don't worry about a thing,' I soothed, imagining Francesca sitting sobbing into her wedding dress, bundled on her lap. 'There's lots of time. I'm going to call you back in ten minutes with details of a hotel for tonight. OK?'

'OK, Isabella. *Grazie molto*.'

'No problem at all,' I soothed. 'Just keep calm. Now, have you called Roberto to tell him what's happening, or shall I?'

'It's OK. Look, my phone is losing battery now,' Francesca added nervously.

'OK, I am going now but I'll call you back. Bye, Francesca.'

I zoomed upstairs to the office and, true to my word, arranged a hotel in Madrid, taxi and a complimentary bottle of champagne on arrival for Francesca. I did my best but the hotel wasn't luxurious, there were no good rooms left, but at least she didn't have to sleep in the airport, clutching her wedding dress and wondering when eight a.m. would finally come.

When I called Francesca back, I gave her the name and address of the hotel and told her to run a big bubble bath, order the best thing on the room service menu and get an early night. A car would pick her up at six a.m. for check-in.

*

The morning of Francesca's wedding finally arrived and it was chaos. I made it to the hotel in Palma just shortly after the bride and went straight to her suite. The hotel was beautiful. A grand, ornate palace buried deep in the Arab quarter of the city with a chic, minimal interior. Inside, the white marble hallways, free from embellishment, were filled with the scent of cedar incense and silence. I walked lightly and awkwardly on tiptoe, to minimise the click of my vintage mules, which echoed loudly as I searched for Francesca's room number. Five minutes later I was still wandering down identical hallways, cursing the unhelpful design (roman numerals for room numbers, painted the exact same colour as the walls they were placed on) and my shoes (three-inch heels rather than skyscrapers, but my feet were already calling out for flats). Through the emptiness I could just make out the faint sound of giggling. I followed the noise and it eventually led me to Francesca's door.

Inside, the bride's best friends and bridesmaids were lounging, sipping champagne and nibbling on the lavish, complimentary fruit basket, their flawless, tanned bodies delicately wrapped in the most luxurious Italian underwear. They were lazing on the white leather chaises painting their toenails, and draped across the four-poster bed swathed in acres of voile, gossiping in Italian. I turned towards the window, feeling uncomfortably British.

The putty-coloured floor-to-ceiling shutters were open on to the vast decked terrace, on which sun loungers, a full-size lemon tree and a dining table created an oasis with views of the cathedral. It was a wonderful day for a wedding, I thought, looking up at the pure blue sky which was dotted with just a few clouds as fluffy as the towels draped over the arms of the sunbeds.

From the bathroom I could hear Francesca sploshing around in the bathtub, chatting loudly to a friend in the shower. I couldn't imagine any of my more reserved British brides being so open and free.

'*Ciao*,' said the girl wrapped in a crisp white towel, who'd opened the door to me, before raising a crystal flute of champagne to her lips.

'Hi, I'm Isabelle. I'm helping Francesca to organise the wedding,' I replied, slightly embarrassed, as she wriggled the towel up over her perfect cleavage.

'Ciao, Isabelle,' she purred. 'Francesca!' she shouted in the direction of the bathroom. 'Eeeesabelle.'

'No, no, really, don't disturb her if she's bathing, I'll wait,' I replied, self-consciously.

I wandered on to the terrace, took a seat, pulled out Francesca's schedule from my bag and slid my oversized sunglasses from my head to look at the itinery. Everything was organised and, right now, there was nothing to do, yet, glancing at my watch, I realised that the make-up artist was late and I instantly felt nervous.

I peeked back inside whilst I dialled her number. To the left of the bed Francesca's dress hung from the single door handle of the wardrobe on a purple velvet hanger; a sheath of 'Francesca cream' silk with a corseted back, it was simple, but stunning. To the right, a pile of rich-red Cartier jewellery boxes were scattered on the bedside table, beneath which lay a pair of exquisite damson satin Gucci shoes studded with gleaming white diamante. The colour of which would match Francesca's bouquet. We'd agreed it would be a strong statement.

'Isabella?' It was Francesca, standing in front of me on the terrace, her lythe bronzed body enveloped in a white towelling robe. Her face was free of make-up, her wet hair was combed back and beads of water trickled on to her robed shoulders; she was glowing. 'Come, *bella*, meet my girls,' she said excitedly, taking me by the hand and dragging me away from my paperwork shield.

Francesca treated me like a long-lost friend. She wasn't in the least bit worried that the make-up artist was late, she was more concerned that I see her dress, have a glass of bubbly and join in the girly fun, but I sensibly declined and asked if she thought Roberto would like me to check on him. She translated this for the girls and they roared with laughter.

'Isabella,' she started, in her pretty accent, 'the boys, they are having sauna. Then they will get ready. They will take more time than us girls! Maybe you check the make-up artist is not with them!'

As the girls laughed again, I made my excuses and headed for the church. It was a busy Saturday morning in Palma and I wiggled my way through the city on my Vespino, looking up at the stately buildings, peering into lavish shop windows and dodging shoppers idly walking through back streets. Eventually, I followed the sweep of the traffic along the Maritimo, looking out at the gleaming white boats on the water, passing joggers and rollerbladers, all taking in the view.

The church was a few minutes from the city along the coast. Set in a pretty garden, with a domed roof and views of the sea, it was one of Celia's most popular. As I swooped off the main road and parked under the shade of a eucalyptus tree, I saw that the church grounds were buzzing with activity.

From the parking area I could see a large group of Spanish wedding planners in the distance. Two, in harnesses, scaled lampposts to wrap them in white ribbon, others decorated the outside altar with a lavish spray of flowers and covered the remaining space with candles, laid out chairs with spotless white covers in the garden, and unfurled the longest white carpet I'd ever seen. I peeled the riding helmet off my head, placed it on the seat as I smoothed my hair back into a ponytail, and locked up the bike. I stood up to gather my things and took a moment to take in the scene. The Spanish team were dressed entirely in black, clutching clipboards and speaking into mics wrapped round their cheeks. They appeared to be fiercely organised, like a team of overgrown ants, scurrying about their perfectly ordered business.

As I made my way towards the church clutching my mobile, handbag and helmet as my heels sunk into the gravelled drive, I felt like a shoddy impostor. In the distance, I could hear the sound of a ceremony already taking place: the German Wedding, I presumed. I weaved my way through the sea of white wedding chairs ready for their reception, the quickest route to the front of the building, desperate to see if it was running on time. My florist would arrive in just twenty minutes to start constructing the elaborate hanging displays that Francesca had ordered. As I contemplated the enormity of her task, I heard garbled Spanish orders on walkie talkies and, seconds later, was confronted by a shrieking Spanish wedding planner, waving his arms dramatically, wanting me to clear his 'set'. I froze, momentarily mortified. Dozens of the workers in black turned to feast their eyes on me, before I tottered back on my tracks.

I took the side gate that led down a cobbled path to the front of the church. Here, a small white van was parked and from the double doors at the back I could see a waiter setting out champagne flutes on silver platters. As I made my way, trying to avoid him, presuming he was with the Spanish wedding planners, he stopped to wave. It was Alfonso, a friendly waiter from a restaurant Celia used for some of her wedding receptions.

'Ah, Isabelle! *Como estás?*' he asked.

'*Muy bien, y tu, Alfonso? Va bien?*' I answered, asking him how it was all going.

'Isabelle, you organise this wedding now?' he asked in English, loosening his bow tie as the sun beat down on his back.

'Yes, the wedding at four p.m.,' I replied.

'Ah, no, Isabelle. *This* wedding? *La boda Aleman.*'

'No,' I answered, '*una boda Italiano!*'

'*Dios mio!*' he exclaimed, '*hay una mas boda Española también!*' Alfonso revealed, telling me there was a Spanish wedding that day too. He, it transpired, was organising cava and canapés for when the German wedding ended. These were to be served on the small terraced area in front of the church, so that the guests could enjoy the views of the sea whilst they toasted the newly married couple. I could feel my face turn white as I realised that Francesca's guests were scheduled to gather for her ceremony at precisely the same time. Worse still, if they lingered even longer, my bride might even arrive whilst they were still celetrating the previous wedding – a complete disaster.

I had to think fast. I told Alfonso my situation, my guests would be arriving at three-thirty; the bride, at four. Then I called Maria. She was the person I'd hired to make sure that all of the wedding guests got on to the coach to take them from the hotel to the church. She would make an announcement on the bus in Italian, to tell Francesca's guests to make their way to the front of the church on arrival, so that they didn't think that the grand ceremony set up in the garden was for them. And, so that I had time to make sure that the German drinks reception had ended before they gathered at the front of the church, I used a stalling tactic; I called the string quartet we'd hired and asked them to come fifteen minutes early. If they played outside so that they blocked the way to the front of the church, I could then make sure that the German drinks reception at the main entrance had ended before my guests wandered round to take their seats. Without Celia there for support and advice, I could only hope that I'd done the right thing.

The afternoon was filled with activity. I jostled with the other wedding planners when they disapproved of the string quartet taking up an unconventional position, primed the videographer of our new plans for his shots, and spoke sweetly to Alfonso, hatching a plan to move the German drinks reception to a lower terrace if it overran.

Finally, as the German newly weds left the church, I was ready. Despite the scale of her extending ladders, I snuck the florist and her vast supplies of cream peonies past the celebrating entourage and into the church to work her magic. Then I apologised profusely to the priest conducting the Italian ceremony for the consumption of alcohol just outside the house of God. As he darted inside to prepare his papers and put on his robes, I went back to the car park. I had to convince the string quartet to 'borrow' some chairs from the local bar to take up their places, ready for the Italian guests.

When the coach arrived, I'd never seen such a well-dressed cortège. Francesca's girls were vivacious in glamorous 'red carpet' dresses. Buffed, groomed and accessorised to perfection, they smoothly negotiated the cobbled steps leading down to the church in strappy jewelled Manolos, the sun catching their glossy 'up-do's', glistening lip gloss and acres of honey-coloured skin. The men followed, their handsome faces shielded by dark sunglasses, their tanned, taught bodies in sharply tailored suit jackets, crisp white shirts, dry-clean-only jeans, and the sharpest Italian leather shoes. Only the Italians could get away with wearing jeans to a wedding, I thought, guiding them towards the string quartet, blushing slightly at the devilishly good-looking men when they smiled in my direction and at my now dishevelled and stressed-out appearance. I turned round to see that it was in fact the photographer they were smiling at. 'Don't be shy now!' he was laughing ironically as the men turned yet again to pose.

'*Ciaaaao, bella*,' one impossibly good-looking male guest drawled, extending an arm to me. His cream jacket was impeccable and a large expensive-looking watch was just visible under a perfect white cuff. His face was warm and open, his angular jaw slightly stubbled, and his eyes were hiding behind Prada shades.

'Dante,' he offered, pulling me towards him to kiss my cheeks. He smelt clean, of soap, fresh lemon and warm vanilla – it had to be Aqua Di Parma cologne.

'Isabelle,' I managed, taking in a sharp breath, feeling heat prickling my cheeks.

Dante left my side and, as my eyes followed him dreamily, I realised that the guests were heading towards the string quartet on their own.

'Crap!' I cursed, running after them, wanting to make sure they didn't pass the musicians. I *had* to make sure the coast was clear at the front of the church first.

I trotted past the Italian guests inelegantly, hoping no one would notice me as my hair worked its way loose to bounce around my shoulders. Speed was of the essence. Outside the front of the church, the German bride and her entourage were in party mood. Alfonso's 'flying buffet' was in full swing, the guests were laughing, chatting, clutching their brimming champagne flutes. There was no sign of them moving.

I looked behind me, at least none of the Italian guests had followed me to the entrance of the church, but I had no time to waste. I started to usher the celebrating party on to a lower terrace, out of view from the front of the church. Alfonso, to my relief, interrupted conversations to do the same. I apologised, explaining in very sketchy German that another bride was about to come – which, thankfully, the newly married couple accepted graciously.

I glanced nervously at my watch: 3.47. According to my schedule, I should already be calling the bridal car to give the driver his cue, having checked the priest was ready and all of the Italian guests were seated. Not only was I running late, but, glancing at my schedule again, I read the words 'Izzy to hand out Order of Service', and my heart raced. The Order of Service booklets which Francesca had painstakingly translated into Spanish from Italian, and which I had taken so much time in finding the right 'Francesca cream' paper for at the printers, were, I realised, in the basket of my Vespino. There was nothing for it. I took another jog to the front of the church, past the immaculate Italians, hanging my head in shame.

'Eeeeesabelle!' I heard a male voice call. I thought it might be Dante but I didn't dare stop. I pretended not to hear. At this very moment in time, someone else's romantic day was much more important.

Scooping up the booklets carefully bound with damson silk ribbons, I breathed a sigh of relief. At least I hadn't lost them. Tucking them tightly under one arm, I called the driver on my mobile to give him the all clear as I walked back towards the guests, composed myself and put on my best 'wedding planner' smile.

Celia had told me *never* to call the driver until I had carried out all of the final checks in the church – music, flowers, priest, seated guests, it all had to be perfect for the bride to make her entrance – but, today, I had no choice but to take the risk. Francesca would already be panicking. I greeted her guests, announced that they could take their seats, and gave the lead violinist a wink, her cue to lead the musicians inside. I led the way and, once at the heavy church door, did my best to look calm as I handed each wedding guest a pristine Order of Service. From where I stood I could see the priest standing silently by the lectern, the peonies piled high in the huge glass bowls above him and Francesca's candles by his side, at the altar. It was a sight that steadied my nerves. Everything was going to be OK, I told myself, grinning at yet another guest, offering yet another booklet. The wedding car, I calculated, should be arriving at any moment. I gave a nod to the strings to be silent and quietly slipped through the back door to greet the bride as her guests anticipated her arrival.

The elegant vintage Bentley I'd booked for Francesca rolled down the drive. The driver, in full tails and hat despite the heat, jumped out to open her door. She looked beautiful. I welled up a little as I greeted her. Careful not to spoil her make-up with my now damp cheeks, we air kissed.

'All ready?' I asked.

'I am sooo excited, Isabella!' she replied, 'sooooo excited.' She looked radiant. Her bridesmaid took her arm and they glided down to the church doors. I cued the quartet and felt like a proud, emotional aunt as I heard the gasp of guests marvelling at how beautiful she looked above the sound of the strings. I waited until Roberto had taken Francesca's hand at the front of the aisle and beamed her a smile before I slipped on to the last pew at the back.

It had been a crazy scramble, but from this point onwards, the service was seamless. Well, almost. After the priest's welcome in Spanish, and then Italian, I could hear some of Francesca's girls giggling. I followed their gaze and looked up. The gentle gusts from the electric fans were causing the peonies in the glass bowls to dance. I darted to the electric box and turned the big clunky switch to 'off' before any could fall to the floor. Francesca, eyes transfixed on Roberto, thankfully didn't notice.

As the ceremony ended and the couple kissed passionately, not once but twice, for the photographer, I threw open the heavy wooden doors so that the newly weds could lead their procession outside.

'EEESSSSABELLA!' I heard Francesca shout at the top of her voice. I was running by the second syllable and presumed that some of the German wedding guests had made their way back to the terrace. But by the time I had gently squeezed past the other guests, I could see no one but Francesca and Roberto.

'Francesca?' I asked, out of breath and panicked.

'*Bella*, we just wanted to say thank you so much, before we have the photographs!' Francesca cooed sweetly.

'Oh, no problem. Really, you shouldn't hold things up for me.' I smiled, blushing but relieved.

'Well,' started Roberto, 'also one little thing. A favour, please,' he sing-songed, in his rich accent. 'We leave the wallet in the hotel room and now we realise is impossible to pay for the wedding reception without!'

'Oh!' I gasped, 'no problem. I will leave Maria to get your guests on to your coach. Your driver will follow whenever you are ready, no rush, and I will go back to your hotel room. Tell me, where will I find the wallet?'

'Grazie, Isabella!' Roberto started. 'We leave the keys at the hotel reception. The wallet is either in our suite or in the boys' room. You remember the room the boys are sharing. Just look for the Gooochi. The large brown leather Gooochi, is inside.'

The Gucci, the Gucci, I mused, thankful that I could whiz there quickly on the Vespino.

By the time I arrived at the hotel I was hot and nervous. I couldn't imagine not being at the reception venue to greet the bride, groom and their guests, to make sure that the cocktails they had ordered were ready to be served and that the chill-out DJ was already playing on the wonderful outside terrace, overlooking the sea. At best, I'd calculated that the journey from the hotel Francesca was staying in to the hotel the reception was being held at, was twenty minutes in good traffic. But what if they didn't have the wallet and they couldn't pay?

As I finally tapped my nails on the marble desk, waiting for the receptionist to bring the keys, I called the maître d' at the reception venue, to make sure that everything was running to schedule.

'Hola, Isabelle. Where are you?' Catalina asked, surprised to pick up a call from my mobile.

I explained what had happened and Catalina laughed. 'No problema,' she told me, 'tranquillo, everything is fine, take your time.'

I ran up the flights of marble stairs, first of all to the suite. Francesca's girls had done a great job of tidying up; the bed was crumple-free and dreamy, the furniture free of make-up bags, shoes, accessories and dresses. But no sign of the brown leather Gucci. My eyes searched for it amidst the sea of pristine white furnishings, to no avail. The Gucci hadn't been kicked under the bed, wasn't concealed inside the vast wardrobes or even by chance, in the decadently minimal bathroom. I glanced around for one final check before heading quickly down another two flights to the boys' room, my heels echoing throughout the empty halls.

I reached the door puffing, catching my breath. I slid the credit-card-style key into the sleek electroninc lock and pushed the handle open. In complete contrast to the still, pristine building, the room inside was chaotic, a designer jumble. A sea of crisp, white unworn under-pants emblazoned with Dolce & Gabbana and Armani littered the floor, burnt-orange Hermès boxes and freshly ironed shirts were strewn across the unmade beds, Prada ties were discarded on chairs in loose bundles, a mountain of sunglasses, some idly left open, covered a bedside table, and a pair of Missioni specs had fallen on to the floor amidst silk socks, jeans and leather belts. I glanced around in search of the Gucci, feeling uncomfortable at being there. 'The Gooochi,' I mocked to myself. There was a large Louis Vuitton holdall on the floor by one bed, a Prada overnight bag and a smaller matching flight case on a sofa, but no Gucci. As I wandered tentatively into the bathroom and marvelled at the sheer volume of grooming products on the floating glass shelves, my phone rang.

'Catalina?' I asked, recognising her number. 'How are things?'

'Isabelle. When you come? I have a small problem,' she asked, sounding panicked, drawing in a breath. 'The guests, after the one cocktail, compliments of the couple, they are ordering many more drinks. Many. But when we give the bills, they are not paying my waiters.

You said they know to pay. We don't want a problem and we don't want to upset any client.'

'OK, don't worry, Cati,' I soothed. 'Francesca told me they would make sure that their guests would be prepared to pay for their own drinks. Give me thirty minutes and I will be there to remind them, when I give them their wallet – it will look very casual, don't worry.'

'But Isabelle, you don't understand. The bar bill is already nine hundred and eighty euros and the bills . . . are many. I need to get this organised.'

'Wow! OK, don't worry, I will be there soon.' I clicked my mobile shut and decided there was nothing for it, I had to start moving things around a little in the bedroom to spot the Gucci through the mess. I shunted a Vuitton holdall and moved clothes carefully, engrossed in my mission and clock-watching all the while. Then, from nowhere, I heard a male voice speak in Italian. I jumped. My heart hit my throat and I turned round slowly.

'Isabelle.' A velvety, thick accent uttered. '*Scusi*. I did not mean to scare you.'

I didn't quite recognise him at first. Without his sunglasses on, I could see Dante's face for the first time. His eyes were green, sparkling and mischievous and rimmed with the longest black lashes.

He took my arm to steady me. I felt faint. Embarrassed. His hand felt warm and soft on my arm.

'Oh, hi,' I stammered, feeling wobbly. 'Francesca and Roberto asked me to come and search for their wallet. They left it behind.'

'I know.' He smiled sexily. 'Roberto, he thought you need help, and this room is messy, you know, from the boys.'

'OK.' I blushed, trying to get back to the task in hand. 'The wallet is in the Gucci.'

'The Gucci?' he purred. 'Roberto's Gucci is not here. It is in the suite. Come, I show you.' He turned to face me now, taking my hand, which still clutched the credit-card-key, opening my fingers gently, like the petals of a flower.

I pulled my hand away, embarrassed.

'Isabelle?' he asked softly. 'Are you sitting for dinner with us? I hope so,' he answered himself, before I could tell him that I would not be.

'Look. I must get the wallet,' I replied, trying to focus, amazed he was being so forward. 'And no, I am not coming to dinner, I have to work, make sure everything is organised,' I said matter-of-factly, turning to head for the door.

'That is a shame,' Dante answered. 'A shame.'

He still had my arm in one hand and he pressed it a little, to turn me back to him. My head was in a spin. I knew the maître d' was waiting for me, I knew there was a problem at the hotel and I still had to find the wallet and get back to the cocktail reception. But as I turned back to Dante, he was much closer now, his eyes on mine. His breath was warm and sweet and his mouth was full and sensuous. I studied it, despite myself. And before I knew what was happening, his soft, generous lips were on mine. He took the back of my head in his hands, very softly. He rested his other hand on the small of my back, against the cool silk of my dress.

'I must find the wallet. The Gucci,' I whispered, pulling away slightly. I felt woozy. This was delicious.

Dante's hand slid to my neck and gently pulled my head to his chest. 'But you're still in shock, I think, Isabelle,' he offered.

I wanted to move, but I nuzzled at the warm scent and soft dark down at his chest. I raised my head again, remembering myself and why I was here. He took my hand again and put it back to his chest. Then, with his, he slowly undid the buttons on his shirt. I wasn't sure if I was in complete shock by his actions, or stunned by the perfectly sculpted, tanned torso before me, but I froze. Dante threw the shirt to the bed. I still couldn't move. He sat on the edge of the bed, pulling me towards him.

'If you are not coming to dinner, Isabelle, we should get to know each other now,' he stated.

I stood in front of him, transfixed. Was this really happening? This perfect, beautiful, Italian man wanting me? Then I panicked. I was sweaty and dishevelled from running around all day. I tried to remember if my underwear matched, wondered if my make-up had run down my face . . .

'Please, Isabelle,' he soothed, pulling me closer, 'it is fate we are here.' I was now teetering over him, at that point where gravity dictated that I had to pull myself back or fall on to the bed. I gave in and flopped down beside him, as elegantly as I could. He started to undo the fly of his jeans, whilst covering my neck in tiny kisses. I snuck a look as he used the other hand to push the denims over his hips, pulling with them the top of his crisp, white briefs, revealing a delicate line of paler flesh, that hadn't seen the sun. My heart raced in double time. His lips moved to my ear as he eased his jeans over his muscular thighs.

'Isabelle,' he whispered softly, making me tingle.

'What does it mean, this Isabelle?' he asked.

'It's just a name,' I replied, perplexed at the question, taking a peek at a sculpted, bronzed thigh and secretly hoping now that he wouldn't stop.

'Dante,' he started, with a boyish chuckle, stroking the silk at my chest, 'it means in Italian, "endurance".'

And with that I blacked out. I literally fainted. I

didn't know that I was about to go, my body gave me no warning, I just slipped away into a heady, dark nothingness that seemed to last for ever.

I heard my name. 'Isabelle, Isabelle.' It was Celia, clutching a cup of water in one hand and wearing a stern expression. 'What*ever* happened?' she asked crossly as my eyes flickered open. 'The hotel reception called me,' she added impatiently. It took me a moment to come around. As I remembered where I was, I remembered Dante. An image of his dancing eyes, his perfect buffed body flashed momentarily in my mind, but as my eyes searched the still messy room, I could see within moments that he had gone.

Of course I made it back to the wedding that afternoon, tended to the bride and groom's every whim, and tried to avoid Dante's gaze.

After bundling me into a taxi with the wallet she'd miraculously found, Celia had returned to oversee the wedding she had organised, some forty minutes' drive away, having accepted my explanation of panic and dehydration for collapsing in the hotel room with a raised eyebrow and a disappointed smile. She had obviously thought I was made of stronger stuff. Nevertheless, I should have been relieved that the day continued so smoothly, that Roberto had ended up picking up the bar bill, that Francesca was happy with the food, that the service and weather had been so spectacular. And I should have been able to focus, but I still felt groggy. With lacklustre enthusiasm, I checked on the arrangements for the dinner whilst the cocktail and canapé reception entered its final half-hour.

'Isabelle, you are OK?' Catalina asked with concern, as I skipped three names on the table plan and forgot the 'favours' on two tables. 'This is not like you,' she added, placing the missing items on the tables behind me.

'Oh Cati, I'm fine, thanks, really. I just got a bit hot and stressed earlier at the hotel. I might just take five minutes when we finish here, before I move guests for dinner,' I replied, taking in the view.

The dining terrace was perched on the cliff's edge. Below, an infinity pool in smooth limestone led seamlessly out to sea. It was perfectly calm, clear and almost tropical. The water close to the rocks faded to palest jade and despite the depth of the ocean, it was possible to just see the golden sand at its bed, a shoal of small grey fish and a gnarl of black rock. On the horizon the sea glittered under the sun, a full, yellow ball against the clear sky. I took in a breath. The clean smell of sea salt helped clear my head a little. The noise of the waves lapping against the rocks was soothing.

'Isabelle, please,' Catalina pleaded. 'Take this chair, for a moment.'

I smiled gratefully. Cati had turned round one of Francesca's smart cream-covered wedding chairs, so that I could turn my back on the view and see her elegant tables as well as the guests at the reception, on the terrace above.

I took a seat as she turned to check on the chef. 'OK, Cati, you win, just for a moment,' I answered gratefully.

The spot was perfect for people-watching. Above me, I could see the beautiful Italians milling under the grand stone arches of the hotel, lounging in small groups on the generous cream sofas and chairs, endlessly toasting, chatting, laughing, posing for photos in the warm early evening air. The girls looked incredible in their dresses. I could spot a Pucci pattern here, a silk jewel-coloured Lanvin there, and a wonderful piece of 1950s vintage that was straight out of a Fellini movie. As I gazed at an impossibly pretty girl in a delicately pleated Feretti dress, I saw a hand rest gently on its rose-coloured angel wing sleeve. The hand belonged to Dante. He greeted the girl with a kiss on both cheeks and perched on the end of her oversized chair, his arm draped nonchalantly over its back. He flirted, talking closely, whispering in her ear, making her giggle with laughter before taking her hand to sit still and attentive, whilst the rest of the table continued to roar with laughter and gesticulate wildly.

Still watching, almost guiltily, I didn't feel a pang of envy, I just felt inadequate. The beautiful Italians reminded me of the beautiful people of Notting Hill, the magazine girls Harrisson hung out with, the models, the budding actresses, the creatives, the fashion stylists like Remi, who all seemed so glamorous and so together. And as what appeared to be a beautifully directed Italian perfume ad unfurled before me in all its hazy perfection, I was reminded of the time I had hung out with Harrisson on one of his photographic shoots. The time I'd been mistaken for someone who was there to fetch the coffee. I always felt, in those situations, that I didn't fit in. It wasn't just that I never quite seemed to wear the right clothes, be daring enough, fun enough or at the right place at the right time, it was the expectation that all of those things were what counted, what mattered. That to fit in to that particular world, you had to do something or be somebody who stood out, without making a complete fool of yourself. And during my time in Notting Hill, I felt like I had only managed to achieve the latter. Here in Majorca, I realised, I had started to become more confident. Celia had trusted me to do more than be her lackey, I mused, as an ugly image of Maddy popped into my head. I had been able to take control of the weddings I was looking after – under Celia's watchful gaze, of course. I'd learned a little

Spanish, I'd found it relatively easy to acclimatise, and I was, I admitted to myself, enjoying the job. Maybe, I wondered, watching Francesca and Roberto embrace for yet another photo, this was where I was supposed to be.

I watched as a waiter drifted into view, a white napkin draped over one arm, a silver platter of canapés held high on a cupped hand. As he passed the DJ, nodding gently to the chill-out beats that drifted over the guests, I checked myself again. Maybe I was being unrealistic. Was Majorca so beautiful that it was clouding my judgement, lulling me into a false sense of security and well-being? Would I soon need a big London fix? After all, the reality was that I was living in someone else's house, depending on them for work when I had just let them down. As I glanced at the guests again, I saw Catalina come into view. I realised that not only was I late in seating the guests for dinner, but also that my life was still in a complete state of flux.

One, Too Many

Celia sat in a high-backed wicker chair carefully positioned beneath a shady canopy of vines, her legs neatly crossed, reading a well-thumbed paperback. It was the first day she'd taken off in weeks, but she still wore a stiff formality that prevented her from at least appearing to be relaxed.

From my bedroom window, I'd seen her leave the house for church earlier that morning, a green vintage crocodile handbag swinging from the elbow of one arm as she curtly told Pepillo to stay and closed the heavy wrought-iron gate behind her to briskly walk, the way that she always did, down the country lane. Seeing her slight frame fade from view, I'd decided that despite it being a Sunday, I would press ahead with the wedding preparations. Since Celia had been called to the scene of my fainting episode at the Italian wedding she had been aloof, not once mentioning the incident, and I was eager to get back into her good books.

I sat with my inbox open and my diary spread in front of me, loose leaves of paper fluttering in the warm breeze that seeped through the open window, as I tried to concentrate. It was peacefully quiet. No telephones, no distractions, just the sound of birdsong. A golden light had filled the room, reminding me that most people would be outside, enjoying the sunshine before long lunches in the local restaurants or walks by the sea. I forced myself to focus, lifting my head three hours later, when my grumbling stomach signalled that it was time to take a break.

Downstairs in Celia's kitchen, I prepared myself a *Pa Amb Oli*, toasting two large slices of yesterday's rustic bread, rubbing a clove of garlic, then the pulp of a fresh tomato, on each one and drizzling the slices liberally with olive oil, topping them with shavings of Manchego cheese and shiny jet-black olives. I eyed the olives greedily, popping one into my mouth whilst pouring myself a long glass of sparkling water, watching the ice cubes I'd placed at the bottom crack on contact with the liquid. Celia, I could see from the kitchen window, was still reading. She'd turned her chair slightly, to remain in the shade, and had adopted a wide-brimmed, chic straw hat with a silk scarf tied at the middle as an extra precaution. She looked engrossed in the book, a PG Woodhouse, or a Jane Austen, I presumed. Thinking it best not to disturb her, I wandered out into the garden in search of my own quiet spot. On my way, I picked up the copy of British *Vogue* I'd left on the kitchen table. It had been a ridiculous luxury to sign up to an overseas subscription, but I couldn't go cold turkey completely, I needed a fashion fix, something of London that would be waiting at the postbox Celia had in the local town; news from the real world, I'd figured. It might only be for a short while, I'd convinced myself, I could always cancel it.

I took the cobbled-stone path lined with long-stemmed daisies, their yellow flowered heads turned upwards to soak up the sun. It led past a twisted olive tree, a row of bright green succulents, and down to a pretty patio. Here a wooden bench nestled between French lavenders and bright red hibiscus, with a view of the valley. I put down my plate of food, my glass, and finally my magazine, enjoying the warmth of the sun on my back. As I started to sit I heard a low growl. A small dark shape ran at top speed towards the bench. It was Pepillo, his one good eye bulging, his small pink tongue hanging out of the side of his mouth. Before I could stop him, he'd thrown himself at my plate, swiping half of the *pa amb oli*. I stood for a moment in disbelief before instinctively chasing him barefoot. His legs were short, his body thick and stout, but he was fast, winding his way round the garden he knew so well, dropping the olives and cheese as he flew past the carefully tended bushes and plants, looking for shelter under which to devour his oily catch.

'Pepillo! NOOOOOO!' I called after him angrily, my stomach still rumbling with hunger.

Then I was stopped dead in my tracks. It was, at first, like I'd hit a wall. I'd had my eyes on the cheeky runt and not where I was going, but as I turned my head, I realised I'd run into another person. In shock, I let out a girly shriek.

'Steady on there,' the voice said, seriously.

I gazed up to see a complete stranger before me. A man, late thirties maybe, tall, mid-brown hair, pale skin, glasses; definitely English.

'What the—?' I started crossly at the intruder, spying Pepillo crouched under a large leafy bush, devouring my lunch.

Then the penny dropped. The voice. The voice from the phone. Well-spoken, a public school tone, it must be Tomas. Celia's Tomas.

'Sorry . . .' I started again, trying to find my manners. 'Isabelle,' I said firmly, extending a slightly oily hand. 'I hope I didn't hurt you.'

'Tomas.' He smiled thinly, before shaking it.

'Ah, *Pa Amb Oli*,' I explained, embarrassed. 'A little bit of oil.'

He rubbed his hands together, in a no-nonsense way that reminded me instantly of Celia.

'Good for the skin,' he quipped, 'but maybe not for dogs. I see you know Pepillo,' he continued in his very proper accent. 'He's quite a character.'

Character! I unwittingly raised an eyebrow. 'You're right there! Well, I suppose you're looking for Celia,' I finally offered. 'I'll point you in the right direction, then maybe I can fetch you something? A drink maybe?'

Tomas didn't answer but followed my lead to the back of the house. Pepillo, crumbs still stuck to the spiky, greying fur around his mouth, trotted closely behind us.

'Tomas!' Celia piped from her chair, squinting to see him against the sun, her hat now in her hand. She stood up to greet him, all smiles. 'What a surprise.' Despite our conversation just a few days before, she appeared to be pleased to see him. They embraced formally on the lawn, briefly kissing both cheeks, Pepillo jumping up at Tomas's shins as they did so. Before they parted Celia took a moment to look up at her son; he smiled warmly back at her. I stood a little way back, on the cobbled terrace, feeling slightly awkward.

'Come,' I heard her say, finally. 'Have a cold beer with me on the terrace.'

I started to turn to walk to the kitchen now, to allow them some time together and to prepare myself another lunch, preferably something that Pepillo couldn't steal.

'Isabelle?' I heard Celia call. 'Isabelle, meet Tomas.'

They were walking over and he looked a little nervous, maybe remembering our phone conversation, I guessed.

'Yes, we just met,' I replied, trying to manage a knowing look at Tomas. 'Shall I fetch you something to drink? I was just about to get something for myself.'

'A beer would be lovely.' Celia smiled a thank-you and Tomas nodded in agreement. 'And do join us,' she added.

The old flagstones in the kitchen were cool underfoot. From the window I could see Tomas and Celia chatting, sitting at the table on the shady terrace. Before long they were deep in conversation. I rooted at the back of Celia's fridge for the coldest amber bottles of beer. It was a large white cabinet, circa 1950s, with rounded corners. I pushed the chrome handle to close its sticky seal then wandered over to the pantry in search of some nibbles. Whilst I poured the beer into long glasses and decanted generous helpings of almonds and olives into china dishes, I snuck another look at mother and son. Tomas looked more relaxed now. His stiff posture had softened, he had rolled up the sleeves of his pale blue shirt and his fingers traced the lace pattern on Celia's antique tablecloth as they chatted. He peered up at Celia intermittently through his foppish schoolboy fringe, his large, clear eyes animated behind his rectangular glasses – simple black frames, the kind an architect wore. Beneath the table his long legs were crossed at the ankles, his knees bare beneath neatly pressed chino-style shorts. His style was nondescript, functional, with little regard for fashion. It made him appear older than his years.

I joined Celia and Tomas outside, the afternoon air was warm and scented, the view from the
terrace of the mountains and the valley below was
wonderful.

'Isabelle has come to help me with the business,'
Celia explained to Tomas. She was eyeing my casual
dress and unbrushed hair with a look of disappointment
as I placed a glass of beer in front of him. I sat down,
grabbing a handful of nuts, hungrily pushing them into
my mouth, instantly regretting my greediness as Celia
looked to me for a response.

'Yes,' I managed, after a few seconds of fast,
unladylike munching that I was sure made me look like
a guinea pig that had been starved for a week, 'it's been
a wonderful opportunity, I've really enjoyed the work
and, of course, the island.'

'Well, you make it sound like you're leaving already,'
Tomas laughed.

I looked at Celia, embarrassed. We hadn't yet
discussed what would happen at the end of my trial
period, but she overlooked it.

'So, how is work for you, Tomas?' Celia asked.
'Where are you with the Ph.D.?'

Ph.D., I mulled. That explained the khaki shorts, the
intellectual glasses, the serious demeanour.

'Yes, extremely well, thank you. The paper I'm
currently working on is coming together and I'm just
contemplating my next project.' Tomas looked
thoughtful. I imagined that he often did.

'Tomas is studying botany,' Celia announced proudly
in explanation, ignoring his last comment. 'It's always
been his passion.'

'Oh, right.' I smiled, not knowing what to say.
'Really, I should leave you two to it,' I added quickly,
excusing myself from the table. 'I might sneak in

another hour or two in the office. It's been good to meet you, Tomas.'

'Likewise,' he replied formally, without warmth.

Back upstairs in the office I could hear the couple's non-stop chatter break intermittently into laughter from my open window and another beer bottle fizzing open and being glugged into a glass as the sun began to fade from view. Later that evening I came downstairs to find that Tomas and Celia had gone out. There was just Pepillo stretched out on his rough, chewed blanket on the kitchen floor, asleep. It was the first time for ages that I'd felt that I could have done with some company.

I wasn't sure how long Tomas planned on staying and I don't think that Celia knew either. She didn't mention the matter and spent long days in the office as the weddings were gearing up towards peak season. Celia still took the lion's share of the organising, be it a small ceremony and celebration for twenty, or the elaborate three-day event she was preparing for three hundred people at the end of my stay. Surrounded by endless piles of flower orders, coach quotes and catering contacts, I was Celia's support network, fixing the details she didn't have time to organise. Some of which seemed strange and abstract to me when they weren't part of the weddings I was taking care of, yet sourcing a tutu so that a pet chihauhua could be a 'bridesmaid' for a Paris Hilton-esque bride or a taper to light a ten-foot high candle definitely made a change from my usual tasks. Meanwhile, Celia seemed tired and preoccupied. On the wedding days themselves, we often worked on the set-up from mid-morning, leaving, exhausted, only when music and dancing was in full swing well after midnight. There'd been little time to think about anything else.

'Isabelle?' Celia had asked late one afternoon, rubbing her brow with a perfectly manicured hand, 'I think I'll have to work late tonight; I need to meet a photographer regarding the big wedding next month. It's the only time he'll be on the island and the brief is complicated.'

'Shall I do it for you?' I offered, noticing that she looked shattered and pale. 'Why don't you relax, spend some time with Tomas?'.

'That's most kind of you, dear,' she replied, 'but it's not quite as simple as that. In fairness, by the time I've explained everything to you, I could have done it, but, on the other hand, I had promised Tomas we'd go out for supper. He's cancelled a drink with an old friend to make it and I do feel terrible having to cancel.'

'Mother, really!' We turned to see Tomas standing at the open office door, laughing.

'You're working far too hard, but there's really no problem with tonight. I shall call Marta and reschedule. I doubt she's made other plans at such short notice. Really, you simply should have said.'

Celia looked apologetic. 'Oh, I'm sorry, darling,' she said, startled by the interruption. 'I've been trying to race through everything and make this meeting another time, but it's just not going to work out.'

'Don't fret, honestly. It was only supper,' Tomas reassured her. 'We can do it any time.'

They both looked at me, momentarily.

'Why not take Isabelle with you?' Celia suggested brightly, as if she'd stumbled upon a great idea.

Tomas looked awkward. 'Certainly,' he fired, as his good manners had taught him. 'How about it, Izzy?'

*

I'd convinced Tomas to jump on the back of the Vespino that night to the port. He'd shot me a strange look at the suggestion but we'd headed off almost straight away, him wincing as I kicked up the stones of Celia's gravelled drive with too much throttle from my back wheel. I let out a giggle. I could only imagine that Tomas's female friends back home were more delicate and bookish.

Winding down Celia's lane the wild flowers were colourful against the stone walls at the foot of the fields. Jasmine and nasturtiums climbed the gates of the houses and the bells dangling from the necks of the sheep and goats rang out as we rode past them, the bike a little heavier than usual with the extra weight of another person. Tomas, I could see in my mirror as we swooped down through the local village, was careful to keep a gentlemanly distance, despite the limited space on the bike's slippy leatherette seat. As we slowed to descend through the dusty local town, the older men of the village had gathered to play *boulé*. Under their flat corduroy caps you could just see their lips pursed in concentration. Animated discussions about the game gave way to a roar and all hands were thrown into the air to dispute a move in the sand as we drove by.

We picked up speed as we passed a long line of town houses, shutters closed against the warm evening sun, and again as the road opened on to a smooth dual carriageway. We sped by the open fields, lush bougainvilleas, and a donkey taking his own stroll by the roadside. Tomas, I could see, gripped the bar behind his seat tightly as we finally slowed to join a line of traffic leading down to the port. His arm swung in front of me to point out a space in the busy car park.

'Well spotted!' I shouted back in his direction,

pulling over between the large BMWs, Wrangler Jeeps and hire cars.

The sea glimmered in front of us, the masts of yachts bobbing gently on the water.

'Beautiful evening,' Tomas commented when I'd turned off the engine. We took off our helmets and turned to face the sea.

The port was bustling with life. Spanish families were taking their evening promenade along the paved walkway, their children riding bikes, the older ladies immaculately dressed, their hair set and their thin legs in thick tan tights, despite the warmth of the evening sun. English and German tourists ambled amongst them, easily visible in their summer shorts and floaty dresses so early in the season. We followed the little wooden bridge over the water, strolling past the fishing boats, which, Tomas explained, still hauled their catches into the tiny harbour, despite it being mostly filled with sleek motor boats and beautiful teak-hulled yachts. Their bright orange and yellow fishing nets were stretched out to dry in the sun.

'Do you sail?' Tomas asked, as we took in the sweep of the port, framed by mountains on all sides and topped with an almost impossible number of houses and lush, green trees.

'No, I've always wanted to. What about you?'

'Yes, love it. In fact, I really think you see a different Majorca from the sea.'

Our conversation was still stiff and polite.

'Shall we go for a drink?' I asked, hoping it might loosen him up a little.

'Good idea,' he replied with a smile. 'I know just the place.'

I couldn't imagine what Tomas's type of place would

be. We passed the front line of pretty tourist restaurants, bars and shops, rows of tightly packed tables commanding their own prized slice of the promenade, overlooking the water. Most were at the foot of traditional town houses, all painted a different colour, something of their charm preserved. Tomas turned a sharp left and I followed him up a steep cobbled street that wound through back streets of fishermen's houses; once humble homes, I guessed they'd now fetch millions of euros in the newly inflated market. The road continued away from the seafront and past a pretty church that Celia used for ceremonies. Tomas took another diversion, up yet another side street, narrow and filled with flats.

'I promised we'd meet Marta,' he said, breaking the silence now, 'she can't make it for dinner, but she has time for a drink. I hope you don't mind, I think you'll like her.'

'OK, sounds great.' I nodded. Marta, might be less reserved, more fun, I thought.

We finally came to a discreet open doorway. With no sign outside I was surprised to see Tomas look back at me, to signal that this was our meeting place. A little old man was sitting in a red leatherette chair outside, a small yellow canary in a cage hung up on the wall behind him, in a spot that was sheltered from the sun.

'*Buenas tardes*,' he greeted us in a gruff Majorcan voice.

'*Buenas tardes, Paco, como va?*' Tomas answered. The old man looked again, closer this time. Recognising Tomas his face lit up and he stood, grabbing his stick, to greet him like a long-lost son.

I followed Tomas to the bar. Still talking to the old man in Majorcan he pulled up a tall mahogany stool and placed his wallet on the marble-topped bar. I copied him.

It was a small room, no larger than a living room and the bar ran the entire length, down one side. On top of the original, ornate, patterned-tiled floor there were five small wooden tables with rickety old chairs. In the corner, a huge old-fashioned television in a heavy wooden box blared with a Spanish soap opera, the women in full make-up and stiff hairstyles shrieking at each other at top volume from the wobbly set.

'Wow. You speak Majorcan?' I asked, genuinely in awe, when the old man had shuffled his way to change the TV channel.

'Yes of course,' Tomas laughed. 'I spent all of my holidays from boarding school here, from the age of twelve. I also speak Castellano as well as Catalan. But it's really no great shakes,' he added, as if not to boast, pushing the rim of his glasses back with a finger.

'So you went to boarding school in England?' I asked.

'Yes. Mother thought it most important.'

The old man appeared at the other side of the bar, ready to serve us a drink. We ordered a bottle of the local white wine, which the man served in short, wide glass tumblers, and a large bottle of soapy, sparkling water. To my surprise, Tomas lit a cigarette.

I turned to the door. It was still open, and the sun cast a single shaft of light on to the ceramic tiles, bringing the pattern to life. There was so much I wanted to ask Tomas about Celia, I didn't know where to start.

'Marta!' I heard Tomas exclaim excitedly, before I could fire my first question. As I looked up, a girl in her twenties stood before us. Dark, wide eyes like saucers, shoulder-length hair as glossy as melted chocolate, her nose sprinkled with freckles. She was beautiful. She stood with a straw bag slung over the shoulder of her small but voluptuous frame. Beneath a simple white cotton dress and jacket, the skin on her bare legs was a deep shade of olive, and she wore simple white pumps on her tiny brown feet. She smiled widely, genuinely, before throwing her arms round her old friend. They chatted away in Spanish, as if nothing else in the world existed. I turned to study the long glass cabinet of tapas, feeling very out of place.

'Marta,' Tomas finally stopped to announce, 'this is Isabelle. Isabelle, Marta.'

'*Hola*,' I offered with a smile, feeling deeply inadequate, wishing I'd maybe put on some lippy or at least had changed.

Marta beamed me a warm '*hola*' back. She turned away quickly to greet the old man, with kisses on both cheeks. '*Marta que guapa, siempre guapa*,' he enthused at her beauty.

Tomas pulled up a stool for Marta. She ordered a *vino tinto* and the little old man proudly presented her with an earthenware dish of *caracoles* from the tapas cabinet.

'Her favourite,' Tomas explained with raised eyebrows.

'Are they snails?' I asked, looking at the tiny shells covered in coriander seeds, trying not to crinkle up my nose at the thought.

'Yes,' he said, before turning to chat to Marta once more. But it wasn't like Tomas to forget his manners and, after a few minutes, he suggested we move to a table so that we could chat more easily.

'So you come to Majorca to work, Isobel?' asked Marta in a soft, honeyed tone, changing my name to the local equivalent and picking the snails from their tiny shells with a small, long-handled fork. Her eyes were inquisitive and I could see now, quite enviably, that they were free of make-up.

'Yes, I'm working with Celia, Tomas's mother, organising weddings,' I replied. She raised her eyebrows and nodded in recognition.

Marta, I discovered, worked at the local vineyard. It had been in her family for generations and now it was the turn of her and her brothers to learn each step of the wine-making process and the secrets of its success, so that they could carry on the family tradition.

'Marta has a lot of fun organising the tastings for the English,' Tomas chuckled.

'Yes, my God, Isobel!' she exclaimed. 'The English, they drink so much. And they take all of the free bread and cheese and sometimes my brother and father have to ask them to leave before they are too drunk to stand!'

I blushed, embarrassed. 'We have this at the weddings too,' I explained.

'I do not understand, Isobel,' Marta asked, 'why the English eat so little good food and drink so much.'

I could only look perplexed. 'Yes, I know,' I replied, remembering my Mojito-fuelled fun in London.

Tomas ordered more wine and eventually went in search of Paco, the old man, for more tapas, as Marta and I started to descend into girly chatter. I noticed that Marta's eyes followed Tomas as he left the table, lingering on his back.

'He is a good man, Tomas,' she said, matter-of-factly.

'To be honest, I barely know him,' I answered, wondering if there had been a little more history between them than 'just friends'. 'What's he like?'

'He is *muy simpatico*, you know? And very kind. Handsome too, no?' I wasn't sure what to say. I certainly hadn't thought about whether he was good looking or not. To me he just seemed a little stuffy, cerebral and well, tweedy.

'He cares a lot about the environment,' Marta started again, this time in a low whisper.

'So how did you two meet?' I asked, intrigued.

'At the vineyard,' she started lowering her gaze to her glass. 'He was interested in the grapes, the vines; you know, how they grow,' she explained.

'Ah, yes, the botany,' I confirmed with a smile.

'Yes,' Marta confirmed. 'And now Celia uses the vineyard to host some of her weddings.'

Tomas came back to join us, cutting our conversation short and Marta soon made her excuses. She had to be home for a family dinner at ten o'clock.

'Are you sure you won't eat with us?' Tomas asked as she got up to leave.

'No, really, I promised my grandmother that I would come now, she will have made something for us all to eat together. But next time.' She smiled at us both.

'Nice to meet you,' I said, standing to kiss Marta goodbye in the local way.

'*Igualmente*, Isobel.' She smiled again as she turned to leave.

After a few glasses of wine I peered again at Tomas, remembering Marta's words as he filled up my glass. I felt a little hazy, a comfortable, happy hazy, from the red wine and the warm evening. The bar had started to fill with a few locals. The small room was filled with smoke and loud chatter.

'So, shall we stay here and sample some more of Paco's tapas, or go somewhere else to eat?' I asked him, now analysing his features.

'Paco would be mortified if we don't stay,' he laughed

apologetically. 'Do you mind? He makes a mean tortilla with salad if you want something more substantial.' I still couldn't see what Marta saw.

I let Tomas ask Paco what was fresh that day and he bought delicious plates of food *para picar* – to pick at and share. There were earthenware dishes of tasty salted cod, richly flavoured meatballs, a dense slice of tortilla and a freshly chopped *trampo* salad, amongst the endless servings that emerged from Paco's tiny kitchen. Tomas seemed to relax a little as we hungrily clinked our forks into the dishes. Paco looked on proudly, smiling. I wasn't sure if it was a particularly warm evening, the number of people in such a small space, or the effects of the wine, but the bar seemed to grow warmer. Tomas undid the second button at the neck of his shirt, his posture softening as he leaned into the back of the wooden chair.

We started to chat about England. The things Tomas missed when he'd come back from boarding school to Majorca; cups of strong tea, a good game of rugby, waking up to snow. And his life there now, in the wild Scottish Highlands, where he could be closer to the plant life he studied.

I dipped a slice of crusty bread into a dish of dark olive oil and it dribbled down my chin as I took a bite.

'Oops,' I laughed, wiping the oil from my chin and looking at Tomas to see if he'd noticed.

'You don't seem to have much luck with bread and oil,' he replied, referencing my scrape with Pepillo. 'Or with hot hotel rooms either,' he added in his cut-glass accent, with a mischievous grin.

I felt my mouth open wide in shock. 'Celia told you about *that*?' I shot back at him, reddening.

'Yes,' he laughed at my embarrassment. 'I'm quite surprised,' he added, 'I wouldn't have put you down as a wilting flower.'

'I'm not,' I replied defensively before laughing it off. 'I'm not sure what happened.'

'Really?' he asked a little too knowingly, teasing me like an older brother might. I raced to move the conversation on.

'So, you and Celia talk then,' I started. 'You're close?'

Tomas leaned in a little. 'We haven't always been,' he started. 'I think things will be a little better now. I hope so.'

'She seems pleased to have you in the house,' I replied, worrying that I'd probed a little too deeply.

'Yes. She does, doesn't she?' he pondered moment-arily. 'Mother, I've come to understand, just isn't the maternal type. I guess you can't really blame her for that,' he explained. I wasn't sure if it was the wine talking, but he continued. 'She had me at the end of her modelling career, that's when she met my father, and she sent me off to boarding school whilst she enjoyed a few more wild days in London. But when my father died, years later, she found it so difficult. We all did . . .' he explained.

He paused for a second. 'Father and I had been so very close. He was the one I spent time with, doing the things that boys do, and when I returned from school, she was cold. It was inevitable that I reminded her of him, I'd idolised him and we'd become so alike.'

Tomas looked thoughtful now. I wanted to ask how his father had died, but I didn't dare.

'But you think things are better now?' I said instead, trying to pick up the tone.

'Yes. I think it helps that I'm older. I understand her better. And I think she's finally accepted me, too. She's definitely mellowed with age.'

I couldn't remember the last time I'd heard a man talk so openly about his feelings.

'Sounds like Celia's led quite a life!' I answered, wanting to know more without being too nosy, too personal.

'You could say that. You should ask her about it, the parties and the rock stars she knew . . .' Tomas started. 'I was never that interested, having grown up with it.'

There was a pause. Tomas looked around the bar and smiled at Paco to get his attention. The old man shuffled over to clear our empty dishes.

'So what were you doing before you came here?' Tomas asked finally.

'I worked in TV in Notting Hill,' I started. 'It's a long story, but I think I started to look at it like you looked on Celia's clique in London . . . except I didn't know the celebrities or go to any wild parties. I'm not nearly as glamorous,' I giggled.

Finally we had something in common.

'So do you think you'll go back?' asked Tomas, signalling to Paco for the bill.

'Do you know,' I replied honestly, 'I'm really not sure.'

The air felt fresh and invigorating as we left the bar. The moon perched high above the mountains cast a golden glimmer on the water. The sky above it was clear and domed.

'I love that you can see the stars so clearly here,' I said dreamily, staring at the sky.

Looking up, I felt a little giddy, having come from the heat of the bar, and perhaps having drunk a little too much *vino tinto*. Crossing the wooden bridge over the water I felt a plank wobble under foot and stumbled slightly into Tomas.

'Careful there, Izzy,' he chuckled, putting an arm round my waist to steady me, pulling me closer.

His arm felt comforting and warm. 'Oopps, sorry!' I giggled, embarrassed. 'Must be the wine.' I looked up at Tomas. A smile flickered over his face. He moved his arm and I stepped aside awkwardly, looking ahead. He was different to the guys in Notting Hill, I mused. More sensitive. And maybe it was that sensitivity that Marta found attractive.

Solid Gold Princess

'**I**sabelle!' the voice on the phone said urgently as I uttered 'Hello?' It was early and I'd run, wrapped in a towel, from the shower to grab the receiver before the call went to answermachine.

'You have to come quickly, we have problem. A big problem with the wedding,' the voice continued.

It was Miguel Angel, the owner of one of Majorca's finest boutique hotels and the venue for the wedding later that day. His voice was deadly serious and I felt my heart skip a beat.

'*Hola, Miguel Angel. Qué tal?*' I answered nervously, my hair wet and stuck to my back.

Miguel started to talk very quickly, very seriously in Spanish, not once pausing for breath. His words seemed to merge and float over me.

'I'm so sorry, Miguel, I can't understand,' I finally interrupted when he paused. 'Can we try in English?' I pleaded, with a little shiver.

'Isabelle. You come?' he asked. He was unsure of his English on the phone. Face to face, it was easier for us to understand each other. '*Es muy importante*,' he added.

'Of course, Miguel, no problem. In one hour,' I assured him, nervously.

'*Perfecto, Isabelle. Gracias. Hasta luego*,' he replied quickly, hanging up. I couldn't begin to think what might have happened.

I went in search of Celia and found her taking a leisurely breakfast on the terrace downstairs with Tomas. In Majorcan style they were drinking freshly squeezed orange juice and strong milky coffee and devouring sweet, sticky-bottomed *ensaimadas*, the local pastries. Celia's table was dressed with fine bone china and silver; the lady herself, in vintage Dior.

'Morning!' I chirped, hugging the towel self-consciously. 'Sorry, not quite dressed yet.' I made excuses for my appearance as Celia and Tomas looked up from their plates. 'Err, seems to be a problem at the hotel today, Celia,' I added in explanation. 'I have to go and see Miguel Angel straight away; he just called, says there is a big problem.'

Tomas smiled sympathetically.

'OK, dear,' Celia answered nonchalantly. 'I'm sure it's nothing you can't cope with.'

'Yes, right,' I replied, realising I'd have to sort this one out alone, all part of my trial period, I guessed.

'I do hope everything is OK, Isabelle,' she added. 'Call me if you need to.'

I hurried upstairs to get myself together. The drive to the hotel was at least forty-five minutes. Packing my fake green Marc Jacobs shopper I mentally ran through a check-list in my head as I stumbled to step into a dress. I left my bed unmade as well as my face, stuffing a bulging make-up roll into the bag so that it wouldn't close. A few moments later I dashed for the door and out to the Vespino, my hair still wet under my helmet.

*

When I arrived at the hotel the owner greeted me at the door. 'Isabelle. Welcome,' he started warmly, looking relieved. 'Please, come.' He walked over to the quiet lobby.

It was a bright, sunny day and the hotel looked the best I'd ever seen it look. The bronze water feature glistened at the entrance in the sun, a contemporary foil to the traditional stone façade. Inside, the décor was sophisticated, a sea of white furnishings, modern art adding vibrancy to the walls. We sat below a picture window, with views across the hotel grounds and its field of golden corn. A bowl of simple water lilies lay in front of us on the low, white table. I perched on the edge of an L-shaped sofa that looked like it had never been sat on, crisp scatter-cushions on top of the immaculate upholstery. I was careful not to crease them.

'*Café?*' Miguel Angel asked, before we started.

'Thank you, yes, that would be very kind,' I answered as one of Miguel's attentive staff joined his side.

'Now, what I can help with?' I asked, hesitantly.

'OK, OK,' Miguel started. It was his way of creating a pause, so he could find the words in English.

'OK, Isabelle. How do I explain? OK, today . . . after the ceremony of the wedding, there must be no more celebrations at the hotel.'

'What?' I let slip in shock, before I could muster a diplomatic answer. 'No more weddings this year?'

'No, Isabelle. No dinner, no music, no dancing.'

I couldn't believe what I was hearing. I waited for Miguel to continue.

'OK,' he tried to smile, 'you see, because of the friends and family of the bride and groom I am worried about the hotel.'

'Why are you worried?' I asked quietly now, my head spinning.

'Well . . . You know, Isabelle, this hotel is owned by two very old brothers. Priests. That is why we have the ethos of *tranquilidad*.'

'Yes, of course, Miguel Angel,' I encouraged.

'The hotel is *muy preciosa*. We want to keep it a tranquil, beautiful place . . . and this is why I explain to you and Celia that only certain guests are right to stay here, *si*?'

'Yes, of course,' I assured him, 'we understand this.'

'Well, these are not people for this hotel,' he continued matter-of-factly.

'Why, Miguel Angel?' I asked sympathetically. 'What have they done?'

A waitress, dressed head-to-toe in black, a pristine white napkin draped over her arm, placed an elegant cup and saucer by my side and a plate of tiny pastries. '*Complementos of Chef*,' she explained. I was hungry, but the offering made me feel even worse about what Miguel was trying to tell me.

'Last night, Isabelle,' he continued, 'these people go from here to the local town. And they go to *restaurante*. There, it was busy night. They have live piano music, so many Spanish people come.'

I took a sip of coffee. The first of the day. It was hot and rich, the milk fuzzy against my top lip.

'These people, they are forty persons. They order food. But then, they do not want to wait in the *restaurante* so they do not take the food when it come. They are already in the bar, you understand?' My heart was sinking. 'Then, in bar, they drink, very much.'

I nodded, recalling the conversation I'd had with Marta the night before.

Miguel's face was cross now as he spoke. 'The

persons, they laugh at the pianist and, how you say, make the fun of him.' I nodded, for him to continue. 'Then, one man, he attacks the pianist. You know, is violent.'

'You mean he hit him?' I asked in disbelief.

'Si, black eye,' Miguel confirmed. 'And the *restaurante*, they call me about this, because they know these are people from my hotel. They know they are here for the wedding.'

'Oh God, I'm so sorry . . .' I started, shocked.

'Isabelle,' Miguel continued, his face quite red now, 'you understand, I cannot have this here, in this small town. It is not good for the hotel. And another thing. I don't want these people to have party here tonight. I don't want trouble. I don't want to call police. To have things in the hotel broken, my staff treated badly. You understand, Isabelle?'

'Yes, of course, I understand, Miguel Angel. Really, I do.' I was still taking the story in, but I knew the wedding had to go on. The bride and groom had paid eighty per cent of the bill upfront. The bride would be devastated. Their guests, however rowdy, had travelled to Majorca to celebrate. I thought for a moment.

'Look. What would you say if we talk to the groom and the best man?' I asked him. 'Get their assurance that nothing will happen here tonight?'

'I am not sure, Isabelle. I am not sure it is good idea any more,' Miguel Angel replied honestly.

'It is important for our company that you are happy, Miguel Angel,' I continued, looking around once more at the beautiful hotel. 'We want to work with you, maintain a good relationship, and we don't want any bad feeling. But we also have a responsibility to our client. Let's just see what they have to say. Then you can tell me if you are happy for the celebrations to continue,' I said hopefully.

Miguel Angel looked sceptical. I was almost begging now, as an image of a drunken guest swinging for the pianist filled my mind.

Miguel nodded reluctantly in agreement. 'OK, Isabelle,' he answered. '*Vamos a ver* . . . let us see.'

I got up from the lobby and wandered outside to call the groom from my mobile phone. The last thing I wanted to do was to have the conversation from the almost silent reception area. Guy answered instantly. He was apologetic and appalled. The culprits had been a group of his 'lads' who had gone out to 'get smashed' and he had no idea what they'd been up to. I liked Guy, he was always sweet and charming; an Essex boy with a big heart and rough edges.

'You see, Izz,' he explained on the crackly line, agreeing to come and speak to Miguel Angel, 'it's no excuse, but they're just making a weekend of it.'

I snapped the phone shut and looked up. Two groups of girls in tiny bikinis were sunbathing around the infinity pool, gossiping, soaking up the sun.

Guy strode across the lawn, wearing a pink Hackett T-shirt with a small Union Jack on the sleeve and long, baggy shorts, his feet in bright red Havaianas.

'Michelle,' he started, his arm outstretched to shake his hand. 'Mate, I'm sorry.' He always called him Michelle in his boy-racer accent, 'w' sound with the l's in the girl's name.

Miguel Angel accepted his hand and winced a little as Guy squeezed it a little harder than he was used to. 'The boys, you see,' he started to explain, screwing up his face, 'they've let me down. But it was just a bit of fun that turned bad.' His eyes were full of concern.

'I understand that it wasn't you,' Miguel Angel replied, 'but I cannot have this in this hotel.'

'Look,' Guy said, 'I've already worked out who was behind it. I've spoken to those involved and I've got their word that nothing'll kick off here.' Guy looked genuine enough.

'OK,' I said, trying to defuse the situation, 'at least this happened last night and hopefully now it's out of their system. Better then, than tonight.' I looked at Miguel Angel for his thoughts.

'And these people,' I continued, purposefully asking Guy a question to which I knew the answer, 'they're not staying at the hotel, are they? They're nearby?'

'Yeah,' Guy responded on cue. He'd taken the five-star hotel for three nights, all twenty rooms were filled with his guests.

'So they know to be on their best behaviour here? That this is a special place they need to respect?' I was feeding him lines now.

'Course, Izz. And Michelle, I've got me best man on it, he's going to keep an eye out. Head off trouble before it can start.'

Miguel Angel listened thoughtfully. 'Well, Isabelle,' he concluded, 'if you are to be responsible, then I think we do something, but at the first sign of trouble, we call the police, we stop the party.' His face told us that he meant it.

'Course,' Guy answered. 'Thanks, Michelle. The future Mrs would kill me if the wedding don't 'appen. You understand?' His face was deadly serious.

Miguel Angel laughed. 'Yes, of course. In Majorca, what the woman says, goes.'

With a huge sense of relief, I now pressed on with the wedding preparations, sending Guy back to his room with another warning.

'He really is serious, Guy, you know that, don't you?' I stressed.

'Sure,' he replied, his head hanging in shame. 'Not sure what else I can do, really.'

'Just get your best man and maybe a couple of good friends to keep watch tonight,' I warned. 'Make sure the lads don't hit the bar too early before the ceremony and that they don't get out of hand later. That way, you won't need to worry and spoil your day.' I smiled. I felt sorry for him.

'Thanks, Izz,' he replied. 'And please, not a word to Nicole.'

'Course not. Why would I worry the bride? Now, tell me the name of your best man and I'll hook up with him.'

'Bulldog,' he replied, matter-of-factly. 'You can't miss 'im. Big bugger, he is, but soft as a puppy.'

Fantastic, I thought. Fantastic!

The ceremony would be held in the exquisite chapel that had been part of the old *finca*, now the hotel, for centuries. It was tiny but ornate, holding just sixty people, but the bride and groom were happy to leave the doors open in the heat of the sun and to let a few more of the guests spill out of the back on to the lawn. I directed the hotel staff as they positioned an additional fleet of white chairs, with large bows, to the rear of the pews and out on to the grass. Here the guests would still see and hear every moment of the ceremony.

Afterwards, the bride and groom would lead a procession towards the hotel gardens, where the canapé and champagne reception would take place on the summer terrace at the cliff's edge, overlooking the sea. I walked the route now, turning the plan of the day over in my head. The sun was already high in the sky and warm. I took off the cotton jacket I'd slung over my dress and felt for the waiters, who were lifting the large rattan furniture and low tables to create chill-out areas, and setting up a bar in the shade.

'*Buenas, Isabelle.*' They waved, calling me over.

'*Hola! Como estamos?*' I said, asking how they were. Alfonso, the maître d', shot me a pained look; he was moving a nasty-looking floral display.

'What's that?' I asked him. He looked at me again, embarrassed.

'Isabelle,' he started, 'the florist. But not very good style for this hotel, maybe?' he answered apologetically.

'No, Alfonso,' I answered him with a chuckle, 'don't worry! These aren't the flowers for the wedding.'

'Yes,' he said. 'They tell me, flowers for the wedding.' He looked down at them in dismay. It wasn't that Alfonso was a snob, the flowers just weren't good. They'd been fashioned in a stiff triangular shape, in pinks and mauves, the oasis foam clearly on show, barely hidden by a metallic bow tied around the base of the plastic pot they stood in.

'No, really. It's a mistake. Nicole has ordered white and green flowers. Very beautiful ones, from one of the best florists we use in Palma.'

I turned round to see the florist in question standing behind me with his three assistants.

'*Hola, Isabelle!*' they chorused.

'The van is parked on the gravel drive. Is it OK? We have so many heavy displays to bring,' Bertrand asked, kissing me on both cheeks. The Frenchman had a wonderful shop, impeccable taste and was a fantastic floral designer.

'Yes, sure,' I said, shielding my eyes with my hand. 'I'm sure it's fine. Do you have everything you need?' I answered, but Bertrand didn't respond, his eyes were fixed on Alfonso, still clutching the shoddy flowers behind me. Bertrand was passionate about his work and something of an artist. Bad design upset him.

He nodded slowly, looking chic, as usual, in a cute neckerchief, T-shirt and simple marine-blue pants, as they headed back to unload their kit.

'Alfonso!' I gasped with Bertrand out of earshot. 'What do you mean, they're the flowers for the wedding?'

'They are all here. In the chapel, in the *restaurante*, all like this, all the same,' he replied sadly.

I thought for a moment. Nicole had organised the flowers through Bertrand and me. Why would others arrive?

'Did Miguel Angel—'

'No!' Alfonso laughed, as though it was the most ridiculous thing he'd ever heard.

So that left one person, I figured: Guy. Guy came to Majorca four times a year on holiday and the last time we'd met, he'd been quizzing me about our suppliers, telling me, with his family background in retail, that he was a brilliant negotiator on prices. He was a business-man in his own right and clearly had plenty of cash, but it seemed that Guy loved nothing more than a bargain.

'Guy?' I asked as a male voice answered the phone. 'Really sorry to disturb you, but can you tell me anything about some flowers that have shown up which Nicole hasn't ordered?'

There was silence.

'I'll come down now,' he stammered, sounding perplexed.

I met him at the entrance to the hotel and we walked round to the chapel. Here, Bertrand and his team were lifting the huge urns, which they would be filling with large blooms of hortensia and the sweetest-smelling roses, into place.

'Come inside,' I urged him. 'See what I mean?' I pointed to the displays on the altar, all the same as the first, with day-old carnations and spindly sprays of white gyp. The beauty of the chapel, with its gold candelabra, frescoed ceiling and delicately faded stained-glass window, only highlighted their ugliness.

'Jesus. They're terrible,' he admitted, walking over to one. 'Nothing to do with me.'

'Well, you've been at the hotel for a day, so I know they aren't left over from another event, but leave it with me, I'll get rid of them,' I started, still unable to solve the mystery. Then Guy froze. He'd pulled out a card from one of the pots and now looked at me, red-faced.

'Izz, think I owe you an apology,' he said with an embarrassed smile. 'This card is from a florist in Santa Ponça who I got a quote from. But I didn't ever confirm it, I didn't ever call her back. Didn't think she really understood my English . . .'

'Ah, that explains it,' I realised out loud, 'they would have done the job on trust rather than let you down for a wedding.'

Bertrand was standing at the door. 'Isabelle, dahling,' he purred, 'OK if we come inside to finish arranging the displays?'

'Of course,' I answered. 'I'll just move out what's here.' I shot Guy a look, scooping up the unwanted flowers into my arms. 'Then I'll roll out the red carpet for the aisle when you're done.'

'What is thees, Isabelle?' Bertrand started, eyeing the wilting blooms in amazement. 'Theees, theees, *merde!*' He raised his voice now, his eyes aflame behind his glasses. 'I cannot bear theees.' He poked at the flowers. One of his assistants shot me a sorry look.

'Incredible,' he added, 'theees work, it is

deeeesgusting. I cannot put my work amongst theees!' he whined like a diva.

'No, no, Bertrand, you misunderstand. I'm just moving them out of your way. They are not here for the wedding,' I replied in a calm voice. 'Nicole only wants *your* flowers.'

It was best to remove all the flowers from Bertrand's sight, as quickly as possible, I realised, as he stormed past me to go back to his van in a Gallic strop.

Guy gave me a sorry look. 'Won't have to pay for those, Izz, will I? As I didn't confirm 'em?' he begged, as I raced to remove all of the other flowers the Santa Ponça florist had left around the hotel before Bertrand and his team could follow with theirs.

'Well, you should, really,' I replied honestly, 'but let's worry about that after the wedding.' I smiled, letting Guy go back to his suite to get ready and have some lunch whilst I smoothed things over with the maestro of floral design.

I walked up to the window of Bertrand's car; he was still sulking, sat sitting silently inside with the air-conditioning on. I made him click open the central locking and tried to soften his mood by explaining the story of how the flowers had got there, as I slid into the passenger seat beside him. 'Silly boy,' he said of Guy, 'why employ you and then think he can do better, no?'

'Nicole would have killed him!' I shot back. 'Imagine!' Just as we were mocking the faces the bride might have pulled as she walked into the church and saw the 'bad flowers', Celia's car drew up beside us. She emerged looking elegant and composed, removing her headscarf and 'Jackie O' sunglasses. I stopped contorting my features and got out of the car like an obedient schoolgirl as she walked purposefully towards me.

'Everything under control, Isabelle?' she asked, as I crunched over the gravel drive to greet her. 'I hadn't heard from you, so thought maybe I should come and check on things.'

I realised my mistake instantly. 'Celia, I'm so sorry, I should have called, but I've not stopped!' I was breathless even now, still clutching a black sack filled with some of the sad, broken flowers. 'Things seem to be back on track though, so everything else should run smoothly for the rest of the day,' I assured her. But these were words I uttered a little too soon. At that very moment the sound of shattering glass seemed to echo from the front of the hotel. Our shoulders rose in tandem. I ran inside.

I paced through the calmness of reception and the beautiful lounge, eventually finding myself in the chaos of the restaurant. The floor was completely covered in glass, the waiting staff in a panic, frantically trying to clear it with glossy steel dustpans and brushes.

'What happened? What happened?' I screamed, at anyone who would raise their heads to listen. But as I looked in front of me it was obvious. The seamless line of full-length glass windows leading out to the dining terrace had completely shattered, covering Nicole and Guy's beautiful white linen-covered tables outside in a million tiny shards. They glistened in the sunlight, playing on the otherwise perfect setting.

'Izz?' I heard a male voice say. I looked behind me to see that Guy had wandered into the restaurant.

'I heard a crash, what's happening?' he asked me nervously. My instinct was to try to make myself very large, in a pathetic attempt to block out the scene behind me. I could only hope that the Christmas bulge I'd still not beaten, was helping me master being a human screen.

'Oh, it's the acoustics in this place; a waiter just dropped a tray of champagne glasses in the kitchen,' I lied, putting my arms in the air to make a bigger shape and reinforce another lie. 'It's fine, sounds worse than it is!' I was laughing now, almost hysterically. Guy made an exit and I told him to come and see the restaurant when we'd finished creating the tables, for the best effect. I breathed a sigh of relief as he turned to leave. The tough Essex boy seemed a little on edge now.

One of the younger waitresses, still sweeping the glass from the white marble floor, looked tearful, mumbling, 'Miguel Angel will be very unhappy, very unhappy,' in Spanish, over and over again. But still the maître d' was nowhere to be seen and there was no time to waste. Over at the bar I rummaged through a list of names and numbers in a leather book by the telephone and rang the first *cristalero* I came across.

'*Hola, puedes ayudarme?*' I pleaded, asking for help, trying to think of how I'd explain what had happened in my limited Spanish. But he couldn't, and '*si*', raising my hopes, followed by '*mañana*', dashing them, was the one phrase that all of the busy glaziers uttered.

As Celia emerged to join me, Miguel Angel in tow, the young waitress and I had conspired to get a local DIY man to board up the windows with MDF. It was the only thing that could be done with so little time. Celia looked suitably impressed.

'But what will you do to conceal the ugly brown boards?' she asked.

'The hotel has some white muslin that I've seen before. Maybe, Miguel Angel, we can drape that over as curtaining?' I asked politely. 'I'll then see if Bertrand can cover some of it with any leftover flowers he might have' – I hoped he'd forgiven the earlier episode – 'or ask the lighting technician to place fairy lights behind them, to create an illuminated wall as the sun goes down.'

'Very well,' Celia said with a little smile, as Miguel Angel checked the restaurant meticulously for any further damage, 'why don't I check on the bride whilst you organise that? You have checked on her already, though, haven't you?'

'No, Celia,' I admitted, 'I haven't yet; she was next on my list, once I knew things were underway here.' I looked down at my feet, wishing I could be quicker and prevented some of the calamities of the day.

'Yes, quite right,' Celia retorted, to my relief.

'She's very nice, Nicole. I think you'll like her, Celia. She's very natural, pretty and organised. I'm sure she'll be composed and have everything under control,' I enthused.

'Great,' said Celia.

'She's staying at the Agrotourisme hotel down the road with her bridesmaids. I'll fetch the bouquets from Bertrand so you can take them with you. The car, as it says on the schedule, is due to arrive at three p.m. to pick her up and bring her here for three-thirty. Thanks, Celia.' I smiled.

Bulldog, when I finally met him, was like no other man I'd ever set eyes on. As the wedding drew closer and the guests started to gather on the lawn for pre-ceremony drinks, I checked in with Guy to see if his nerves were holding up. But I couldn't focus on him. He proudly introduced me to his best man before I could speak. 'This is my main man, Bulldog . . .' he started excitedly, presenting him to me like a kid does at 'show and tell'. 'He knows his mission for tonight, don't ya, Bull? Done it a million times before, aint ya? The stories we can tell, ay?'

Bulldog let out a laugh, a wheezing, almost soundless laugh, like Mutley from the kids' cartoon series *Wacky Races*. The man mountain had a face only a mother could love, the physique of a heavyweight boxer (complete with a wobbling waistline), and a flamboyant sense of style. He'd encased the wobble in a loud pink shirt with a large Harry Hill collar and matched it with a silk tie and socks in the same dazzling hue. The latter were just visible beneath his black snakeskin shoes. He looked like a thug from a Guy Ritchie movie, with the dress sense of De Niro in *Casino*, save for a diamante earring, heavy silver identity bracelet, and flashy, chunky Rolex, which chinked as he rubbed his bald head.

'Pleased to meet ya, miss,' Bulldog said, in a soft, high voice. It wasn't unlike David Beckham's. I thought he was joking and started to giggle, but to my amazement he paused, blushing, and I stopped instantly, the smile fading from my lips.

'Yes, you too,' I replied, not knowing what to call him, 'it's great you can help us out tonight, to make sure the guys don't drink too much. Of course, the hotel owner wants everyone to have fun, but—'

'There are limits,' Bulldog interrupted, flashing me a smile, keen to show he understood.

'Yes, and with that large case of Red Bull we had to order in for the party . . .' I started.

'Don't worry yourself, Izz, it's all under control,' Guy assured me again. He looked quite handsome in his suit. Pale grey, a mod cut. His hair looked good. 'Bull is a teetotaller,' he added in explanation, 'he's in the God-squad!' He laughed.

'Right, then, brilliant,' I replied, not knowing if they were having me on. 'I need to go and check on things for later, so I'll see you in a while . . . unless there's anything you need, Guy?' I added, remembering my role.

'You're all right,' he answered, which, relieved, I took as a no. I wanted to do some final checks and see how the MDF construction was coming along.

I stopped at reception, eyeing the girl there with curiosity. '*Hola!*' I singsonged, about to pass. 'Everything OK?'

The pretty girl was new that day. Her desk was surrounded with wicker baskets filled with bottles of olive oil. She was looking at a printout of the guest list for dinner, making labels on her computer to stick on to the oil bottles.

'*Si, Hola*, Miss Isabelle,' she replied. 'But please, I no speak good English.' Her Spanish accent was thick, her face kind and attentive.

'It's better than my Spanish already!' I said jollily.

'Oh, sorry, I no understand,' she replied.

'Don't worry. Err—'

'*Una* question, Miss Isabelle,' she interrupted. 'I do bottles.'

The hotel offered the bottles of oil as an alternative to a name card; a souvenir that people could take with them, with the name of the bride and groom on the label. God, I thought, her English seemed OK, but it would be tricky for her to tackle Nicole's unconventional abbreviations.

'Who this "Moose" person? How I spell it?' she asked.

'It's a nickname,' I explained, going over to look at the list.

'So it's not real name. How you spell real name?' she asked. I really wished my Spanish was better.

'No, it is the name for the bottle,' I tried to elaborate.

'You mean yes, it is not the name for the bottle?' she replied with big eyes.

'Ah, yes, that was my fault, bad English,' I explained.

'No no, *I* bad English,' she interrupted before I could continue.

'OK,' I started seriously now, forcing a smile, this was turning into a farce. 'Please, can you write the names as they are on the list?'

'Of course!' she answered as if I had been suggesting something completely different and she had been doing that all along.

'*Muchas gracias*,' I said, maintaining the grin as I waltzed past the desk to the restaurant.

Toleo, my MDF man, was busy trying to make minimum mess in the otherwise pristine environment as he constructed our emergency fix for the smashed windows. He looked disgruntled at the maître d', Carmen. She had appeared and told me now, with a sorrowful look, that the accident had been her fault. The wind had picked up, causing the door she'd left open to smash, along with the windows in the same frame. Toleo looked grumpy, not having relished a call-out on a Saturday.

'But it's fine now, Carmen, don't worry,' I said, trying to console her. She still looked a little shaky. Our conversation was cut short by my phone ringing.

'Izz, it's Guy,' he announced, his voice urgent and tense.

'Hi, Guy, everything OK?' I asked, sensing it wasn't.

'Izz, I've messed up.' He laughed. 'Look. You know I went ahead and booked the Rolls-Royce for Nicole . . . the special Silver Shadow you said wasn't available because it was a non-runner?'

'Yes, of course.'

'Yeah . . .' he paused. 'Well, the one I booked, it's stuck on the Maritimo, that main road in Palma down by the sea.' I couldn't quite believe what I was hearing. 'She's gonna KILL me, Izz,' he added, desperately.

I felt sorry for him and guessed that the car in question had been one and the same. We'd offered Guy a long list of alternative vintage cars, knowing that this particular Silver Shadow, his dream car, was in no fit state to be relied on till it was fixed after the season, but he knew what he wanted and only that one was going to do. Guy had convinced me he'd found his own alternative and had been adamant about booking it himself. He'd been so confident that Bertrand was poised to fill the back shelf with flowers and the exterior with bows.

'OK, no need to panic,' I gulped, 'we still have an hour before the wedding. We can fix things. Now, what do you mean "stuck"?'

'I mean stuck,' he was panicking now, 'broken down with steam pouring out, the geezer told me at the garage. Says it's creating a right jam.' This didn't sound promising.

'Right,' I said firmly. I wanted Guy to let me deal with things now. 'Give me the number of the garage. I'm going to cancel the car. I don't want to risk them trying to get it started, it might break down again.' I was surprised at hearing my own voice, how decisive I was being.

'But Izz, the car, it works with Nicole's dress, the whole thing. It's part of the dream,' he argued.

'Guy, I'm sorry, please trust me on this one. The important thing is getting Nicole to the ceremony. Let me call and see what other Rolls-Royces they have. And if they can't supply one, I'll try the other companies we use. But speed is key now. Even if she arrives by taxi.' As soon as I uttered those last words, I regretted them. Guy exploded.

'My Princess ain't arriving in a bleedin' taxi!!' he shouted.

'No, of course not, Guy. I'm just being practical. Look, I'm going to make the calls now, I'll ring you back and let you know how it goes. Does Nicole know?'

'No, not yet. Look, sorry, Izz. I know I just lost it, I just feel so bad about it. It's her day, you know. I want it to be perfect for her.'

'I know, and it will be. It's all a bit stressful,' I cooed. 'I'll just call her and tell her a slightly different car will be arriving, once I've arranged things.' Guy finally agreed and was all apologies as we hung up.

I sat down inside the restaurant and called the garage who'd rented Guy the car. They were initially confused that I was ringing, but when they realised Guy was my client they were apologetic, saying that Guy had insisted and they'd tried their best. I believed them. They were happy to scrap the order and were more concerned about clearing the steaming Rolls from the Paseo Maritimo. The local police were at the scene as we spoke. The bigger problem was that, on a busy Saturday, most of the cars were out, already hired. There were certainly no Rolls-Royces available now. In fact, they had just one car left. A brilliant red American Ford Mustang. Not just any Mustang, but a Mustang with yellow and amber flames emblazoned down its sides.

I hung up and put my head in my hands as I raided my contacts book for all of the vintage and classic car specialists we had relationships with on the island. No luck. Twenty minutes later, my mouth was dry from panic and pleading and there were clearly no other options. I called Guy.

'Guy? Izzy. Look, I've really tried my best,' I said, bracing him for bad news. 'All of the very best cars are already booked for today.' I was trying to keep things short.

'Right. So, go on, Izz, what's left?' he asked, nervously.

'A Mustang,' I said gingerly.

'A Mustang,' he repeated, letting it sink in.

'Yes. The only options are a Mustang, or a taxi.'

Then he asked the question I'd been dreading. 'What colour is it?'

'Red with . . . err, flames,' I replied quietly.

'This is a wedding, not *Starsky and Hutch!*' he shrieked. 'White might have just done it. But red with what, go-faster flames? You're kidding me!' He was a little calmer by the end of the sentence. 'Look, Izz, I'm sure we will laugh about this and tell our grandkids one day,' he said, realising he'd been a fool, 'but is there nothing at all?'

'No, nothing,' I stopped him. 'I'm sorry, Guy. Look, we've not got much time now. Nicole will be ready and waiting, the car should already be there by now. Taxi or Mustang, I need to book it,' I urged him.

'All right. Well, I still want her to have a chauffeur, so it's going to have to be the Mustang. But look, Izz, do me another favour, will you?' he asked, his voice pleading. 'Tell Nicole yourself, will you? I don't want to call her, she just might not show up!'

'Of course I'll call. You mustn't see or speak to her before the wedding, it's supposed to be bad luck.'

'Yeah,' he laughed in relief, 'these kind of things might be why.'

With the phone still clamped to my ear, I wandered back past the girl on reception to make the call to Nicole. She was still there spelling out names on the guest list, sticking the labels on to the bottles.

'Miss Isabelle?' she called as I rushed past. 'This name, "Big Tone", is mistake?'

I beamed her another smile. 'No,' I sighed, 'it's as it is on the list.'

*

The guests had started to fidget in their seats and become impatient. They'd already waited an unexpected forty-five minutes for the bride. Some had tried to sneak a glass of beer or champagne to their seats. I couldn't blame them, but as the priest looked on in disapproval it was my job to play the party pooper.

'I'm so sorry, sir, I know it's a warm day and that you are waiting, but this is a religious ceremony and I will have to ask you to leave your drink at the bar.' It was the fifth time I'd mentioned it and I heard my voice becoming slightly monotone with repetition. The man nodded politely, but as I turned, I saw him hide the glass underneath his chair.

I waited nervously at the edge of the grass, waiting to spot the bridal car, to signal for the music to start up for her entrance. I'd already called Celia to tell her about Guy ordering the car, as an explanation as to why a Mustang would be showing up. Celia, unflappable, had not sounded the least bit surprised, and had said she would tell Nicole herself. 'Best in person, rather than on the phone,' she'd advised. Meanwhile, I called Bertrand. The florist was also expecting to work his magic on an elegant Roller. Being expected to decorate a car painted with flames would just about tip him over the edge.

As I looked out towards the wonderful entrance of the hotel with its long driveway lined with olive trees, I realised that there was nowhere the car could stop at a place where the guests wouldn't see it. There was nowhere it could park and be hidden.

I called Celia again, checking my watch. The car, by all accounts, should have arrived ten minutes ago and the ceremony was running almost an hour late.

'Yes,' Celia answered in a curt tone. 'Yes, the car's

just left,' she confirmed. 'Nicole was not too happy, we had a . . . well, a moment. And let's just say I think she's had quite an afternoon getting ready with the girls.'

I wasn't quite sure what Celia meant. 'But anyway, she seems more composed now.'

I breathed a sigh of relief.

'Bertrand, however,' she added, 'is not!' We both laughed knowingly. 'I'm on my way now,' Celia added, before hanging up.

Celia arrived just before the wedding car and joined me in waiting for the bride. Beside us, the photographer stood waiting, poised to capture the moment of her arrival. I warned him about the car.

'Look, there's been a problem with the car; the bride's coming in another, one she might not like,' I told him, 'so it might be best not to get all of the shots with it in view.'

Before he could answer, the Mustang swooped down the driveway, the flames clearly visible as it passed the wizened olive trees.

'Ah, I see what you mean,' the photographer chuckled. Poor Nicole. The guests, having waited so long for the bride, started to filter out of the tiny chapel on to the grass, to see her arrival. I tried desperately to marshal them back inside.

'Please, if everyone could take their seats,' I bellowed as best I could above the kerfuffle as unkind nudges and sniggering erupted amongst the gathering crowd at the sight of the car. 'Please be seated ready for the entrance of the bride,' I repeated.

I turned now to see if Celia had greeted Nicole. I could see a foot, in an elegant white satin shoe, peep from the door of the car. The door, I noticed, had a slight dent in it. 'Not exactly a "mint vintage",' I muttered to myself in further dismay as the foot met the grass. The chauffeur emerged first, to hold the door open for the bride. He looked strangely out of place in full uniform by the side of the American car. With the door open, I could see Bertrand had kept his promise and filled the back shelf with simple white flowers, but he'd obviously thought better of tying bows on the wide, slightly battered bonnet.

Guy, obviously worried for his girl, had, somewhat untraditionally, come to the entrance of the chapel. I waved him back inside, but he held his ground, so I let him win the stand-off and nodded for the music to start. The guests piped down. All was quiet now, just the sound of *El Divo*, Nicole's mum's choice of CD, as the bride emerged from the car.

I did a double take. What had happened to the sweet, natural girl I'd met just a month before? Nicole was the first bride I'd seen in a mini-dress. It was white, short *and* low. Her over-tanned cleavage was bulging beyond the tightly fitting corset, there was more than an ample amount of curvy leg on show beneath a wisp of net, the top of one thigh sporting a red lacy garter. And on closer inspection, as she started to walk towards the aisle, I now noticed that she had also dyed her long flowing hair white to match the dress. Over the classical boy band I heard the click of a camera next to me as the photographer started to shoot. I turned to see a glimpse of Bulldog from the corner of my eye. He was kissing his crucifix, wiping his eyes dry with a tissue. Maybe he was religious after all.

Then, without warning, on seeing Guy, Nicole, whom I could only guess by Celia's comment had indulged in a bit too much pre-ceremony champagne, shrieked at the top of her voice in a pure Essex accent: 'Bet you didn't fink I was coming, eh, Mister? Sending me that bloody rotten car! Who d'ya fink I am?'

175

I froze in shock. The priest looked horrified. The guests were silent. I could see Celia, just out of their sight, laughing almost uncontrollably. I caught her eye and we giggled together.

So it had been a day of disasters, but they'd been ones out of my control and I'd gone a long way to fix them, I reflected, surprising myself. And noting Celia's face, as her laugh faded to become a warm smile, perhaps she thought so too.

Sóller and Bust

Celia recounted the tale of the disastrous Mustang wedding car, the shattered hotel glass and the shrieking bride to an amused Tomas the next morning at breakfast. It was the first time I'd seen her come close to gossiping about a wedding, the first time she'd spoken about a bride in any context other than business, and she seemed to be relishing it. Her steely eyes twinkled as she paused to politely chew her herb omelette and pat the corners of her mouth with a linen napkin, her gaze drifting out to the mountains beyond the cool, shady terrace.

Pepillo sat patiently by Tomas's side, hoping for a falling toast crust as Tomas allowed himself to laugh, his shoulders rising with each chuckle. I felt my cheeks burn.

'Your mother called last night,' Tomas told me, changing the subject, as we washed down our final mouthfuls of toast with tea.

'Oh?' I managed. I'd asked her only to call me if she really needed to.

'She just called to see how you were, I think,' he added politely, placing his knife down on his plate. 'I said you'd call her back.'

'Right, thanks.' I smiled, before getting up to clear the dishes.

'Now,' Mum had started when I called later that morning, 'you didn't tell me there was a young man living in the house with you and the wedding planner,' she quipped eagerly with an enquiring tone. 'I've not told your father, obviously,' she added, as I imagined the gossip flying around her knitting circle.

'Really, Mum,' I whispered, making sure no one could hear me from Celia's vast, echoy hallway.

'He's Celia's son and he's visiting, that's all,' I assured her, trying not to rise to it.

'Well, I must say, he sounded very nice, dear. Lovely manners, well spoken—'

I let out a small groan. I ran my finger across the heavy mahogany telephone table. 'Is everything all right at home, Mum?' I asked, trying to change the subject.

'Yes, of course, same as usual. Your father's fine.'

'Oh good. I was worried something might be wrong,' I admitted, relieved.

'Oh no, dear, not at all,' she insisted, before probably putting her hand over the receiver. 'Pick up a lottery ticket on your way to the post office, dear,' she whispered urgently to poor old Dad.

'Hmmmm?' Mum asked, coming back to the conversation as I heard the front door slamming behind him.

'You were telling me how things are there,' I reminded her.

'Oh yes, absolutely fine, dear. Although Mrs Bartholomew from number twenty-six has had a bit of a fall.'

'Mrs who?'

'Oh, you know, the old lady down the road; the one your father never liked. But I did pay her a visit, to be neighbourly whilst she's laid up.'

'Look, Mum, it's lovely to hear from you, but I really should go, what with this being Celia's phone and a long distance call . . .' I explained.

'Yes, quite right too,' she agreed before adding, 'your father can't imagine what the food's like there, Isabelle. What are you eating?'

'Mum, the food's great, really. Tell Dad I think I've even gained a few pounds. That will make him happy.' I looked down at my waistline; it was probably true.

'So when are you coming back home? Your father and I *have* been wondering.'

Finally, she'd let slip the real reason why she'd called the previous day. She always mentioned Dad when it was obviously her who was wondering.

'Not really sure yet,' I answered honestly, 'but I'm having a good time, working hard, everything's fine. Look, I promise to call you again as soon as I have a better idea of what I'm up to.' I felt guilty now for not having called sooner.

'Yes, do. And, as I said, the boy sounded very pleasant,' she said.

She couldn't resist it. She was infuriating. But I had to admit to myself, that it was good to hear her voice.

'OK,' I giggled, 'but really, he's not my type. Speak to you soon and love to Dad.'

'Yes, Isabelle, and remember, don't gorge yourself on that greasy Spanish food or you won't be anyone's type either.'

There was never a case of winning with my mother.

'Take care of yourself now.'

That afternoon was long and lazy, the kind that siestas were invented for. I took a good book and holed myself up in my room, lying on top of the cool cotton sheets on my bed, shutters closed tightly against the heat and glare of the sun. When my eyes felt heavy from reading, I let the book fall to my chest and drifted off to the sound of cicadas across the valley, a constant reminder that the true heat of the summer had arrived. It felt luxurious not to stir till early evening when I wandered down to the kitchen in search of a long cool glass of water, my throat dry and my head still fuzzy from sleep.

Tomas ambled downstairs in pretty much the same state, fully clothed, save for his shoes and glasses. He rubbed his eyes and ran a hand through his now messy hair, nodding me a hello as his face contorted momentarily with a yawn. I picked up a bottle of water and angled it towards him, he managed a smile, so I poured the contents into a glass jug and filled it with ice, slices of lemon and fresh mint leaves, a delicious trick that Celia had taught me. We both grabbed a glass as we wandered out into the garden.

'God, siestas are good,' he yawned again. 'I think I'm destined to become an English eccentric, taking a few hours each afternoon in the dark English winters.' His voice was low and his eyes were still screwed up and struggling to open against the bright sunlight.

'You're right!' I laughed. 'But it would be such a waste to take one every day.' I took a sip of water.

'But you just do more at the end of the day,' he answered seriously, as if I was nuts. 'Take tonight, for example . . .' he continued, one hand shielding his eyes. 'Fiesta night in S'Arraco. OK, so it starts early for the children, but it will go on till the early hours. If you don't have a siesta you miss all the fun!'

'I didn't really have you pegged as a party animal,' I smiled, 'but I know what you're saying.'

'Is that a challenge, Izzy?' he asked, trying not to sound wounded.

'A challenge?' I queried.

'Yes. To see if I'm a party ... what did you say, "animal"?' I'd never heard him sound so public school. I couldn't help but laugh.

'Oh, I see,' I replied, suddenly understanding. 'So you want to go to the fiesta?'

'Well yes, why not?' said Tomas, grinning.

Later that evening, we approached the small neighbouring village of S'Arraco as the sun began to fade. It was a pretty place, with a main road of elegant stone houses with elaborately decorated façades and narrow pavements brimming, this evening, with excited children. Some wore smiles under faces brightly painted as butterflies, lions and clowns, others grasped the hands of Mum, Dad or older siblings, a little wary of what to expect as the sound of music started up and a small procession of mime artists on stilts kicked off the evening's entertainment.

The kids looked mesmerised as a man in a top hat and stripy tights sang and told jokes, honked the nose of his fall guy counterpart, and announced that his female companion would somersault, back flip and ride her unicycle as the procession clowned their way towards the square. When they reached the top of the road, there was a human surge, as children and families in the know rushed to stand beneath the church tower.

I looked questioningly towards Tomas, then back to the scene. Two señoras appeared at the highest stone window to throw sweets to the crowds below. The kids didn't flinch as they were pelted with bright-coloured *caramelos*. Instead, they giggled and bobbed to sweep their hands across the ground, scooping up the tiny treasures they hadn't yet caught. I moved forward to join in the fun, passing a flying sweet to a little girl behind me, perched on her daddy's shoulders, before raising my arms up with the crowd as the señoras shouted for us to be ready, in the hope of catching more. When I paused to look behind me, I couldn't help but smile; Tomas, in his very British way, was standing happily observing the scene from the sidelines, towering above the only other people not joining in the fun – a group of silver-haired grannies. I went back to grab him by the arm.

'Come on!' I pleaded with him, as I saw what was happening next. In the middle of the square, a gigantic white machine was being filled with bumper-sized packs of popcorn. Behind it, two huge speakers started to play Spanish Euro pop at full volume. As the kids moved in front of them to dance, I pulled Tomas towards the stage by the material of his shirt. I'd attended too many weddings this season to still harbour a British reticence to join the dance floor without a drink. Tomas yelled above the beats, I could just make out the words: 'You are crazy!'

'Let's dance!' I shouted, above the noise, finally wrenching a reluctant Tomas to the dance floor to the hilarity of the older girls and boys. He looked totally dumbfounded and embarrassed, but eventually shuffled from side to side and, when I looked next, he had taken a little girl's hands in his, to twirl her round. A few moments later a rotund man with a black moustache climbed up to the giant machine to launch it, and a powerful spray of popcorn was unleashed into the crowd. Dads now ran to the dance floor, untucking their T-shirts from their jeans to catch the popcorn in the fabric to give to their kids. Tomas did the same to his dancing girl's delight. She squealed as her mum moved over to us, and flashing us a large smile she pushed handfuls of flying kernals into her mouth and pulled it out of her hair simultaneously. The music seemed to get faster. The kids sang along to the songs and their hips swayed to the Latino pop beats as the corn kept on coming. We tried our best to keep up and Tomas, now laughing, kept catching my eye. Finally, defeated, we dragged ourselves off to the sidelines, bent double with laughter. I'd never seen him so relaxed or having so much fun.

'Let's get a beer,' I managed as my cheeks ached with laughter and my legs felt like jelly. We scurried off to a bar at the side of the square with its doors flung invitingly open, its chairs outside already taken, and the pavement awash with people.

We sipped on the cold amber liquid from lukewarm plastic glasses, transfixed at the scene in front of us. The dancing had now taken on a different pace, the music was traditional and families gathered in large circles, performing folk dances in perfectly choreographed time. Arms were elegantly curved above heads, feet skipped and tapped beneath them.

'You learn these dances at school,' Tomas explained.

'Go on, show me,' I pleaded, but he just laughed, wiping his brow with a handkerchief.

The sun had almost disappeared but its heat still resonated. With the music still too loud for us to talk, we stood together for the first time in comfortable silence, watching the fiesta unfold before us. Behind the music equipment, a race track with small go karts had been set up for boys and girls, who, with large helmets strapped tightly on their tiny heads, weaved their way through an assault course of tyres. A climbing wall was another feature off the square to the left where the smallest children seemed able to haul themselves up with the agility and speed of Spider-Man. To the right, stalls selling barbecued *butifarron* and *sobrassada*, the local sausages, were doing a roaring trade with the less energetic.

'So what happens later, "party animal"?' I finally teased Tomas, who clearly had given up on dancing.

'Lots more eating, drinking and merriment,' he replied with a matter-of-fact tone and a smile. 'This is Spain, what else is there?'

It might have been the heady atmosphere of the fiesta or a cup too many of beer, but later that night Tomas asked me if I wanted to go with him to the mountain town of Sóller the next afternoon and I agreed. He'd said that for his research he had to visit the botanical gardens there and suggested that we might go for supper afterwards. It wasn't until I got to my room after we'd got back, shut the door tightly and started to undress, that I realised this would be a proper date. A date with Tomas.

'A date . . . a date!' The phrase ran through my mind again and again as I peered helplessly into my wardrobe. It was a word that felt so alien. I hadn't been 'on a date' for what felt like months, years! 'Gardens, then dinner . . . gardens and then dinner,' I pondered out loud to clothes piled high around the stuffed rails. Jesus! How was it possible to dress properly for both? The first suggested a romantic tea dress, fresh, natural make-up and sweet, strappy sandals, the latter something sexy and alluring that wouldn't show the consequences of a nervous slip of a fork with a stray strand of spaghetti. I was definitely out of practice when it came to 'date' dressing, let alone combining two disparate activities.

'We may as well have planned to go rock climbing before clubbing,' I snapped out loud to myself, frustrated. But that wasn't all that was concerning me.

The final part of my nervousness was that this was Tomas. Cerebral Tomas, classic Tomas; the man more concerned with plants than fashion, a breed of man I wasn't used to. I wanted to make an effort, but I also knew how he felt about his mother's former fashionable life. This would take time and a lot of thought.

Maybe it was more appropriate to dress down, I pondered, perching on the edge of my bed to eye the wardrobe from a different perspective. Maybe I was just thinking about all of this too much, I resolved, moments later, picking myself up again. Back in front of the wardrobe I prised the tightly packed hangers apart in turn, dismissing one by one my trusty old favourites as 'too twee', 'too retro', 'too worn', 'trying too hard'.

Then it came to me. Hallelujah, I still had it. I'd brought it with me. My emergency, multipurpose, all-occasions dress. The super-flattering-super-slimming-super-expensive dress. Tomato red with a floral print and a plunging neckline, perfect. I imagined my hair up and red lippy to match and let a smile travel across my face.

I started with a spritz of girly, floral Chloé scent and some pretty undies. I pulled down the dress from its hanger, letting the cool silk fabric slip through my fingers. I threw it over my head, searching blindly and inelegantly for the arm holes. I'd done well to put it on before doing my hair, I thought, still flailing as it suddenly got stuck around my midriff. I gave it a yank, but it wouldn't budge. So I gave another. It succumbed without a rip and felt tighter than I'd remembered as I willed it down over my frame, but the cool silk still felt good. No one likes to have to wrestle to fit into a frock, but at least I could still get into it, I thought, pushing an earring into place. Now I just had time to fix my face and tie up my hair.

'Right, heels!' I decided, having created a scruffy 'up do' that would look like I hadn't bothered. Yes, heels. That's what I needed. Not too high, but just high enough to give my walk a wiggle and my legs a bit of length. I grabbed a pair of studded Marni sandals with a two-inch wedge and deliberately mismatched a handbag for the evening. I slung in a few essentials. I was ready to go, but paused at the door momentarily to practise holding a smile across my nervous features before venturing downstairs to the kitchen, where I knew Tomas would be waiting. It would have been so much more romantic if we had arranged to meet somewhere else.

Tomas was sipping a beer and chatting with Celia. He was wearing a fresh shirt and khaki pants, one hand fiddling with a bunch of keys.

'Ready?' I chirped merrily as Celia eyed me with a strange distaste. Maybe Tomas had told her this was a date. Maybe I had interrupted an important conversation.

'Yes, ready,' Tomas agreed. We eyed each other nervously as we headed off.

The journey to the north of the island was long and awkward. It seemed that although we'd spent the last weeks chatting endlessly at home, now that we were on a date, something had changed. As the road through the mountain tunnels stretched on to the motorway, I let the familiar scenery whiz by and concentrated on trying to find something interesting to say to break the silence. I asked Tomas what he expected to find at the gardens, but he met my question with an academic answer that I didn't know how to respond to and fell quiet again. I nodded and smiled, pulling down the mirror in the visor above me to check my face. But my face, it transpired, wasn't the problem.

As Tomas focused on the road, I'd angled the visor

discreetly downwards. The mirror had revealed that my cleavage was oozing over the top of my underwear and appeared to be fighting its way out of my dress. I wouldn't have been too alarmed if I'd mastered the kind of neat, heaving bosom a dress department creates with a sturdy corset for a Merchant Ivory film, but I hadn't. I'd managed something far less attractive. My bra was instantly visible, its pattern jarring in the plunge of the neckline, and at the same time it seemed to have created almost four breasts out of two, cutting across them like a cheese wire. I let out a stifled gasp. How had I not noticed? Probably the deadly combination of rushing and the absence of a full-length mirror, I realised. The dress, I now saw, was not just a bit tighter than it had been, but much tighter. The fabric, once loose and body-skimming, was now clinging hungrily to every curve. I snapped the visor up, blushing, and tried to compose myself. There was nothing I could do. I made an effort to block out visions of lumpy thighs and splitting seams, Tomas was far too gentlemanly to comment and maybe if he focused on the plants, he wouldn't notice.

'I love this part of the island,' said Tomas, finally breaking my thoughts on the offending bra as we pulled off the motorway. 'It's a different Majorca beyond the mountains,' he continued.

The long straight road ahead of us stretched as far as I could see and disappeared in a dusty heat haze. Fields of almond trees lined both sides and the occasional palm tree shimmered, its leaves high enough to catch the only breaths of wind.

'I loved it when I came here with Celia,' I replied dreamily, still peering out of the window. 'The first wedding we worked on together was in Deià, but I didn't get to see much of the countryside.'

'I'm almost glad,' he said seriously. 'I can show you it

all first, then.' He flashed me a smile. It was the first flirtation.

I smiled back, realising I was all butterflies. I wasn't sure if I still felt flushed from my horrid 'bra' realisation or if the sun beating on Tomas's car, a car without air-conditioning, wasn't helping . . .

'Are you quite all right?' he asked concerned.

'Yes, of course, thanks,' I answered, realising how flustered I must have looked.

'That turning goes to Orient.' Tomas pointed, his eyes wandering. 'Beautiful.' He said the word slowly, with emphasis.

Tomas continued to point out the landmarks and tell anecdotes about the places we passed. I found myself feeling calmer as we approached the mountains and the tunnel that had been carved through the rock. We paid the toll and drove into the darkness.

'It's amazing they can do this!' I proclaimed with childlike wonder, looking up at the vaulted ceiling above us and reading the neon signs, flashing their warnings in Majorcan. The temperature dropped as we ventured further into the tunnel and I welcomed the coolness and the relief from the glare of the sun on my eyes.

'When I was a child I used to try and hold my breath as we drove through tunnels,' Tomas chuckled, 'but obviously this one is only a few years old, which is just as well as it would turn anyone blue to attempt it!'

I let out an ungainly laugh; it was a laugh that sounded like relief.

Tomas looked at me a bit surprised, then laughed himself. A more relaxed, giggling kind of laugh rather than his usual deep tones. Finally, it felt like we'd broken down our very British self-consciousness. Now we could get on with the date.

As we reached the other side of the tunnel a new

vista opened up in front of us, the clear blue sky emerging like the first few moments of a movie rolling in full Technicolor from the darkness of an auditorium.

'So, Izzy, old girl, this is Sóller,' Tomas announced as I squinted to see against the bright sunlight.

Mountains reached high above us on all sides, stone houses teetered on their terraces amidst the lush green pines and fruit trees. As we descended to the bowl-shaped valley that contained the town, the winding road sent Tomas's small car swaying with every turn, giving me a giddy, fairground-ride feeling.

As the road finally fell straight I looked right, at Tomas's instruction, and could see Sóller's traditional stone buildings and the vast Gothic church, rising up in the middle. I looked forward to exploring later but for now, we had to visit the gardens and I was surprised when Tomas swiftly pulled over, almost immediately in front of a simple stone building.

'Are we here?' I asked, not able to see any sign of any gardens. The stone building appeared to be a house.

'Yes, this is it!' replied Tomas cheerfully as he switched off the engine.

I opened the car door and rushed out to join Tomas, who, obviously keen, was already pacing purposefully ahead. As I reached his side he slowed down to match my pace and we strolled beneath a shaded canopy towards the house. A lady at a small ticket office waved us in with a smile.

Stretching out beyond the house were a series of small but beautiful terraced gardens, each packed with plants and flowers, a narrow stone pathway, and a series of dry-stone walls winding between them.

We paused to take it all in and I snuck a look at Tomas. He was smiling.

'Each terrace contains a different ecological group of

plants, each one simulating their natural habitat,' he explained.

'I can't believe it's so green or that anything grows in this heat,' I replied, feeling the intensity of the afternoon sun.

'On the contrary,' Tomas started, 'this Balearic flora and fauna has adapted itself to survive dry conditions very well, requiring very little water and using the least energy possible over the hottest months. Some even send out a toxic substance to ward off herbivores!'

'Really?' I asked, genuinely interested, although he sounded a bit 'text book'. 'That *is* clever.'

Tomas smiled again and we strolled on.

As we wandered between the terraces, Tomas took great pride in explaining a little about each garden, from the mountain flora to the plants from the river beds. He told me interesting facts about some of the Balearic species, their origins and why some are vulnerable. I listened and, to my surprise, I became transfixed. The final garden was my favourite, with a pretty running stream or *torrente*, which looked and sounded wonderful in the heat of the afternoon. We laughed enviably as a tiny bird swooped to take an early evening dip in the cool water.

Tomas crouched to show me a rare and pretty species of flowering shrub that originated from China. I found myself kneeling beside him, wobbling on my ridiculous wedges as he carefully brushed over the leaves of a plant with his thumb to explain its make-up. I was listening with my head on one side as Latin names rolled off his tongue while he pointed out the smaller samples all planted in neat rows, each group meticulously marked with a small white stick and a name. It was then I realised that of course it wasn't the subject matter I was finding engaging, it was Tomas. The simple language he used to help me understand, his obvious passion for plants. It was all very intimate. For the first time, I was finding Tomas quite sexy, noting the gentle way he caressed the plants carefully, never once damaging the tiniest leaf, fern or herb with his now dusty brown hands. How he peered over the top of his glasses as he spoke to me, his eyes intently studying the flowers and then me. The gentleness of his low, soothing voice. The smoothness of his sun-kissed skin . . . Tomas stood up to continue our tour, suddenly interrupting my thoughts.

The gardens felt like ours that day, so quiet, with just a bright blue sky above us and no one else around. There was a greenhouse filled with seedlings, an immaculate museum and a wonderful wooden-clad library still to explore, but Tomas lost me when he started to talk about palaeontology and other scientific research. And I remembered that he was there for a purpose.

'I'm going to go for a wander for a while,' I announced suddenly. Tomas looked hurt.

'You have to do your research, remember?' I reminded him.

'Yes, yes, of course,' he said blushing and looking at his watch, 'and I've been going on for far too long, I expect.'

I left Tomas to it, and saw him pull out a notebook and his reading glasses as he wandered back inside to the collections and the library, before I turned to descend the stone steps.

If I was being truthful to myself, I had two things in mind on suggesting Tomas studied there and then. Firstly, I wanted to fix the silly bra and damned dress once and for all. I had seen the dress in all its full-length glory in the highly polished glass of the doors leading to the cabinets when I should have been peering at fossils.

I looked ridiculous, the dress as tightly stretched and inelegant as I had feared. Secondly, I'd decided that it would be quite romantic for Tomas to come and find me and I wondered how long it would take him. So whilst Tomas licked the tip of his pencil, jotted notes and read about the plant life of ancient Majorca in Catalan dialect, I went in search of a quiet bush behind which I could do a bit of my own 'flower arranging'.

My inclination was to walk as far as I possibly could away from Tomas (despite my calves aching, in objection to traversing uneven stone pathways, in inappropriate heels) and then to weave my way to a secluded, shady spot. Finally, with no one around, I felt pretty safe taking shelter under a large magnolia tree, with a row of box hedging in front for extra cover.

I stopped, turned my back to the house and wriggled the clasp fastening on my bra with both hands. I looked down towards the ground and let out a sigh of relief as I unhooked the material. Next, I slid the dress from one shoulder, then the other, to quickly take off the offending item from underneath. It was a two-movement motion and I managed it in super speed, checking over my shoulders as I pulled the dress back up and rearranged my chest. Now, the moment of truth. I looked down. Much better. No nasty cheese-wire bra in mismatching fabric and the line of the dress looked and felt smoother. Now all I had to do was to make sure I'd stay in it and get the bra into my handbag. Ah! Handbag. I didn't have it any more. I looked around my feet. Nope. I peered my head around the tree but I couldn't see it anywhere.

'OK, Izzy,' I told myself, 'better fix the dress fast and then go back for it.' I stamped a foot at myself in annoyance. I looked down at my chest again. Would I really be OK without a bra? Or would I shock Tomas? I pondered momentarily. Then, on seeing the magnolia tree in front of me, I had a cute idea. I'd place a flower just where my cleavage was most visible and fix it with a hairpin. Genius!

I was feeling quite pleased with myself as I plucked a perfect, milky white flower from the tree to fasten it with a long, pointed pin from my bird's nest hair do. To do a good job, I slipped the top of the dress off my shoulders once more, to fasten it from the inside. But then I realised someone was watching.

'What *are* you doing?' I heard a man's voice ask in a stern tone.

I turned to face the voice and saw Tomas standing directly in front of me with a well-dressed, elderly man. Both stared at me, outraged. I was still clutching the bra in one hand and holding the loose fabric of the dress closely against my breasts in the other to conceal them, my shoulders bare.

'I was just going to find my—'

'Handbag,' he finished the sentence for me, holding it up in the air like a prize.

'Err, yes!' I agreed with an apologetic smile, desperately trying not to look half naked.

The man Tomas was with was obviously Spanish. He dropped his eyes to the floor respectfully, but he didn't leave Tomas's side.

Maybe I had got this all wrong, I thought during an awkward silence that seemed to last a lifetime. OK, so he probably wasn't used to being on a date with a girl who takes her bra off in a public place, but there wasn't any need to shout and be all prudish about it . . .

Tomas handed me the bag and I grabbed at it with one hand, clutching the fabric even tighter to cover my chest with the other. But I moved too fast and forgot that I was still clutching the bra and it fell to the ground.

Flustered, I bent down to pick it up but when I stood up again, the shocked expressions on Tomas's and the stranger's faces made me jump. I didn't need to look. I knew instinctively that I'd let go of the dress. It had slid to my waist, where it stuck, as it had earlier that day, refusing to budge. I felt a warm breeze against my bare nipples and let out a horrified scream. Running further along the path and into the bushes I heard Tomas's companion proclaim '*Madre de Dios!*'

Behind the bush, I wrenched up the dress. 'Bugger ... bugger ... bugger ... bugger ... bugger ... bugger,' I muttered loudly under my breath. My mind whirred back to the incident with the priest in Deià when I'd first arrived. How many men would I expose myself to on this island?

'Izzy?' I could hear Tomas calling. 'Izzy?'

I didn't answer. I was mortified. I could have stayed hidden behind the box hedging all night. Or, at the very least, until Tomas had left. But I didn't have a choice. He found me, and this time he was alone.

'Where did I leave it?' I asked him, my cheeks aflame as I tried to fix the subject on the bag. But he just chuckled.

'Tomas, I'm sorry,' I started apologetically, feeling ridiculous. 'I know what this might look like, but I was just ... erm ... erm ... just got a bit hot and uncomfortable and wanted to adjust my frock.'

I finished fixing the flower in place, busying my hands as I waited for his reply.

When I looked up, Tomas was moving towards me, reaching out his arms. But then, as quickly as I had looked up he stopped and his face changed. 'But why,' he said, 'why would you do that?' he asked, pointing. 'Why would you pick a flower here?'

'Pick a flower?' It was then that I saw them. The

wooden signs every few metres stating 'Please do not pick the plants' in three different languages.

'Oooohhh!' I realised out loud, my cheeks flushing a deeper crimson. I was speechless. Flower picking to Tomas was obviously a definite no-no. I shrugged my shoulders and averted my gaze, unable to look at him. 'God, sorry,' I mumbled sincerely. 'What do I do now?'

Tomas burst out laughing. 'Nothing,' he said. 'Nothing.' He didn't sound angry any more. 'It looks lovely and you've made an afternoon of botany a bit racier than I could ever have imagined.' Tomas, still chuckling, took my hand in his and we walked back through the gardens.

'Do you think anyone will notice?' I asked concerned as we approached the house.

'Don't worry about a thing,' Tomas replied, as we both spotted the Spanish man who dropped his eyes again as we passed.

'Who's he?' I asked Tomas.

'The patron of the gardens,' he replied nonchalantly. 'Ready for supper?'

Run, Run, Run

As the heat of the sun began to fade, Tomas and I took a leisurely walk through the town of Sóller. We made our way through the narrow backstreets lined with handsome stone town houses and Tomas, being a gent, never once mentioned the incident in the gardens. We chatted instead about the houses. With many of their grand teak doors thrown open to invite in the cool evening air, we couldn't help but peer into the vast entrance halls. Immaculate and traditional, they appeared to have remained unchanged for hundreds of years. Some of the houses stood proud and grand with Juliette balconies, pillars and decorative façades. From the hallways of others it was possible to see through to gardens filled with orange trees, vines and pots of brightly coloured flowers as old ladies in pinafores came out to leave the house at the cooler end of a long hot day.

'Watch your back,' Tomas would warn me every now and then, when I became distracted by a heavy wooden antique chair, a glass lantern or a floor covered in Moorish tiles, before gently coaxing me on to the smooth cobbled pavement in front of him to avoid a car careering round a corner.

'This way,' he'd direct me next, disappearing down another street and eventually off the road through a smoothly cobbled walkway. The street, quiet and peaceful, save for the gentle trill of birdsong, was lined with rows of terracotta pots filled with plants. Tomas took my hand and we turned on to a busier road now, a tram track cutting silver grooves into the dry, dusty tarmac.

'That's the market.' Tomas pointed to a large cream building that was closed up for the day. It looked stark and perfunctory, without any decoration. 'But this, I think, should be our first stop.' He signalled across the street. 'What do you think, Izzy?'

'Great idea. I love ice cream,' I answered with childlike glee, following his finger to an impressive *gelat* parlour, with coloured tables and chairs on the pavement outside. I sped up to peer inside.

'Sooo many flavours.' I beamed excitedly back at Tomas.

'And all made here in Sóller, too,' he added. 'I can highly recommend the almond.'

After some deliberation and indecision I settled on lemon, then mango, then finally praline and demanded a lick of Tomas's as we continued our stroll towards the square. We chose a shady stone seat beside a fountain, and looked up at the impressive Gaudi-esque church and stately town hall at the plaza's core. We watched the children playing, the people drinking and chatting merrily at cafés and the little mahogany and brass tram as it rattled straight through the bustle of it all.

'Hungry, Izzy?' Tomas asked gently, breaking the comfortable silence between us.

I hadn't given it a thought, but as I glanced up at the town hall's clock and saw that it was almost nine, my stomach seemed to grumble loudly on cue.

'Yes, I think I must be,' I laughed.

'I've booked a table over there,' Tomas continued, pointing to the far corner of the square where a small restaurant sign hung above a white entrance, next to a tiny grocery shop.

'Looks perfect.' I smiled. I suddenly felt self-conscious again, remembering that we were on a date. This was the part where I was expected to make scintillating conversation, make him laugh, be attractive, be alluring. The thought of it all only made me nervous.

'What kind of food is it?' I asked as we wandered in the direction of the restaurant, avoiding a little old man with a stick and a horde of tourists.

'Traditional Majorcan,' Tomas replied. 'It's very good.'

'Fantastic,' I enthused, looking forward to sitting down amongst the tables balanced precariously on the pavement outside.

'It specialises in local delicacies such as rabbit and snails,' Tomas continued.

'Yeah, right!' I jibed, laughing. He was joking, surely? But he didn't answer.

As we approached the doorway and Tomas spoke to the waiter in Majorcan, I saw the restaurant's little rabbit logo entwined with its name in the sign and realised that he was serious. I gulped. I almost dreaded being handed the menu.

'Thought we'd sit inside,' Tomas explained, as a distinguished tall, white-haired man pointed to our table and pulled a chair out for me in an old-fashioned gesture. 'It will be more comfortable.'

I looked around. The restaurant had a terracotta-tiled floor, bright white walls and lots of charm. There were wrought-iron candelabras, chandeliers laden with candles, and alcoves stuffed with coloured-glass jars, table lamps and paintings. The tables were dressed simply with white paper cloths on top of checked linen and comfortably spaced throughout the ground floor. It felt a few welcome degrees cooler inside and it was also calmer, being away from the crowds. I looked around at the other diners in the half-full restaurant. There were two young families, a couple and one large family spanning several generations, all chatting happily in Spanish, and I gazed up to see a mezzanine level where another group were balanced above us.

'It's still a tad early for dinner,' Tomas remarked, looking around slightly nervously at the many empty places.

'I just can't get used to this ten o'clock dinner time thing here,' I agreed, leaning in closer to him to whisper, 'even though it's hot, I can never wait until then! But there are some people eating already,' I quickly added, not wanting Tomas to feel that he'd brought me somewhere lacking in atmosphere.

He nodded in agreement as the waiter returned and peered over his round horn-rimmed glasses till he found a pause in our conversation to politely hand us the menus. Each was an A4 tome of loose sheets in several languages, laminated in plastic and bound in dark brown leatherette. I decided to battle along with the choices in Spanish, to impress, and began to study the first page.

'The Spanish is on page two,' Tomas informed me a few minutes later as I squinted to make out the strange words. My face must have given me away. 'The first page is in Majorcan,' he added.

'Thanks.' I smirked, relieved. I hadn't understood a single word.

Tomas, I discovered, had been right about the meaty

local delicacies, but even I had to admit that when a tray of sizzling *caracoles* wafted past on the arm of a waitress, the toasted aroma of the coriander and cumin did smell good. Not that I'd ever dream of ordering snails. I followed my finger down the menu for something simple and safe. Something that even I couldn't turn into a disaster.

'Would you like a drink, Izzy?' Tomas said, interrupting my pondering. The white-haired man had silently returned and looked at me impatiently for an answer as people gathered at the doorway to be seated. I let Tomas order some wine and dived for the local cracked green olives and bread in an earthenware dish when they were brought to the table with the bottle. To my delight, the *pan moreno* was lightly toasted and the top two slices were smothered in tomato and drizzled generously with olive oil. It was delicious.

After a glass of smooth, chilled white Rioja I finally started to relax. I stopped looking down to check that the magnolia flower was still doing its job, and I stopped fiddling with the table decoration and the droplets of condensation on my glass as I spoke. At some point, after a hasty second glass to quash my nerves further, I also stopped being concerned about being a witty, informed date and, feeling the heady effects of the wine, decided just to be myself. And it felt good. As the restaurant began to fill, some eager diners waited keenly at the bar for a table to become free, whilst the beaming faces of locals and foreign visitors were warmly greeted as they made an entrance. Even the white-haired waiter softened a little as we congratulated him on his wine and tomato bread; a trick Tomas assured me would gain us seconds. And it did.

Tomas seemed to let down his guard and move on from polite conversation as we shared a platter of *croquettas*. I unashamedly devoured all of the spinach ones, discovering they were the tastiest starter I'd eaten in Majorca yet and Tomas didn't seem to mind a bit. Tomas teased me about the 'garden incident' and we joked about the fact that we were on a date and both living with Celia. For the first time, we really laughed. But Tomas was also serious and generous, asking me all sorts of questions. Unlike Harrisson, he spoke less about himself and seemed genuinely interested in my life and I found the attention flattering. He wanted to know about my family, my friends in London and what I thought of life in Majorca. I couldn't remember a time when I'd spoken so much about myself, I realised as I battled to eat the fish of the day – a locally caught sea bass far too big for my plate and one which seemed to want to escape whenever I paused to speak. In turn, I was keen to find out more about Tomas, but despite my questions and his more relaxed demeanour, he still seemed elusive. He talked about his love of botany, fishing and good wine, and how all of his friends at university were stuffy and square. He loved to come back to Majorca and mix with people who were interested in what he called 'the important things in life' – by which, I discovered, he meant family, food, friends and taking your time to enjoy life.

I tried not to stare at Tomas as the evening grew dark and his face became lit by candlelight, and I tried to ignore the fact that he had opted for the *gazapo*. I hid my disappointment on realising it was rabbit, rather than chilled tomato soup (*gazpacho*) when it was proudly presented to him at the table. In short, I still had a long way to go with deciphering the subtleties of language and dating, 'Majorcan style', but I was having fun doing so.

Dinner seemed to race by. It wasn't until I attempted to excuse myself from the table, dropping a linen napkin on the floor, that I realised I was, yet again, a little giddy from the Rioja. But I also realised that I was happy. I negotiated a visit to the ladies room in a state of calm, despite the fact that it was located outside, up a flight of steep stairs, and consisted of a seating arrangement built into a wooden bench. But it didn't matter. I felt happy and I felt content. Or did I? I started to question, as I washed my hands and looked up at my reflection in the mirror. I looked at the face I'd seen upset so many times before, the one I'd seen let down and the one that had only recently run away from a relationship that finally just might have worked.

None of that matters, I told myself firmly as I tossed a paper towel in the bin. 'Don't ruin it before it's begun,' I chided myself and made sure that I was still smiling when I returned to the table.

Later that night, when we finally made it back home, we stumbled noisily through the back door into Celia's kitchen.

'Shhhhh,' I told Tomas noisily in giggles, concerned at the thought of waking Celia. I felt like a naughty schoolgirl and, tipsy from the wine, Tomas laughed too and pulled the finger I'd placed to my lips towards his chest, pulling me gently into him.

'It's been rather fun,' he said in a low, gentle voice as he stooped to kiss me. It was a soft, gentle kiss that lasted only a minute, but it took me by surprise. Tomas pulled away, keen, I imagined, not to overstep the mark.

I looked down at our feet, where Pepillo was growling.

'He's not sure if I'm attacking you!' Tomas confirmed as the little black dog showed his teeth. 'Maybe that's my cue to say goodnight,' he whispered, kissing me on the cheek as Pepillo let out a single, low bark.

Upstairs I placed the magnolia flower on the table in my room, undressed and lay naked, perfectly still on top of my cool cotton sheets in the darkness. I listened as Tomas climbed the stairs to bed after sharing a nightcap with Celia who was, in fact, still up. I listened as I heard him wash in the bathroom and imagined him taking off his glasses and then his shirt to get into a cold shower, as he said he would, before going to bed. And I giggled to myself at the frustration of going on a date with a man who invites you back only to stay with his mother. Who happens to be your boss.

I woke up early the next morning and pulled the sheets up around myself in the cool dawn air. I'd left my window wide open and the sound of birdsong, cockerels and sheep were an early and discordant alarm clock. I lay with my eyes closed, enjoying the fresh, dewy temperature in my tiny room and the thick cotton against my skin as I mulled over last night's date. I recounted Tomas's jokes and his face when it softened as he let down his guard. I smiled to myself, remembering how good he'd made me feel at dinner, how we'd laughed about the ridiculous 'handbag/dress/breasts/ garden incident' and how I'd spent an evening with a man very different to the one I thought I knew. I'd had a great time. I'd had fun. And this morning, maybe, I wondered, my stomach filled with butterflies, I was awake early because I just couldn't wait to see him again. Suddenly it was a feeling that threw me into panic. The reality, I reasoned with myself, was that I was setting myself up to be vulnerable again. And not just with someone on the island, but with my boss's son. And my job was the only structure that I had. I lifted up my head a little and plumped up the pillow, before sinking my head down into it again. As usual, I'd been an idiot. What was I doing?

For the next few days, I did my best to maintain a low profile in the house. I was polite and friendly to Celia, but made a deliberate effort to stay away from Tomas. I found that I just couldn't face him. I heard myself making excuses to leave a room when he entered and got out of the house on my Vespino whenever I had some spare time, heading to the beach in the evenings, or to the town square for a drink on my own. Finally after two days of my bizarre behaviour, Tomas seemed to get the message and started to do the same. He would disappear off to have lunch with Marta, walk Pepillo, or stay in his room to study and, eventually, I was relieved to discover that our paths, at least for now, ceased to cross.

The office became a welcome distraction. Celia and I had never been busier. I installed myself behind the heavy teak beast of a desk for days which faded well into the evenings as we worked on the last two weddings of the season. The first was a small, intimate event for just thirty guests that I was organising. The second, by contrast, was the largest wedding of the year, with so many elements to it that Celia delegated endless tasks to me without ever having time to fill me in on the bigger picture. I knew nothing of the couple getting married, but I continued to speak to stylists regarding their lavish table decorations, to work on the logistics of the bride and groom's arrival at the church by boat, and to keep in close contact with Marta, Tomas's friend, who was hosting the wedding reception at her family's vineyard.

I buried myself in work. Some days, I only noticed

that the day had ended when the sun disappeared behind the mountains, framed by the picture window in the office. And it was then that I would realise that I hadn't eaten or that Celia and I hadn't uttered a word that wasn't related to weddings in ten hours.

This routine lasted for almost two weeks before I realised that I was focusing on work so that I didn't have to think about the big question that was looming: what the hell was I going to do next? The truth was that I just couldn't begin to address the issue of whether I wanted to go back to London or stay in Majorca when my trial with Celia came to a close. But without a man in either port to complicate the issue, I felt that I would at least be in a position to make a level-headed decision when I couldn't put it off any longer. If only my life was that simple.

'Tomas has decided to extend his visit,' Celia announced merrily one morning in the office whilst sipping her first cup of Lapsang of the day. It was obvious that she was enjoying his stay and her face beamed as she delivered the news.

'Really?' I quizzed, genuinely surprised, almost dropping an A4 file I had been reaching down from the bookshelf. 'Wonderful.' I gulped quickly, forcing a smile as I turned to face her. 'How long for?'

'He's not really quite sure yet ... I suppose it depends on his research,' Celia contemplated, studying her beloved rose bush from the window and keeping a watchful eye on Pep the gardener, who was bent double tending a flower bed in the morning sun.

'In any case,' she continued, her eyes still animated, 'I thought we could do with some extra help with the weddings. An extra pair of hands on the day. Most useful,' she offered.

I struggled to hide my surprise and alarm as I clutched the file and walked back to my desk.

'He's a gentleman *and* dependable,' reassured Celia. 'I'm sure he'll come in very handy.'

'Of course,' I agreed. 'Great!' I managed as an afterthought when Celia turned back to her notebook, her perfectly made-up face full of concentration as she picked up the telephone to make a call. There was no avoiding Tomas if we had to work together.

That afternoon I stared at a blank computer screen, the cursor flashing continuously in a blank email. I'd made a decision not to get involved with Tomas, but I couldn't ignore the small part of me that had been secretly pleased to hear Celia's news. And then, again, I just knew that I shouldn't, couldn't act on those feelings. So what now?

Should I try and be grown-up for the first time in my life and explain to Tomas how I felt? Maybe then we could get along, work together. But when I played the scenario through my head, Tomas and I would be walking along the beach with me sounding like I was spouting a series of well-worn excuses 'I've just finished with my boyfriend', 'I don't want to get hurt', 'we just don't have anything in common. Maybe I just got carried away with the idea of a holiday romance', it was ridiculous. I couldn't face the humiliation of it and I doubted that Tomas would ever believe those tired old clichés. But did I have a choice? If I carried on ignoring Tomas it would make working together impossible and Celia would no doubt notice. I couldn't imagine what he thought. After all, if anyone could object to our date, it should, in theory be him . . .

*

'*Hola*, Raimundo,' I typed, finally starting the email to my trusty Notting Hill pal who always seemed to be equipped with a 'perfect man' scanner.

> I know, I've not written for ages and it's a disgrace, but hoping you will forgive me if you have not already filed to divorce our friendship.

> Need your impeccable advice on men. Have a moment?

> Miss you

> Izzy xx

If there was anyone who knew about guys it was Ray and his reply came back from his BlackBerry within seconds:

> Darling Izzy,

> Contemplated stern pause to make you realise that I have indeed been hurt by said silence and have moved on to find new 'amigas' . . . until I read your plea for man advice. You got me there, spill the beans . . .

> Intrigued of W11,

> Ray xx

I started to fire off a few lines in response. I knew that if I wanted Ray's honest opinion, I had to be frank with him. In truth, this wasn't hard. Ray had advised me through all sorts of man hell, warts and all. He'd tried to warn me off Harrisson for one, of course. Then there was the guy Ray told me could only ever love himself, which I realised was true when I caught him working out in front of the mirror at every conceivable opportunity. He'd grit his teeth, screw up his face and shout, 'You're the man! You're the man!' at his reflection, curling weights with each arm. And he'd also once put me in hospital when I went flying over his dumb-bells in my Manolos.

Then there had been 'X-Box Boy', so perfect in every other way, but so obsessed with computer games that he became a zombie in front of them. At first I didn't mind, it gave me more time to bake brownies, read *Vogue* in the bath, spend endless hours Facebooking and Skyping people I'd spent all day at work with whilst I painted my toenails, but eventually I'd forget he was in my apartment and he'd scare me to death when I walked into my own living room. My neighbours reported my surprised screams to the police and I thought I was going to develop heart palpitations from the constant shocks.

There had also been the good-looking, enigmatic, alternative chemist who was into natural products and refused to wear deodorant. Ray told me he would stink by summer and he was right! There was the high-flier Ray saw straight through, telling me that his lavish presents, impressive job title and flashy persona didn't ring true. I realised why when he finally invited me back to 'his' and I discovered that he shared a house with his grandparents, who slept in the room next to his. And snored. Not sexy! Finally, there had been the drummer in the Indie band who, Ray told me, would never make it. We finished when I could take his delusions of 'breaking America' no more. Months later he turned up at On Fire and failed to make the auditions for a trashy reality TV show. He was last seen working as a 'Kwik Fit Fitter' in Brighton, where he reportedly bores the customers by trying to play car parts as musical instruments. In short, Ray, I deduced, was qualified. And, more than that, I wasn't about to shock him with my bad taste in men with the history I already had.

However, maybe I'd underestimated just how bad Tomas sounded on paper. Ray was unable to get his head around the fact that I'd dated a student. 'At your age, honey? And a Ph.D student in botany, with no interest in fashion? Not sounding very Izzy to me,' he typed back at lightning speed. He couldn't come to terms with the fact that Tomas had chosen to come and live with his mother for the summer.

I found myself making email excuses for my behaviour to Ray: 'I haven't had sex for MONTHS', 'I haven't even set eyes on a handsome beast for LONGER' and, what is worse, 'I am starting to have an affair with ice cream'. But before long I was asking him for his 'man test' verdict and his answer appeared on my screen in clear and very definite black and white.

'Izzy, my love,' Ray wrote.

I think you've spent too much time in the hills away from real people. You know the type, ones with interesting lives, ambition and style. This man is NOT for you. He sounds dull, dull, dull. I'm thinking that if he were a material, he'd be corduroy. He might even be a psychopath. One of those ones who loves plants, secretly hates people.
RUN A MILE!
RUN A MILE!

RUN A MILE!
Preferably in this direction. What are you doing
there in Majorca anyway???

I hadn't quite finished reading this damning report on
my life when I heard someone clear their throat. I
looked up to see Tomas standing at the office door.

'Izzy?' he started, his voice low and warm. 'Do
you have a moment?' I looked round, Celia was
nowhere to be seen. I saved Ray's latest email to 'draft'
and nodded.

Tomas walked over to my desk and perched
awkwardly on its shiny edge. His large eyes peered
down at me with fixed concentration. He wasn't wearing
his glasses.

'Look. I'm going to be here for a while longer, so I
didn't want any hard feelings, or things to be awkward.'

He paused, but I couldn't speak.

'Celia's asked me to help out on the weddings . . . so
I just wanted to check you're OK with that?' he asked.

I felt such a fool. I was acting like a child and he was
being so mature about the situation. 'Yes, of course,' I
managed with a gentle smile, looking up at him,
purposefully trying not to find the golden skin at the
open neck of his white cotton shirt attractive.

'It's just that . . . well, I was wondering what . . . we
. . . we seemed to be getting on so—'

Tomas was struggling to find the words, but I knew
instantly what he was trying to say. At the same moment,
as Tomas continued awkwardly, I could see Celia
approaching the office, through the open doorway
which Tomas had turned his back to.

'Celia!' I announced. 'We were just talking about
working on the weddings together!' I chirped a little too
loudly with relief, stopping poor Tomas mid-sentence.

He shot his head round to see her and looked back at me, deflated.

'Yes.' Celia smiled, looking delighted. 'I think it should be rather fun.'

Later that evening, just before I shut down my computer, I remembered to read the rest of Ray's final email.

'OK, so I guess you won't be running back to London unless I make you see some sense,' he had continued. 'I never thought I'd be the knight in shining armour type,' I read on, with a smile. 'It's such a hideous heterosexual fairytale, that the thought of me in armour, on a horse, is, quite frankly, abominable . . . but I'm worried about you, Izzy.' My smile widened. I loved the fact that Ray was looking out for me. That someone, after what felt like months away from London, was looking out for me, but especially Ray. 'I'm coming over for the weekend,' the email announced. Was he serious? 'I've booked the tickets. I'm all packed. I'll be at the airport tomorrow at six p.m.' I reread the line several times. 'For God's sake, just be there to greet me so I don't get swept away with a mass arrival of tourists heading for a coach transfer. I'll never survive. Ray xxx'

Bless Ray, I thought as I stood peering hopefully up at the arrivals boards in the airport the next evening. I couldn't quite believe that he'd make the journey to visit me here, but then, he hadn't, not quite yet. The monitors flicked through a neverending database of destinations and flight numbers as countless other upturned faces gazed at the screens searching expectantly for the words *en tierra* – 'on the ground' or 'landed'. I'd arrived at five p.m. in a panic, just in case Ray's flight came in early and now, two coffees later, I was 'jangly', almost out of change to collect the car from the multi-storey and eager to get back outside to the real world.

Tomas had very kindly insisted that I borrow his car to collect Ray. A taxi would have cost almost as much as Ray's flight for a round trip via the city, and I knew my guest better than to hope that he'd have travelled light enough, or with something as sensible as a rucksack, that would fit on the Vespino. I'd thanked Tomas graciously, knowing it was a good idea, however nervous I was of driving a car for the first time on the 'wrong' side of the road, and took him up on the offer.

The vast marble arrivals lounge seemed to fill with a neverending surge of bodies. There were families lugging suitcases on trolleys, kids sitting proudly on the top as dads in squeaky new trainers pushed them along. Holiday reps in bright nylon suits jostled for the best spot to hold up their signs. Young trendy couples with soft Scandinavian voices pulled impeccable designer luggage on wheels without breaking into a sweat, and glided across the shiny floor towards the hire car booths. But still no Ray.

I waited behind the shiny chrome barrier that divided me and other pacing, toe-tapping people from the security guards and the baggage collection behind the frosted-glass wall. Next to me a tall, grey-haired man in a blazer sucked his teeth, his scruffy dog lying on the floor next to his feet, watching nonchalantly, far from perturbed by the noise and the chaos in the arrival lounge. I looked down at the dog with envy. When I looked up again, I could see the unmistakable vision of my Asian babe battling against the other easyJet arrivals.

He caught my eye and pushed through the crowd.

'IZZY!' he yelled with abandon.

Ray, in his regulation Dior skinny jeans, was pulling

a sleek leather suitcase on wheels and had a matching overnight bag in apple-green slung low over one shoulder and several bags of Duty Free weighing down each arm. He stretched these out towards me, his arms wide to greet me as he came closer, beaming a big, bleached-teeth smile. His Stella McCartney shades slipped down from his head and knocked us both on the cheek as we kissed hello in fits of giggles. Ray shimmied a carrier bag up one arm, leaving his hand free to push the glasses back on top of his immaculate, black crop.

'You-look-SO-well-I-can't-believe-you're-here,' I said excitedly, almost all in one word. I could feel myself welling up just a little.

Ray stood back to get a better view of me, despite us now being directly in the way of several families pushing buggies, luggage and sports kit, eyeing us with disapproval and steering their children awkwardly round us.

'Well, you certainly don't look quite as desperate as I'd feared.' He smiled, his eyes warm and familiar before giving me a hug. 'It's been AGES.'

'Can we get out of here now?' we chorused desperately as I tried to wrestle Ray to offload some of his Duty Free.

The ride to Ray's hotel was filled with non-stop chatter. He was desperate to fill me in on several months' worth of gossip from On Fire, countless tales from Notting Hill involving who was sleeping with whom, which stores had recently opened and closed, which bars were now best, and the details of his break-up with his hideous ex, Marc. I'd forgotten how quickly Ray spoke, how his mind worked at lightning speed, how hilariously funny he was, and I wanted to drive carefully, sensibly, and not let Ray distract me, but taxis cut us up on the *cintura* and fast Audis and sleek BMWs tried to push us into the slow lane, which, most of the time, was filled with ambling tourists wrestling with maps and therefore was to be avoided. Ray winced visibly at the lane-crossing, the last-minute turn-offs and general unpredictability of Spanish driving. He ran a finger along the dashboard, lifted up an empty box of matches, then a small book on botany, and screwed up his perfectly tanned nose momentarily before he carried on chattering as I crunched through the gears.

I'd decided to take Ray the scenic route into town, past the impressive cathedral and on to the Maritimo, knowing the glamour of the big yachts and the beautiful people rollerblading along the promenade would appeal to him. Then, under the clear skies and heat of the evening, we cut through the old town, through the cool backstreets of the Arab quarter and, finally, to a small plaza that was home to one of Palma's many impressive churches, trendy cafés and Ray's hotel.

'Not bad!' Ray purred before finally pausing for air as we pulled up. He checked out the modern glass cube that somehow worked seamlessly with the historic building and nodded in appreciation.

'It's supposed to be THE place to stay right now, so I think even you'll like it.' I smiled, admitting, 'I'm desperate *just* to look inside.'

Hotel Om had been described as the ultimate boutique hotel. Its minimal but exotic Eastern décor was encased in a beautiful and elaborate old Majorcan palace. The original stone pillars, balconies and marble fireplaces had been immaculately restored, I noticed as I checked out the original building while Ray made his way towards the cool, ultra chic black marble reception desk. Ray soon noticed the good-looking guy standing behind it, wearing the trademark Om uniform of a tight vest in unbleached white cotton and was swiftly informed that he was booked into the most expensive room in the hotel, the 'Attico'. We raced, like kids, into the glass lift to check it out.

Ray's room key, dangling from a large leather tassle with the Om emblem charm attached, opened an impressive set of intricately carved wooden doors which led theatrically into a luxurious but minimal suite. I tiptoed after him, whilst he threw down his luggage in the middle of the floor and strode over to turn on the air-conditioning, as if he already felt at home. He found the CD player and kicked off his funky retro trainers, revealing perfect, brown feet as some gentle chill-out beats filled the space.

'Right, fridge?' Ray announced purposefully, padding across the marble floor. 'We should celebrate with a drink!'

'Good idea,' I agreed. 'This place is amazing!' I said, keen to explore. 'Seems a shame you didn't bring someone with you to share it!'

I looked around, feeling a messy, awkward addition to the impeccable suite. The bedroom featured a vast, high bed swathed in raw silk and topped with a wide, thick, carved wooden headboard that matched the doors.

'Well, you never know, I might not wake up in Palma alone in the morning, not with a palace like this to woo a Romeo,' he joked as I pushed open another set of heavy double doors with impatient curiosity.

'Wow, have you been out here?' I yelled back to Ray. The bedroom led on to a terrace decked in black bamboo with its own hot tub, dining table, dark wooden loungers and large cream scatter cushions. The view over the rooftops of the city was incredible.

'Did you find the mini-bar yet, Izz?' I could hear Ray

calling from inside. 'Priorities, Izzy, priorities.' He knew me too well.

I wandered back into the bedroom and through to the lounge, my eyes searching the room for the fridge. Two plump cream sofas with oversized mocha cushions were in the centre, a projection TV screen above them, and there was a toffee-coloured leather chair that looked elegantly battered and expensive, and some sophisticated lighting and Asian art. But as for the mini-bar—

'Ah, got it!' I heard Ray shout from the other room. 'Panic's over!'

I found Ray popping open a bottle of cava.

'Amazing bathroom, you *MUST* see it ... I could spend all weekend in there alone ... but why do these places insist on all of this concealed storage? he asked as I stood in the doorway. 'I can just imagine unpacking, going clubbing and never finding anything the next morning ... disaster!'

'They concealed the mini-bar?' I asked with surprise. 'I thought the idea was to tempt us?'

Ray smiled. 'You've got a point. Let's take these outside, shall we, and you can start to tell me what's been happening.'

'Sure.' I smiled back, momentarily mesmerised by the only colour in the bedroom – a beautiful lilac and green speckled orchid sitting on top of an antique oak chest.

'What's that?' Ray asked, putting his glass down as he followed my eye line.

It was an envelope, a silver envelope, with 'Hotel Om invites you ...' delicately scrolled on the front. Ray scooped it up, opened it impatiently, and read the contents out loud. 'Four complimentary tickets to Om Beach, our seafront club, tonight. An exclusive VIP invitation for you and your guests,' Ray announced with excitement dancing in his eyes.

'Well, that's settled. How fab!' He laughed. 'We'll have a drinkette now, maybe grab supper, if you fancy, or tapas, or whatever it is you have here, then go!' Ray decided. 'And why don't you bring along Tomas and what did you say the ex-model was called, Celia? She sounds amazing. It'll be a ball.'

Ommmmmmmmmmmmmmmm!

Once I'd got my head around the idea of going out, *really* going out for the evening, for the first time in months, I started to look forward to some fun. With Ray in town, I decided, it was going to be like old times, but in the sun, as if we were both on holiday. Ray convinced me, over that first glass of cava, to invite Tomas and Celia but not to go back to the house to get ready.

'Just call them!' he insisted. 'I have this amazing embellished vest top you should throw over those jeans and heels and you'll look fabulous, Izz,' he pleaded, obviously not wanting to risk me driving back south and not coming back.

'*Buenas tardes*,' Celia answered the phone merrily.

'Celia? Hello, it's Izzy,' I answered her.

'Hello, Isabelle. Has your friend arrived safely?' she asked politely.

'Yes, thanks, Celia. I have my friend here and he has some complimentary tickets to a lovely sounding late-night bar and nightclub in Palma Bay . . .' I covered the receiver with my hand as Ray giggled loudly at my genteel description. '. . . and anyway, we thought how nice it would be if you and Tomas joined us there,'

I continued, trying not to look at him.

'Oh, how very kind,' Celia answered in her usual polite way. 'Of course, we'd love to, it sounds wonderful.'

'Don't you want to ask Tomas first?' I replied, a little taken aback by her instant enthusiasm and expecting that a club wouldn't be his or her scene.

'No, no, dear. He'll be delighted, I'm sure,' Celia protested. 'He was just this moment telling me that he doesn't have plans for this evening.'

I could imagine Celia at her telephone table, jotting down the address in her perfect hand.

'Yes, Tomas will know it,' she assured me. 'We'll look forward to seeing you there at ten-thirty!'

Back out on the rooftop terrace we decided to order room service, light the candles and get ourselves ready, replacing the soothing chill-out for some obscure club CD that Ray had packed with him. And, of course, whilst we groomed, we laughed, picked at our food, preened, and finished the bottle of cava.

'Maybe the guy from reception will be there tonight,' I teased Ray as we sat, finally ready, amidst the candles twinkling against the clear night sky. 'I could see you checking him out.'

'Well, he *was* cute,' Ray agreed. 'I *am* single and shamelessly checking out everyone, Izz!' he laughed, peering over the edge of the balcony at a group of tight-bodied Latino guys chatting below.

The city seemed to be just waking up after a lazy siesta. At just before ten the square's bars were filling, the locals were taking their pre-dinner drinks, groups of kids were hanging out, gathered around the fountains as well-dressed thirty-somethings made their way towards the hotel.

'Quick drink downstairs before we go?' Ray asked, surveying the scene and as keen as ever to bar-hop en route.

'You know,' I pondered, looking at my watch, 'I don't want to be a bore, but I'd hate to be late for Celia and Tomas, so why don't we just head there?' I replied cautiously.

'Yeah, you're right, we should get going,' Ray said, taking me by the arm. 'Still drinking Mojitos?'

Om was already heaving with its Saturday-night crowd when we arrived. The bar – long, white and all shiny surfaces, bathed in golden light – was filled with attractive Europeans, tanned and dressed up for the night. Unlike Notting Hill, there wasn't a desperate scramble to get served at the bar. Instead, the Spanish seemed to languish in flirtatious bar chat, checking each other out and greeting friends with kisses. Like most things in Spain, waiting to be served was part of the process and not to be rushed.

'Cool place,' Ray said as we made our way past the DJ to look outside.

Giant torches dramatically illuminated the way, Moroccan lanterns and Thai screens cordoned off a VIP area.

'It's great to be in a club where you can actually get out of the sweaty dance zone and chill outside by the pool. I likey,' Ray said, eyeing three large four-poster sun beds swathed in organza. 'They look like fun!' he added before we continued on our tour. Ray always liked to check out a venue first, before deciding on the best place to start the evening and where he planned to party later. It was an art he'd developed, which was a bit like Feng Shui.

After the obligatory circuit we joined in the hustle of

the bar, still catching up and chattering all the way, Ray breaking away intermittently to try out his pigeon Spanish on good-looking *chicos*, whom he tried to involve in our conversation, to their bemusement. As I slipped off to the ladies, leaving Ray with two perfectly mixed Mojitos for old times' sake, I realised happily, as the music started to get louder, that I was having a good night. It was fun to be out, tottering on heels, being with an old friend. I felt a sudden sharp pang for London.

Back by the bar, my eyes scoured the room for Ray. No Raimundo to be seen. I wandered outside to see if he'd taken up position by the pool and it wasn't till I came back inside that I realised he was already on the dance floor. The party had clearly started.

Ray saw me and beckoned me over before I could think twice about whether or not I wanted to dance. I smiled and shimmied a little as I made my way to join him, deciding decisively not to be self-conscious and just to enjoy myself.

'Izzy, this is Xisca, Pedro, Jessica and Ana,' he said, introducing me to a whole group of new friends he'd acquired in record time.

'*Mucho gusto*,' I said, nodding, wondering quite how Ray had achieved it. He and Jessica were cooing over Ana's scarlet satin stilettos as Ana made tiny, accurate dance steps towards a tall, well-dressed *chico*, her hips swaying sexily to the beat.

'She's fierce!' Ray laughed as Ana spun round and came almost face to face with her *guapo*, leaving him staring at her back, her long dark hair flying behind her in the wake of her neat salsa move. She opened out her arms as her footwork became faster, her eyes flashing wickedly as she moved back towards us in a salsa, not once glancing back. The chico in question was mesmerised.

As we watched, giggling, my eyes surveyed the crowds and I picked out a face watching intently from the sidelines. Tomas's. He was stood standing stiffly, awkwardly, in his usual uniform of crisp shirt and khaki pants at the side of the dance floor. Those same clothes, which he wore whether he was engrossed in research, just at home, or at a wedding, seemingly without much consideration, were suddenly conspicuous amidst Palma's best dressed. He looked out of place and slightly embarrassed, but as our eyes met, his face became soft, his eyes smiled, crinkling at the corners and a slow, 'Hi' travelled across his lips. He raised his hand simultaneously, in the first motion of a wave.

I started to raise mine, in polite response as Tomas's eyes moved to my left. I turned instinctively to see what had caught his eye and saw Celia chatting closely to Ray on the dance floor. She was throwing back her head in laughter, a head that was neatly swathed in a brightly coloured turban that gleamed in the lights. She wore an elegant silk kaftan, heavy bangles and the highest heels I'd seen her in, heels that just had to be seventies YSL. She looked incredible. Ray took her by both hands, inviting her into a dance as I made my way over to join them.

'Hello!' we boomed in competition with the music, kissing each other on both cheeks.

'I see you've met Ray!'

'Yes, he's quite a mover!' Celia answered with a girlish grin, elegantly swaying like a flower child at Woodstock.

I turned to find Tomas in the crowd again. He should come and join us, I thought before I found him staring intensely back at me, still planted in the same spot. I made a cup with my hand and mimed drinking and a shrug to beg the question, but he shook his head with a smile and indicated with a wave that I was to go back and have fun.

Celia's moves became even more wild and exaggerated the longer she danced, her face animated as she moved.

'*Loving* Ceels,' Ray whispered, leaning over to me, as the DJ kicked the music up a gear.

I smiled back. 'I can hardly keep up with her!' I said in awe. 'Shall we grab another drink? Maybe we need refuelling . . .'

'God, yes, great idea,' Ray answered, leading me off the dance floor, past a black girl dancing barefoot in white jeans and a jewelled bikini top. We decided to get drinks for everybody and find a table, so that we could then gather together and chat.

The bar was heaving now and the Spanish had sauntered in to the party after their ten o'clock suppers. Ray and I patiently joined the relaxed wait to reach the front of the queue.

'Izzy,' Ray started seriously after a comfortable silence as we both surveyed the scene. 'Tell me, what's the deal with Tomas? What's the latest?'

'To be honest, there really isn't a latest,' I admitted. 'I got freaked out after the date and I've shied away from addressing the situation. I've just kind of ignored it, hoping it would go away and that maybe we can carry on being friends like before . . . it's not like we ended up in bed together,' I added, in a pathetic attempt to justify my actions.

'So what are you putting the whole thing down to?' Ray asked. 'Man drought? Boredom? A new-found passion for botany?'

I smiled, embarrassed as a girl in a strappy, mint-green dress pushed past us. Ray screwed up his nose as she flicked her long glossy hair away from one shoulder and into his face.

'OK,' I started with a sigh. It was time to be honest. 'Firstly, Tomas isn't really my type.'

Ray raised his eyebrows in a 'hallelujah' gesture, I smiled and continued.

'We didn't really have anything in common,' I said as Ray made another shock-horror face that broke into a smile.

'He just happened to show up at Celia's and I guess I got carried away with the romance of the situation.' Ray nodded, encouraging me to continue.

'You know as well as I do that if we were in London, I wouldn't have gone on a date with Tomas at all, but maybe that was part of his attraction?' I asked, out loud. 'He wasn't the kind of guy to try and impress me by booking a table at a cool new restaurant or getting tickets to a premiere or the latest must-see in the West End, and I guess that was part of the appeal; I was looking for something different ... you know, I was searching for a new start, I suppose – and I thought, maybe, that I needed a different kind of man, too ...'

'I get it, so what happened?' Ray asked seriously now as we edged our way forward towards the bar.

'I panicked. We got on OK, we had fun, but I started to wonder if it was all very real. Like everything here, my job, staying with Celia ... it's all felt so temporary and I started to wonder what dating him would be like if I decided to go back to London. And that's when I started to think that I was just heading for another disaster.'

'God, you women are hilarious!' Ray jibed, smiling at me. 'You only went out once!'

'I know!' I smiled back. 'But I couldn't help it!' I admitted. 'And I started to think that Tomas was more likely to suggest we dodge the grey army at a "racy" date at Kew Gardens on a drizzly afternoon than humour me with an art house movie with subtitles where I could eat my body weight in popcorn. I'd never get him to a romantic evening ice-skating at Somerset House,' I said, remembering my most favourite date with Harrisson ever.

Ray nodded knowingly. 'Exactly! You're still the same person, Izz.'

'I know! I know! He'd never understand why I would need to leave him to ramble in the Highlands for heather samples whilst I insisted on staying in front of a log fire with woolly socks on, a pile of newspapers and a glass of red wine until he returned,' I agreed, 'and God forbid that he'd ever suggest fishing . . .'

Ray winced visibly in shock. 'Fishing?' he asked in horror.

'Fishing,' I confirmed.

'It's worse than I thought!' he joked.

'Then, I imagined going back to England, renting a flat and trying to find a new job, and I knew that Tomas wouldn't fit into my life there,' I confessed. 'I know it sounds crazy but I kept imagining us wrestling for the remote control when he wanted to bore me with *Gardeners' World* when I wanted to watch reruns of *America's Next Top Model*. There would be no room for his gardening books amongst my self-help shelves and Vreeland tomes. No room for scraggy, weedy specimens amongst my Diptyque candles. He'd hate the self-obsessed, bitchy, shallow friends I adore and the fact that I'd insist on getting trolleyed with them three nights a week on outrageously priced cocktails that aren't even any good.' I was on a confessional roll and Ray laughed in recognition.

'But you don't *know* that!' he argued, his voice shrill

above the music. 'Don't you think you might have got a little ahead of yourself?'

'Yes, yes, definitely! Of course!' I agreed, shuffling forward as we edged ever nearer to the bar.

'Look,' Ray started, his voice more serious than I'd ever heard it before. 'I'm sure he's a nice guy, and maybe he's not right for you. I've not even spoken to him and, believe me, I will be vetting him closely when I do . . . but all I can tell you, honey, is that I don't need to engage with this guy to know that he's totally fallen for you. He's not taken his eyes off you all night . . . and, Izzy, look, this is so obviously not a place this guy is at home in, but he's come down here to meet your friend *and* he seems to be having a good time, just watching *you*. If I had any reason to think that he isn't a genuinely nice person, I'd say it was freaky. Knowing what little I know, I'd say that he's really into you.'

I gulped and took in a breath before giving the barman, who was now standing in front of me waiting impatiently, a diamond gleaming in one ear, my order of drinks. I turned back to Ray as the barman reached for glasses before turning to face the optics.

'But of course there is something bigger going on here,' I admitted, leaning against the counter. 'The last thing I needed after Harrisson was to get caught up in another relationship that was doomed to fail before it got going. I have to protect myself. I've come here to get away from my troubles with men, not to make more problems for myself.'

Ray looked at me square on, his eyes wide. 'There's no easy way to tell you this,' he started, 'Harrisson . . . he's . . . met . . . mmm . . . someone else.'

I stared at Ray in disbelief.

'*Cuarenta y dos euros*,' the barman interrupted, his hand outstretched for the cash.

'The rumour is . . . well, he's met some posh bird and they're engaged,' Ray added in a quieter voice, full of regret.

Before I knew it, I'd let a glass of white wine and a Mojito I'd been holding slip to the floor.

Ray rushed to help me, the barman shot us a disapproving look, then shouted at another bartender in an enraged Spanish voice for him to clean up the mess. I was momentarily mortified. Not at the broken glass, wet toes or shriek from the chiquita whose dress I'd covered in mint and sugar syrup, I was mortified about Harrisson. I felt my heart sink. I felt weak. I hadn't been ready to hear this. To hear that there was someone that Harrisson was prepared to marry who wasn't me. To think I'd been organising weddings all season and Harrisson's moneyed miss had been planning their own.

'C'mon, Izz,' Ray soothed apologetically, taking me by the arm. 'I had to tell you and there was never going to be a good time.'

I smiled a watery smile.

'Where's your tan gone?' he asked, his hand on my now pale cheek, talking to me as if I were the only person in the room, despite the attention the broken glass had attracted. 'You're not going to let that slimeball ruin our night, are you?'

'No,' I muttered miserably. I wanted to cry.

'Look. I've got the barman to make more drinks, just wait here a sec and I'll grab them,' Ray ordered kindly, as if I were a child he was about to bring sweets to, for comfort.

I watched Ray walk back to the barman. He'd come all this way to visit me, I thought. He'd been worried about me before. And maybe he'd also come over to tell me this. I couldn't let him down now.

I was determined not to dwell on Harrisson for the

rest of the evening, and just to have fun. After all, things were over, what did I expect? Well, I hadn't expected him to rebound and marry a perfect posh bird quite so quickly, but wanting Harrisson to stay single and pine for me, for more than a few weeks, would be unrealistic.

I glanced around. Celia and Ray had become entrenched in a conversation about fashion and modelling in the Sixties. Ana was finally chatting to the *guapo*. I saw Tomas making conversation in Spanish to Ray's new friends and I joined in with my limited vocabulary and slow pronunciation, determined not to sit on the sidelines and think too much.

When Ray and Celia got up to dance with a group of tight-bodied young guys, I watched Tomas break into a smile.

'She's in her element, Izzy!' he told me. 'It was good of you to ask us. She loves to dance more than anything.' His face was sincere and warm.

'Not really your thing, though?' I asked.

'Is it that obvious?' he replied with a laugh.

'We could always leave them to it?' I suggested, a little tired myself. There was no way I was going to be able to drag Ray away from Om in a hurry. 'There are shuttles to the hotel.'

'Would it be rude?' Tomas asked, ever the gent.

'You really don't come clubbing often, do you?!' I teased him. 'Of course it wouldn't be rude!'

We went back to the hotel where we picked up Tomas's car, and he drove us home, kindly offering to lend it to me again to pick up Ray the following day and take him to the airport. The journey seemed so long in the dark and we soon fell silent. A text message beeped from my mobile phone, waking me in my seat: 'Im bck at the hotel now w. some1 ...' It was Ray. '... Celia!' he added. 'She's such fun! xx' I tried to show Tomas but he preferred to concentrate on the road ahead.

I smiled and sent a message back before trying to drift off to sleep, my mouth dry and my head aching. It was a familiar feeling. Too many Mojitos, I told myself, just like when Ray and I used to go out in Notting Hill. Must take Ray to the airport tomorrow, I reminded myself, and his voice filled my head with that previsit question, 'What are you doing in Majorca anyway?' It was my last thought, along with a lasting image of Harrisson. As my head slumped back into a delicious sleep, Tomas steered his way back home, the bright lights of oncoming traffic flickering through complete darkness.

13

Back to the Future

As Celia, Tomas and I left the house to travel to the final small wedding of the season together the next day, I dwelt on my time with Ray. It had been so good to see him that the meeting up for breakfast, before dropping him off at the airport, had been emotional and had left me a little wobbly. Now, in the car and back at work, Tomas's presence had an effect I hadn't been expecting. I suddenly felt part of a family outing that I had no right or inclination to attend, whilst at the same time I didn't feel part of anything. I was genuinely happy to see Celia and Tomas getting on so well and becoming close again, which was clear from the endless chattering and laughing about their nightclubbing which eminated from the front seats of Tomas's scruffy car. But there was something about it that jarred with my homesickness and my doubts as to whether I fitted in on the island. I felt like an outsider, an impostor. I cringed remembering Celia's line that we would all have 'fun' and dwelt on Ray's email question: 'What are you doing there in Majorca anyway?' I had an uncontrollable urge to write myself some kind of sick note and head home to hide under the duvet for the day. A wedding was the last place I wanted to be. Just get on with it, I told myself as Tomas took a turn off to the east of the island and I tried to stop myself from wallowing in negative thoughts. Get on with it and don't blow it now! I was thinking about my apprenticeship. This was, after all, the penultimate wedding of my trial and I had to keep all of my options open for the future.

I sat quietly in the back, windows wound down, brooding about my predicament. It was a beautiful sunny day but my mood was more akin to Central London in February; cold, grey and sombre and I just couldn't seem to kick it. I had precisely an hour and a half to buck up my ideas, paste on a smile and get into wedding mode. But adopting a perky, efficient and helpful persona felt as fake as being expected to pull on a chicken suit and entertain a rabble of five years olds at a party. Eventually I stuck my head in the wind stream of the open window, closing my eyes so that the sun could beat on my face. I let my mind drift and blanked out the cheery sound of Celia and Tomas from the front. The air was balmy, the sun was hot on my skin, and I allowed my eyes to rest for a while longer than I should have done.

'Izzy, Izzy.' The next thing I knew, Tomas was calling my name, shaking me gently by the arm, breaking a dreamy, woozy sleep in the heat of the afternoon.

'Huh?' I answered in a daze, my mouth dry and my eyelids reluctant to open against the bright sunlight.

I sat up in the back seat and caught a glimpse of myself in the driver's mirror. 'Christ!' I muttered, startled by my own appearance. My hair was a frothy bird's nest, a long deep crease had appeared on one side of my face from using my arm as a cushion, and I had smudged the make-up beneath my eyes.

'God, sorry!' I excused myself to Tomas, wiping the

kohl away with an index finger. 'Must have dropped off.

'What's the time?' I asked quickly, my mood lurching from sleepy to panic.

'It's OK, Izzy, don't worry,' Tomas soothed. 'Take your time, it's only two-thirty.' He passed me a bottle of water. 'We've got two hours before the ceremony.' I unscrewed the top and took a long drink.

Usually two hours was very little time to prepare, but today's wedding was small and simple: a total of just thirty guests gathering at the tiny Sanctuary perched high up on a hillside for a ceremony and then trans-ported by coach to a nearby restaurant for celebrations in the gardens.

The couple had made the planning a breeze. Sue, a nurse from Nottinghamshire, and Graham, who ran his own IT company, were easy to please and down to earth. They'd been together for six years, Sue had told me, when I discovered that their three children would be taking key roles in the ceremony. As I took a minute to fix my hair in the driver's mirror, I remembered Sue telling me their story.

They'd met walking their dogs in their local park. Her Spaniel had run after Graham's Terrier's ball, caught it, and refused to give it back. 'I knew,' she told me, 'after I'd finally chased my dog Stanley down to the lake and prised the ball from his chops . . . and when, totally embarrassed, I looked up at the owner and saw Graham's face, I knew that he was the one. Graham said, "Don't worry, duck, you can buy me a brew and Sam here a biscuit" and the rest, as they say, Izzy, is history.' Conversations with Sue had always run that way, I mused, pushing a kirby grip into place and feeling the gentle scrape on my scalp of its pointy end. She'd end up telling me a chapter of her life story when I'd only called to ask her what shade of orange she'd like the roses in her bouquet to be. She'd ramble on for ages and then answer 'Oh, flowers! Silly me. Whatever the florist thinks will be nice, they know best . . . got to run, I've got a fish pie in the oven for the kids.'

I grabbed my bag, slipped on my strappy flats and handed the water back to Tomas. There was no more time to waste. I wanted everything to be right for Sue and her family. 'Rustic,' she'd told me when I'd asked her how she envisioned her wedding, 'natural and relaxed.' I'd discovered that there was a lot of organising that went into making a wedding look effortless and the final test now, was bringing it all together.

'OK, ready,' I said to Tomas. 'Thanks.' I smiled at him as I stepped out of the car. I could see Celia walking away in the distance, taking small, calculated steps towards the entrance of the Sanctuary in her smart heels, neat, crisp blouse and flawless cream fitted skirt, barely creased despite the journey. It was a sobering sight.

Tomas and I headed after Celia, taking in the incredible panoramic view, which stretched across the countryside for miles and down to the sea. The Sanctuary seemed to tower above this part of the island, watching over it, its tiny chapel full of history and atmosphere, tucked inside an old stone façade, weatherbeaten, due to its exposed position.

'OK.' I cleared my throat, getting down to business. 'So the coach will drop people here,' I told Tomas, pointing. 'Then, they need to be directed through the large wooden door and through to the courtyard before the ceremony. We'll offer them water, which we'll stack in the bucket in the well, whilst they wait to go into the church.'

Tomas humoured me, nodding, taking my lead, but I sensed that he had already been fully briefed by Celia.

He took a folded piece of A4 containing all of his detailed, timed notes out from his pocket, confirming that my senses were spot on, and waved it at me.

'I've got that covered, Izzy, it's in your memo here. I assure you that I did take time to read it. I'll set up the water from the cool box, don't worry.'

'Thanks,' I smiled, 'and don't forget—'

'That the Spanish guitarist will arrive at three-forty-five to set up and the coach will arrive at four?' he interrupted. 'No problem, I'm on to it.' He smiled, giving me an officer's salute.

I giggled, despite myself, and went off in search of a shady spot from which to call Sue. I settled on the covered steps that led to the chapel.

'Izzy!' she sung excitedly on hearing my voice. 'Isn't the weather wonderful?' I'd never heard a bride sound so elated.

'Isn't it! I'm so pleased for you,' I answered, genuinely. 'Now, how is everything? Is the make-up artist there with you?' I asked, hearing children squealing in the background.

'Oh yes! You won't believe it,' Sue said, desperate to tell me, 'she's worked real magic. You might not recognise me, Izzy . . . and as for the hair, I can't believe it's my own!'

'Of course I'll recognise you, Sue. You're the one in the big white dress, right?!' We both laughed.

'No really, Izzy, thanks for everything. The babysitter's just in the room with us so that the kids can get used to her before we leave. She's been great. We got the children ready together, so I've had plenty of time to enjoy being pampered . . .'

'Perfect!' I cooed. 'Can't wait to see you all . . . anything you need? I'm just at the church and could be with you in ten minutes by car . . .'

'Don't think so, duck,' Sue replied, 'Graham's even sent over a bottle of bubbly but I daren't have any. I'm so excited I think it might tip me over the edge!'

'OK, Sue . . . Ring me if you need anything, and if I don't hear from you, the next time I call will be to tell you that your car is waiting outside and that all the guests are being seated so that you can set off with the little ones and your dad, OK?' I paused, then remembered. 'Do you need me to check on your dad to remind him of the times and to see if he's got everything he needs?'

'No, really, Izzy, we're all sorted here.'

'Great, everything's looking wonderful here, too,' I reassured her, looking around, totting up the jobs left to do in my head. 'Have a lovely time.' I signed off, snapping my phone shut and seeing Celia in the doorway.

Celia smiled down at me, but there was something behind her expression. She looked concerned.

'Everything OK?' I asked tentatively. I felt a thump in my heart, worried that there had been an oversight . . .

'Oh yes, wonderful, dear,' she replied, but her eyes looked a little watery and her bottom lip quivered.

'Are you all right, Celia? You seem . . .' My eyes searched for Tomas, but he wasn't anywhere to be seen. I stood up to join her, taking her arm. She looked a little unstable.

'Come on, Celia, talk to me,' I gently pleaded, wondering what on earth was wrong and if I had enough time to deal with whatever it was before the wedding. This wasn't like her.

'You'll see,' she said. 'Come.'

I followed Celia up the stone steps and inside the chapel, wondering what I'd find, what disaster might have occurred.

'Wow!' I gasped, catching a sideways glance at Celia who was welling up again. It was breathtaking. Flowers filled the chapel. The florist had come early that morning to work her magic, leaving abundant arrangements of delicate roses to rest in the cool darkness of the closed-up chapel. Now that Celia had eased the tall, heavy wooden doors open, the scent of perfectly opened roses filled the tiny but impeccable room, from its humble worn-stone floor to the chandelier that glistened high in the domed ceiling. I looked towards the altar. It was beautiful in its simplicity; a simple raised platform, a single wooden cross on a natural stone wall behind, and a garland of pure white roses across the heavy dark wooden table. To the right, another smaller, decorative altar gleamed gently beneath the darkness of an arch, lit now by hundreds of tiny candles. The pews, just eight rows on two sides, were decorated with simple cream silk bows and between them there was a scattering of petals along the aisle. Of course, we'd seen the chapel before, but today, there was something about it that seemed particularly special, as if these few adornments had given it new life, made it shine.

Celia took my arm. 'Terrible line of work, this,' she mocked. I glanced at her about to smile, but quickly turned my head, as I heard a gentle, familiar clearing of a throat behind us.

Tomas stood in the doorway with Ramon, the Spanish guitarist. 'Look at you two!' he laughed. 'Not getting carried away, are we?'

'Of course not!' I answered embarrassed, breaking from Celia's arm to greet the guitarist.

Behind the altar I rummaged through two cool, dark, airless rooms, searching for a chair for Ramon to perch on whilst he played his classical twelve-string. There was a kitchen, with perfunctory utensils, a scrubbed wooden table, and a small stone pantry housing all manner of cleaning materials, buckets and mops and, above them, a row of immaculate white, green, gold and claret-red priests' vestments. It was in the next room, a teaching room, decorated with nothing but a large blackboard and a large refectory table, that I picked up one of many uncomfortable-looking wooden chairs and waddled awkwardly back to the altar with it. I put it down momentarily to turn the large iron key to lock off this part of the church, always kept out of sight.

'*Yo la tengo!*' I exclaimed to Ramon, lifting the chair up slightly to show him, before placing it carefully to the left of the small, decorative altar where he would accompany the bride's entrance.

Celia and Tomas were nowhere to be seen and, looking down at my watch, I guessed that the coach must have arrived. How quickly two hours had passed, I realised, heading out to find the ushers amongst the guests, so that I could tell them where to stand to hand out the Order of Service booklets whilst Celia and I seated everyone else.

Ramon had already wandered out to the courtyard, where he would play for half an hour as guests gathered waiting for Sue's arrival, but he was far from ready to strum. He was lighting a cigarette and his guitar, I could see as I looked back through the open chapel doors, was laid across the small altar. He saw my expression of scorn as I emerged down the steps and into the daylight but he simply shrugged his shoulders.

'*Cinco minutos?*' he asked, raising an eyebrow.

'Ramon, NO, *ahora!*' I demanded back. He jumped a little and stubbed out his cigarette on the courtyard patio that Tomas had so obviously swept. I looked at him, outraged, till he picked the butt up.

At the front of the Sanctuary Celia and Tomas already had the guests in hand, leading them to the courtyard, whilst seeking out the key people for the ceremony.

'Ramon's all ready,' I whispered in Celia's ear as she directed people towards the courtyard.

'Ah, here's David, the reverend, I'll go and meet him,' I added. Celia nodded.

David was a well-mannered but difficult man and, unfortunately, the only English-speaking reverend operating in the north-east of the island, so for months I had courted him for Sue.

I had liaised with him on every detail for the ceremony. I had passed on his recommendations and his prerequisites, taking his advice and relaying it with a cheery explanation of, 'He knows what's appropriate, Sue, and what will work best.' In the end, Sue and Graham had had to fit in with his wish for a particular time for the ceremony, his choice of religious readings, and had narrowly escaped his insistence on hymns, one battle I fought for her and successfully won. The ceremony plans, it seemed to Sue, were slipping from her control. 'He might want the hymns, Izzy,' Sue told me, 'but we certainly *do not*. Please kindly inform Reverend Meade that this is my big day, will you, duck?'

David had not been thrilled to hear that a classical guitarist would provide the processional and recessional music, but I'd joked with him that at least I wasn't asking him if they could play a Kylie CD. 'Now, Isabelle,' he'd retorted in his quiet, mannered tone, 'you may joke, but I take these matters *very* seriously. I was once at a marriage ceremony where a young usher thought it very funny to play a different track on the Cliff Richard CD he'd been in charge of operating, to the one he'd been told to play ... so the bride and groom left the Catholic church to "Devil Woman" that day, rather than "Congratulations". And, of course, they couldn't just turn round and do it all again!' I shuddered in horror at the mere thought of Cliff Richard playing at a wedding.

David and I made our civil greetings and I showed him round to the courtyard, explaining where he could change into his robes. He looked preoccupied, nervous; a trickle of sweat lined his forehead and damp patches had appeared under the arms of his short-sleeved shirt.

'Can I get you some water?' I offered, concerned, but David wasn't paying attention.

'What on EARTH is going on here?' he exclaimed without warning, his voice raised as he entered the chapel.

Ramon, I realised, had not removed his guitar from the altar and was nowhere to be seen.

'David, I'm so sorry,' I started, blushing, 'I have asked the guitarist to remove this and to start playing.'

David shook his head and fell silent before walking towards the rooms behind the altar.

'Sort it, Izzy, will you please? I'm really very unhappy about this, it's unacceptable, most disrespectful.' His voice was calm and low again, but filled with repressed anger.

Weddings have an ability to enforce a particular mood and discipline and, within ten minutes, the event was in full swing and David and I were back on track. The guests were happily helping themselves to water and chatting in the courtyard with the sound of Ramon's beautiful guitar playing in the background.

The ushers, smart in pale grey suits and crisp white shirts, stood each side of the entrance to the chapel as Sue and Graham's guests were seated. Graham stood at the front, nervously shuffling from foot to foot as the men around him teased him that Sue wouldn't show. Moments later, dead on four-thirty, his bride arrived outside.

Sue looked incredible. As I met her at the wedding car, skipping out of the way of the photographer, she emerged with her dad and children, all smiles. I had never seen a bride look so radiant, so perfectly happy. She wasn't the youngest or the prettiest bride of the season, but there was something about her relaxed attitude; how she gently reminded her children of their roles, beaming excitedly, so keen to enjoy every moment, that made her the most beautiful bride to me. I gave her a reassuring smile and slipped inside to the back of the chapel, ready for her to make an entrance.

Megan, Sue and Graham's three-year-old daughter, entered the church first, her dress a dainty pink tulle, flowers in her hair and a serious expression of duty on her cherubic face. An 'ahh' rose from the crowd as Ramon's delicate guitar playing accompanied her with a Latin version of the 'Wedding March'. Megan scattered even more rose petals down the aisle ahead of her mother's entrance, careful not to slip in her ballet shoes as she walked. Just behind her, her sister Emily followed, holding hands with her five-year-old brother Michael, so cute in his tiny grey waistcoat and trousers, a single orange rose button hole on his lapel, and a cheeky smile on his face that threatened misbehaviour at any moment.

Celia, Tomas and I stood at the very back of the chapel. I clutched the remaining Order of Service booklets in my hands and studied one, noting each step of the ceremony, so that I didn't need to meet Tomas's gaze. I could feel him looking down at me as I read and we stood silently, slightly closer together than was comfortable. As Sue and her father entered the chapel a sudden spontaneous round of applause filled the room. It was a noise I'd not heard before in a church and it took me by surprise. It started as a reserved gesture, but grew in magnitude to whooping and whistling as Sue and her dad Keith walked in. I teetered on my tiptoes to see David's face, hoping he wouldn't disapprove, but to my relief he joined in, clapping slowly, smiling with the rest of the congregation. I teetered again to try to see Sue's expression, but could only see her back, her arm linked with her father's, their feet perfectly in time. The guests looked on in delight. Ladies in hats, men in suits and well-behaved children had all become part of the ceremony and only added to the heady atmosphere.

As Sue and her father reached the altar, the chapel fell respectfully silent and Ramon played a little more of the march, before gently fading out the tune on his guitar. The Reverend David Mead stepped forward and the service began.

David performed a warm, personal ceremony for Sue and Graham. The couple stood holding hands throughout, their children looking on in wonder, Graham giving Sue's hand a little squeeze whenever she got emotional. There was a pause in the service for 'Ave Maria', which Ramon played seamlessly and which had many ladies reaching for their hankies. The reading by Keith was full of love and so obviously heartfelt that it left everyone moved. Sue and Graham repeated their vows carefully, with solemnity and passion. Of all of the elaborate, expensive, showy weddings of the season, this felt the most real, the most intimate and the most romantic. It was, I decided, glazing over dreamily in the back row, next to Tomas, the kind of wedding I would want myself.

'Well . . .' Celia had started warmly at her debriefing for Sue and Graham's wedding the next morning, 'didn't it go well!' We sat around the table in the shade of the terrace, Tomas and I with notebooks and pens poised like eager pupils, both slightly dishevelled after the late night and long drive home. It was early, but the sun was already large and bright in the sky, casting a slightly milky heat haze above the mountains and bathing Celia's carefully tended hibiscus, fuchsia and bougainvillea in brilliant light.

Despite the heat, Celia served piping-hot coffee from a silver pot that looked like it would cause a stir on *The Antiques Road Show*, tsking gently as a tiny splash hit the pure linen tablecloth. Her platinum hair was carefully coiffed into a neat chignon and secured with an ivory pin, her make-up was immaculate; her crisp white shirt-dress was neatly pressed and adorned with a jewelled belt and an African bangle. I felt a mess, as always, in comparison. How does she do that? I wondered to myself after her introduction, zoning out a little with tiredness and feeling an ungainly bead of perspiration above my top lip. How *does* she do it?

'Susan and Graham seemed perfectly happy with everything,' she continued. 'Am I right, Isabelle?'

'Oh yes, I think so,' I replied on cue, having caught the line just in time. 'Sue was ecstatic, although, to be honest, she seemed so determined to enjoy herself that anything could have happened and she would have thought it was all wonderful!'

'I think you're doing yourself a disservice there, Izzy,' Tomas interjected. 'It really was rather well put together.'

I blushed slightly at the praise. 'Thanks,' I uttered almost quietly.

'So, nothing we could have improved upon?' Celia

asked, her head cocked slightly on one side, like an exotic bird.

'Well, there was . . .' I started, but then decided not to tell Celia about the incident with the guitarist wanting a cigarette and leaving his guitar on the altar for the Reverend to find, in case it backfired on me.

'Well, what?' Celia pursued.

'Oh, just that if I was going to be very picky, I'd say that the first course was a little slow to come out, especially when the speeches had run to the minute, as we told the kitchen they would,' I fumbled.

'Well,' Tomas defended, patting Pepillo who had come to sit by his shins in the sun, 'I didn't notice and I didn't see anyone complain; I think you're becoming as much of a perfectionist as Celia.'

'That's no bad thing at all,' Celia quipped, studying me thoughtfully. 'No bad thing,' she concluded quickly. 'Let's spend time chatting through some of the outstanding tasks we should divide up for the final wedding of the season.'

I stifled a yawn, aware that I was contorting my face unattractively, but unable to stop it. My legs felt heavy and tired beneath the table, my eyes dry and frazzled, willing me to close them, my own unwashed hair, laced with cigarette smoke, made me feel queasy. This wasn't, I personally thought, the best time to talk about the next big day. This seemed like the perfect day to indulge in some mindless filing, gentle office cleaning or some light research, preferably followed by a big lunch and a long siesta, but Celia, as always, was fired up with enthusiasm.

'Right-o,' Tomas agreed. 'Yes, do tell me more.'

'Oh God!' a voice groaned inside my head. 'That's two of them.'

Celia's list of tasks filled another hour's discussion,

the plans were complicated and the budget was sky-high, even higher than I'd thought when I'd first started helping Celia with the wedding.

Tomas, as keen as his mother, picked up the final organisation of the stag party and hen night. This would include a yacht charter with beach paella for the young guys and an eighteen-hole golf tournament for the old guard, who would be arriving on the course, having completed a tour of the island in vintage cars. For the girls, he had to negotiate a package for a spa day at one of the best five-star hotels on the island, including a champagne reception and lunch. The 'hens' would then be transported by a fleet of limos for an evening of music, drinking and clubbing in Porto Portals, the most glamorous port on the island. I doubted, somehow, that they would be wearing L-plates and glittery head boppers for the occasion.

'Remember, Tomas,' Celia had warned as he took copious notes, 'the budget is generous, but do make the calls in Majorcan so we can get local rather than tourist rates; I imagine it will make quite a difference when you include all of the trimmings . . . Not to mention the fact that each part of the spend will be gone through with a fine toothcomb by the client. Like everyone, they want value for money.'

'Of course,' Tomas agreed, nodding.

'And if the spa menus look like Chinese to you, I'll help you out with what to offer the girls,' I chipped in, dreaming of massages and hot tubs.

Celia turned to me next. As I was in contact with the vineyard, I would be overseeing the final points of the design and set-up of the event, including logistics. This would free up Celia to focus wholly on catering and all of the elements of the wedding ceremony.

Celia unfolded her map of the venue, unveiled her

lists of notes, and started to explain what she had planned. My mind ached within minutes.

First, there was the arrival of the bride and groom by boat from the church (which I had made a start on planning), and a short transfer to the vineyard from the harbour side to organise. Second, there was the set-up of a cocktail bar in the old olive press at the vineyard for the canapé reception, which would utilise the courtyard as well as the other historic rooms on the ground floor of the *finca*. The olive press room was cool, dark and still home to the original machinery used to make oil, but for the wedding it would be filled with candles and a team of 'mixologists', who would be providing a bespoke cocktail made from local oranges and brandy. The main issue to resolve, Celia informed me, was the fact that there was no electricity in the room, so the guys would need to come with ice prepared in buckets and pre-pressed orange juice, and I had to calculate the volumes required. Then, there was the question of uniting the other rooms with the courtyard, offering suggestions for their use and decoration.

'All this preparation, cost and trouble for just one hour's drinks and canapés?' I asked, laughing. It was almost incomprehensible.

'Yes, for just one hour,' Celia confirmed seriously. 'We need to create something special in each room so that the guests utilise all of the spaces,' she said, frowning slightly. She then moved on to the plans for dinner.

It transpired that the bride wanted to emulate an elaborate table decoration on a vast upstairs terrace for a lavish three-hundred-place setting that she had ripped from the pages of *Vogue Living*. The magazine was Australian, and sourcing the identical items on a small Spanish island, for a reasonable price, would be no mean feat. The stylist commissioned to perform the task, Celia explained, was now working in the wake of two who had failed to impress the bride with their efforts and had little time to pull off the almost impossible. Celia warned me that this was a job that needed managing. The budget for the table was large and the end results had to justify it. The magnitude of the task gave me goose bumps. I was just thankful that the caterers had been chosen and the menu, wines and champagne had been agreed. But that wasn't the end of dinner. Oh No!

There was also, Celia informed me, the task of finding a lighting company to illuminate the mountain behind the dining terrace as daylight faded. Then I needed to get the correct permits from the local town hall for a short firework display to coincide with the cutting of the cake. After this, the congregation would be split into ladies and gents who would be entertained in separate rooms.

The gentlemen would retire to the cigar room, which Celia had (thankfully) already organised with Marta. It was to be staged within a grand room on the second floor of the *finca* with a 'private gents club' feel, filled with vintage leather armchairs, an open fireplace, and a large antique table which could be stocked with single malts, a lavish cheese board and fine cigars.

The ladies, during this time, would gather in the 'gossip parlour'. This would be situated in a room with huge white French refectory tables and twinkling chandeliers, which lent itself perfectly to the theme. Here a fleet of male dancers were booked to serve drinks in outfits Celia described as male versions of 'Playboy Bunnies', before ripping them off to perform a sexy dance routine. Celia, to my relief, had found an agency to provide the troupe, but I couldn't resist trying to argue that I needed to vet them as Celia gave me a wicked smile and Tomas raised an eyebrow.

'All this, before embarking on the rather larger task of organising the music and dancing for the evening session,' Celia continued, getting back to business.

Her music agency had sourced a band, which had won client approval, but the final details of designing and executing the Moroccan-style theme including a late-night chill-out area, still had to come together . . . and fast. The bride, I learned, had recently been to Marrakech to source lanterns, cushions and Bedouin throws, the visible evidence of which Celia eagerly awaited.

'She went there just to research the wedding?' I asked out loud, pushing Pepillo down as he jumped up at my chair.

'No!' Celia replied, keeping a straight face. 'Apparently, she went for a party which a friend of hers flew all of her guests out to. Really,' Celia confirmed, seeing my jaw drop. She continued to flesh out details and elaborate plans, and by the end of the briefing my head was spinning.

'We haven't even got to the third day of the event!' I suddenly realised out loud.

'Yes, quite,' Celia replied with a smile, 'but you'll be pleased to know that I've found a super yacht which is coming from the mainland for their charter and I am on to the catering and a DJ.'

I feigned relief. With so much to do, I could see why Celia hadn't wanted to waste another day. But the couple getting married were still a mystery to me.

'So,' I asked Celia, as she started to gather up her paperwork in a neat pile and check her smart Mont Blanc diary for meetings. 'Who are the bride and groom?'

'Oh, media types,' she answered, dismissively. 'He's

an up-and-coming film director, she's a model,' she
sighed. 'I've known her mother for years ... they still
live in Chelsea.'

Tomas, I could see from the corner of my eye, was
shuffling in his seat uncomfortably. I could imagine that
compared to the hours he spent conducting his solitary
research, with just specimens and books for company,
the idea of working on such a vast event with Chelsea
types was a concept alien to him.

As the meeting came to a close, Tomas silently stood
to leave the table but Celia stayed sitting thoughtfully,
appearing to study her notes but clearly not reading
them.

'I was thinking ...' she said, finally breaking the
silence, 'as they are from your world, I thought you
might want to "lead" on the wedding day, Isabelle?'

'Me?' I answered, a little shocked by the enormity of
the task.

'Yes, of course. You, Izzy,' Celia confirmed with a
smile, looking bemused.

The next few weeks were filled with frantic preparations. Although the sun beat down on Celia's stone
house, inside we were almost oblivious to the outside
world as we worked. With Celia's heavy, old-fashioned
phones clamped between our chins and shoulders, we
simultaneously tapped out emails and planning
documents. The rickety old fax machine sucked in our
orders and splurted out information as though it was
taking its last breaths. We received huge parcels stuffed
with Moroccan cushions, lanterns and Kilim fabrics, all
carefully wrapped in jewel-coloured tissue paper. It was
only when I dashed out to meet contractors or to see
Marta at the vineyard, that I enjoyed the big blue skies,
the warm, fragrant air and the searing sunshine.

With each trip to the vineyard I began to know Marta a little better and before long I found myself saving up a list of queries as an excuse to visit. With all of the family working hard on site to produce the vineyard's own successful wine, she was always there and always happy to see me. The whole family would greet me warmly. Marta's father Raul, a gentle, serious man, was in charge of the general running of the vineyard; her older, cheeky brother Paco was head of production; Francesca, Marta's vivacious mother, looked after decoration at the events whilst Marta worked on logistics. For larger events, Marta would enlist her sweet younger brother Juan, his wife Ana, and her pretty teenage sister Margalida to help out. They seemed to be one, big, happy family, all working together, breaking only to enjoy a long lunch in the middle of the day, to which extended family members, babies, children and Marta's grandmother would arrive with a dish to add to the table.

Whenever I visited, Marta would invite me to share a cool glass of water with her from the vineyard's natural spring and we'd take a seat in the courtyard shaded by a lush canopy of vines to chat. As the weeks went by, the water turned into a small tumbler of the vineyard's wine and we'd spend an extra hour chatting after our planning. Marta, I realised, when I first met her that night with Tomas, had been shy. Now, she told me stories of the events and the wine tastings she had organised. We swapped notes on 'bridezillas' and eventually, I, too, was being persuaded to stay for family lunch. I'd succumb, embarrassed that I had nothing to add to the spread, but it didn't seem to matter. Lunch was very social, filled with lively chatter in the local dialect, which the family kindly peppered with English and Spanish as I struggled to understand. Marta served the youngest wine of the vineyard in brown ceramic jugs, sharp cracked olives the family had picked and pickled from their own trees and bread baked freshly in the vineyard's brick oven. Three courses followed. They were humble, traditional and simply delicious, making the most of the fresh, local produce.

At the end of those long, hot days, when I returned to Celia's later than I should have, I'd catch Tomas coming home from his tour of golf courses and spas around the island looking increasingly tanned. He'd shoot me a smile.

'They're all starting to merge into one,' he admitted one afternoon, clutching yet another handful of brochures and price lists along with Celia's digital camera as he came to say 'hello' to Celia in the office and to report back to his groom on his findings.

'Can't say I have any sympathy,' I teased him, glancing over at Celia.

'Do you hear that?' she asked, ignoring me, her face intent on identifying a noise. 'That ringing?'

We all fell silent and listened out for what I assumed would be a bird.

'No, nothing,' Tomas answered. But then it became clearer and increasingly louder. The ringing sounded familiar, a tone I hadn't heard for a long time; it was my English mobile phone. I kicked off my shoes underneath my desk and rushed up to my bedroom barefoot, avoiding Pepillo, who was sprawled across the cool tiles in the hallway.

'Hello?' I finally chirped, out of breath, desperate to catch the caller before they rang off.

'Izzy? Are you all right?' the voice chimed back. 'Sounds like I've interrupted a saucy siesta!'

It was Ray.

'Hey!' I replied excitedly. 'I just ran for the phone.

Sorry about the heavy breathing!' I giggled. 'God, it's GREAT to hear your voice!'

'Yes, thank you, dahling! But you'll have even more of me soon, lucky old you!' he quipped.

I fell silent, not understanding Ray's outburst. Was he working up to asking me if he could plan a visit? That would be so Ray, slag off the place, then want a free holiday . . .

'The wedding, Izzy! I've just fished out the invite, it was so long ago that I sent the RSVP that I'd totally forgotten the details. So, imagine, I'm standing in the flat, looking much better without Marc's things – never did dig his style – did I tell you we split? We're through?'

He continued at lightning speed before I could answer, 'Anyway, so I was thinking, God, was the invite for one or do I need to find a hot date to take? And that was before I could even think about what on earth you wear to a wedding in the sun. Then, whilst contemplating a new Jill Sander suit I'd seen in Arena Homme Plus, I saw at the bottom of the card, all embossed and rather impressive, the location, in Majorca, AND the name of your company . . .'

There was a pause.

'Can you believe it?'

'What, that you've split with Marc? Honey, I'm still over the moon since you announced it on your visit!'

'No, Izzy! That I'm coming to the wedding! Well, I should say *we're* coming to the wedding . . . Everyone's coming!'

I turned to face the mirror on my dressing table, catching my horrified reflection. 'Everyone? What do you mean, everyone?' I could hear the fear in my voice.

'You know . . . Remi, LOADS of magazine types, TONS of people you know from Notting Hill, HALF of

On Fire, including Maddy D-P herself, according to her new PA – not a patch on you, babe, natch . . .' He was on a roll and it was frightening. Absolutely, bloody, buttock-clenchingly frightening. My face in the mirror grew pale with shock and I failed to hear the rest of the list.

'Izzy? You still there?'

'Huh? Sorry?' I mumbled.

'Earth to Izzy? . . . Look, I can't wait to see you,' Ray continued.

'Yes,' I managed slowly.

'Well, you don't sound very excited,' Ray whined, disappointed.

'Can't wait . . . to see you too,' I managed. 'No, really . . . I can't, but it's all a lot . . . to take in,' I admitted nervously, making my excuses to sign off. A hell of a lot to take in. I had no choice but to hide the horror I felt on discovering that my old life would be following me to Majorca. I did my best to calmly pretend that everything was perfectly normal in front of Celia and Tomas, but the more I thought about it, the more my paranoia increased. There would be people who would judge me, people who would think I'd run away to hide, people who would want to see me fail, and people who might tell Celia or, even worse, the bride, how things had really ended at On Fire. I hated the fact that I was concerned about what they would think, but I couldn't deny that it bothered me. Enormously!

By day, I checked and double-checked every detail of my planning meticulously. By night, I started to have my own wedding-anxiety dreams, those 'what if' night-mares, suffered by the most nervous brides.

I dreamed of Maddy (my evil former boss) making a huge scene in the church on spotting me, demanding at the top of her screeching voice that the wedding be stopped as it would undoubtedly be a disaster. That Remi (my self-obsessed former friend) was poking my belly and laughing and yelling 'TTY!' (taller, thinner, younger) on greeting me in front of a fleet of impossibly thin bridesmaids as I stood before them in just a tiny bikini and a snorkel. That Celia had raised her hand when the priest asked 'Does anyone know of any reason why these two people should not be joined . . .' 'Yes,' she had keenly interrupted from the back, 'I need to fire the wedding planner!' I imagined the cortège giggling, fingers pointing from guests shadowed in the pews and whispers from behind raised hymn books. I imagined the snide comments from the office bitches on seeing me dressed in last season's clothes, fighting the contented Spanish spread my figure had developed and witnessing my sad life after television.

As the days passed, the dreams increased in their frequency and I almost always awoke feeling humiliated. Finally, one morning, as I opened my eyes and realised that I'd had my first good night's sleep in ages, I bolted upright in bed. I couldn't believe that I hadn't yet considered it: there was a fair chance that *he* might be invited. Harrisson.

I hid my eyes in my hands and let out a frustrated 'Arrrrgggggghhh!', shaking my head from side to side. I wanted to crawl back beneath the covers and hide till the whole wedding was over and it was safe to come out again, knowing that the people of Notting Hill were on a return flight home, but it wasn't an option, not even for a few hours. This morning, Marta was expecting me at the vineyard.

I was thrown into a panic, my stomach was groaning anxiously and I felt dizzy with nausea. I skipped breakfast, grabbed my documents, and jumped on the Vespino, taking the winding mountain road up to the vineyard to meet Marta. My mind was swimming but the fresh morning air went some way to easing my head a little and the road, dappled in shade and lined with pines, provided a cool retreat for a few minutes. I even felt my shoulders drop a little as I listened to the sound of birdsong, as the olive trees parted to reveal views of the mountains as I approached the grand stone *finca*. I eased back the throttle to gently ride to the top of the drive, past the fields of vines and gardens bursting with colour. Marta was already waiting for me at the entrance to the *finca*, waving. As I stopped the engine and took off my riding hat she came running straight over.

'Isobel, *Hola!* I thought I hear your bike,' she started in her almost perfect English, calling me by the Spanish version of my name as always. 'But you are early, no?'

'Am I?' I answered, oblivious to the hour, my head still racing. 'Is it OK to start early for you?' I asked.

She shrugged her shoulders and nodded happily in response before greeting me with a kiss on both cheeks and a smile.

'Anyway, how are you?' I continued, still flustered. 'Beautiful day, isn't it?'

'Of course it is a good day. This is Majorca!' she giggled back. 'Come, let's have some coffee,' she said, slowly leading the way. 'And maybe you'd like an *ensaimada*?'

I looked down at my watch as I followed Marta through the vast wooden doors which guarded the front of the *finca* and led to its rustic stone courtyard. She was right, it was only just eight a.m. and Marta, I noticed, as my eyes followed her small frame draped in a white cotton kaftan, was barefoot.

'I will just get dressed and make the coffee,' she said, signalling for me to take a seat and pushing her hair out of her face. 'Then, Isobel,' she announced seriously after a pause, 'you must tell me what is wrong.' Before I had the chance to answer or protest, Marta had turned to head inside.

Alone in the courtyard I fumbled in my oversized tote for my meeting notes. 'How had Marta known?' I asked myself, cussing at how the bag seemed so large that finding anything was impossible. 'How had she seen that I was upset?' I rummaged through old receipts and chewing-gum wrappers that lurked with other debris in the bottom of the bag. I discarded a lip balm and finally pulled out my paperwork and a pen, placing them on the wooden table in front of me. I took in a deep breath. The sun was just starting to peep through the lush, green vines entwined with bunches of fat black grapes that provided a canopy over the courtyard, its heat already strong, despite the hour. I took another breath. 'Mustn't well up,' I told myself. 'Get a grip, Izzy.' I had to preoccupy my mind. I let my eyes study the space and went through a mental checklist for the wedding decoration, my new favourite game.

The courtyard suddenly felt very large with just me in it. I imagined it filled with people at the champagne reception and deliberately tried not to visualise their faces. 'This is work, Izzy. Come on,' I told myself, looking around. There was an old stone well, which Marta's mother Maria had decorated with a tin jug filled with cream flowers on a rope pulley. Behind the well, a flight of stone steps led up to the second floor of the *finca*, which I would be covering with sumptuous Moroccan cushions for the wedding. To my right were three handsome wooden doors decorated with heavy ironwork. I walked over to them, to see if they would open at a gentle push, to remind myself of the layout. The first door led to the olive press room where the 'mixologists' would produce their cocktails. Here I had to cover every stone surface in candles and Moroccan lanterns and remove the ceramic pots and hand-blown olive jars that were usually there. The second door led to the old stable complete with sawdust floor and antique horse riding tack. I'd enlisted the help of Marta's brothers to help move in some tables, chairs, flowers and patterned tea glasses, for those wanting to drink somewhere out of the heat. The third, generous room, was home to the cellar or *bodega*, and here I would place vast wooden bowls filled with oranges on top of the scrubbed wooden tables which Marta used for the wine tastings, and drape the furniture with Moorish throws. I made notes and took measurements inside the cool, dark, rooms, counting invisible candles, estimating how many chairs would be needed in each, imagining piles of cushions.

'*Vale*,' Marta said softly from the doorway, making me jump slightly. 'Come, let's sit.'

Marta's face beamed a smile, a happy, contented, relaxed smile. In under ten minutes she'd switched her kaftan for a simple lemon cotton sundress and flat rope-bottomed espadrilles, and had managed to produce a tray of coffee, hot milk and sweet flaky *ensaimadas*.

I pulled out a chair and sat back down.

'*Mira*,' she said, pushing an *ensaimada* towards me and pouring the coffee into tiny *cortado* cups, 'tell me what is the matter.'

'No, really, I'm fine,' I protested at the pastries as well as the shoulder to cry on.

Marta flashed a raised eyebrow and an unbelieving look.

'Let's start with the arrival of the guests, shall we?' I asked, trying to change the subject to the wedding as I nervously scratched at a large mosquito bite on my leg.

'Isobel!' Marta protested. 'It's OK . . . *por favor*, let's talk first, eees OK, you can talk to me,' she pleaded gently.

I felt my eyes sting with hot tears and I fought them back. Marta looked away, embarrassed, and over to her brother crossing the courtyard, nodding him a silent *hola*. When she turned back to me, the tears were streaming down my face.

'Sorry,' I snuffled, reaching for one of Marta's paper napkins on which to blow my nose and pat my eyes dry at the corners. 'I'm just being silly.'

'I don't think it's silly if you are sad,' Marta soothed, placing her hand on my shoulder from across the table.

'I'm not really sad,' I managed, my throat tight, 'I'm just . . . well . . .'

'You're worried about the wedding?' Marta asked, encouraging me to tell her more.

'Yes, I guess . . .' I sobbed.

'Ah OK, but you are good organiser, Isobel, you have nothing to worry about,' Marta said kindly, her accent thick and her eyes wide, as she passed me another napkin.

'It's not really about that,' I replied, forcing a smile, tipping my head back to stop the tears. 'This isn't like the other weddings.'

'Because at the vineyard we must organise everything, not like hotel?' Marta enquired. 'Because you are worried about generator, decoration, all the things usually already there before you think about the wedding?'

'No,' I interrupted her. 'That's OK. It is more . . . work,' I said with an attempt at a laugh, 'but it's OK and I trust we will all work together well to do this . . .'

'*Sí!*' She beamed at me. 'Good collaboration!' She paused. 'But then I don't understand.' Marta gave up her guessing game to pour herself a second coffee.

'It's the people who are coming to the wedding . . .' I said very quietly.

Marta looked puzzled.

'The people I used to work with . . . in London,' I explained. 'The people I used to know, who lived where I lived . . . I just found out that they are coming.'

'Ah, but this is nice for you, to see friends . . . and . . .' Marta stopped mid-sentence as I gave up the fight with the tears and resorted to incomprehensible sobbing. She waited till I gained my composure.

'You don't like these people?' she asked, looking at me with surprise.

'Some of them . . . but, well, some of them . . . are not so nice.' I felt foolish now. 'I don't know where to start, Marta,' I answered, genuinely. 'Well, one of the people who I think might come, is my . . . my . . . ex-boyfriend.'

Marta's eyes grew even larger. Our coffees and pastries lay untouched in front of us.

Composing myself enough to elaborate, I started to tell Marta everything, right from the beginning. I explained how I'd melted into a jelly-legged wreck when I'd first started to date Harrisson after the photo shoot at The Love Café. And how, after he'd taken me out to congratulate me on getting the job at On Fire, we'd started to see each other regularly. I told Marta how I'd been so impressed by his arty job and the celebrities he worked with, his good looks, designer clothes and velvety voice. Marta giggled and finally took a sip from her coffee cup, relaxing back into her chair to enjoy the tale.

'I was happy to listen and be bewitched as he held court every time we went out together,' I explained. I told Marta how I'd enjoyed the chase and unpredictability of our dates, of not knowing when he'd turn up and whisk me away for dinner, an afternoon at a fairground or to a party in Paris. 'The pure escapism and romance of it all,' I sighed, remembering those weekends he'd book us into luxurious hotels or drive down to the seaside, so we could eat fish and chips out of newspaper, walking along the promenade. It had all seemed so glamorous and so much fun. My mind drifted as Marta broke off a small flaky piece of *ensaimada*. I remembered how I loved falling into Harrisson's bed after Sunday lunch on a drizzly grey afternoon and escaping from the real world till Monday morning came around.

'I felt lucky to be dating a man who was exciting, unpredictable, always up to something different,' I continued. 'I didn't mind that he'd get caught up in work for weeks on end and not call. I told myself that of course he'd be busy. I didn't mind that he showed little interest in my life – my past, my family, my friends, my job. I told myself that of course he had much more exciting things to preoccupy him. But after a while he made me feel that, somehow, I was not quite deserving of his attention. Everything seemed to come before me. Work, friends, "the something urgent" that would crop up on a Friday night when he had promised to take me to a club ... or on a Sunday when we'd planned to go to Tate Modern. I began to become paranoid he was two timing me, dating other girls, but I was never really sure.' Marta, relishing the last few bites of her *ensaimada*, gave me a knowing look. 'Whether he was or not, he let me down one time too often and in the end, I blew my top, told him I was sick of it.'

'And then you told him it was over?' Marta asked, licking the tips of her fingers.

'Well, not exactly. I didn't have the courage. I just left London and he left me a message on my mobile to say that he guessed it was over.'

'So he doesn't know you are here or organising the weddings?'

'No, I don't think so,' I answered, realising that it could also be a shock for him too, if he did show up. My stomach grumbled again at the thought. 'And I have been told that he is engaged to marry.' Marta let out a little gasp in sympathy.

'Oh Marta, there is more,' I added. 'The people who are coming, some of these friends, they are from the last company I worked in, and I was . . . well, sacked.'

'Sacked?' Marta asked, rolling the word around her mouth, screwing up her face, not knowing the term.

'Fired,' I said uncomfortably. 'They asked me to leave . . . and the woman in charge, who fired me, is coming as well!' I could hear a catch in my voice as I said it.

'Oh, don't worry, Isobel, this sometimes happen,' Marta soothed. 'I'm sure you did nothing bad . . .' She moved on pretty quickly, not probing or asking any questions.

'So,' she added decisively, 'there is only one thing for it.'

'There is?' I asked, hoping she had some genius escape plan.

'Ah! Yes, you're right,' I said, butting in, the obvious suddenly hitting me between the eyes. 'The guest list . . . I need to check the guest list. I'm such an idiot! I could have done that this morning!'

'No, Isobel, it is too late for this now. Whether he come or just these other people. You have to look *guapisima*!' Marta's eyes danced with excitement.

I cringed. It was almost a reflex action.

'No, no, Isobel . . . *mira*,' Marta started to explain forcefully, with the wag of her finger. 'If they are coming, they are coming, there is nothing you can do. So . . . you must be prepared. You do your job and you look your best so that you feel good – you know, have the controls on the day, and so that he, this man and these friends you tell me of, they see that you've moved on and are successful and happy, no?'

'Really? You think?' I asked.

'Yes! We must go to Palma. You must have the right thing to wear and maybe we do something with your hair . . .' Marta trailed off, studying me intently.

'Palma?' I repeated, surprised at the suggestion. 'Marta, you're so sweet. You're right, there is nothing I can do, I just have to do my job. But really, I can find something to wear at home and maybe just take a little more care when I get ready.'

'Pah!' Marta dismissed with a wave of her hand. 'This is not the same, we have to go shopping in the city for you. Why not today?' she suggested, pleased by the thought.

I hadn't realised that I'd become quite so keen to break the shopping habits of a lifetime, habits that had been teetering on the ridiculous side of obsessive consumption, till I'd left London. Something, I realised now, had changed when I came here. The clothes I'd brought with me had become worn old friends, I'd stopped lusting after the latest dresses, coolest jeans and killer heels in magazines, my *Vogues*, left unread on my bedside table, had been usurped by Celia's Penguin Classics. And I certainly didn't miss my London routine of agonising over what to wear to work. These days I loved nothing better than adopting a safe uniform I didn't need to think about and spending more time in bed in the mornings. The only time I'd tried to dress for a date . . . well . . . I looked up at Marta. Maybe I'd gone too far? Maybe this was Marta's way of telling me? Perhaps I was turning into a slob, one of those women who's ridiculed and made-over on TV, who started out looking a little jaded, but ended up going through the ringer to explore parts of her body she didn't know existed in communal changing rooms and wearing clothes so inappropriate for her age that her teenage daughters had no choice but to disown her . . .

'Isobel!' Marta pleaded again, bringing my paranoid thoughts back to the present. 'Come, there is no reason why we cannot go now!'

It was obvious that Marta wasn't going to take no for an answer.

'I just take this inside, then we go,' she announced. 'The time, anyway, is only nine-thirty.'

'But the meeting?' I objected pathetically.

'We will talk on the way!' Marta replied, her back to me as she carried the tray away.

'Celia is expecting me in the office after . . .' I yelled back, making another excuse, but it was no use, Marta had disappeared.

I let out a deep sigh and looked up. The sun was playing shadow chase on the table, shafts of white-hot light cutting through the vines as the almost breathless, warm breeze gently ruffled the leaves. It would be hot in the city, I thought. Steamy. And I'd be worrying about the work that awaited my return to the office . . .

'You look . . . how do you say in English, grumpy!' Marta quipped, laughing as she appeared again, with a straw bag slung over her shoulder. 'Isobel, this should be fun,' she added, waving her car keys at me with a grin.

Marta, I discovered, was the owner of a battered, white Renault 4 that looked like it might have been used as a stock car, or at least had lived a long life as a workhorse. Its bodywork wore its scars and scrapes proudly. Inside, the shabby plastic seats were ripped and smelt of ripe tomatoes, the floor was littered with cardboard wine boxes, carrying the vineyard's logo, and a sad, forgotten cat basket lay on the back seat. Marta had parked under the shade of a generous mulberry tree, but heat seemed to pour out of the creaky doors as she opened them for us to climb in. She shrugged her shoulders saying, 'This is normal,' with a smile, and I followed her lead of waiting a few moments for the fresh air to circulate before getting in beside her.

As I opened my bag to check I was carrying money and a credit card, Marta revved up the engine and sped off with a start, rocking us in our seats. My eyes were still focused on my handbag and my stomach lurched forward. Marta, it was apparent within five minutes, was a crazy driver, all last-minute turns, late signals and frantic horn-blowing at any opportunity. I couldn't believe that the same girl behind the wheel was the pretty, shy thing I'd met with Tomas just several weeks before.

Despite my reticence, the drive to the city was fun. Marta asked, 'You want air-conditioning, Isobel?' and wound down the windows when I nodded. 'You want music?' she asked next, turning the huge dial on her ancient, hissing radio till it found a channel. '*Estupendo!*' she proclaimed at finding a channel devoted to Spanish pop beats, and she sang along enthusiastically, tapping the steering wheel in time. 'This song is *numero uno!*' she announced happily, a little figure of Jesus swaying in time from her rear-view mirror.

Marta took a call on her mobile as we approached the city on a route I'd not yet explored. She clamped the tiny phone between her shoulder and her ear, talking quickly in her sing-song Spanish as she changed gears and steered, taking on the traffic, speeding against expensive sports and hire cars. The road circled statues, grand avenues and historic stone buildings before widening to four lanes. The city was already busy. Cafés were full of workers taking their morning break, of ladies dressed in high-heeled shoes and smart clothes, rushing to appointments, tourists ambling lazily in the heat, Spanish kids in jeans, hanging out on school holidays. She drove into the middle of the lanes and down to a car park that seemed to be situated in the middle of the road, without slowing down. Then she negotiated the steep slope down and we parked up, keen to leave the heady fug of the heat below ground and to emerge in the middle of the city.

'You like Palma, no?' Marta asked as I looked around me. The architecture was impressive. The Ramblas, lined with flower sellers, trailed off to our left, the road leading to the grand historic centre to our right.

'Yes, it's beautiful,' I replied, taking it all in.

'But it's big, no? So . . . where shall we start?'

It was a good question. I looked down at my watch. It was wonderful to be out of the office, exploring again. It was something I only ever did in my spare time, which, with weddings most weekends, was seldom. It felt decadent. A little bit naughty . . .

'Tranquilo!' Marta soothed, seeing my clock-watching. 'We can just pick a few shops where we can get something special!' she said excitedly. 'It need not take so long.'

'Good idea,' I replied, gratefully. 'How about we start at Corner?' Corner was a series of boutiques in the city that stocked the trendiest designer brands, the kind that the wedding guests would be turning up in.

'Sure!' said Marta. 'This way!'

We headed down the Borne with its wide

pedestrianised centre lined with bronze sculptures and bright red petunias in terracotta pots, and took the turning that led into the Centro Traversial, a narrow winding street of neverending steps lined with lovely shops and cafés. The first Corner store was just at the beginning, actually on the corner itself.

The white marble floor and fierce air-conditioning was a welcome respite from the heat outside and gave me goose bumps. A smiling assistant greeted us as we cooed over the Miu Miu shoes and bags on display at the steps that led upstairs to the clothing collections.

'*Que preciosa!*' Marta cooed, engrossed in a rail of Etro dresses of Paisley chiffons, swirling patterns and beautiful colours, perfectly displayed.

'Maybe a bit much for the planner?' I asked her, gawping at the prices in disbelief. 'But they would look wonderful on you,' I said truthfully.

'In-cre-dible,' Marta whispered to a Marni dress, its sheer fabric covered in an op-art print.

The shop assistant trailed close behind us, pretending to dust a shelf, or move a handbag slightly to a better position, obviously wanting to help with a size, or secure a sale. I wondered how she kept up the pretence of being busy. The shop was so immaculate, what could there be to do? The piles of Seven jeans were folded just so, a dust-free portrait of Audrey Hepburn smiled down on a collection of precisely presented accessories. It even smelt clean; a lemony, zesty clean.

My eyes feasted on the clothes. The simple silk separates on the Miu Miu rail were smart but still quirky and beautiful, in classic colours, but still way over my budget. The Paul Smith collection made me think of England, giving me my first fleeting pang of homesickness. But none of the garments seemed realistic.

'Marta,' I said softly, so the assistant couldn't hear, 'I think this is a bit out of my league, price-wise. Let's go!' Marta nodded and led the way out. Back on the street we contemplated the other Corner boutiques before moving from our spot. This had been the middle-range; the one that stocked Chloé and Prada was just not a consideration. From the prices I'd seen last year in London, nor was the third store that featured Marc Jacobs, D Squared and Stella McCartney ('Who?' Marta asked, but it wasn't worth explaining).

'I have it!' Marta exclaimed as we meandered up the steps of the street in search of inspiration.

'The discount Corner, you know it?'

The words sounded heavenly to my ears. Discount. That sounded good for once. 'Sort of labels for less?' I asked.

'*Exacto*,' Marta confirmed, gently tugging at my arm to change direction. We paced down through the backstreets, arm in arm, past the back entrances of shops, towards a narrowing alleyway. Here, I found to my delight, was the store that my favourite labels came to rest in when they didn't get snapped up in the sales. It was a treasure trove of seasons past. Shoes piled high on top of boxes, rails jammed full of colourful garments, and thick velvet curtains for a changing room, all jostled for space.

Hmmm, I contemplated, wincing at a lime-green Pucci print top that greeted me at the doorway. No wonder it didn't sell. On closer inspection of the rails I found a beautiful Gucci dress in too small a size, a pair of beautiful silver heels that were just too high and a few signature pieces that screamed too loudly of particular seasons.

Marta was wrestling with a pair of toffee-coloured sandals, trying to manipulate the supple leather to make them fit, laughing with the shop assistant in Spanish. I trawled the rails avidly, deciding that if I could find something classic in my size, it wouldn't matter that it was from a previous collection. At least it would look classy.

'What about theees?' Marta said excitedly, picking out a demure Prada dress which would cling to me in all of the wrong places.

'Not sure,' I said honestly. 'Thanks, though,' I added as I turned back to the rails and as I did, I saw them. A simple, crisp, cotton shirt in the sharpest cut and a pair of simple Miu Miu marine-blue cigarette pants in beautiful brushed cotton. Items I'd never look twice at in England.

'*Puedo probar?*' I asked the assistant, rushing to the changing room to try them before getting an answer.

'Isobel?' Marta called moments later from the other side of the curtain. 'Let me see!'

Before I showed the outside world, I studied my reflection. I'd never dressed this way before, but somehow it seemed to work. Maybe that was the appeal. It was smart, European, sophisticated. I span around momentarily, straining to see from all angles, and decided that it was also flattering.

'*Que guapa! Que elegante!*' Marta shrieked with delight as I drew the curtain back. The shop assistant nodded and then held up a finger to signal she had an idea. Moments later she rushed back with a pair of the softest Spanish leather pumps and a great pair of sunglasses.

'Very Jackie Onassis!' she proclaimed in her broken English.

'*Si!*' agreed Marta.

I had the assistant wrap the lot in an instant. At eighty per cent discount, I'd have been crazy not to, I thought as Marta and I left the shop, saying our '*Hasta Luegos*' to the sweet assistant. And besides, I needed a replacement for the shoes Pepillo had chewed, I justified, before I gave way to a pang of guilt.

'Coffee?' Marta asked, as I slung the bag of designer goodies over my shoulder.

'Yes, I guess we still have the meeting to go over,' I said, smiling.

14

In Control

A day out of the office had been just what I needed. Maybe shopping was still my therapy, I mused, as I closed my bedroom door on the outside world to marvel at my recently purchased treasures that evening. In the cool atmosphere of my dark room, windows and shutters closed tightly against the still-scorching sun, I laid out the contents of the shiny new bag on my bed. I carefully unwrapped each of the garments, leaving a pool of aqua tissue paper to rest on the cotton sheets as I lifted up the items to inspect them. I noted the perfect crease of the pants, the subtle, soft colour of the pumps, the intricate, stitched detail in the shirt, the way that everything smelt the way only new clothes do, a state in which I'd never enjoy them again. I put on the sunglasses and checked my reflection in the mirror. I played around with my hair, pulling it off my face, checking my profile, remembering Marta's advice to do something with it, but not knowing what. Then I let it drop loose with a start, on hearing a firm knock at my door.

'Oh, hi!' I smiled at Tomas, who was eyeing me strangely from the other side.

'Hello, Izzy,' he replied formally, standing back awkwardly from the door. He paused for a moment, a puzzled look crossing his brow.

'Izzy, sorry, but I have to ask . . . why are you wearing sunglasses indoors?'

'Ah!' I giggled, pulling the door to behind me, so that he wouldn't see the decadent spend sprawled out on my bed. 'Just, well, you know, resting my eyes,' I replied pathetically, 'instead of having a siesta.'

'But it's almost seven-thirty!' he blurted, baffled.

Tomas, I could see, had just showered. His skin smelt fresh, his tan glowing against a crisp white T-shirt. His hair was still wet from a wash and neatly combed back. Beneath his glasses, a line of freckles I'd not noticed before danced across the bridge of his nose.

'Celia's been in the office all day,' he explained, 'so I thought I'd take her out to the port for a drink. Thought you might like to join us?'

'That's very sweet of you,' I replied, noticing the colour of his eyes magnified by his accidental tan. 'I've been out of the office myself quite a bit today, so I thought I'd do some catching up this evening,' I said, resisting the lure of a long drink and a sea view. I still felt guilty about my impromptu trip into town.

'Not to worry,' he said, making his excuses to whisk Celia away. 'I'll leave you with Pepillo.'

'Sure.' I smiled, gritting my teeth at the thought of the scraggy runt.

Home alone, I wandered out into the garden. The sun was still bright in the sky and a milky heat haze still lingered over the mountains, but the evening air felt several degrees cooler and a welcome relief from the intense heat of the afternoon. A dragonfly darted over Celia's well. A wall of succulents had unfurled the pink petals of their flowers to bask in the rays. Out beyond the terrace, the stone pathway of Celia's garden felt warm and smooth under my bare feet. The heady scent of the pale pink rose bush was delicious. I took a seat, in one of Celia's favourite spots, and took in the view. The house and the valley were perfectly quiet and for the first time in weeks, I just sat, enjoying the stillness.

I felt like a different person from the one who had started the day. I had a new outfit, one that was grown up and sophisticated, to show that I knew what I was doing. I had resigned myself to the fact that the wedding guests were coming and I would do all I could to be ready for them. And if that included Harrisson, so be it. My outpour to Marta, I had to admit, had only confirmed my feeling that the whole dynamic of the relationship had been wrong. I just had a few details to iron out in the planning and I was all set . . . but not quite. First, I had Marta to thank.

Later that evening I made myself a large salad and ventured up to the office to give Marta a call. With my stomach rumbling hungrily for food, I found myself answering emails between mouthfuls before making the call, the plate balanced precariously on my desk. Waiting in my inbox was a sweet thank-you note from Francesca, my Italian bride, who'd just returned from a honeymoon in the Maldives, two new enquiries from girls wanting to plan weddings for the following year, and several polite 'to do' lists from Celia. I got stuck into Celia's notes straight away, prioritising a list of jobs to tackle. With few distractions in the office, the atmosphere almost museum-like, the light soft and the temperature comfortable, I became engrossed in work, soon forgetting the time and almost half of my supper. Finally, as I let out a yawn and indulged in a stretch, noticing a blaze of purple and red sunset over the valley like a vibrant watercolour painting, I decided it was time to forget about work. I picked up the heavy, old-fashioned phone and dialled Marta's number.

'*Si, digame,*' a voice demanded grumpily, an elderly voice I recognised as belonging to Marta's grandmother.

'*Buenas noches, soy Isabelle,*' I trilled gaily.

'*Hola, Isobel!*' Grandma replied, in a now friendly tone. '*Como va? Momentito, por favor. Maaaaarrrttta!*' I heard her screech loudly, her hand over the receiver. A gentle commotion followed in the background.

After a few moments, I heard the patter of Marta's tiny feet on the terracotta floor.

'Hola, Isobel!' she said happily. '*Va bien?*'

'It *is* going well, thanks to you, Marta!' I replied jollily. 'In fact, I was just calling to thank you for today. I really appreciate it and everything you have done for me . . . *muchisimas gracias!*'

'*De nada, Isobel!* I hope you feel better about the wedding, *si?*'

'Yes much, much better, thanks,' I replied gratefully. 'Not just about the wedding, but about *everything* . . . You know, Marta, when I first came to Majorca I felt that nothing would go right,' I confided, staring out of the office window as the sky darkened to a deep violet. 'I messed up my other job, the one I told you about. I made mistakes. And I doubted that I could take on anything with responsibility again. But now I feel that maybe I *can* do it, maybe I can do something well. I just need to focus, not be distracted, because with the right people helping me, people like you and Celia, I can learn and I can become more confident. I didn't ever think it was possible before. I felt as though I would always be running from one disaster to another . . . and not just with work, with relationships too.'

'*Si*, this Harrisson, no?' Marta agreed.

'Yes, exactly, but friendships too. You know, today was so special because you were so selfless taking me shopping.'

'Self . . . less?' Marta asked, rolling the new word around her mouth.

'Yes, not selfish . . .' I tried to explain, but Marta's silent response seemed to call for an explanation. 'For example, in England, I'd go shopping with my friend Remi and it would always be about her grabbing the best bargains, being competitive about what she already owned, or had to have, and I always ended up feeling too fat, frumpy or unfashionable to have fun . . .'

'Nooo!' Marta said, her voice low in disbelief. 'This is no friend!'

'Really. There was one time, when we were going to a party,' I explained, 'and Remi had borrowed a stunning, gold lamé Gucci dress from the wardrobe department of a magazine she'd just styled a shoot for. She told me that she'd ordered it in for the shoot, knowing that she could wear it that night and that no one would ever know . . . and then she told me that she'd take me shopping, because she wouldn't be seen dead with me if I didn't look right at the party. Can you believe that?' Marta let out a little gasp. 'Then, when we were shopping, she decided that she'd look much better in the outfit she'd picked out for me and bought it for herself! Just as the shops were closing.'

'So you had nothing to wear?'

'Exactly. Well, I did have plenty of things at home which I would have worn, but she'd convinced me that all of them made me look like a total monster!'

'Dios mio!' Marta exclaimed. 'Here in Majorca, this is not what friendship is.'

'I see that and I know we've not known each other long, and that I don't speak your language, but I wanted to tell you just how much I appreciate you taking me shopping.'

'But Isobel, this is how friendship is, you don't need to thank me. One day, you may do something for me . . . and in the meantime, we do things together, no? Have a good time, enjoy life . . .'

'Yes! I'd like that,' I answered, smiling to myself. 'But I don't know how long I'll be here . . . I'm waiting to see what happens at the end of the wedding season. After this final wedding I will have to decide whether to stay here, or go back to England.'

'And you don't know yet?'

'No, I guess . . . not.'

'But Isobel, it doesn't matter, we are friends now, no? I am here for you, even when you are in London.' Marta paused. I couldn't imagine having such support from someone I had so recently met in London. I'd seldom had such understanding or unconditional friendship from my family, let alone a friend!

'You know, Isobel,' Marta continued, 'you have friends in Majorca, people in Majorca who care about you. There is one person in particular, with whom you could be very, very close . . .'

I didn't know if it was Marta's English or if I just didn't understand what she was getting at.

'There is?' I asked.

'Si,' Marta said. 'Tomas.'

'Tomas?'

'Si, Isobel, Tomas . . .' Marta repeated before pausing. 'Isobel, you do know that he . . . how you say it . . . is in love with you?'

Matrimonial Mediterranean Media Madness!

An unwelcome beam of bright white sunlight streamed through a gap in the shutters, the sound of a proud but discordant cockerel echoed through the valley, signalling the start of a new day. Not just any day, but the day of the big wedding, *the* wedding, *that* wedding, the wedding I could do nothing to avoid! It had arrived so quickly and the preparations had taken so long, that, as I dressed, it was almost impossible to believe that the dreaded event had finally arrived.

I carefully stepped into my new cigarette pants, making a concerted effort to slow down my mind as it raced through a mental checklist. I buttoned down the crisp, white shirt, focusing on staying calm. As I combed my hair and willed it into a sleek, neat ponytail, I pushed all thoughts of weight gain, inadequacy and nervousness at seeing former colleagues to the very back of my mind. I'd managed, so far, not to let these bubble to the surface and I'd not even entertained Marta's crazy idea about Tomas. Today, I had to give everything to the wedding, to the bride and to Celia. It was, I realised, everything that I'd worked towards since I came to Majorca. I owed it to myself to do a good job. I knew that my performance would determine if I was able to stay and seeing half of Notting Hill in Majorca would help me decide if I wanted to. But right now, that idea was just too big to consider. I wrapped it up neatly in a mental box and stored it for later.

Downstairs, the kitchen was silent. Pepillo lay fast asleep on his gnarled blanket, a single fly buzzing above his water bowl. A pot of late-night coffee had been left to go cold on the top of the oven and Pep, the gardener, I could see from the window, had just arrived. His flat corduroy cap was pulled down over his head against the sun and he was clasping a plastic supermarket bag filled with tomatoes from his own garden, presumably a gift for Celia, in his work-worn hand.

Careful not to splash the water, I refilled the stainless-steel coffee pot, sliced some of yesterday's bread, and scrambled some local farm eggs, marvelling at the golden yolks as the silky orbs slid into the white china bowl. I ate breakfast alone, with Pepillo at my feet. He had awoken excitedly on hearing the toaster whirr before he could even smell the toast browning. I dared him to chew my new pumps and threw him a crust as a precaution. He chomped it noisily, his one good eye firmly fixed on my plate in the hope of more.

As the kitchen clock struck nine, I washed my dishes, handed Pep a cup of strong black coffee in exchange for the tomatoes, and piled the vibrant fruit into a wide ceramic bowl.

I grabbed my bag, popped on my shades, and headed out to the Vespino, feeling the crunch of the gravelled drive beneath my new slippy leather soles. My day was always going to start much earlier than Tomas's and Celia's. I'd been invited to join Layla, the bride, and her bridesmaids at the end of their champagne breakfast, to go through some final checks and to see if they needed anything before they began to get ready. At first, I'd been nervous at the thought. I'd imagined seeing Remi and countless modelling friends of the bride looking beautiful yet still bitching over who the make-up artist would tackle first, who had the best tan, the best date, the best dress, the best pedi, the best wax! Revving the bike, I shuddered again, then immediately stopped myself. I *had* to stay positive. Best to see the bridesmaids first and to check that Layla was OK, before tackling the rest of the day, I told myself. Besides, I figured, seeing Remi, an old friend, a friendly face, should kick off the day to a good start.

The journey to the city was hot and hectic. Weaving through the rush-hour traffic and avoiding a constant stream of indecisively driven hire cars, I swooped down into the city and into the historic centre, passing the narrow streets that led to the various five-star hotels that the guests were staying in. In the months leading up to the wedding, there'd been an almighty battle for the most desirable addresses and the most lavish suites. Those that had been featured in *Condé Nast Traveller* magazine, enjoyed column inches in glossy Sunday supplements or had the most glamorous reputation, were highly coveted. Never before had I encountered such room-envy. Never before had guests been cheeky enough to try to book themselves into the same boutique hotel as the bride behind her back, when she had reserved all eleven rooms just for her family and bridesmaids. And the groom's all-male stay at a well-known hotel with its own chic beach club, had been unsuccessfully boycotted by several single girls. Celia, as always, was not going to stand for such behaviour.

Layla's choice of hotel was a grand, stately building with high-corniced ceilings and vast marble halls, where elegant Spanish antiques and original features had been mixed with luxurious, contemporary finishes. There was a decadent bar, a lavish wood-panelled dining room, and a black-slate swimming pool graced the roof, enabling guests to swim or sunbathe on vast grey steel loungers, whilst enjoying views of the cathedral. I parked the bike, pulled off my riding hat, smoothed my hair back into place, and took a very deep breath. I'd booked the girls the sumptuous chill-out area on the terrace, usually closed for breakfast, so they could enjoy the exclusive use of the area whilst they nibbled on fruit and croissants. I was hoping it would earn me some early brownie points and put everyone in good spirits for the day.

Crossing the street, swinging my bag over my shoulder and checking my mobile for missed calls, I walked purposefully towards the etched-glass doors at the hotel entrance. But before I could reach them, I looked up from my phone on hearing an enormous and very English commotion. A hysterical girl was running out on to the street. Dressed in a tiny chartreuse silk slip, she was wailing incomprehensibly. I felt my jaw drop. Was she OK? Was she being chased? Under attack? A shiny black bob framed the now bright-red face, moving like a shampoo advert in slow-motion as she shook her head in utter despair. As passers-by made way and a moped performed a skidding emergency stop as she stepped out into the middle of the road, I came to a shocking realisation. It was Remi. I picked up speed, to reach her as quickly as possible, and began to decipher her cries of despair. 'MOTHS ATE MY PRADA ... MOTHS *ATE* MY PRADAAAAA!' She stopped dead and fell silent on spotting me.

'IZZY!' she screeched.

'Are you all right?' I asked. 'How are you, it's great to see you, Remi!'

'No, I'm absolutely bloody not all right,' Remi started, the redness of her cheeks still glowing furiously, a stray eyelash fluttering on an angular cheekbone.

'Izzy, you HAVE to help me,' she demanded assertively. 'I'm *supposed* to be the Maid Of Honour. I'm also *supposed* to be at Layla's champagne breakfast in precisely five minutes. But no! *Nothing's* that simple!' Remi whined like a spoilt brat. 'I was just going to hang up my outfit for today as I got dressed to go downstairs and I unzipped my holdall to find THIS!'

I squinted in the sunlight. Remi was clutching a chiffon wisp of a dress, so small I'd not noticed it. The dress, I could see now, was a complex swirl of subtle-coloured fabric, delicate figures hand-painted on to the silk. It was gorgeous. The kind of dress most of us only dream could morph into real life from the fashion pages of *Vogue*.

'It's lovely . . .' I muttered, but Remi's face searched mine for another answer. 'So, what exactly am I supposed to be looking at?' I asked after a pause, quietly, confused.

'THIS, IZZY! Don't tell me you don't see it. THIS!' Remi pointed to a hole. A hole the size of a five-pence piece on the neckline of the dress.

'Ohhh.'

'*OH?*' Remi said. 'This is a *disaster* and you say *OH?*'

I let out a sigh. This wasn't the greeting I'd hoped for.

'Come on, Rem . . .' I offered supportively. 'You're not going to let that ruin a fabulous dress, are you? Now, why don't I ask housekeeping if they have a sewing kit, or, better still, don't you have some amazing necklace that you can throw over it?' I suggested hopefully. Her emerald-green eyes were wide with fury and impatience. I had one final thought. 'Layla's final dress fitting is at eleven-thirty, maybe the designer can—'

'Look,' Remi interrupted, 'can't you just see if there is a store in this backwards Spanish town that has another one of these?' I couldn't believe my ears. 'I know you're expected at breakfast,' Remi continued, 'that you're paid to pander to Layla, but I have to look good too . . . or . . . or I'll be letting Layla and all of the guests down.'

I put my arm round Remi's fragile shoulders and spoke very softly.

'Remi, I am really sorry about the dress,' I soothed. 'Let's go inside for breakfast as planned . . . then maybe afterwards, you can nip into town . . . if there's one person at this wedding who has the skill to put together the most incredible outfit in an emergency, Remi, it's you. You do it for a living, for God's sake!' I tried a giggle to convince her and lighten her mood, but she glowered at me.

I took her by the arm and held open the glass door of the hotel for her to slip quietly back inside. I watched as she silently climbed the sweeping wrought-iron staircase, her face still furious. 'So, how are you, Izzy?' I mumbled to myself in disbelief as her thin, tanned legs disappeared from view, my eyes lingering on the staircase. And, just as I was considering how beautiful the metal work was and the seamless turn in the heavy wood balustrade, I heard a horribly familiar voice, directly behind me.

'Well, dahling,' it chimed discordantly, in a familiar haughty tone, 'get me a quote from Abramovich's fiancée today and we'll go to press . . .'

My shoulders stiffened, my neck tightened, I instantly froze. The subject matter wasn't television, but

I didn't need to turn round to know that the voice belonged to my past and to Maddy Davenport-Parker. I instinctively snuck behind a vast white marble sculpture of a female water carrier, waiting to see if her conversation continued.

'Dahling, you don't need to remind me that it's a Saturday! Or that Roman will most likely be on his yacht . . .'

Maddy, I could see, was not just making a quick, casual call on her mobile. She and a young, chiselled, deeply tanned, highly muscled guy, dressed head to toe in white, had in fact set up an impromptu office on the couches just left of the reception desk. Maddy was perched on the edge of a squishy cream couch, her wafer-thin titanium laptop set up on a glass coffee table in front of her.

She was barking into her high-tech phone and frantically clicking her mouse whilst the receptionist struggled to take hotel bookings and answer enquires from guests.

Peering around the outstretched arm of the statute, I could see the chiselled guy desperately searching for a waiter, to bring Maddy yet another machiatto latte, her Botoxed brow increasingly furrowed with stress. Maybe, he was her new assistant, I mused, as he flapped nervously around her. Lost in the strange scene, I'd not considered how I'd disappear undetected from view. Feeling and looking vaguely ridiculous, I contemplated an escape route. To the rear of reception, the sumptuous bar led on to the terrace, where I should have joined Layla and the bridesmaids at least half an hour ago, I realised with a start, looking down at my watch.

I stepped out from the safety of the statue. All I had to do was to turn, keep my back to reception and keep walking. Surely no one would notice my exit. But then it happened. With one swift turn, my handbag swung out, clobbering the marble lady clumsily around her bust, knocking her off balance. I threw myself forward to steady her, one hand round the statue's cool, slim neck, the other on my bag, and let out a sigh that both had steadied and the marble lady hadn't toppled over. I glanced heavenwards and took in a long, deep breath in relief.

'Isa-belle-Mistry,' Maddy's voice slowly and loudly projected from the couch, emphasising each syllable of my name. I felt my heart sink into my chest. It was too late to hide again.

'Isabelle *used* to be my assistant,' Maddy announced to anyone who could hear. The chiselled guy gasped knowingly and I felt my cheeks flush crimson with embarrassment.

This was all I needed. Maddy and the chiselled guy were staring at me intently, waiting for a response. There was nothing for it, I cleared my throat and faced the situation head on.

'Maddy, hi!' I beamed, with a wide wedding-day smile, walking over to the couch.

Maddy didn't get up. She crossed her legs and studied me, inch by inch; the jewelled platform espadrilles on the feet of her pin-thin legs looked impossibly heavy and vulgar.

She didn't introduce the chiselled guy. Seconds passed in awkward silence and I didn't have seconds to spare. I was supposed to be in control of the wedding. Just as I opened my mouth to make my excuses, Maddy beat me to it.

'Isabelle, I really should thank you,' she said finally. 'Thank you very much indeed.'

The comment was more baffling than any slight

could have been. She sounded as though she'd been in therapy.

'If you hadn't . . . let's say . . . *opened up* the situation for me at On Fire, I'd still be there now, kowtowing to the board, to commissioning editors, and married to that fat slimeball of an MP . . .' I stood dumbfounded. 'I would never have met Johan!' she enthused, eyeing him as if he were supper. 'We would never have become an item!'

I shot Johan a pitying look.

'How hot is he?' she asked, out of character, as if he wasn't there. I squirmed. Maybe the therapy had been some weird sex-yoga thing. 'He's been invaluable in the new business,' Maddy continued, deliberately planning a pause, so that I'd ask exactly what her new business was.

'So what are you doing now?' I asked obediently on cue, clocking up the minutes. I only hoped this early run-in would help things go smoothly with madam later on.

'I have a *hugely* successful dot com, an online therapy and support portal for celebs who've been wronged by the press . . . well, after my experience it seemed to be the right thing to do. Now we're a really strong network . . . I'm just working on organising a retreat in India with meditation, Indian head massage, et cetera, et cetera, for this autumn – which, incidentally, I might film as part of a series for my new production company. AND, of course, I have my own column – you *must* have seen it . . . I succumbed to the deal *just* to show how we can all manipulate a situation in the media and turn it around to our own advantage,' Maddy continued until I finally managed to get a word in as she paused to take a breath.

'Well, it's great to see you and hear about your

exciting new ventures,' I managed with as much sincerity as I could muster, 'and sorry to cut things short, but I'm organising a wedding here and I really must check on the bride.' By the time I was halfway through the sentence, Maddy had already mentally dismissed me, ordering Johan to dial another call. He looked up at me fleetingly like a dumb, obedient puppy, his manly fingers fumbling to press the digits on Maddy's tiny phone.

As I turned to walk through the bar to the terrace I could feel Maddy's eyes on my back and hear the affected insincerity of another conversation. I didn't dare stop walking until I reached the dark cocoon of the bar. If a bartender had been serving behind the highly polished black marble slab, its shelves stocked with expensive-looking reserves, I'd have succumbed, even at this hour. Instead, I checked my reflection in the glass of a picture and finally went to greet the girls.

A gentle breeze carried the sound of girly laughter and chatter. Swathes of cream organza billowed at the open glass doors, signalling the way to the terrace and masking the view beyond the bar. But as I held back the curtains to step outside, there was no one to be seen. It was deserted. A silver tray of champagne flutes, two empty bottles of Tattinger, several porcelain plates piled with half-eaten croissants, and a cut-glass bowl dripping with grapes were the remnants of the champagne breakfast. The spread was sprawled on a low basketwork table surrounded by wide, matching chairs strewn with bright-patterned cushions. A linen napkin had strayed on to the floor, a forgotten room key on a tasselled fob glistened on the table beside a small mountain of cream and gold wrapping paper scrunched into a ball. My stomach leapt with nerves, frustration and disappointment at having missed the first meeting of the day.

I looked out over the rooftops and up to the clear blue sky above. My eyes scaled the grand exterior of the hotel building and I realised that the laughter was resounding from the balcony of the bridal suite. 'Bugger,' I mumbled under my breath. Nothing had gone well so far. But I wasn't going to let that deter me. I waltzed straight back to reception, deliberately evading any eye contact with Maddy and a forlorn-looking Johan, telling the girl on the desk that I was heading up to Layla's room.

I took the stairs instead of the lift with a sense of purpose and on reaching the top floor, gave the tall wooden double doors a distinct knock. There was no answer. I turned the heavy bronze handle gently and silently walked inside. My eyes met a bustling 'girly' scene. A fleet of model bridesmaids were having their poker-straight hair 'blown out' and teased into up do's, their gossip rising above the buzz of hairdryers. A sultry, dark-haired girl with legs like Bambi was stretched out on a chaise longue in a rock chick T-shirt and bikini bottoms, calling room service to order more champagne as a stylist pulled at her tresses with a paddle brush. An elfin blonde with an edgy crop keenly directed an unhappy make-up artist with a sentence that started, 'When I was in New York during fashion week . . .'

The bridesmaids' soft candy-coloured dresses decorated the antique armoires and the impressive four-poster bed on padded silk hangers. Their satin shoes were lined up in a row, as if waiting backstage for a catwalk show. There was no sight of Remi. She must have gone in search of another outfit, I guessed.

Directly to my right, with her back to the door, Layla teetered on an elaborately carved wooden chair in front of a matching dressing table, its surface covered with vases filled with delicate cream antique English roses, which I'd ordered for her as a gift from her father. The scent of the flowers filled the room. Layla was wearing the most exquisite wedding dress with a neverending train. The designer and his team were gathered around her, pinning up the hem, sewing flowers made from freshwater pearls on to the bustle and cinching in the corset with a generous bow. I could see her face in the reflection of the dressing-table mirror. She was animated, engrossed in conversation with the designer, blissfully unselfconscious. She was beautiful. Long red hair fell around her shoulders in natural waves, her skin was porcelain-pale, and she had the largest, baby-blue eyes. Suddenly I was aware that they'd caught mine, watching her.

'You must be Izzy!' Layla trilled.

The bridesmaids stopped to take a look at the new girl in the room.

'Yes . . . sorry, didn't want to interrupt, nice to meet you.' I blushed.

'That's OK, I won't come and kiss you, though.' She smiled, her voice friendly and distinctly well educated. 'I'm under orders to stay still for Michael.'

'Of course! Oh, and I'm so sorry I didn't make breakfast. Something cropped up that made me run late,' I replied.

'Oh, don't worry about that,' she said, a look of concern crossing her face.

'Of course, everything's fine now.' I smiled, to reassure her. 'Is there anything you need?'

'Gosh no, Izzy, really! I'm sure you've got plenty to do. I've got the girls if I need a hand.'

'OK! And you've got my mobile number should you need *anything*,' I added. 'Your make-up artist is booked to arrive in an hour,' I reminded her. 'Flowers at two, and I'll be back here by then, to leave the bouquets for you.'

'Wonderful, thanks,' she said sincerely, before checking the back of her dress in a full-length mirror.

'Your dress!' I offered, turning back before leaving, 'it's incredible.'

'Thanks!' Layla replied. 'Loving it,' she said to Michael. Suddenly the cliché of the 'big meringue' seemed very out of date.

Right, I thought, shutting the door tightly behind me, back on track, feeling good. I mumbled the words out loud to myself, keeping up my positivity and checking my notes. The neatly collated sheets of A4 were my Bible and I scoured them for the phone number and address of the boys' hotel. Walking back down the grand hallway towards the staircase, I called ahead to the groom.

'Max?' I asked as a deep, public-school voice answered the phone.

'Yuh?' it answered curtly.

'Isabelle calling, your wedding planner. Good to speak to you . . .' The greeting was met with silence. 'Thought I would pop over and see if there's anything you need, if it's a good time.'

'That's rather good of you,' the voice replied cheerily, to my relief. 'But really, I don't think there's any need. Everything is perfect here. I'd rather you take care of Layla,' Max said considerately.

'Well, if you're sure?' I started. 'I've arranged lunch in the hotel's grill room for you guys at one-thirty as you know,' I said, checking my notes. 'You have exclusive use of the gym, sauna and pool all day, your Swedish massage is booked for three, and your cars will arrive at four-thirty, to get you all to the church well ahead of the bride. Did you see the revised time on my email last week? It's due to a concert in the city; we need to make a detour around the closed roads . . .' I took a pause for breath. 'The only thing I thought you might need is a call to housekeeping, for ironing? Something I was going to check for you when I reached the hotel.'

'We did that this morning, thanks, there's no need to worry,' Max confirmed. 'But thank you, Isabelle. I must say, I've been incredibly impressed with the organisation.'

I grinned from ear to ear on hearing the compliment, yet I was still nervous, not knowing if the day would live up to everyone's expectations.

'I don't know if Celia mentioned it, but I work in film. We always need good fixers like you, to scout for locations, work with caterers . . . similar game, really . . . so please promise to come and see me when you're back in London, won't you?' Max's voice was kind and sincere. I wasn't sure what to say. He seemed to be offering me a job. At a film company. In London. Something I'd always dreamed of!

'Sorry, I know this probably isn't the time or the place,' he added apologetically. 'Always working, even today . . .'

'NO! Not at all. Thank you, Max, that sounds fantastic!' I said excitedly. 'You have my number if you need anything before I see you at the ceremony,' I added, remembering the job in hand. 'If I'm not coming down to see you, I'll send the florist's assistant to reception, to buzz the best man to collect the button holes.'

'Perfect. See you in church!' he said, signing off.

I let my arm fall to my side and stood for a moment, taking things in. It was a good sign, a good omen, maybe. An indication that new opportunities awaited me back in London after all.

I turned to walk down the staircase, now a little more confident. Maybe today would work out OK, I pondered, looking at my notes to see the first jobs awaiting me at the church. With my head bowed to read, I suddenly felt a blow to my side that knocked me off my feet. I saw the papers fly above me in slow motion, as I felt my legs give way. I ended up on the solid wood floor, feeling the soft thump of an awkward landing.

'GOD, so, so, sorry . . . shit!' I heard a man's voice say behind me in a rush and a panic. I didn't look round, I was still shaken. I tried to move up a little, reaching out an arm to grab the bottom of the balustrade to help me pull myself to my feet. The man's hand clasped mine, pulling me round to him, so that I faced him as I sat on the floor.

'Izzy? I thought . . . I thought it was you. Are you OK?' The face looking back at mine, so handsome and full of concern, belonged to Harrisson. 'God, I'm such an idiot. I'm so sorry,' he continued. His eyes, searching mine, seemed to be smiling and saying so much more. 'I was in such a hurry, I wasn't looking. Are you all right?' he rambled.

My eyes welled up instinctively. I told myself not to be stupid, it was just the impact of the blow, I told myself.

'Yes, fine,' I replied as businesslike as possible in the circumstances, whilst looking for my paperwork now scattered in an untidy trail down the staircase.

Harrisson didn't gather them up, like the guys do in the movies, his eyes meeting mine as we stood up. No, Harrisson tried to gather me up. Literally. Scooping me up to my feet in his powerful, hundred per cent white cotton-clad arms.

'Look, really. I'm fine,' I protested. His familiar,

warm, firm hand lingered on the small of my back as he made sure I was standing and steady.

I smoothed back my hair, nervously. God, I bet I looked a state.

'You look . . . really . . . well, Izz,' he said as we stood awkwardly.

'I am, thanks,' I replied defensively, not wanting to ask how he was.

'No, I mean you look great,' he corrected himself.

I didn't answer. 'What are you doing here? Are you coming to the wedding?' he asked, suddenly. 'I thought only the bridesmaids and Layla's family were staying here?'

'They are and I am,' I replied matter-of-factly, avoiding his gaze and trying not to dwell on the fact that he smelt so good.

'Oh . . .' he said awkwardly, not knowing, it seemed, what to say. I'd never seen Harrisson speechless before. He was the socially confident guy. The person who always told the jokes at parties, the guy who held court.

'I'm just here to see if there's a room for us. Stazi's gone nuts on seeing our hotel, hates it, and I heard that there is an extra room here, which isn't taken.'

'There is, Layla didn't fill it,' I said. Harrisson looked bewildered. I was determined not to ask if 'Stazi' was the fiancée. 'I'm organising the wedding.'

He smiled.

'That's great, Izz. Good for you,' he said genuinely. I felt patronised, regardless. 'I knew you'd do something fantastic, end up successful, doing a great job . . .' His hand took my arm. His touch was tender. I had to break away.

'I really have to get to the church,' I said, pulling away.

'No, Izzy, don't go,' he said pleading, his voice

dropping to a gentle tone. 'I, well, I've really missed you
. . . you know?'

'No, I *don't* know,' I replied, trying to put a stop to
the conversation. I couldn't meet his gaze. 'Don't!' I
said, firmly. 'You've already told me that you're here
with someone else.' I broke away, pacing down the stairs
as fast as my legs, would go, picking up the papers as I
went.

I didn't look back, I headed straight for the door,
feeling like I wanted to shout, really loudly, at the top of
my voice like Remi had that same morning.

The venue for the wedding ceremony, a hidden palace
in the grounds of the city's cathedral, was a short
distance from the hotel and I decided to walk there,
despite the intense heat of the midday sun. I had to
clear my head. I had to try to find some calm before I
met the priest and the florist, be all smiles, be
professional. Yet despite my best intentions, my journey
there was a blur. I hadn't been ready to see, let alone
meet, Harrisson, I now realised. I thought that if and
when I did see him, I would be in control. Cool, calm
and collected, standing back as all of my plans for the
wedding came together. But nothing could have been
further from the truth.

My still wobbly legs carried me through the Arab
quarter of Palma, the tall elegant buildings towering
above me in the narrow backstreets, providing some
welcome shade on my sticky back. My mind tried to
search a database of Notting Hill faces for a 'Stazi', it
replayed the scene in the hallway, as if someone had
rewound a DVD for me to watch on a giant screen. I
climbed the endless stone steps up to the cathedral,
slipping to the left at its magnificent entrance and
towards a simple set of heavy wooden double doors

opposite, guarded by the Guardia Civil policemen. The men stood silent and serious, deep-green berets on their heads despite the heat, guns on display in their holsters. I showed them my pass and my name on a fax from the palace, and they opened the huge doors, one on each side, so that I could enter.

Inside, the cobbled-stone courtyard of the palace was peaceful and I was pleased to spend a moment alone. With the hum of the city and tourists roaming beyond, I felt safe behind the high stone walls. I took a seat for a moment on the grass of a raised flowerbed, shaded by tall palm trees, enjoying the sound of the marble water fountain trickling by my side. I looked around, trying to get my focus back for the day. I knew I had to walk away from Harrisson, he still had an incredibly powerful effect on me and my emotions, but it was no longer an effect I wanted in my life. This had to be the final goodbye. A very definite goodbye.

Behind me, a row of grand stone arches and pillars led to a stately government building. Behind its tiled roof, the cathedral rose majestically, its spherical stained-glass window and intricately carved spires in full view. I looked up, captivated for a moment. I had suggested that Layla and Max get married in the cathedral itself – they were both Catholic and had almost three-hundred guests, enough not to be entirely lost within it, but they'd fallen in love with this little jewel of a building when Celia had brought them to visit and I couldn't blame them. It was beautiful as I looked at it now, at its elaborate marble arched doors, turrets and incredible windows. Eventually, we persuaded the authorities to let the wedding go ahead at the palace, despite their maximum capacity being too small, by allowing some of the younger guests to spill out into the courtyard. We'd waited, with bated breath, to see if the

King of Spain might need to use the palace himself, for his own worship, which he reserved the right to do up to three weeks before the event. It had been difficult to tell a bride that there was another person who could take precedence on her wedding day, but she'd been patient.

The ring of my mobile phone made me jump with a start. I'd been daydreaming, I realised, as I searched for it desperately in my voluminous handbag.

'Hello, Izzy speaking!' I chimed on autopilot, without checking the number on the display panel.

'Izzy ... it's Remi,' the voice replied unexpectedly, sounding subdued, almost humble. 'Look, I got your number from Layla ... I just wanted to apologise.'

'Oh Rem, it's fine really. I know everyone gets stressed at weddings, I'm used to it,' I told her truthfully, although we both knew she had acted appallingly. 'Now, tell me, did you have any luck in Palma?'

'Yes!' Remi said with excitement. 'You'll see.'

'I guess I will,' I agreed, looking at my watch, realising I had better buck up and get down to business.

'So how's the organisation going?' Remi asked, considerately – especially for her.

'Yes, good,' I said.

'I kinda get it,' she said, 'you know, the gorgeous lovely things, parties, the great hotels ...'

'I know, could be worse!' I agreed, laughing.

'Look, sweetie,' Remi said, cutting the conversation short, 'I know you're working, but I hope we can catch up for a drink later, yeah?'

'Yes sure,' I replied, 'that would be good.' I was genuinely pleased by the idea.

As we spoke, something caught my eye. I could see two figures, I was sure, beneath the shaded arches of the government building, on the steps, looking intimate.

Strange, I thought, walking over to investigate, as the courtyard was closed to the public for the wedding. I'd had to give a full list of guests and contractors, names to the guards and the office. It would be an offence for anyone unauthorised to be here.

'So . . . Izzy, are you there?' Remi asked, her words drifting over me.

'Sorry, Rem, need to go, speak to you later,' I said quietly, careful not to disturb the intruders as I hung up.

I didn't know whether to call the guards or spring on the couple myself, but my dilemma was quickly answered. As I walked closer, I could see a guitar case had been placed at the couple's feet, at the bottom of the steps. They were both guys, dressed in suits. On closer inspection I could make out that one of them was good looking and had a sharp haircut, very sharp. It was Ray, I realised, as the couple remained too engrossed in conversation to notice me, and, as I squinted to get a better view, a musician I eventually recognised as Ramon.

Ray looked up, flashing me a smile as Ramon lit a cigarette. Ray gave me the 'Do not disturb' signal he'd always used and I turned on my heels, leaving him to his usual charm offensive. I could imagine Ramon, anarchic, wild and ruggedly good looking, would be just his type for a holiday fling.

That afternoon the palace was adorned with thousands of cream antique roses, candles and an aisle an inch deep in candy-coloured rose petals. The deep-green velvet-covered pews were moved into position for the guests. Pre-ceremony drinks were set up in the courtyard on a long white cloth-covered bar. Ray had disappeared, giving me a 'see you later' wink and a big smile, as Ramon picked up his guitar case and put Ray down.

Celia and Tomas were on hand to help. Tomas, I had to admit, looked so different; handsome, in fact, in a smart black suit and sharp white shirt. I caught Celia eyeing him proudly and remembered that this was the closest they'd been, the most time they'd spent together, for many years.

As the guests started to make their way into the courtyard, admiring its beauty, the photographers, bartenders and guitarists took their positions. Tomas, on Celia's suggestion, took up a post at the entrance with the guards. Celia discreetly asked several twenty-something girls in tiny dresses and killer heels to remove their handbags from the shiny copper bucket that adorned the antique well at the courtyard's centre. They rudely complained at there being no cloakroom in response. 'I'm sorry,' I heard Celia apologise, 'but I'm yet to find a church equipped with a cloakroom,' to the amusement of several older ladies within earshot.

The courtyard soon filled with media types, predictably using the situation to network. There were the families, the rich old guard taking a weekend away from their country piles, 'Mummy', wearing all of her best jewels, and 'Daddy', wishing he was out shooting. There were Layla's modelling friends, willowy girls looking beautiful, but slightly out of place with their edgy dresses and London haircuts. There was a fleet of Notting Hill mummies draped in designer dresses, their toddlers accompanying them as matching accessories. And there were Max's public-school chums, bumbling Boris Johnson types, downing a class or two of cava to muster the courage to speak to the models.

Celia and I conducted a head count fifteen minutes before the bride was due to arrive. Predictably, many guests had decided it would be OK to be fashionably late. We signalled for the ushers to take their positions at the entrance to the palace and encouraged guests to be seated. I called Layla's hotel room, and spoke to Remi.

'So sorry, Rem, it might be a little longer than planned before you can leave with Layla and the girls,' I told her. 'Let Layla know for me that Max is here and everything's fine. You should leave in ten minutes, the cars are already waiting.'

'Don't worry, Izz,' Remi assured me, 'Layla's very laid back about it.'

'Great,' I said with relief. 'I think that some people take the time of the wedding as the time that *they* should arrive, rather than the bride, these days,' I said hanging up.

Max fidgeted nervously at the end of the aisle, tanned and immaculately groomed in a sharp navy-blue suit, his back to the door. The priest, visibly rehearsing his lines, shot him smiles of reassurance from the marble altar. The guests continued to waltz in late. Girls used the aisle as a catwalk, parading their finery, checking the pews for the best-looking guy to squeeze in next to. Some familiar faces emerged at the last moments, seemingly convinced that their celebrity status might have meant that they would have been mobbed if they had arrived on time. Amongst them was a well-known chat show host, a soap star, a TV chef and his family, along with several fashion designers and models, all acting conspicuously inconspicuous. Layla's mum, forever the fifty-something fashionista, arrived in a Philip Treacy hat in the shape of a swan and a figure-hugging Vivienne Westwood dress. Max's mother looked on in disbelief, nudging her stuffy husband at the sight of their new in-laws. Harrisson entered, trailing behind a glamour puss with a sour face who I presumed was 'Stazi'. He reluctantly followed her, his face unhappy, wearing a look of defeat. Before I could study the situation further, the wedding cars arrived – three slick black vintage Bentleys, with wide white silk bows tied to the door handles and a lavish display of roses on their back shelves.

Celia gave the signal for the musicians to play and an authentic Majorcan folk band which Layla had requested walked down the aisle in traditional medieval costume. The beautiful bridesmaids followed, eight of them walking to the beat of the traditional goat-skin drum, their pale-pastel dresses shimmering, their eyes focused forwards, their hands clasping the palest pink bouquets. It was an unpredictable spectacle. A mix of old, rustic Majorca and new, carefully considered and very British chic.

Lola was next to make an entrance. A naughty two-year-old flower girl, who had to be held in the tight clasp of her mother till the very last moment, then pushed gently in the direction of the aisle. She was undeniably pretty: a blond head of curls, a tiny-sized smock dress, a face fixed with a wide, cheeky grin. She relished the attention and started to meander her way slowly to the front, forgetting to scatter the petals as she'd been shown how to do so often, eventually dumping them all in one heap from her pretty Bo-Peep basket as she reached the feet of the priest.

With all eyes on the sweet and innocent Lola, Remi, as Maid of Honour, took a quiet few steps into the palace. After the little one had been dragged to the side of the front pew by a firm, taloned female hand, there was a collective gasp from the congregation as all eyes rested on Remi. If her first choice of outfit had been inappropriate, the replacement was just ridiculous. Traversing the aisle on angular futuristic wedges, she was wearing a deconstructed sailor's outfit which I could only guess she'd fashioned herself at the very last minute. I groaned, remembering my words to her, feeling vaguely responsible. A Breton sailor's top had been distressed, ripped, torn and adorned with a necklace made from a plastic lobster and shells; tiny white shorts studded with gold buttons had been fashioned into a skirt, with wisps of chiffon trailing from the seams; and a sailor's hat with elaborate gold braiding was perched at a jaunty angle on top of her immaculate black bob. Remi's face was deadly serious, her walk exaggerated, her mouth ablaze with bright red lipstick. Lola let out a scream, terrified, as Remi reached the altar.

The congregation was all whispers. The priest raised his hands for quiet as the bride stood at the door with her father, waiting for the sign to proceed. She looked radiant. My eyes studied the room. A hundred girls visibly melted at seeing their dream come to life. Layla was beautiful. Her baby-blues eyes sparkling with anticipation, her dress and bouquet pure perfection, her smile genuine and natural. Max turned to face her, a proud look crossing his face. I glanced up at the domed ceiling, feeling emotional. The stonework was intricately carved, and light flooded through the brightly coloured stained-glass windows. Beyond the open doors of the palace, chairs disappeared impressively out into the courtyard. My eyes followed the line outside and back again to the congregation, where I spotted some familiar faces – the now heavily pregnant receptionist from On Fire, and shop, club and restaurant owners I'd not seen in months. Maddy, I could see, was seated near the front, clinging on to Johan, as she dramatically cried fake tears. Celia and Tomas stood at the back, looking on happily. Tomas proudly looked over the scene that she'd created, attentively leaning in to reassure her with what I assumed were calm words. There was something very caring but strong and so attractive about him in that moment, that I gave Tomas a double take. To my embarrassment, he caught me doing so and I blushed as his eyes clocked mine, becoming wide behind his glasses. His eyebrows raised for a moment, before a warm smile beamed across his face as his eyes lingered on mine. As the room fell silent, I finally broke away from his gaze.

'We are all gathered here today ...' the priest announced.

For me, words had never rung so true.

Oh No!

I snuck out of the side door, leaving Celia to oversee the ceremony and Tomas to co-ordinate the coaches for the guests. A prebooked cab was waiting to whisk me away to the vineyard from the bottom of the cathedral steps, so that I could check the final preparations before the guests' arrival.

It was a relief to leave the intense atmosphere of the cathedral and to get out of the city.

I felt my whole body relax as the driver put his foot down, his windows open to let in the breeze and the late-afternoon sun as we climbed the winding motorway to the countryside. I was already exhausted. My mouth was dry and my stomach was groaning with hunger. But there wasn't time to think about myself. Today was all about making things perfect for Layla and Max.

The *finca* sat majestically above endless rows of vines. The driveway to the vineyard had been lined with torches, staked into the ground, which would be lit at nightfall. At the entrance to the house, I could see a vast team of people, scurrying to get the venue ready in time.

I waded my way through stylists, florists, lighting technicians and waiters, to try to find Marta. The rooms looked incredible. The courtyard had been transformed, the 'mixologists' were perfectly happy in their candle-lit oil press, the stable room and *bodega* were ready for the final touches, and the Moroccan elements were a huge success. Everything, at first glance, was fantastically impressive.

'Isobel!' Marta greeted me on the staircase, now lined with plump Moorish cushions. *'Como va?'* she asked, kissing me warmly on both cheeks and giving me a squeeze.

'Marta, fantastic to see you.' I laughed with relief on seeing a genuine, friendly face. 'Everything looks amazing, you've worked so hard!'

'No, this is normal.' Marta smiled back, proudly.

'Mira . . .' she said excitedly, 'Come, see.' She turned to walk back up the worn stone stairs.

Marta and I helped her mother with the final decorations in the ladies gossip parlour, inspected the cigar room and checked the bars and the concealed catering set-up in the grand salon. The stage was set for the band and the chill-out area was great. I resisted the childlike urge to bounce on the low Moroccan day beds and mess up the exotic cushions. Instead, we cleared the set for the florists to rig their final displays. Marta took my hand, pulling me outside. The mountain was ready to be illuminated at the flick of a switch, the terrace was ready for the speeches.

'Just already the tables to be finished,' Marta announced, her English wavering with tiredness as we looked down to the swarm of stylists balancing oranges in tall, tiered copper vessels.

'Isabelle!' Ute, the stylist in charge of the production, was calling me over. 'We have problem,' she announced in her thick German accent. My heart raced at the expression.

'I have two hundred and ninety-eight oranges, sliced, left to dry and ready for the name cards,' she said matter-of-factly.

'Great, yes, that's right,' I said, confirming the numbers.

'Now you put the cards,' she announced.

'Me?' I asked, knowing the client was paying thousands of euros for her company to look after the table decorations.

'Of course,' she said coldly. 'That job is not styling.'

I looked at the vast terrace, the endless table, dressed and beautifully ready, the two hundred and-ninety-eight oranges, one at every elaborate place setting, ready to be filled, and gulped.

The cards, I knew, had not been put into the order of the table-plan. That, I'd made clear at my briefing to Ute, was for her to organise before the wedding day. But I guessed she'd forgotten. Ute was unshakeable. I checked my watch. We still had forty minutes before the guests were to arrive and an hour during the canapé reception, when the area was concealed from view, so that it could be revealed later. Almost three hundred people scrabbling for seats without name-cards would be a disaster. An animated discussion followed on the terrace. I had the other rooms to oversee, Marta was busy briefing her waiting team, and Ute was being paid for a job she was trying to delegate. I stood my ground. It felt good. I was confident and the conversation even ended in smiles, with Ute's assistants shuffling the cards. I promised to return in an hour to check the names with Ute, once the canapé reception was in full swing.

The courtyard of the *finca* was a hubbub of celebration that night. The guests were inquisitive, exploring the rooms, drinking merrily. I caught snatches of gossip between people I'd known in Notting Hill as I passed them unnoticed. I stayed ignored by many people I'd once worked with. Others greeted me over-enthusiastically to draw me into loud conversations about their latest projects, as they tried to impress a colleague or rival. The waiters circulated silver platters of canapés endlessly. The mixologists served their cocktails till they drained a barrel of local sweet orange liquor. I searched for Remi, but on seeing her draped around a well-known Arab billionaire, decided that I'd chosen a bad time to take her up on that drink. The party, at least so far, was a great success. I checked on Layla and Max, queuing for their attention amidst their well-wishers, to find that they loved the results. I checked in with a happy Celia and then slipped upstairs, pleased to get away from so many people for a moment, to check the table for dinner. The doors to the rooms on the way had been deliberately cordoned off. But as I walked through the hallway of the *finca* and passed the cigar room, I could hear inappropriate noises coming from the terrace; quiet but discernible noises. Through the dark green wooden shutters, I could just see the shadowy figures of Ray and Ramon, entwined on a wide marble table-top. I giggled to myself and carried on walking. It was so typical of Ray.

The terrace, when I reached it, looked stunning. The design was opulent, like a lavish banquet, the orange and white colour scheme bold against the rich green of the mountains beyond. The stylists had lit the candles early, to complete the effect. I checked each name, crossing them off my list one by one, the double barrels, triple barrels, exotic and famous, with a now smiling Ute. Marta strode over, bringing us both a welcome glass of cava from the reception downstairs. We toasted with a celebratory *'Salud!'* and I took a sip, feeling the refreshing cool bubbles on my tongue. But there was still too much to do to relax. With Ute keen to pack up and Marta checking the bar was adequately stocked for the evening session, I slipped away into the gardens beyond the terrace. There were still ten minutes to spare before seating the guests and some quiet time, away from the all-too-familiar faces, was what I desperately needed.

The early evening air was starting to cool, the sun was setting spectacularly over the mountains and the sound of cicadas resounded throughout the valley. The *finca*'s gardens were rustic but pretty in the dusky light, brimming with wild flowers, simple daisy-like marguerites and well-established fruit trees. But the delight to my eyes was the sight of a single rickety wooden chair and a simple table that had been placed in the shade of a leafy tree, giving the perfect view of a field of vines below. I wandered over to take a seat for a moment, to pause for breath, give my legs a rest and finish my glass of cava. I slumped into the chair, pleased to feel its support against my tired bones. With no one around, I let out a large sigh. 'That's the worst bit over,' I told myself, feeling the twinge of an ache in my calves. The ceremony had gone well, everyone was enjoying the canapé reception, and the rest of the evening was planned to schedule. I felt a mild sense of relief. It was strange to think that in just a few hours' time, after so much work, the whole event would be over and we'd never see the couple again. And maybe, I wondered, looking down to the vines below, their dark leaves shimmering in the fading light, in just a few days' or weeks' time, I could be on a plane back to England, never to organise another wedding again. I still hadn't entertained the thought. What did I really want? I started to ask myself. What did I want to do? Where did

I want to be? Would Celia want me to stay?

But before I could answer my own questions, a tall, shadowy figure emerged, seemingly from nowhere, to stand in front of me.

'Christ, you scared me to death!!' I said, my heart thumping in double time.

'Izzy, I'm sorry, I had to find you,' the voice said slowly, calmly, its tone deep and sincere. It was Harrisson. 'I came through the gardens from the opposite direction . . .' he added, explaining his silent approach. He really wasn't making today easy. There'd have been a time when I'd have been desperate for Harrisson to have come running after me. But now, I genuinely wanted him to walk off into tonight's perfect sunset with his new bride-to-be. It would make my life so much simpler.

'Look, I need to talk to you,' he pleaded.

'I don't really have much time,' I protested truthfully, standing up from the chair and picking up the now empty glass. 'I need to get back to help seat the guests for dinner,' I explained, starting to make a move towards the steps.

Harrisson reached out, placing his warm hand on my arm to stop me, his touch familiar, his breath sweet.

'I need to explain, Izzy, please,' he argued. 'I did a lot of thinking that day you called me on the shoot, you know,' he started, as I pulled my arm away.

'That was a long time ago,' I said, trying to turn, to leave, but he continued to talk, regardless.

'I realised that I'd taken you for granted. That I should have treated you better. That I'd been an idiot, thinking that you'd always just be there . . . I realised that all I really wanted was you. And that it was too late.'

I looked at him disbelievingly, his face shadowy in the fading light.

'I'm not a complete idiot, Harrisson,' I said firmly. 'Why do you say these things, turn up with a new girlfriend and expect me to buy them?'

'Because, it's not that straightforward,' he replied.

'Looks pretty straightforward to me,' I answered, hearing the anger in my voice.

'When you left, I really lost my way for a while,' he said, his voice almost childlike with the admission. 'I just missed you so, so much.' He paused, swallowing hard.

'Sure, I had work, I was flying, shooting, but I was a mess. I was going out and getting wrecked every time I was back in London, trying to forget you. And then at a party I met her . . . Anastazia.'

I looked down at my watch. I wanted to run, to get back to my job, escape, but something inside me knew that I'd never get this chance again, to hear the story, to hear what had happened, and my curiosity glued me to the spot. I'd give him two minutes, I bargained with myself, as he continued. I looked up at his face, trying not to find him attractive.

'It all happened so fast. It was just supposed to be fun, to get you out of my system . . . but then I got offered a job in New York, a great job in New York. Art directing a fantastic fashion magazine, with an amazing penthouse apartment on the Upper East side . . . and before I knew it, I was making plans and Stazi was making herself part of them.'

I couldn't imagine anyone 'making' themselves part of someone else's plans, but Harrisson tried to convince me otherwise.

'She's just so pushy, she basically told her family that I'd proposed, so when I arrived for what I thought was just lunch on a Sunday, they congratulated us and shot me a thousand questions about the ring, children, how I was going to look after her in America . . .'

I stood aghast, my mouth wide open.

'So why didn't you just tell them that wasn't the plan?'

'You haven't met her family, Izzy,' he explained, pathetically. 'Bulldozing aristocracy, very strong, influential; they're not the kind of people you say no to. And why should I? I've told her, Izzy, that *she* has to tell them. Tell them that there's no engagement, that she isn't coming. That I was going to ask you . . . to . . .'

'What?' my mouth fired before my brain got into gear.

'. . . to come to New York, to live with me, be with me, spend the rest of your life with me . . .'

I stood in silence, stunned. This was too much. My mind was racing, my life in Notting Hill and my time in Majorca flashing before my eyes as they prickled with tears. I felt confused. None of this made sense. In just a few hours, the madness of my old London life, my friends, the pace and excitement of the media, had all flooded back, not least with the idea of Max's offer of a job back in the city and my mind whirred with the heady pull of it all. Yet it was a pull that had me torn in two directions. The pull of a city like London or New York and a life with Harrisson that still held the promise of excitement and glamour, and the pull of the complete opposite; a life that was determined to leave precisely all of that behind.

'I will do anything to have you back, Izzy. You belong with me,' Harrisson pleaded. But did I? Really? I wasn't so sure. Over the past few months I had come to love the island, I'd come to value different things. I'd felt happier and more comfortable than I had for a long time.

'Izzy, please . . .' Harrisson begged now. His eyes were sincere and I had never seen him look so determined. But even if my feelings for Harrisson and my old life were still strong, it just didn't feel like either of them were my future.

Lost in my thoughts, I barely heard the sound of someone clearing their throat from the steps behind us. I looked up. It was Tomas. Kind, dependable Tomas, the man who evidently loved me. And I realised, at that precise moment, that although we had yet to give our relationship a chance, what I really wanted was to stay here, in Majorca, with him. I looked at Tomas and smiled, wondering how much he had heard, and presuming he was waiting to take me back to seat the guests for dinner.

'So, Izzy,' Harrisson continued desperately, oblivious to Tomas's presence, 'I have to ask you—'

'Will you marry me?' Tomas interjected.

little black dress

**brings you fantastic new books like these
every month - find out more at
www.littleblackdressbooks.com**

Why not link up with other devoted Little Black
Dress fans on our Facebook group? Simply type
Little Black Dress Books into Facebook to join up.

And if you want to be the first
to hear the latest news on all things
Little Black Dress, just send the details below to
littleblackdressmarketing@headline.co.uk
and we'll sign you up to our lovely email
newsletter (and we promise that we won't share
your information with anybody else!).*

Name: —————————————————————

Email Address: ————————————————————

Date of Birth: ——————————————————————

Region/Country: ————————————————————

What's your favourite Little Black Dress book?
——————————————————————————————

How many Little Black Dress books have you read?————

*You can be removed from the mailing list at any time

Pick up a *little black dress* – it's a girl thing.

TRASHED
Alison Gaylin
PBO £5.99

Take two suspicious, Tinseltown deaths and add them to the blood-stained stiletto of a beautiful actress who's just committed suicide ... Journalist Simone Glass is finally on to the story of her life – but is she about to meet a terrifying deadline?

Hollywood meets homicide in Alison Gaylin's fabulous killer-thriller.

978 0 7553 4801 5

SUGAR AND SPICE
Jules Stanbridge
PBO £5.99

After the initial panic of losing her high-flying job, Maddy Brown launches Sugar and Spice, making delicious, mouth-wateringly irresistible cakes. Can she find the secret ingredient for the perfect chocolate cake – and the perfect man?

A rich, indulgent treat of a novel – love, life ... and chocolate cake.

978 0 7553 4712 4

Pick up a *little black dress* – it's a girl thing.

ITALIAN FOR BEGINNERS
Kristin Harmel
PBO £5.99

Despairing of finding love, Cat Connelly takes up an invitation to go to Italy, where an unexpected friendship, a whirlwind tour of the Eternal City and a surprise encounter show her that the best things in life (and love) are always unexpected . . .

Say 'arrivederci, lonely hearts' with another fabulous page-turner from Kristin Harmel.

978 0 7553 4743 8

THE GIRL MOST LIKELY TO . . .
Susan Donovan
PBO £5.99

Years after walking out of her small town in West Virginia, Kat Cavanaugh's back and looking for apologies – especially from Riley Bohland, the man who broke her heart. But soon Kat's questioning everything she thought she knew about her past . . . and about her future.

978 0 7553 5144 2

A red-hot tale of getting mad, getting even – and getting everything you want!

Pick up a *little black dress* – it's a girl thing.

IT SHOULD HAVE BEEN ME
Phillipa Ashley
PBO £5.99

When Carrie Brownhill's fiancé Huw calls off their wedding, running away from it all in a VW camper-van seems an excellent idea to her. But when Huw's old friend Matt takes the driver's seat, could fate be taking Carrie on a different journey?

978 0 7553 4334 8

'Fulfils all the best fantasies, including a gorgeous, humanitarian hero and a camper van!' Katie Fforde

TODAY'S SPECIAL
Alan Goldsher
PBO £4.99

When chef Anna Rowan and boyfriend Byron Smith are asked to star in a reality-TV show about their restaurant, TART, they find themselves – and their relationship – under the hot glare of the TV cameras. Do they have the right recipe for love?

978 0 7553 3996 9

A.M. Goldsher serves up another deliciously quirky and original romance.

You can buy any of these other
Little Black Dress titles from your
bookshop or *direct from the publisher*.

FREE P&P AND UK DELIVERY
(Overseas and Ireland £3.50 per book)

TO ORDER SIMPLY CALL THIS NUMBER

01235 400 414

or visit our website: www.headline.co.uk

Prices and availability subject to change without notice.